TWILIGHT OF THE SERPENT

THE SERPENT SERIES

SZ ESTAVILLO

ONE

THE VICTIM'S SHADOW

HE WAS EVERYWHERE AND NOWHERE, all at once—playing with her mind, pulling her back to what had been. How she'd fallen on her knees. Yes, on her knees, begging for him to stay. Cheonsa Soo-Min had made a fool of herself, shattering her pride for Merrick Winslow—the man who once owned her soul, piece by aching piece.

Until the day it was suddenly all gone.

Meeting Merrick had shown her that love could be something pure, untouched by doubt. A piece of him had fused with her soul, leaving an indelible imprint. It flooded her neural pathways with familiar songs, the waft of scents from another time, light laughter lingering like an eternal echo—preserved in a capsule that kept it alive day after day, month after month, year after year. Together, they'd built a list of innocent first-time moments. With age, their souls had matured into a scorching kind of lust slipping beneath a new dawn of discovery, like the first time she demanded that he take her completely and the first time she'd willingly dropped everything for him.

Cheonsa would move wherever the military took them, so as long as they were together.

It was the first time she'd ever put aside her feminist liberalism, wild independence, and thirst for being a forever vagabond. With Merrick, she could be that gypsy and have someone with whom to share her love for travel.

How could she have been so wrong? Cheonsa didn't see it coming. A knock on the door pounded almost as forceful as her heart, threatening to crack her rib cage, and she was back again.

Opening the door. Cheonsa? *Yes.* You've been served. *I've been what? Served what? Hey, asshole, I asked you a question!* The stranger walked away—he didn't even flinch. What was in the manila envelope? Opening it gently. To hell with this. Ripping it open. Divorce papers. *Divorce papers?* Dialing Merrick. Voicemail. Dialing Merrick again. Voicemail.

No. No. No.

What did she do wrong? Running to the closet. Empty. How could she not notice he'd moved out his clothes? What kind of wife doesn't notice something like that? Was this because of her master's degree? Her new executive job? The marketing director position was her dream. He'd celebrated with her just two days ago with a bottle of fucking 2010 Château Lafite Rothschild—a fourteen-year-old French award-winning wine.

He cooked her dinner, accenting the ambiance with candlelight and then ending the night with passionate love.

Knock. Knock. Knock.

Knock. Knock. Knock.

She dragged her leaden body up off the sofa, dread consuming her. There was nowhere to run. Yes—he was everywhere and nowhere—always lurking. No one would ever believe her. Five years post-divorce, he still haunted her, pulling the strings like a puppeteer.

Knock. Knock. Knock.

Knock. Knock. Knock.

"Cheonsa Soo-Min? We need to have a word with you. Please don't make this harder on yourself," boomed a deep male voice. The authoritative tone behind the closed door left no doubt—cops. There were cops outside. "Another freeway chase won't look good in court. We can get you on evading the police —it's not gonna look too good with the warrant out for your arrest."

Her mouth went dry, and air left her lungs. Before she could register the decision, her legs carried her to the bedroom. Cheonsa lifted the corner of the curtain just a touch—their squad car blocked her vehicle from leaving.

Fuck. Fuck. Fuck.

How did they find her new hideout? Merrick. He did this. Grabbing her passport, plane tickets, and the lone bag she'd pre-packed, Cheonsa hesitated only for a moment—then reached for the gun. They weren't meant to find her. She was supposed to be heading to the airport in an hour and didn't want to have to go with plan B. She brought her things to the door and opened it, coasting on neutral. The officers stood casually and, by the look on their faces, clearly didn't expect her to put up a fight.

Both officers smiled at her with forced politeness. "I'm Officer Reed, and my partner here is Officer Taylor," Officer Reed began, his tight, fake grin still firmly in place. "We can make this real easy. Most likely, you won't spend too much time behind bars if we can get your cooperation."

"We've got you blocked this time around. They wanted to bring SWAT out, but a little thing like yourself—we told Chief Johnson that we could handle you all by ourselves," added Officer Taylor.

Both were armed, though they hadn't drawn their weapons —why would they? She clearly wasn't meant to be a problem. The officers glanced at a picture up on the wall. In it, she was at least a mile ahead of the rest of her peers. The framed news article she'd been proud of read: *Cheons-nado Secures Another Victory: Named All-American In Track and Field Triumph!*

She'd earned the nickname in high school and throughout college because, much like a tornado that swept through any obstacle in its path, she'd outrun almost all the long-legged gazelles twice her size.

"We know you can move those pretty legs of yours. Told Chief Johnson, 'Sure, she can run—but let's see how she holds up against the men's team. Women's track really doesn't count as the big leagues, does it?'" Officer Reed mused.

The sexist comment made her blood boil, reducing her to something fragile—like she was made of porcelain or some shit.

"Calling the colonel three hundred and fifty times," tsked Officer Taylor, "kinda breaks the protection order."

"You two green cops are too naïve to be doing a job that's supposed to be about protecting innocent victims." Cheonsa pointed her Glock 19 at their faces. "Never called or contacted him—I changed my number, you stupid fucks. You're trying to arrest the wrong party."

"Put the gun away," Reed said anxiously.

"We have all the evidence. Had you left the colonel alone as he'd asked, we wouldn't be in this situation," Taylor said, each reaching for their weapons.

"Don't you fucking dare," Cheonsa bit out, then ordered. "Both of you in here now—in the kitchen." She had a modern farm table with metal legs that weighed over a hundred pounds. The two officers entered. Cheonsa confiscated their weapons and threw them on the sofa. "Handcuff yourselves to the table."

"Making a big mistake. This'll make your case a whole lot worse. He warned us that you'd do something like this. Look, Colonel Winslow still cares about your well-being and mental health. He'll talk to you, alright, face to face. We got the go-ahead in advance cause we know your resistance to speaking with law enforcement. He's on his way and'll be right here in your living room to talk witcha. No cop. No PD mediator. None of that. Okay? You can speak with your ex-husband like you've been wanting—promise—no strings, no calling backup," Officer Reed said.

"We could have this place surrounded by twenty, thirty squad cars—it's just us, alright, and Colonel Winslow," Officer Taylor insisted. "The aftermath of a divorce can be traumatic. Went through it myself just last year."

For the first time, Cheonsa's hand began to shake. "Shut the fuck up!" she jabbed the gun in their direction, voice pitching high on hysterics. "Cuff yourselves, NOW!"

The officers delayed no more and did as she asked.

"Did you say M-M-Merrick is on his w-way?" Her eyes misted, heart ramming through her chest like a malfunctioning train.

"Well, yeah, he volunteered—insisted that you'd listen to him," Officer Taylor said. "It's an unconventional method, but we often call upon relatives and loved ones in difficult situations when we've run out of options."

"Said I never once called the piece of shit. Haven't been harassing him," Cheonsa snapped. "Don't you see? You've got it the other way around. He's been calling himself, emailing himself. He hasn't left me alone in five long years. This won't end until I'm dead. My cold body will be on your conscience."

Both officers glanced at each other and exchanged an unmistakable "oh brother" look, the kind who'd heard countless crazies and criminals claiming they were innocent.

"Colonel Winslow divorced *you*," Officer Reed said dryly. "The restraining order is against *you*—ain't on him."

"Look, Miss Min, we've got all the phone records, all of them emails—they point in your direction," Taylor chimed in before Cheonsa could say anything.

There was no use in even trying to defend herself. Despite being handcuffed to her dining table—nearly as heavy as she was—the officers glared at her like she was a pathetic, love-struck, obsessed bitch. Cheons-nado who could run on the field but not from the man who had broken her heart. She knew she shouldn't have deleted all of the initial messages and emails Merrick had sent, dismissing them at first as just a rebound phase. He'd go away after a few months and take the hint after she ghosted him. But "no" wasn't an answer that Colonel Merrick Winslow took.

She threw the gun on the couch, freeing up her hands. She had one large piece of luggage and two smaller carry-ons. Snatching the officer's keys, she ignored their filibustering. She'll have to run back in the house and do a second sweep-through in case she forgot something.

"C'mon, Cheonsa," Reed pled, "if you turn yourself in right now, we can strike a plea deal. This little incident will remain between us. You can get in a whole lotta trouble keeping police officers hostage like this. Turn yourself in, and we'll have us a chat with the DA."

Rushing out, leaving Reed and Taylor's angry shouts to snap at the air like tethered dogs, she tossed her suitcase into the trunk of her car, grateful that she'd packed light. Without a second thought, she climbed into the squad car, blocking her vehicle, and maneuvered it out of the way. Just as she was about to run back in to double-check if she'd missed anything, the low rumble of an engine cut through the quiet. She hopped back into her car as a massive black Ford F-450 roared down her street, prowling to a stop in front of her rental house.

I forgot something. Think Cheonsa—what did you forget? The gun!

She had tossed the gun on the couch, preoccupied with trying to hustle the bags in the car.

Merrick. He was handsome as ever: sandy blond hair parted and gelled neatly to the side, like that perfect next-door neighbor. He still had that goody-goody vibe he could never shake off, which worked in his favor. It allowed him to rise through the ranks year after year. That church deacon, organ donor look—a saint in the flesh. Everyone loved Merrick. Her friends and family—they worshipped him. Even his subordinates looked up to him. *Leave it to Psycho to ruin her own marriage,* everyone thought. Some even had the nerve to say it to her face. Forget about how his parents looked at him. He was the youngest child of three and the only boy, making his two older sisters jealous of their little brother, who could do no wrong. The perfect soldier born to a fiercely patriotic family.

He could put her on the shelf, dust her off, and play with her whenever it suited him. He could file for divorce, walk away while she crumbled—sobbing, makeup streaked, snot and tears mingling in an undignified mess. He could mock her in private, laughing at her pain, and then step into the light, spinning his lies so convincingly that everyone believed him.

Colonel Merrick Winslow was God.

Fear froze her vocal cords as he stood just a few feet away, looking at her with that same *you're pathetic* look—now laced with something darker. A devilish desire. Property, that's what she was. Ownership was what he wanted. I'll-have-you-when-I-want-you-lust.

He walked up to her vehicle and leaned into the open passenger window.

"I'll give you a head start," was all he said, beaming those straight white teeth, promoting that good-boy, charming smile. "Go ahead. You'll be late for your flight. Besides, you won't want to stick around to find out what you did."

What she did? Alarmed, Cheonsa watched as her ex-husband strode casually into her home. Her hands were quaking so badly she could barely start the car. Just as she reached for the shifter to reverse—*Bang! Bang!*

For a cold, terrifying thirty seconds, she couldn't move. Merrick walked back into view, her own gun gripped in his gloved hand. A twisted grin spread across his blood-smeared face, the splatter painting his handsome features like some macabre trophy. With a mocking regal flair, he gave her a prom-king wave goodbye.

Reversing the car, she peeled out of her driveway and sped to the airport, hoping to catch her plane to Brazil. All the while, she knew that no matter where she went in the world, her perfect, charming ex-husband would find her.

TWO
THE HUNT BEGINS

DETECTIVE ANAYA NAZARIO prepared for utter misery between the expected sleepless nights of breastfeeding every two hours, diaper changes, and, worse than seeing dead bodies, her mastery over fear of intimacy. What scared her the most was that at any given moment, she could relapse and start drinking again. But once Ariabella was in her arms, all of her fears dissolved. The connection she had with her daughter was unlike anything she'd ever experienced. It had even surpassed the love she felt for Blake Huxley—the proud father of their precious daughter.

Nazario had stalled moving in with Huxley until a week before Ariabella was born. Fear of commitment was her hard-earned flaw and the reason she was sure she'd struggle as a first-time older mother in her forties, but when postpartum depression never paid a visit, a new ache had softened her hardened exterior. Her daughter turned her into putty, as four months of maternity leave was painfully short. It was four months to the day since she'd given birth, a fact that hadn't slipped past her or Huxley. If she counted back—ten months, one month before her due date—she could pinpoint the moment everything changed. Their daughter had spent three-quarters of a year growing before the world got to meet her, and now, at three months old, she was already slipping through time too fast.

As *Master of Puppets* blared from her phone—her ringtone from her favorite band—she met Huxley's sympathetic eyes.

"It's a good thing we staggered our leave this way." Huxley rocked Ariabella, who looked like a small doll in his muscular arms.

"Wish I had another four months," she sighed.

"You could request more time off. We could both be off work together."

The phone continued to ring—it was Chief Johnson.

"Chief Johnson would understand, being a father himself, but I don't think it's a good idea. Best you take your paternity leave now as we planned, and I head back," Nazario reasoned, feeling her heart constrict as she looked at her daughter's tiny pink fingers resting against her plump cheeks. As hard as it was, they couldn't both take off at the same time, not with their jobs being so demanding.

Huxley nodded in defeat. "You're right. Bet that's a cold one on that line. Best answer it, then. Sorry, babe."

"Nothing to be sorry about. It is what it is." Her shoulders sagged as she slumped into her recliner and answered, "Detective Nazario here."

"You don't sound very excited," Chief Johnson said.

"I'm not, sir."

"Can get someone else, your call."

"You know I won't let you do that."

"Your trainees—"

"You mean Taylor and Reed? Them smart asses wet out of the academy?"

"You're not gonna like this."

"Don't tell me, do we need to write them up?"

"Negative," The chief blew out a rowdy exhale into the receiver. "They're cold."

"What?" Nazario launched to her feet. "Both of them?"

"Unfortunately—got an anonymous tip. Caller ran their voice through some kind of AV Voice Changer Software. Sounded like a creepy-ass bootleg Darth Vader filter. Said Taylor and Reed would be marinating in their own juices for two days, so be prepared for some real funk."

"Goddamn it." Nazario raked a hand down her face.

"And there's something else. Looks like this'll be your third femme fatale."

"You're kidding me? How're we certain our perp's a woman?"

"They were there to arrest her on a warrant—stalking. Don't know much other than our suspect spent months in a psych hospital. Looks like she killed Officers Taylor and Reed before fleeing the scene." The captain paused for a beat, then pointed out, "Given your and Wilson's track record with the Bridge Killer murders—and you and Huxley handled Von Schlange—figured this would be a slam dunk."

Nazario adjusted the phone, exhaling a weary breath. "Wilson's heart attack kept him off that one. And as for the Serpent Woman—she got away, remember? Not so sure that one counts toward my so-called 'good' track record, sir."

"Well, it's on record as a suicide," Chief Johnson said, but they all knew better. "She and her dog didn't survive the cliffs, and that's *that*."

Although Nazario couldn't prove it, she knew Dr. Wilder Friedrich—a.k.a. Von Schlange—was alive and hiding somewhere, likely under another alias.

"And Wilson?"

"Already spoke with him," the chief said, "and of course, he wants you to stay with the baby. Gus was in here with him, and she put it to him straight. Said there's no way in hell you'd say no to this investigation."

Augusta "Gus" Humphrey was Captain of Gang and Narco, and while Wilson was close to her, Gus was her best friend. Nazario was honored to have officiated the wedding between her best friend and her bride, Quinn Ellison-Humphrey. Quinn was an investigative journalist who bonded with Gus over their mutual love for crime stories. She'd only gotten certified because Gus begged her, and Nazario could never say no to her best bud of twenty years. Their marriage was the first LGBTQ+ wedding for the force, connecting blue and rainbow folks in attendance.

Put those two together, and there were plenty of drunks, especially some of the officers who loved to party together. The eclectic bunch was fun to be around, but difficult as hell. It was an eye-opening experience to be the sober one, having to watch everyone chug free booze and get all stupid. Temptation sucked ass, but Nazario refused to slip up. Her daughter gave her a reason for staying sober. While Huxley only drank on occasion, he stayed sober that night with her, which she appreciated.

"Gus is right on the money," Nazario said, returning to the conversation with her boss. "I'll give Wilson a ring now."

"Don't bother," the chief said, "he's already on his way to pick you up."

"Y'all know me too well," Nazario said.

"By the way, how's Ariabella?" he asked, then added before she could reply, "I love that name. How did you two come up with it?"

"I liked Bella, but Blake wanted an A-name after me. Thought it was stupid. But, he liked Aria, and well, we put it together and *voila*."

"Well, it works!" complimented Chief Johnson.

"She's an easy baby. Smiles all the time. Our little miracle," Nazario said, watching her daughter sleep in Daddy's arms. "Thanks for asking, Chief. How's the wife situation?"

"Better. Not giving me so much shit. It helps now that I cut back my hours. Not pulling sixty a week, no more. She said she might call off the divorce, but that's a big maybe."

"A maybe is still better than a no. You know, taking time off hasn't been half as bad as I figured it would," Nazario said, her heart hurting at the thought of having someone else watch her daughter—just as Wilson pulled up. She let the captain go and kissed little Ariabella on the forehead.

"Cold ones?"

"Two officers," Nazario filled Huxley in. "Taylor and Reed."

"Damn," he said. "Those two rookies with the tasteless sexist jokes you round-housed to the ground?"

Nazario flushed, as it wasn't her proudest moment, but with a fourth-degree black belt in taekwondo and veteran mean streak, they should've been glad all they got were bruised egos and a few superficial scrapes.

"Yep," Nazario said, "and it looks like they pissed off the wrong woman."

She gave Huxley a quick peck, wiping her wet eyes as she left her sleeping newborn behind. *Mommy'll be home soon*, she thought, never imagining how hard it would be to juggle motherhood and her detective career.

Detective Isaac Wilson appeared in jovial spirits, munching on a bag of baby carrots courtesy of the heart attack that had separated the pair for about a year, placing her old partner on desk duty and a dull diet of healthy shit. Finally, they were back together just like old times after a baby and a "fat man's death scare," as Wilson called it. But he was no longer overweight, having shed half a century off the scales. Her longtime partner of more than fifteen years had a whole new wardrobe of skinny jeans, fitted shirts, and snacks for bunnies instead of his usual In-N-Out, Double-Double, Animal Style.

The only time she got to see Wilson was during her baby shower and when Ariabella was born. He'd missed all the cross-country fun as Huxley and she had chased down and faced Von Schlange, the Serpent Woman, only to have her slip through their fingers. The near-fatal heart attack had her partner laid up in the hospital for about a week. However, the recovery took much longer, involving rehab and a major lifestyle change that included a Fitbit and a diet made for birds.

"Well, hot damn, has it been a minute or what?" Wilson beamed brightly at her from the driver's side as she climbed into his Chevy Tahoe. "Don't even look like you popped out a baby."

She clasped his hand, but it wasn't good enough. He leaned in for a bear hug.

"You look amazing. Damn, is that a medium you're wearing or what?"

Wilson belly-laughed. "More like wearing a skin suit. Think I need ... whatchamacallit that—*er*—surgery rather."

"Skin removal surgery?"

"Yeah, got the stuff hanging all around me in all the wrong places, like wet laundry. Was on my first date in God knows how long—four, five years—and finally thought I was gonna get laid until I took my clothes off, and the whole thing turned into a downhill toboggan ride with a wonky steering wheel and no breaks."

"What happened?"

Wilson paused to look down at his phone at a text message Nazario could see was from Chief Johnson. He punched in the location in his GPS, and they drove toward the scene of the crime.

"Absolutely nothing. Zero. Zip. Nada. She gave me a look—

like I took a dump and forgot to flush—kinda look. Next thing I know, Peter Pan couldn't get flying. Totally limp like a scared, shriveled-up turtle tucked away in its shell."

"Sorry, Wilson. You can get that surgery. Check to see if insurance will cover it. Bet you money it's covered."

"Can't. Took way too much time off work as it is."

"Dude, but if it's reducing mobility and making things hard—"

"Shit—soft is more like it!" he said, and they shared a laugh, reminiscent of the old days.

It was nice seeing him again. After all this time, they'd picked up where they last left off, making the drive to the crime scene feel like a short ride despite Los Angeles traffic stopping up the 405 like clogged pipes. Los Angeles County was a wider net than many expected, especially for the LAPD's homicide division. They weren't used to driving all the way up to Topanga Canyon, but it was a western county and still considered an L.A. zone. As they followed the robot lady, the GPS took them through parts surprisingly rural.

Hell, if Nazario didn't know any better, it looked like they were in a whole other state, like bum-fuck Montana. Not that she had any beef with the "Treasure State." Huxley had family there, and they'd babymooned in Glasgow, a tiny town in northeastern Montana, mostly agriculture and ranching, during her third trimester last Christmas.

There really wasn't much of anything; Glasgow made Bakersfield, California, look like a metropolis. As dusk settled with the resting sun, the sky boasted coral and auburn hues that looked as ginger as Gus. Her best friend had finally grown out her hair after surviving a double mastectomy and breast cancer. Her fiery red curly hair looked radiant against her all-white tux. Nazario still couldn't believe Gus had married her badge bunny date after only dating for six months. It was a colorful LGBTQ+ wedding, and the first Nazario had ever been to.

Meanwhile, the only reason she didn't have a ring on her finger was that Nazario didn't do commitment all too well. But the birth of Ariabella had surely softened her icy heart—just a little. The road Wilson turned on went from smooth pavement to a narrow gravel road, literally taking them to a small old house in the middle of nowhere. The bumpy ride jolted her mind back to the present.

"Who'n the bleep would wanna live out here?" Wilson crunched loudly on a baby carrot. "Closest sign of civilization is twenty miles away."

"At least."

"Chief thinks we got another Madame Mayhem on our hands. And just when I thought we had a little breathing room."

"Can't undermine the stronger sex."

"Hey, hey—got my full endorsement on that. Hellova lot stronger than my weak ass. Shit, tell all my fam my partner can pull off some mean Jackie Chan kicks on my blubbery ass, and I'd go thump. Don't play with Nazario—fourth-degree in whoop-ass and one mean bitch you don't wanna tangle with."

Nazario raised a dark brow at her partner and snorted out a chuckle. Her taekwondo training had earned her the 'don't fuck with me' spot on the LAPD. She'd successfully taken down Connor Morris, a.k.a. Speed, and earned a torn ACL and meniscus in the process, requiring her busted knee to undergo emergency surgery. It resulted in a cumbersome leg brace—an unwelcome badge of honor. It made going to the bathroom a spread-eagle affair, not to mention the sponge baths that turned into a comedic, soapy stand-up routine. Still, Nazario took down the SOB. Worth it, whether she had to hobble around for three months or not.

A cloud of dust swallowed the car as they pulled up to an

unpaved dirt lot, which held a lonely little cottage that looked too depressing for life to inhabit. The lights were all out, and the sleeping sun tucked away behind the Santa Monica mountains left shadows that kept the secret of what had transpired in its arms. A lone patrol car sat abandoned in the driveway. Nazario and Wilson peeked inside the windows and found nothing out of place. Nazario touched the hood of the car out of habit, and as expected, it was cold. Her heart took a nosedive to her feet as Wilson shared a knowing look. They moved slow. Careful. Guns up.

"LAPD!" Nazario's voice boomed, but it emptied into the same void that had made everything a little too still.

"Anyone home? Knock, knock—got a box of thin mints that're real tasty."

"You wish. Those thin mints are what gotcha that heart attack in the first place." Nazario gave her partner a sideways glance. Wilson had a habit of popping jokes—and back in the pre-heart attack days, he'd eat junk food anywhere. Rotting corpses regardless. "Looks like we're clear."

Speaking of stench, it was in her nose and down her esophagus. Dead bodies had a unique kind of odor that, once experienced, stayed with you like a core memory infused in your senses forever.

"Hmmm—I can taste it. They been cooking here for some time," Wilson said, like he was talking about pork chops instead of two cold ones—team blue and all.

Nazario yanked her shirt over her nose, but it barely helped. She gagged, coughing as her eyes watered. She'd handled worse without so much as a flinch, but ever since the baby, her senses had turned against her—stronger, sharper. The stench clawed at her throat, refusing to be ignored. She didn't always get queasy, but on occasions where decomposition had started to rot the body after a few days, it did get to her. Wilson, on the other hand, had a nose and stomach made of steel. Nothing made the man sick. He could still eat a full meal right after a grisly homicide scene and, more impressively, munch on a jelly donut during one.

Wilson walked in first, and she shuffled in behind. She could hardly make out a thing in the dimness that obscured her vision before her partner flicked the light on. Everything inside was quite orderly. She'd half expected the décor to have a woman's touch. However, the inside appeared to have been pre-furnished at a garage sale. The sofa was at least a decade old, with a small hole eaten away in one of the cushions. The coffee table was scratched up from wear and tear, yet remained sturdy.

The walls were adorned with old black-and-white Western photographs—a relic of a bygone era that no one in the twenty-first century would choose for decoration. Nazario paused at a framed article praising Cheonsa's impressive speed in track—something they had in common. The small abode reeked of old mothballs and the decomposition of human flesh, spreading through the air like malicious fungus.

But it was curious where their 'brothers in blue' were located—slumped over, handcuffed to an oak dining table as old as everything else but as strong as the tree it had been made from. Nazario squatted down for a closer look, shirt still covering her nose and mouth. Blow flies and maggots had already started to infest the body. In the spring month of April, they had some rain, making it humid enough to attract the flies. There weren't too many, though, since the wounds on both bodies had been the point-blank gunshots to their head.

But the blowflies sure loved the rigor mortis stench and feasting on the corpses that looked at least a few days old. Headlights showed through the windows, and a white coroner's van pulled up. They were early, since they couldn't haul the bodies away until the Scientific Investigation Division (SID) had arrived. Other than the grotesque fly food, it hadn't been as ugly a scene as the ones left behind by The Serpent Woman—Von Schlange or Dr. Wilder Friedrich—who, if she were still breathing air somewhere on Earth instead of six feet under, would most likely be going by yet another name.

"These blowflies," Nazario admitted, "are making me a tad sick. I kinda get post-pregnancy sickness ... if that's even a thing. Never had a single day of morning sickness until after I popped my daughter out."

"Nah, this isn't postpartum anything—just plain nasty, is all it is." Wilson crunched loudly. Nazario glanced at him sideways, unsurprised. She hadn't realized he'd brought his bag of baby carrots with him. He turned to her and offered the bag. "Want one?"

"Speaking of nasty, you realize that's what you are, right?" she muttered, still breathing in her shirt.

He let out a low, hearty chuckle—classic Wilson, just as Nazario's phone chimed with a text. She looked down—it was Ellen Yang from the Scientific Investigation Division. Ellen and Chuck Whittier were leads on SID.

Yang: *Running late ... sorry we got lost.*

"Lemme guess, they couldn't find this place?"

"Correctomundo."

The coroner and his assistant walked in. Wilson filled them in on the delay as Nazario wandered around. There was nothing amiss in the living room or the small kitchen except for the two cold rookie officers, who seemed to have at least gone out via quick and painless execution. Nazario walked to the back room and had a look around. Grandmotherly paisley wallpaper stained yellow with age plastered the single bathroom that looked no bigger than a porta potty. In the back, there was a separate office and a bedroom with the bed neatly made. The closet hung friendless hangers.

Digging in her pockets, Nazario pulled out disposable gloves and snapped them on. She opened the bedroom's dresser drawers, but they were empty. Nazario wondered if she had missed anything and walked back to the officer. There was a printer that didn't look too old planted against the wall next to the window across the desk. Following her instincts, Nazario strode toward the printer and noticed a small stack of paper about an inch thick facing down. It looked like someone had printed not just one or two things, but a whole stack—of what? That was to be determined.

The first page told her what they might expect from the rest of the material.

"Wilson," Nazario hollered, "think we got something over here."

Wilson came in and looked over her shoulder as they read together.

from: Cheonsa Soo-Min <csoomin@gmail.com>
to: Col. Merrick Winslow <mwinslow@gmail.com>
date: Apr 19, 2024, 2:43 PM
subject: i'll find you

I will always love you. No one will ever love you like I do. No one can give you the kind of love that I can give you, Merrick. Wherever you go, I'll find you. You are my home. You are my life. I will always be your wife. I will always be your first love. You can't do this without me. You miss me—I know you do. It'll just take time, you'll see. Every time you leave again, it makes me want you more. I crave your touch, your body. You think the grass is greener on the other side. You'll realize that it's all the same and what you had with me was better than anything you could get anywhere else.

You'll regret leaving me. You'll regret being with those other bitches. And they're all bitches. I promise I'll find you and we'll be together again.

Til death do us part, Merrick. I keep my vows.

With all my love,
Your Cheonsa …Your Angel

Wilson whistled. "Looks like we got us a Jodi Arias on our hands," he tsked, taking out another baby carrot and crunching obnoxiously in her ear. "I know what it's like when it's one-sided. When they can't stand to see your skin hanging all over you, unable to find my—"

"Hey, Bugs Bunny, can you put the carrots away?"

He shoved the small bag into his inside blazer pocket. "Well, alright then, Grumpy. Can't wait to see what the colonel has to say about his ex."

from: Col. Merrick Winslow<mwinslow@gmail.com>
to: Cheonsa Soo-Min <csoomin@gmail.com>
date: Apr 19, 2024, 7:28 PM
subject: Re: i'll find you

Cheonsa, for the last time, please leave me the hell ALONE! Told you a million times and you just don't get it. I've happily moved on, and I want you to do the same. Get help! You're in violation of the MPO and the civilian restraining order. These are no-contact, and I'm forced to get the law involved. I've warned you that if you do not stop the stalking, the harassing—I won't be giving you any more opportunities to get yourself right.

Your chances are all used up, and this time, I'm not bailing you out.

W-

THREE
THE SERPENT'S NEW SKIN

THE EARLY MORNING sun stained the sky with smoldering embers, transforming gray clouds that lingered near the horizon into fierce streaks of flame. Dr. Agatha Jones grazed her fingers across the top of Zeus's head as together they watched the horizon of Rio de Janeiro get kissed with a lavender rose hue.

From their luxurious high-rise executive suite, they enjoyed a perfect panoramic view of Guanabara Bay. Agatha and her beloved German Shepherd were early risers, consistently waking several hours before the first light of dawn. Despite Dr. Damião Sequeira's persistent advances, she kept him at a careful distance. They shared the spacious two-bedroom, fully furnished apartment, complete with elegant peroba wood and marble flooring. Damião was her roommate and nothing more—despite his striking dark hair, olive skin, and alluring Brazilian accent.

She couldn't risk getting caught up in anything romantic. Agatha was still on edge, still getting used to being called by her given middle name, still getting adjusted to living her life as Dr. Jones and not Von Schlange. Gone was who she truly was—

Wilder Agatha Friedrich had died the day her sister Sammy had died. She could never go back to who she'd been, especially given that Damião had only known her as Wilder.

Zeus knew all of her, though. He was her best friend, confidant, and faithful companion no matter what she called herself or how many varying IDs, passports, and aliases she owned. Agatha finished her coffee, laced her running shoes, and got Zeus's leash.

"Zeit zu rennen?"

Zeus, who only understood German commands, scrambled to his feet and barked once, announcing that he was indeed ready for a run. His attention shifted behind her, alerting her that they were no longer alone. Agatha turned around, and Damião's bronze torso screamed out against the white walls. He rested his forearm above his head, leaning it against the doorframe of his bedroom. He wasn't a hulking bodybuilder but was muscular in a natural, organic way. His physique resembled a cobra: broad in back and chest, narrowing gracefully to a tapered waist.

Agatha's eyes flitted away, trailing down to the ground, her leg absently kicked at the air. She cleared her throat.

"May I come?" Damião said, then pivoted to Portuguese. *"Ir correr com você?"*

One thing that came quite easily to Agatha was linguistics. She spoke English, German, Spanish, and having lived in Brazil for about a year, Portuguese hadn't been all that difficult to pick up. After all, the romance language had similarities to Spanish.

"Sim," she answered, letting him know he could come on the run. "Hope we didn't wake you? Zeus's bark is a little loud."

"Não ... was overthinking the marketing for our clinic, couldn't sleep. Was thinking that maybe we, I dunno—"

"Hire someone?"

"Thought I could handle it, but it's a lot of work and requires a seasoned digital marketing pro who knows what they're doing. Prefer someone who's social media savvy. Maybe one of these college grads. It's a unique model. I know you said Seattle has one that treats humans and animals, but it's the first of its kind around here. Would you be okay with that? I mean, neither of us is on social. We don't have to put your picture up. I'll honor that, but we need someone to help us. What do you think?"

Hesitating for a beat. "As long as it's your face," Von conceded, "and not mine that's on the website."

"*Ótimo,*" he exclaimed cheerfully. It indeed was great, Agatha thought. Their veterinarian and family clinic was unique and cost-effective, providing affordable care for low-income populations and pet owners who didn't want treatment to feel like a mortgage payment.

"How 'bout we run first, do business later?"

"I know Zeus, he can protect you, but I get worried when you *correr* alone."

"Been fine so far."

"Brazil isn't Beverly Hills—it's very dangerous."

"And I'm not your ordinary woman," she said, her warning carrying a tone of gravity that shadowed his face with fear.

"*Não,* of course, definitely not ordinary—but who wants boring?" He retreated to his bedroom and, regrettably, put on a T-shirt and running shorts. She might've lingered a little longer, but her eye candy had a respectful disposition that made him too polite to ogle without eliciting feelings of guilt. His breathable running shirt stuck to his form, carefully molding itself to his svelte frame. He looked as good with clothes on, and she wondered why she'd stubbornly kept her relationship with her roomie strictly platonic.

"Ready?"

"*Sim* ... you lead, I'll follow behind."

Every time she heard yes in Portuguese, it always reminded her of a SIM card. But *sim* meant yes—much like *sí* meant yes in Spanish, just without the 'm'.

They jogged along a familiar path that led into the Tijuca forest, famous for the giant Christ the Redeemer statue perched on Corcovado Mountain. But her favorite part was the breath-taking, towering trees that provided a rich biodiversity of flora and fauna. There were at least ten kinds of tree species, but the Brazilwood was her favorite because it boasted vibrant green foliage. When cut, Brazilwood, also known to the locals as *Pau-brasil*, had an earthy, sweet aroma, but with age, the scent deep-ened into a tender vanilla sandalwood laced with spice undertones.

Agatha felt alive and one with the forest, embraced in nature's grasp. The air was clean and refreshing, like a burst of country in her lungs. As she jogged, Zeus fell a step ahead, guarding at her left. She'd worried about his hips with age, but he seemed to have defied any signs of hip dysplasia, which was typical for German Shepherds and larger breed dogs. The early morning was gorgeous. It was a good choice they'd made to live close to the Tijuca forest instead of in the city.

As they ran, the high-pitched chirps, trills, and whistles of the vocal marmosets swung from the fig trees. These small, charming monkeys were 20 centimeters (8 inches) in length with distinct gray, brown, and gold dense fur and long tufts of white or black furry ears that wildly extended on either side of their heads. The marmosets had long tails that helped with balance when leaping from branch to branch. As a veterinarian, Agatha loved these morning nature runs that connected her to the wildlife.

The fig trees embraced her with the mild, sweet scent and a

woody undertone that came from the leaves. But when the trees were ripe with figs, the aroma was even more pronounced. On average, the trees grew to an impressive 9 meters, which was roughly 30 feet tall. However, some soared to an astonishing 15 meters—50 feet tall. It made her feel protected, enclosed in Mother Nature's majestic embrace.

The sun's rays filtered through the trees, casting playful shadows that flickered and danced along the trail as they ran. Agatha knew that Rio de Janeiro's poor air quality was largely due to heavy traffic, industrial activities, and extensive local mining. The extraction of iron ore, gold, bauxite, nickel, tin, niobium, and other rare earth elements had caused significant land degradation. This widespread activity contributed to deforestation in parts of the Amazon, worsening Brazil's environmental and health concerns even further.

Her daily jogs through the Tijuca Forest brought her as close to clean air as she could get. The blend of organic scents from the various tree species, paired with the calls of different birds, created a wild symphony. Birds like the Toucan, Rufous-bellied Thrush, Saw-billed Hermit, Dusky-legged Guan, Blue Manakin, White-necked Hawk, Brazilian Tanager, Yellow-legged Thrush, Slaty-breasted Wood-Rail, and Channel-billed Toucan, each with its unique beak, color, size, and musical tone, all contributed to the richness of Brazil's biodiverse rainforest.

There had been only one sighting of the ocelot. They were smaller wild, cats that surprisingly, scared her more than the time they'd been detoured by a boa constrictor that had been a sandy brown-gray color that blended with the soil beneath it. It had been more than 3 meters long—10 feet and robust in thickness. It glided across their path, and for twenty minutes, she and Zeus had remained still as a statue. It took its time and finally slithered away.

Agatha, who'd grown out the hair on the right side of her

head, had concealed her own serpent—a beautiful, detailed tattoo in red ink, etched across her scalp, its fangs landing at her temple. Von Schlange had, for now, been buried beneath the hair growth that hid her venomous strike. But she'd never stopped going to the gym, so Agatha's toned body had grown into itself. Her biceps and upper chest were now defined like a well-sculpted athlete. She wasn't as big as some women who were professional bodybuilders. However, she was muscular enough to turn heads and intimidate some of the gym rats.

She did miss Von and even Dr. Wilder Agatha Friedrich—her birth name. But Dr. Agatha Jones had grown on her. Prior to her move to "the land of the samba and soccer," she'd done away with Wilder and became Von Schlange—Schlange, as her father had named her post-surgery, the one that extracted her female parts, making it impossible for her to ever carry a child.

"You made my daughter a *schlange!*" her father's voice cracked, raw with fury and heartbreak. The renowned neuro-surgeon had glared at Damião, the man who'd wielded the scalpel. The surgery had been necessary—but the emergency hysterectomy cost her more than just her health. At thirty, she'd been thrust into surgical menopause, her life forever changed.

Schlange: the German word for serpent. The hideous dark red and thick keloid scar in the shape of a large snake remained on her belly like a private accusation, a silent witness to the violence she had endured, survived. Yes, Von Schlange was indeed a part of her. But Wilder, the innocent veterinarian, the animal-loving, kind woman who always gave people the benefit of the doubt and saw them for the goodness that they could be, had died along with her unborn child she'd lost to the cruel blade that gutted her open like a pig.

Now, the burn of her quads and hamstrings felt good. Her abdomen, which boasted a six-pack she'd earned, contracted as she gave each forward movement full throttle. They were all her, regardless of what she called herself. They were one with her, each new identity, each name, each trauma that had made her. Though Von had retired, a twisted part of her missed the call, the thirst, and the hunger to right a wrong and to do it in the most inhumane way.

She craved the perpetrators' fear.

She desired their plea.

She yearned for the kill.

Suddenly, a distinct and sharp whistling noise pierced her sensitive eardrums as if a prize had fallen into her lap. The sound continued like a relentless panic. It was coming from a small riverbank. She'd first found the spot for Zeus to drink during one of their early runs—not because she could see it. The rich vegetation—tall ferns, tropical foliage, bromeliads, and orchids—thrived in the moist, organic soil. That's how she'd known a riverbank was near.

"Did you hear that?" Damião whispered.

"Yeah," Agatha said, "it sounds like capybaras—but it's not good. It's the kind of sound they make when they're in danger."

Capybaras were the largest rodents in the world and were endangered primarily because they were often targeted for their fur by poachers.

Zeus's ears perked up to the sharp whistling sound that cried out once more.

"They have to be near that riverbank. They prefer living near water." Agatha clicked her tongue and ordered Zeus, "*Finde es!*"

Obeying her command, Zeus ran westbound toward the river as Agatha and Damião followed. A man clad in camouflage clothing, knee-high waterproof boots, and a matching brimmed sun hat loomed over a capybara ensnared in a poacher's net. In his hand, Agatha recognized the IMBEL IA2. It was a black, sleek, modern rifle made with high-strength polymers and metals with a long barrel and what looked like a flash suppressor at the tip. The suppressor came in handy for poachers attempting to improve shooter concealability and limit muzzle flashes. The IMBEL IA2 weighed around 3.3 to 3.8 kilograms (or 7.3 to 8.4 pounds) and had primarily been designed for use by the Brazilian military. But, due to its capability to muffle shots, Agatha could see why this hunter was using it.

The capybara made another alarming call, and this time, it sounded like a husky bark. Just as the poacher raised his assault rifle, Zeus sprinted even faster, his muscular hind legs powering him forward. He leaped, catching air as his mouth landed with perfect aim, clamping around the barrel. Alarmed, the man jerked backward, finger squeezing the trigger. A shot cleaved the morning air at a diagonal angle, hitting the top of a nearby tree.

Near the poacher's feet, there was a cage trap with at least six pups inside that Agatha could see, which was the average litter a female capybara would give birth to. It must've been the mother trapped in the hunter's snare nearby, the net making it impossible for her to find a way out. The capybara appeared to be the average 35 to 66 kg (77 to 146 lbs), so the net used was likely weighted to reduce escape.

Agatha sprinted toward the man decked out in camo and geared to snatch the mother and her pups. They'd all be killed and stripped of their fur, which would be sold on the black market not only in Brazil but neighboring countries for cold, hard cash. Her thirst to right this wrong returned, and before she could even consider concealing the truth of her character from the man she was sure had fallen in love with her, Agatha drove her body forward at a speed that outperformed her male companion. Her muscular thighs pounded hard, defined calves like a well-oiled machine, taking her to her target.

Damião called after her. His voice lost in the wind, whipping past her as her arms became pistons, cycling her toward the poacher until she caught up with Zeus. Her dog wrestled with the gun, the hunter kicking Zeus in the ribs, but her German Shepherd refused to release the prize he'd been taught to never surrender—guns. Agatha hated them. Zeus hated them more.

Agatha picked up momentum and, as soon as she was within proximity, threw a front strike with her closed fist across the hunter's jaw. Her mean right hook immediately drew blood—sent it gushing from his nose. She'd never stopped pumping the weights since her full hysterectomy—thanks to the attack that killed any chance of ever being a mother. The traumatic event permanently cauterized her old self, giving birth to Von Schlange, who emerged out of hibernation.

The man tried to shoot her but was weighed down by Zeus, who was a hefty one hundred pounds or so of hard-earned muscle. When her fist connected with his jaw and nose, his grip on the rifle loosened. His footing staggered him back. Zeus managed to tear the IMBEL IA2 away.

"*Guter Junge*," Agatha praised Zeus as she snatched the rifle from her dog's mouth. Without thinking, her body moved on its own accord as she swung the rifle, using it to bat the poacher across the face. He fell back, tripping over large boulders and crashing into the riverbed behind him.

"Stay the fuck down," she demanded, and in case he didn't understand English, she reclarified in his native tongue. "*Fique abaixado.*"

The man brazenly grabbed the muzzle of the gun with one hand and wrapped his other free arm around her legs, pulling forward and forcing her to fall backward. Zeus returned to assist, growling as he clamped at the hunter's forearm. But it didn't seem to faze the man, as he stubbornly held on to Agatha's legs, pulling her toward him and using it as leverage to hoist himself up. She kicked her boot at his face hard enough to cause him to fall backward again into the riverbank. His head hit a rock, drawing a stream of blood down his forehead from the open gash.

Damião charged from behind, but the hunter swiftly reclaimed the rifle, spinning it toward them with lethal precision. A deafening crack echoed as the shot whizzed past her, its trajectory aimed at Damião. The doctor instinctively dove to the ground, the bullet slicing through the air inches from where he had stood. Finding her balance, she slipped her legs from the poacher's grasp and lunged forward, her right hook connecting with his jaw. She quickly straddled him as Zeus clamped his jaws harder around the man's forearm, drawing blood. The poacher cried out in pain, releasing the weapon as she took custody of it. Using the handle of the weapon, Agatha slammed it down on his face in repeated blows. She lifted the rifle and brought it crashing down—again and again, each strike more savage, each blow landing with bone-shattering force.

Blood gushed from his nose, and then she hit his mouth with such force that Agatha knocked his incisors—his two front teeth —down his throat. The punishing motion was a repeated action that completely swept over her. That switch in her head, the one that warned the average person to stop, that switch that told her when enough was enough, didn't click on.

"*Pare! Você vai matá-lo!*" Damião cried out, and when his urging went ignored, he repeated in English, "Stop! You're going to kill him!"

The rifle's shoulder stock bottom was bloodied from the stranger's vital fluids.

Agatha lurched the rifle back even further this time and then charged it forward one final time, brutally slamming it in the man's face with all her strength, ripping open a large gash in his jowl, caving in his cheekbone. His mouth—like his face—was full of blood. He groaned, hardly able to mutter the agony he must've been in.

Damião screamed her name, and when she didn't answer, "Von ... Von Schlange!"

Her body froze. Zeus's ears perked as he and his master turned to the voice.

FOUR

THE VICTIM'S NEW ROLE

FROM THE MOMENT the plane taxied onto the runway, Cheonsa Soo-Min could hardly believe she had made it in one piece. Brazil was anything but ordinary. The air carried a collage of wonderful scents—salty from the ocean, hints of tropical blooms, and the unmistakable warmth of the city. Copacabana wasn't far, just south of Galeão Airport, where she'd arrived, its golden sands and crashing waves already pulling at her imagination.

Coffee in Brazil was a celebration, as the country was a major producer and exporter, with countless coffee houses throughout. During the first two weeks, Cheonsa felt like she'd found heaven on earth and wanted to experience everything there was to Brazil. Despite constantly looking over her shoulder, she'd managed to enjoy small pleasures like good Brazilian coffee and restaurants. She admired *Confeitaria Colombo's* imperial charm, renowned for its Belle Époque architecture, regal interior, and elegant culinary offerings that drew countless visitors, but the grand open space made her uneasy.

Cheonsa preferred the *Café Secreto*, literally translated as Secret Café, for its cozy atmosphere and somewhat concealed location. It had little foot traffic and wasn't a typical tourist area. Without local guidance, Cheonsa would've struggled to find *Vila do Largo*—the narrow alleyway that concealed the café house, an inconspicuous hidden gem. Two narrow buildings walled the backstreet. There was something comfortable about the closed-in space. While some might consider it a bit claustrophobic, Cheonsa adored small spaces, tiny studio apartments, and simple living that required only what she could pack in one suitcase.

Ever since she was little, the world had always been experienced through the nose.

Brazilian coffee was coveted worldwide, but even the tastiest and most expensive coffees couldn't compare to the bold richness of a freshly brewed cup in its homeland. She'd barely let herself enjoy it. The sprawling Rio Verde Coffee Plantation was bordered by dense Atlantic Forest, the air thick with the unexpected sweetness of Coffea blossoms—a heady collision of jasmine and orange blossom. Even that scent, decadent and grounding, couldn't push away the weight pressing on her chest.

Merrick was out there.

She could feel it.

Closing in.

Hunting her.

The cops must've thought the colonel was there to uncuff them. To save them.

Had their relief twisted into horror when he raised the Glock?

She swallowed hard.

No.

She had never meant for them to die. But intentions didn't matter when bodies hit the ground. Closing her eyes, she imagined the beautiful partnership between her father and mother— their effortless way toward one another, the humor that never took itself too seriously. What would they think now, knowing their daughter carried a criminal record, one she hadn't even earned with her own hands?

Appa and Umma—her father and mother, Han-Joon Soo Min and Jisoo Soo-Min—shared more than just a marriage. They shared a calling. Appa and Umma met at Seoul National University. The two had the same academic pursuits—but more than that, there was an undeniable chemistry that went beyond their scientific studies of molecules and reactions. Her parents were fragrance chemists and so alike that they were practically one person.

After immigrating to the United States, Umma and Appa loved to work a little *too* much. They'd turned Scents of Han into a thriving small business. Not because Appa wanted his name on the business, but because Umma convinced him it had a catchy ring.

The rich aroma of the coffee plantations intertwined with the sweet scent of the white Coffea blossoms, carried by the salty Atlantic breeze. The humid air clung to her skin, infused with the heady fragrance of wild orchids, frangipani, plumerias, passion flowers, gardenias, and hibiscus—a lush, intoxicating symphony of tropical blooms. They all grew in Brazil's tropical climate. Umma and Appa were at the forefront of her mind and heart as she visited Rio's Botanical Garden—*Jardim Botânico*.

Cheonsa visited just to be close to them. She'd been a late baby as her mother gave birth to her at forty-five, thanks to the miracle of IVF. Scents of Han had been such a popular, charming store that sold original perfumes, candles, oils, and scented lotions in the Manhattan Beach Village. All of the locals in the South Bay loved her parents' store, so it pained her to be near it after Appa had crashed his single-engine Cessna 172 Skyhawk.

She had learned to appreciate life not just with her eyes, but through her nose.

Han-Joon Soo Min and Jisoo Soo-Min would love the many wonderful scents of Brazil, from the coffee to the tropical flowers, the ocean, and the city streets full of eclectic Brazilian dishes and spices that tickled her taste buds. Everything in life was chemistry—a byproduct of interactions, reactions, and inevitable mixtures.

Coffee cherries had to undergo a transformation, and so the processing areas were a hive of activity. Basking under the sun were drying patios that colored long tables with red and green—both the coffee cherries and their green leaves got a chance to sunbathe. But the smoky aroma of large iron roasting drums was hypnotic as they churned while Cheonsa paused to watch. Unique flavors of tangy fermentation added to the plantation's symphony as workers sifted through the cherries with a raking motion that ensured drying was even.

"The fermentation process is quite important," a petite woman standing nearby said, though despite her size, there was something serious about her. She nodded to the wooden fermentation tanks at a distance, bubbling quietly. The air had a lovely post-ripening aroma—a potent blend of earthiness and yeast. The fermented cherries mingled with a woody flavor from the basins. Humming with rhythmic precision, the mechanical depulpers stripped the cherries of their flesh.

"Coffee cherries have an outer layer. The fruit pulp—a sticky substance called mucilage. The depulpers remove it in order to get to the heart of what we all need to stay alert. The coffee bean is inside waiting to be set free, and it takes a long process before the transformation can occur," the woman explained, and Cheonsa couldn't help but wonder if they were talking about something else.

What immediately caught Cheonsa's attention were two

things: the woman's arms were chiseled and muscular, making Cheonsa wonder if the rest of her looked the same, and the second thing—she was American. It was a relief to find a fellow American in Brazil, a small comfort in an unfamiliar place. By her side, a mean-looking German Shepherd sat obediently, its sharp gaze assessing every movement. As she took in the scars along its side and the jagged notch down his ear, she thought of the transformation that came with survival.

People, animals—even coffee cherries—were shaped by trials, enduring long, meticulous processes before revealing what lay beneath. From the hands of the workers to the sun-drying, fermentation, and the final expelling of the pulp and outer skin, everything had to be broken down before it could become something new.

"Are you here on vacation, or are you an expat in Rio de Janeiro looking for a total renovation of your life? To reinvent yourself, as they say?" The woman stunned Cheonsa with her intuition. "Oh, pardon my rudeness, they call me Dr. Agatha Jones around here—but you may call me Von ... Von Schlange—my real name."

Cheonsa frowned at the woman with two names and wondered how many other aliases she had stored in the digital space. Her roots sprouted sandy blond, but her hair was dyed black and cropped in an asymmetrical cut. She'd grown out the right side where it was once shaved. A portion of the tattoo crept across her cheek, temple, and upper brow, partially obscured by hair growth. A rose intertwined with the head of a snake in the design. Von also bore thorny vines with a skull nestled among them and a second serpent coiled elegantly around her neck. There were large holes—tunnels—on each earlobe from what looked like maybe 14-gauge piercings. She knew because one of her good friends in college had the same stretch.

Oddly enough, despite her own fear of needles and aversion to piercings and ink—not out of prudishness but due to a genuine phobia—Cheonsa had to admit that Von's tats and gauged lobes suited her perfectly.

"It's nice to meet a fellow American. Kind of a culture shock, but in a good way," she said, sticking out her hand. "Cheonsa Wi ... um ... Soo-Min. You've got two names, and I can't get my one right."

It was strange saying her maiden name again, as she'd been Cheonsa Winslow for so long. Being a wife was one thing—being Merrick's wife meant everything. Now, every time she looked down at her driver's license, she felt a pang of loss, of failure, that not-good-enough feeling eroding her confidence a day at a time. Ever since her marriage went into the trash compactor, she'd turned shyer. Her voice turned mousy, hands grew clammy, and her heart accelerated. In intimate gatherings or at parties where she had been invited and tagged along as a plus-one, it was much worse. She wanted to crawl out of her skin, sink in quicksand, climb under her bed covers, and hide from the world.

More than anything, what was most noticeable was how difficult it was to look people in the eyes. It was absolutely painful. Nothing hurt worse than the social anxiety that had suddenly manifested the moment she was no longer Colonel Merrick Winslow's wife. The way the other Army wives glared at her with pity and blame, as if it was something she did wrong. She wasn't a better leader. She wasn't Army material. She wasn't strong enough to be her husband's backbone.

Merrick was gorgeous. He had charisma. When he entered a room, people took notice. But what was more impressive was his way with words and his effortless, all-American charm. He was so good at public speaking that he put President Obama to shame. He had been her identity. He had been her everything.

Worse, everyone knew it then and especially now. If he needed witness or character statements, an entire platoon—along with their doting Army wives—would eagerly come forward to tattle on poor Cheonsa, who simply couldn't make the cut in the Officers' Wives Club.

They wouldn't believe her. They didn't know the real Merrick.

The bustling sounds of workers pausing the iron drum, which had been rotating over a flame, brought Cheonsa back from memories of her old life in the U.S. to Brazil. Cheonsa and her unusual new acquaintance stood watching the workers analyze the beans. Satisfied that they'd reached an appropriate roasting level, they extracted them and spread the coffee beans on cooling trays. A couple of loud fans were turned on and directed toward the trays. The fans lifted the scent of roasted coffee beans and wafted it through the air.

"My parents would've loved Brazil."

"How'd they die?"

Cheonsa blinked at Von's directness, keeping her eyes trained on the animated scene before her. Watching a Caucasian couple, most likely tourists, enter a quaint colonial-era farmhouse that had been turned into a visitor's center.

Cheonsa exhaled a tepid breath before answering Dr. Punk Rock, "What ... what makes you think they're dead?"

Von studied her carefully, gaze unreadable. "You talk about them in the past tense without realizing it. There's no hesitation, no mention of calling or visiting, just a quiet certainty. That kind of detachment doesn't come from distance—it comes from loss."

"My parents ... they were fragrance scientists," Cheonsa murmured, her gaze drifting toward the horizon. "They used to say that scents have layers, like memories. The top notes are the first impression—bright, fleeting, gone before you realize. Heart notes. Now, those are the soul, the steady rhythm beneath the surface. And the base notes? They always linger the longest."

"Sounds like the base notes are the foundation," Von said, impressing Cheonsa, who agreed with an eager nod. "Growing up must've been one big sensory experience."

"It was. If I had to choose, I'd prefer to go blind or deaf than lose my sense of smell."

"I can understand. And, sorry for your loss—that's if my assumptions are correct—none of my business, though."

"Appa had his pilot's license."

"Ah ... okay. Technical malfunction?"

Cheonsa cleared her throat uneasily. This Von had outstanding instincts. "Fog. They called it a total whiteout. Appa, he always ignored warnings, said the meteorologist didn't always know what they were talking about."

Cheonsa recalled how the broadcaster warned of a whiteout —fog so dense that it reduced visibility to zero. No condition for flying.

An empathetic smile played across Von's lips. "Sounds like my dad. Try living with a world-renowned brain surgeon who's King Asshole. Ever read *The Psychology of Trauma?*"

"Yes, I have. Love that book. It helped me through my ... well, it helped me through some rough patches."

"My mom's a shrink."

Cheonsa leaned in, her gaze locking onto Von's. The tatted doctor's gray eyes were sharp, cutting through the space between them. Something lurked beneath their surface—something nameless yet electric, prickling along Cheonsa's spine like a violin string wound too tight, one note away from snapping.

"Dr. Katrine Adele Friedrich is your mother?"

Von shrugged, feigning modesty.

"So, you do have a third name, as I suspected—Dr. Agatha Jones, Von Schlange, and Something Friedrich?"

"You got me. Just keep it on the DL. Not a lot of people know this."

"Why trust me?"

"I've got a good read on people. So does Zeus. If he trusts you—I trust you."

"I don't really talk to anyone from my ... from my old life." Cheonsa wrung her hands together, but the shake was noticeable. The doctor, with an assortment of pseudonyms and great instincts, glared down at her fidgeting.

"How long you been divorced?" Von caught herself. "My bad. Think maybe I can be a tad direct. I don't get a lot of Americanos coming around, so pardon me if I'm a little too eager to chat. Don't answer if you don't wanna—and I didn't mean to laugh or talk about me. Tragic how you lost your parents."

"What gave it away?"

"For one: the hesitation over your name—people don't usually stumble on something they've said a thousand times. And two: you're not wearing a ring on your left hand, but you still rub your finger like it's there. That habit takes a while to unlearn."

Cheonsa nodded, looking down at her feet.

"What kind of doctor?"

"Veterinarian."

"I can see that."

"You here on a short stay or longish stay?"

"One-way ticket."

"Whatdaya do?"

"Marketing. Before Merrick." Cheonsa covered her mouth, and her shoulders bobbed, face turning wet from the unexpected tears. "Don't have a job. Left everything. Had to."

Von put a hand on her shoulder. "Hey, hey, it's okay. My clinic's across from the visitor's center. You hungry? I make a mean sandwich. I'm vegan, but Zeus likes the lunch meat, and so does my business partner Dr. Sequeira—Damião Sequeira—he's a meat eater, too."

Feeling foolish, Cheonsa walked with her head down, wiping her face with her hands. At the clinic, she was surprised to discover that it was part veterinarian clinic and part family clinic. The unique setup served both animals and humans.

"Gotta say, never seen a clinic like this before—how original!"

"It was Damião's idea."

"Heard my name," Damião greeted them. Introducing himself, he stuck out his hand. Dr. Sequeira was the dark and handsome type with a lean-built physique that told Cheonsa that he wasn't a hardcore gym rat but the healthy type. He gave her his eyes in the way that a doctor with good bedside manners did, and it was all she could do not to tuck her head in her shirt like a turtle. He sensed her anxiety, and his tone softened. After listening to Von quietly, they both turned to her and offered an opportunity she hadn't expected so quickly.

"We've been looking for a marketing professional. In fact, I was about to post an ad. If you're interested, we'd love to offer you the job. It pays well, and we can even consider a bonus structure, an employee benefits package—things like that," Dr. Sequeira said.

Terrified to answer, she hesitated.

"Something wrong?" Von asked.

"I don't want you guys to get involved," Cheonsa said.

"Involved in what?" Von's disposition turned lethally serious.

Cheonsa shook her head. "It was nice to meet you, but he'll find me. I know he will. If you get in his crosshairs ... I gotta go."

Cheonsa got up abruptly and quickly ran off.

"Cheonsa ... hold up!" Von called out.

Fearing she had said too much already, Cheonsa dashed out

of the clinic, leaving behind Von's worried call. She weaved around the workers and crashed into one who was raking roasted coffee beans, scattering them all over the ground.

"Veja onde você está indo!" the man screamed, and Cheonsa knew enough Portuguese—which was the reason she chose Brazil—to know the busy plantation hand was telling her to watch where she was going.

Not having time to apologize, Cheonsa ran away to her cheap hostel, praying that this Von Schlange—Dr. Tattoos with the many names—would not follow her, and would forget they had met altogether.

FIVE
THE UNSEEN ENEMY

CHIEF JOHNSON LEANED back into his desk chair, scratching the five o'clock stubble sprouting across his jawline, silvery peppered growth contrasting against his deep brown skin. Nazario hadn't seen the chief with a beard before—it looked good on him—except the dark rings under his eyes gave her a spell of worry.

"Moved out, Chief? Thought things were looking up?" Nazario threw it out there. Why skip around it? Wilson gave her a kick with his running shoes. She gave him a 'what?' look, to which he threw a 'you know what' look right back.

"Went downhill mighty fast. Filled up the U-Haul, just wish I was filled up with something other than—fuck, I dunno—'if only' statements running through my head day and night. Like that stupid *Bad Boy's* song from that old *Cops* TV show—hated that damn show but hated that song even more." The chief jabbed a pen in the air at Wilson, who loved being goofy. "And doncha dare sing it, hum it—nothin'."

Wilson surrendered his hands in the air and did his level best to hold his laughter in, but Nazario could tell he barely contained it. He had a bad habit of whistling, humming, and singing, which annoyed everyone.

"Real sorry, sir," Wilson offered gently, "been through a divorce myself. It truly is just an awful, *awful* experience. Even when we left things with 'let's be friends,' it was the hardest thing I've ever had to experience."

That was why Wilson was such a good negotiator, Nazario thought—why she was the more short-fused one of the two, and why they worked well together. Wilson was always level-headed. What was most annoying was that he never got mad. If he ever remotely got upset, he always kept composed. Nazario was a whole other issue.

Chief Johnson raked a hand down his face. "Fuck, man."

"Maybe you should take a leave?" Nazario suggested.

"Nah, if I ain't working, I'm not living. Can't take off. Sit around on my ass, going stir-crazy. Listening to old Bill Withers 'Ain't No Sunshine.' Thinking about what went wrong. Why me and all that nonsense. Crying down a bottle of Hennessy— don't think so." Johnson leaned in and steepled his fingers. "Gimme whatcha got on those rookies—shot upside the head or what?"

"And handcuffed to the kitchen table, a nice sturdy one, too, I might add. Real Australian buloke. You know the buloke is considered the strongest wood in the world? It can withstand more than five thousand pounds of force. Not totally proven, of course. It's based on one study, but I believe it," Wilson said.

"How you know so much 'bout hardwood—'less you count handlin' your morning wood?" Johnson snickered.

Wilson let out a belly laugh.

"In the 'Curious' category for 400, I'd like to know the answer to that, too, Alex," Nazario said.

"You're aging me, Nazario. You realize there's a whole Z generation that'd never get that Jeopardy joke?" Wilson took out his plastic baggie of baby carrots and plunked one into his mouth. Crunching loudly, he shrugged. "I'm a nature man, y'all know that. Fishing, camping—can't be out in nature and not learn a thing or two."

"So, answer me this: what kinda person needs a table that can withstand five thousand pounds of pressure? What kinda person buys an Australian bu-whatever-you-call-it—table? Why not Ikea?"

Wilson cringed. "That's no place for quality furniture. Garbage that falls apart—cheap dorm room crap."

"Hey!" Chief Johnson pointed his pen at Wilson. "You best not talk shit 'bout Ikea. Those are some fightin' words. Gotta dining room table, in fact, bought it at Ikea—still standing, still working—six years running, SIX."

"'Cause I haven't dined on it yet. Get me over for some barbecue, and I guarantee you my fat butt will break that chair."

"My ex-brother-in-law, his ass is a whole lot bigger than yours. At least you lost weight. He, on the other hand, gained by a lot—like over a hundred pounds a lot—and all this year alone. Brotha's at least four hundred pounds now—and that's being generous. Comes over. Empties my fridge down his gullet, eating me outta house and home. That's why I'm divorced, y'know? Wife and I couldn't stop arguing over the fat bastard. That and the long hours. Told her, 'Why you complaining now? Shit—shouldn't've married a cop.' And that Ikea table and its chair have seen more of my brother-in-law's ass than I've seen of my wife's—and it's still holdin' up today."

Refocusing the convo from home décor to its relevancy to the case, Nazario chimed in, "So, off this—who's got the biggest ass—pissing contest. The original question was what kind of person would buy a table that's not your typical purchase like Ikea, Ashley's, Living Spaces. This Australian wood, to me, is more than the strength of the wood. Maybe the person likes to travel? They like exotic things. They'll buy a table just because it's got the word Australian in it. So many people buy Italian stuff for its namesake. Italian shoes. Italian leather. Oriental—excuse me—Asian-made rugs. The hell if anyone even knows if it's all any better than our lame American made?"

"Good point, good point, okay, so we got a potential world traveler, someone cultured, got me a CP yet?"

"Not yet, no, something about the FBI holding onto the files?" Nazario bit out, having a love-hate relationship with the bureau. But since she was freshly moved in with her baby daddy—who happened to be a supervising special agent—she had to play nice.

Chief Johnson gave her an overly wide grin that spread ear to ear.

Narrowing her eyes at her boss. "Better not say what I think you're about to say."

"Oh boy," Wilson said knowingly, "gonna ask us to share our toys, aren'tcha?"

"He's the best, and you know he is," Chief said.

"You're really gonna pull him off paternity leave?"

"It'll only be part-time. Y'all nice and cozy now. Moved in. If you could get through a case when y'all hated each other's guts—you can get through one now in parental bliss."

"Can't we work with any FBI agent other than Blake Huxley?"

"What're you afraid he'll pop the question, and you'll have to consider taking your relationship up a notch?" Johnson jousted with her.

"Doncha even say the M-Word, sir. Doncha fucking say it." Nazario struggled to suppress her panic. "Barely moved in—lemme take it one step at a time. Not ready to pick out wedding dresses or change my last name—baby or not."

"Look, Huxley's one of their top agents. Y'all worked on two female serial killer cases—that ain't nothing. They'd keep throwing y'all together like peanut butter and jelly. Don't matter if y'all gotta personal history or just kicking as homies. Why? Y'all are the two best in the field. Not trying to leave ya out, Wilson. We can't do it withoutcha."

"Guess I'm the bread in this scenario," Wilson chuckled.

Johnson pivoted back to her, gesturing emphatically with his hands like he always did when he was trying to sell her, get her onboard without a stubborn fight.

"It'll be part-time. He'll have plenty of time to spend with Ariabella."

"Since when is part-time a few hours? Part-time is more like forty, and full-time is more like sixty a week—you and I know it. That divorce of yours was more than arguing over Fat Albert. She couldn't handle the lifestyle no more. You—gone all the time. The long hours. C'mon, Chief. Pulling Huxley from paternity leave—we might as well hire a full-time nanny 'cause Mom and Dad aren't going to be around."

"Max twenty hours out of Huxley. Promise. On your father's grave, you got my oath. Plus, we cover the cost of that nanny."

Lucas Nazario, her father, had been the highest-ranking Puerto Rican detective on the force until he was killed while undercover. It was Huxley who had opened up the cold case and solved it, linking the homicide to their unlikely serial killer —Madison Vanwell—her father's jealous lover who objected to the fact that he wasn't planning on leaving his wife. Her father and Chief Trevor Johnson were partners together for years prior to climbing the ranks. If it were anyone else, she would've taken offense to the oath on her father's life.

But she knew where the chief's heart was and that he meant well.

"And who's paying for all this? The bureau or the LAPD?

You guys don't have the budget put together. You do realize how expensive a nanny is? Minimum twenty-five an hour. That's at least fifty-two G's a year. We're in SoCal, not Wisconsin."

"Damn, if kids cost that much, think I'll stick to babysitting my plants," Wilson quipped.

"A cost-effective choice for now," Chief lectured Wilson, who laughed it off, "but good luck getting a damn fern to take care of you when you're old." Chief turned to Nazario with the earnestness of a used car salesman needing to sell a car today, or they don't make rent. "It is in our budget. M'kay. We making it happen. We need you and your Baby Daddy—and that's *that*."

Nazario exhaled a long sigh before finally nodding her agreement.

"Fine. How soon are we talking?"

"Now, don't get mad at him—"

"C'mon, you didn't already arrange this behind my back?"

"We just needed one parental consent before proceeding—Huxley was cool with it," Johnson said. "They released the file over to him since he's the supervising agent and got above top-secret clearance. The files aren't ATS, but they wanted a top agent handling this due to who's involved. He should be here any minute."

"You arranged a fucking babysitter behind my back?" Nazario bit out. "And what do you mean 'who's involved?'"

"I'd imagine we got ourselves a high-profile," Wilson said, "some big wig." He took out a pack of gum from his inside coat pocket. Her partner always had something on him to put in his mouth.

"Gum, anyone?" Wilson offered. "Sugar-free."

Chief Johnson shooed her partner away like he was an annoying fly and continued.

"And you just said yes to my babysitter idea. What's the difference between meeting with the four of us now versus later on?" the chief asked. "I'm her Godfather anyhow. Y'all know I don't have grandkids—sweet Ariabella's all I got for a grandbaby. Got her best interest at heart and yours, and you know it. Would I do anything to jeopardize our relationship? Jeopardize my career and yours?"

"No, sir."

"Mea culpa for the way it went down, but due to the nature of the case, I was asked by people way above me to get Huxley on this ASAP," Johnson explained.

"How high up?" Nazario wanted to know.

"Executive orders—like from the U.S. President, that's how high up," said Johnson.

"Holy moly, cannoli," Wilson muttered, chewing his gum like he wished it were an Italian dessert. "Our first executive order, Nazario. This is going to be a treat."

Had it been anyone else, she'd have let the sense of betrayal eat away at her, let it stick in her mind like Crazy Glue. Once someone was on Nazario's shit-list, there was no turning back. They were dead to her. Some people were forgetful. Nazario had the opposite problem—she couldn't forgive and forget no matter how hard she tried. That was partly the reason why she'd cycle through staying sober and hitting the wine bottles. Gus, her best friend and sponsor, always told her the biggest problem she had was not being able to make amends. She continuously had issues with step eight, which was writing out a list of people that have either hurt you or you hurt them. Step nine was even worse—making amends with each of them.

Fuck all that—was how Nazario handled those steps.

But Chief Johnson had been in her life since she was a baby. He was her father's best friend and partner, and that was not something small. Chief Johnson was more than her boss, more than the first black officer to rise the rank, similar to her father, who held the Puerto Rican title for that. Johnson was a whole lot more to her—he was family.

But what kind of case would involve the sitting president? Who was involved?

Her answer walked through the doors, and Huxley nodded at Chief Johnson before giving her 'forgive me' eyes. Before she could launch into him, he got ahead of her wrath with a parental explanation to ensure their daughter was in safe hands.

"Nana—Mom is willing to watch her since Dad's visiting my younger brothers. She's got the time, and you know she's been dying to watch her."

The Huxley men were all imposing figures, built like thoroughbred horses. Even his father looked like he lived at the gym, and so did his two younger brothers, who shared the same robust physique, though Blake remained the largest of them all. It was evident in the way he entered the room. His six-foot-four muscular frame loomed, making the space around them shrink as if a giant had joined their midst.

Ingrid Margaux Huxley, on the other hand, was a tall, beautiful swan. She moved with a grace that was as effortless as it was timeless, turning heads even in her senior years. She had Huxley's ice-blue eyes and Scandinavian pale features. Nazario had assumed her daughter would inherit Huxley's eyes, but Ariabella had very light brown eyes that were a beautiful golden caramel color. Deep down, she was secretly happy their daughter looked so much like her.

Ingrid was as sweet as she was stunning—the most gorgeous grandmother Nazario had ever seen. She had an endearing Swedish accent that made her enunciate her vowels differently —cat sounded like cot. Desperate for a grandchild that none of the Huxley boys had yet delivered, Huxley's parents had quickly moved from Half-Moon Bay in northern California to

Brentwood—all but five minutes away from their son's home—the moment their first grandchild was born.

Huxley sat down, making his looming presence less pronounced.

When Nazario wouldn't look at him, he pled, "C'mon babe, you really gonna hold this against me? It was an executive order—"

"Don't 'babe' me you could've at least told me Ingrid was coming over. Could've at least told me you were joining this meeting. You being here—that wasn't top secret, was it?"

"It ain't his fault. Put the blame on me. If we had asked you for your permission, would you have agreed?" Johnson didn't wait for her answer to the rhetorical question. "No, course you wouldn't've. This was the only way we could get everyone here —stat."

Nazario exhaled and met Huxley's eyes. As much as Ariabella looked like her, she could see a lot of Daddy in their daughter, too. Before becoming a mom, she could hold on to "pissed off" forever. Now? It was hard to stay mad when the miracle of motherhood and the sweet, precious gift they had together was waiting at home for them. Innocent life: part her, part him. They had their first child in their forties, which was a fucking miracle in and of itself.

When she looked at Ariabella with her bright caramel eyes, curly dark hair, and sweet smile, Nazario knew she was possibly her last good ovum. With a finite number of eggs women were born with, she realized her little gem was the best gift she could've ever received from the universe and the one perfect thing they'd done right.

Chief Johnson was on point. Supervising Special Agent Blake Huxley, Detective Isaac Wilson, and Detective Anaya Nazario worked well together—the trio made a strong team—and they all knew it. When each of them brought their own special skills, it made for a collective dynamic that was the difference between solving crimes and perps potentially getting away with murder.

"It's okay," Nazario told Huxley, nodding to a manila envelope on his lap. "Now, who in the hell is in that folder that would require the Commander-in-Chief to step in?"

"Didn't believe it myself," Huxley sighed, then glanced from the folder back to her eyes. "But I think we might be up against the military. From what we've gathered, it's still unclear whether they're our ally or the enemy."

SIX

THE SERPENT'S RESOLVE

VON SCHLANGE WATCHED Cheonsa crash out of the lobby doors with a look of terror that could only mean one thing—the U.S. transplant didn't come here because she needed a fresh start. After all, Von had fled to Brazil with one goal: to leave her past behind.

Damião frowned. "What just happened?"

"I dunno, but something isn't right."

"Whatever it is, she's obviously spooked by something. I say we put out a proper ad for a marketing specialist, someone without baggage that can come back and hurt our clinic."

"You were the one who offered her a job," Von said. "Now you're ready to give up without so much as wondering what we can do to help?"

"That was before our candidate for the role took off. We have no idea what she's running from, but it can be bad. Real bad. Brazil is dangerous as it is, Agatha. It's best that we leave this one be."

"Can't do that, and you know it. Not my style." She whistled to Zeus.

"*Por favor, não, não, não.*"

"It's not for you to decide. We're going after her," she said, answering his Portuguese with English, then commanded Zeus to follow Cheonsa, switching to German, "*Folge ihr.*"

Language came easy to Von, but so did vengeance.

"Please, Agatha ... I'm begging you. For the love of God, let this one go?"

"It's Von."

"Since when?"

"Since now."

"You can be running into something very dangerous!"

"What makes you think I'm not the one they should be afraid of?" she said, then ran out the door, sprinting after her dog with iron-will determination.

Von would find the girl.

Von would protect her.

SEVEN
THE VICTIM'S SILENT CONFESSION

CHEONSA SOO-MIN RAN through the streets of Rio de Janeiro. A blur of historic buildings—painted in greens, yellows, reds, and oranges—flashed past her, their graffiti-covered walls echoing the city's rebellious spirit. Rio pulsed around her, from the sun-drenched beaches and dense forests to the lively carnivals where music and dance thrummed to the samba beat.

Pristine beaches of Copacabana and Ipanema brought the salty scent that filled her lungs, tinged with the lingering aroma of feijoada from a nearby café. The scent of slow-cooked pork and black beans barely registered as she sprinted through the busy streets, dodging workers and tossing out breathless apologies. Her heart slammed against her ribs, her pulse erratic. She didn't stop. Didn't slow. Not until her aching muscles carried her to the hostel, where she finally sagged against the doorframe, gasping for breath.

After making her coffee, she warmed an inch of milk in the microwave—she liked it creamy. Clutching her Yeti mug, the one etched with CW—a relic from when she was still Cheonsa Winslow—she traced the initials with her thumb. Merrick's one gift she couldn't bring herself to throw out. She stirred in the raw sugar, then took a slow sip before collapsing onto the couch. Nothing could steady her frayed nerves quite like a cup of Brazilian coffee. As she wrapped her hands around the warm mug, she breathed in its rich aroma, letting it ground her. The tension in her shoulders slowly unwound with each sip, lingering adrenaline thrumming beneath her skin.

The hostel was the cheapest place she could find in Rio de Janeiro, offering the basics: a full-sized bed, a writing desk, a tiny bathroom with a shower, Wi-Fi, and air conditioning. The room, measuring 110 to 130 square feet, was quaint and just her size. She disliked giant floor plans and wasted space. Cheonsa loved tiny homes and modern designs that merged practicality with efficiency—living below your means rather than above them.

She didn't need much, and that was what she'd loved about being an Army wife. She loved the mobility of it—living like a gypsy, exploring different countries, experiencing cultures beyond her own. When Merrick decided to buy the Grand Design Momentum 397TH Airstream, a go-big-or-go-home type of toy hauler, he wanted something built for comfort and survival. It was a dream come true with 44 feet of space and off-grid capacity to keep him mobile no matter what. Stateside, all she ever needed was whatever could fit in her suitcase. They'd open a bottle of wine, finish it off while making love, then curl up together in the tight space. It made living a squeeze, but that was her favorite part.

Some of her friends often questioned her closeness with him. Didn't she feel claustrophobic living in such a small space? Wasn't it suffocating, always in each other's business? How did she even find a single moment of privacy? Her reply was always the same. Loving someone meant never seeing their presence as a chore, a burden. She wanted to be close, to experience the world together. As a partner, as a friend, as a teammate, they could face anything—so long as they had each other.

From across the room, a knock on the hostel door sliced through the haze. Cheonsa didn't move. It should have pulled her out of the memory—*reality crashing her into the present*—but it didn't. Not fully. The sound echoed through the small room. Sharp and unrelenting. Reverberating like a lethal countdown. She couldn't rid herself of the stranger standing at her front porch, words clipped and emotionless, delivering a sentence she didn't want to face.

Served.

The rest blurred, but that word remained etched in her mind.

What was almost worse than having been served divorce papers without a single hint, discussion, or advance notice was the look they all gave her. That hidden pity-smile they all had, as if they could hear her words looping in their heads—the way she'd come to Merrick's defense again and again.

What do you have to say for yourself now, Cheonsa Soo-Min?

Pure shame. Utter shock. The loneliness. The years of therapy.

She lost friends, the ones she thought would be by her side. If she was forced to choose between her husband and her friends—she chose Merrick Winslow each and every time. With Umma and Appa dead, he was her family. She had him and only him. When faced with the choice between friends or family, it was an easy decision for her. She could make new friends, but she couldn't replace Merrick. No, she couldn't replace him and couldn't see herself living a day without his sparkling blue eyes, boyish smile, and sexual chemistry. That was a dream come true.

They were perfect together. Perfect for each other. Soul mates for life.

She'd once gushed to her friends about him, and that was all they could recall when questioned by the authorities. Merrick wasn't just charming her—he had a knack for slipping into the lives of everyone around her. He could reach out to her friends directly, smooth as silk, and they'd fall right in line, ready to do whatever he asked. It wasn't just her he had under his spell—it was all of them.

They'd repeat what Merrick would want them to say: he was everything to her.

Oh, that Cheonsa Soo-Min—I hate to say it, but the girl was obsessed. Couldn't quit him, couldn't even breathe without him—or so it seemed. And for what? He wasn't all that. Still, she chased after him like he was her air. She didn't stop until he walked away and left her wrecked. After that, she just unraveled. Totally lost her mind.

She was practically homeless, living week by week on what she'd saved from her parents' life insurance. It wouldn't last much longer. They each had a $250,000 policy, which wasn't a fortune, but together, it gave her half a million. In the five years since her divorce from Merrick, she'd already spent over half, devastated by severe depression that made working impossible. Between rent, food, and traveling when she should've been working, she'd burned through nearly $275,000.

Qualifying for disability turned into a nightmare: she'd been rejected!

Someone tipped off the EEOC and claimed that she was fit for work.

Someone called and had sabotaged her efforts to collect disability.

Someone went through the trouble to send them pictures of her traveling.

The EEOC wouldn't disclose who had tipped them off, but they assessed that Cheonsa had behaved in a way that contradicted their perception of someone who was deemed "disabled" and 'mentally unwell' enough to collect disability checks. To which she argued that people with disability can travel, but arguing with the government didn't help her case.

Cheonsa knew who that someone was, the same one who'd killed the cops.

From the window, she watched her neighbor hang clothes on a line and another sweep their porch. A mother in another unit was feeding her toddler in a highchair and clapping cheerfully at her child for eating their food. Cheonsa sipped her coffee. It was hot enough to burn her tongue a little, but she wouldn't have wanted it any other way. Maybe that was her problem: doing things to herself that caused unnecessary discomfort and even pain.

Knock. Knock. Knock.

Was that in her head?

Knock. Knock. Knock.

Her entire body jolted. It hadn't been in her head, and she never had visitors because she lived a private, incognito life. Cheonsa watched life around her, disengaged and on the sidelines. It wasn't because she didn't want to participate, but because fear of getting noticed held her back.

She got up from the old, worn, hand-me-down sofa, making the springs squeal to life. The quickening in her pulse accelerated into a state of panic. Cheonsa went to her silverware drawer, opened it, and armed herself with a butcher knife she'd bought at the *Pão de Açúcar*—Sugarloaf in English—upon the first day of her arrival in Rio de Janeiro. The high-carbon, stainless steel blade shone under the kitchen lights, sharp enough to debone the meat of a large animal or human.

Knock. Knock. Knock.

Pressing herself against the wall, she clutched the knife's handle with a bruising grip. She inhaled deeply through her nose, though still struggled to breathe, as if no amount of air could bring her calm. Her stomach turned sour, heart accelerating to the point of vertigo threatening to buckle her knees. A visceral kind of fright consumed her. The what-ifs and all the uncertainties that came with her new lifestyle made paranoia the driver behind the wheel. It was no way to live, but ever since she left everything behind, it was the only way she knew how.

"W-w-who ... who's there?" A shiver ran through her.

"Von."

"Dr. Jones?"

"You can call me that, too. But I prefer we drop the doctor prefix."

Her shoulders slumped. With a shaky hand, she mopped sweat off her forehead and unlocked the door, opening just enough.

She peeked out the crack in the door, glancing first at the fierce German Shepherd sitting obediently next to Von and back up to meet those steel gray eyes that looked as sharp as the butcher knife in her hand.

"May we come in?"

Cheonsa wanted to say no and had every intention of closing the door. But there was something about Von that made her pause, made her reconsider whether to trust her as an ally or consider her dangerous. She couldn't pinpoint why she had a gut feeling this woman was someone you didn't want to mess with—call it a woman's intuition or perhaps a sign from the spirits.

Helmeoni, Cheonsa's grandmother, used to always say, "A tiger's gaze can sense hidden danger."

Helmeoni used to always tell her that she had good intuition, but that her heart clouded her judgment. '*Ma-eum-i anin ma-eum*,' she'd say—Mind, not heart—in English. It was those simple words that came back to haunt Cheonsa after the divorce. Had she chosen wrong with Merrick?

Heart instead of the mind?

Was her mind leading now?

"You're safe with us," Von swore, "that I promise you."

Hesitant, Cheonsa opened the door and let the mysterious woman with too many names and her dog in. Von strode casually past, not even giving a quick glance at the butcher knife. But she must've seen it because she said, "Unless you plan on chopping up a salad, you can put that Tramontina down. I know it's a fine kitchen utensil, but I also know that it can cut through just about anything."

Von sought her eyes, but Cheonsa averted her gaze, keeping her hands occupied as she silently complied, slipping the knife away. She paused in front of the coffee, unsure what to do with herself—should she sit or stand?

"Would you ... would you like some coffee? Just made it."

"From the Rio Verde Coffee Plantations?"

"Yeah, is ... is that alright?"

"Best coffee on this planet."

"Cream and raw sugar? Sorry, don't have Stevia."

"Just black."

Cheonsa poured coffee into a paper cup and handed it to Von. "Disposable's all I have ... for now. Sorry, hope you don't mind."

"Stop apologizing."

"I'm sorry, I mean ... okay." Cheonsa finally sat down across from her guest and took a sip of her coffee. The cup danced in her hands as she brought it to her lips, an unsteady tremble hard to hide.

Von glanced at her shaking hands and stared at her until Cheonsa was forced to meet her gaze. "Who you running from?"

"Don't know what you mean."

"What's the real reason you're in Brazil?"

"Needed a change."

Von glanced at her LG flat screen. She'd elected to bring her 32-inch for portability and had gotten rid of the 60-inch that had been in her living room. It was easier to travel with the smaller one.

"Net/Claro, Sky, Oi, Vivo?"

"Net/Claro—had it installed a couple of days ago."

"Same here. Channels and navigation take some getting used to, but there're decent American movies and TV shows that're dubbed."

"I mostly have it for ... for the news," Cheonsa said. "Need to keep track of—well—never mind."

"Keep track of what?"

The palms of her hands turned moist, and her heart drove faster than a racecar, turning a tight corner. "For someone that just met me, you're asking an awful lot of questions," she began, pausing to sip her coffee. "Need the news, is all."

"To keep track of what?"

"Not what—whom. And that's all I'm comfortable sharing. Don't like the way this conversation's going." Cheonsa put down her coffee. "Why'd you follow me here, and why the third degree? How do I know this veterinarian BS isn't the cover story, and you're not some FBI agent on an assignment out here?"

Von chuckled. "One thing I'm not is the law." She took a large gulp of her coffee, likely lukewarm by now.

"I said why're you here?"

"Zeus and I—we have a special set of skills. Call it a tag team effort."

"Yes, you said you could read people, and so can I."

"It's more than that. We can help you, offer protection."

"Don't need protecting," she whispered, her voice betraying

her, lacking the force she had meant to convey. Cheonsa knew she didn't sound convincing in the least.

"Something tells me that you might need a friend, an ally, someone to look out for you," Von ran her fingers along the top of Zeus's head. "Brazil's beautiful, but it can be dangerous. Crime is pretty high, especially gang violence in Rio. However much money you came here with, you'll blow right through it in no time if you don't get your debit and credit cards stolen first. They love targeting vulnerable Americans, promising to help you out as a tour guide or answer any question, and before you know it, they gotcha at gunpoint at the ATM. Homicide rate is around 22%. The law out here isn't the same as it is back in the States. Your body goes missing—and forget about ever being found again. Drop you somewhere in the jungle."

At first glance, Von appeared to be a petite woman. But a closer inspection revealed years of dedicated training to make the veins pop out on her muscular arms, which were lean and strong-looking. Her square, broad shoulders and tapered waist explained why she had callouses on her hands. Von Schlange—Doctor Agatha Jones— born a Friedrich, daughter of a famous brain surgeon and the best-selling author and psychologist Dr. Katrine Friedrich. Regardless of her many identities, Von was not only the only American Cheonsa knew in Brazil, but the only person she'd allowed herself to speak to.

"Help me run the office, marketing stuff. In exchange, you get paid and remain safe."

"You don't know anything. You ... you really don't under-stand what you're getting yourself into. You and Dr. Sequeira should hire someone else. Stay away from me. You guys seem like nice people. But I can't involve you."

Von drained her coffee, crushed the cup with one hand, and tossed it. It bounced off the wall and sank clean into the trash. "Too late."

EIGHT
THE CONCEALED CONNECTION

VISINE DIDN'T DO a damn thing for Detective Anaya Nazario's bloodshot eyes—nor could concealer mask the dark circles underneath them, carved by exhaustion. After a long night of tossing and turning, she'd finally given up the bed for the sofa. Huxley had followed, muttering his thousandth *sorry babe*, like her restlessness was somehow his fault.

She shook her head, exhaling softly. "You don't have to apologize. It's not you."

It wasn't he who kept her up—it was the unknown.

It was hard to sleep since the new case had landed in her lap, blurring the lines between work and personal life once again. She suspected Huxley felt like a third wheel in all of it, especially now that he'd been pulled off paternity leave to partner up with her and Wilson on this case. He wasn't a burden, though—not to her. He was the only part of her life that still made sense. The one thing that couldn't escape Wilson's or her mind was: who the hell were they up against, and why did it involve an executive order? In the twenty-five years she'd been on the force—and damn, did that make her feel old since she'd become a cop at twenty—she'd never once worked on an EO.

Two hours had flown by as they sat in the FBI conference room talking about the EO and getting briefed on unnecessary disclaimers and privacy regulations crap. Nazario's ass hurt from the hard chair as equal parts annoyance and weariness ate away at her patience. They hadn't even opened the damn case file yet, and already the room smelled of musky bodies and cheap chicken teriyaki takeout bowls.

Huxley droned on while Nazario—who'd never called anyone her boyfriend and guessed "life partner" was the term—desperately wanted him to stop. "We have clearance to access classified military data, but confidentiality is crucial. I spoke with Pentagon cybersecurity early this morning, and they want to ensure we use the proper secure channels. Any documents will need to go through me before sending. Clear?"

"Can we get to the mother-effing case file already? We get it. Skip the disclaimer. We got the damn protocol. Let's get this going," Nazario demanded, getting up to toss her empty lunch bowl in the trash.

Chief Johnson shot her a look. "Hope that's not how you talk to your man when he's rubbing your feet at night."

"He needs to rub my numb ass and get going already. Sitting on these chairs is like sitting on a cement slab."

Supervising Agent Blake Huxley gifted her a forgiving smile. "My orders were to be thorough, Honey-pie."

"Well, Honey-pie, you're as thorough as one of them fun tax auditors poking around the office on April 14th," Wilson said with a laugh.

"You know my mama made the best honey pies—homemade custard with a sour cream crust that melts in your mouth." Chief Johnson wiped a hand across his freshly shaved face, exposing smooth brown skin free of the white stubble that'd grown over the two-week post-move-out à la divorce. "Mmm, mmm, mmm. So, *sooo* good."

"You're making me wanna break my no dessert policy, Boss," Wilson said.

"The case. Not honey pies. Not dessert. Not food. The case. The case. The case. Can we talk about the case?" Nazario said, unable to hide her frustration.

"Yes, ma'am, we shall," Huxley said, flicking the overhead projector connected to his laptop from boring DOJ and top-secret legal jargon to an image of a young, modest Asian female with doe eyes and features that were nothing out of the ordinary. She had an unassuming, natural, no-makeup kind of beauty and a youthful look that left her age a mystery. It was difficult picturing this young woman handcuffing anyone to a table, let alone two cops, and then shooting two officers in the head.

"Can't see it—just can't," Nazario said.

"Me either," Wilson said.

"How old is she, even? Looks all but fifteen," the chief said.

"Cheonsa Soo-Min. Korean," Huxley began, "her first name is the Korean word for angel, not that I would call her that. Thirty-five—"

"For real?" Chief Johnson expressed surprise. "Would've guessed no older than eighteen."

Wilson raised his brows. "Not even close to the age I had in my head."

"Definitely blessed with the anti-aging gene," Huxley agreed, then cut to the issue. "Five years divorced."

"So, why were the officers over at her place?" Nazario said.

Huxley changed the slide to a sharp-looking Army officer decorated with too many different ribbons and medals. The one thing she was terrible at was identifying what was what. Meanwhile, Wilson, having come from a military family, had it all memorized. Being the "chubby one," as he'd always tell her, he never did have the discipline or appetite for boot camp, which was why he joined the LAPD instead of enlisting.

Wilson whistled at the officer with short, dark blond hair and blue eyes. They weren't as blue as Huxley's, and he was not nearly as big either. In fact, he had a thin stature but a boyish, disarming charm. If Nazario had to guess, this officer looked like he was the type that could approach anyone and strike up a conversation. There was an aura about him that Nazario couldn't quite place. It was neither a bad hunch nor a good one. Still, of the two, Cheonsa Soo-Min looked much more serious and harder to gauge. Though Nazario made a mental note to herself that the disposition could have something to do with Korean culture.

"A colonel. No wonder they got the EO in place. Mr. Important," Wilson said.

"Colonel Merrick Winslow, Iraq and Afghanistan veteran. Served four tours back-to-back. He received the Silver Medal for Valor during the COP Keating incident. When the combat outpost was surrounded by insurgents in 2009," Huxley explained. "If my memory serves me, it was like sixty U.S. and Latvian soldiers against three-hundred-plus Taliban fighters—a fight that lasted twelve hours straight. One of the most intense battles they had over in Afghanistan. Winslow was also awarded the Latvian medal, an honorary recognition for exceptional service."

"Yeah, I remember that one—a handful of U.S. soldiers died, and around twenty-something were wounded," Wilson added.

"Eight of our men were killed and twenty-seven wounded," Huxley corrected.

"Okay, okay—so, they were married and divorced. Who filed?" Chief Johnson's question sounded less like an inquiry and more like it was dredging up memories from his recent divorce—the one his wife had initiated.

"Lemme guess—she did," Wilson said, glancing at Chief Johnson. "Sir?"

"She," Chief Johnson wagered.

Wilson turned to Nazario last. She rubbed her chin, "My bet's on the colonel."

Huxley cocked a lopsided smile. "A woman's intuition always kicks our asses."

"Yes!" Nazario gloated cheerfully as she narrowed her eyes on the losers.

"How'd you know?" her boss asked her.

"Colonel Merrick Winslow comes across as a very charming, even charismatic leader. He doesn't like to lose, and if I had to take an educated guess in terms of profiling him—think he's a narcissist. A good portion of leaders are. Something about Cheonsa Soo-Min tells me she was more of the beta in the relationship. As an officer, the colonel's likely an excellent logistician. Has to be. Winslow's the alpha type. He's gonna be one step ahead. He'll file before she does. 'I'll leave you before you leave me' sort of thing. I should know. I'm a lot like that. Don't like to lose. Self-professed alpha. Hell, guess I'm a bit of a narcissist since I'd much prefer to be the one to do the leaving."

"Sounds like a personal confession, Detective," Huxley said, "a big step for you."

"Perhaps," she admitted, giving him a wink.

"Nazario, great instinct as always," Johnson said.

"Thank you, sir."

"So, Colonel Winslow divorced his wife. That was what?— Four, five years ago? That's enough time to get remarried, move on with your life. Even pop out a kid or two," Wilson said.

Raising her dark brows in acknowledgment, Nazario nodded at Wilson. "Agree with you there. Find it odd, though, that those emails were sitting there in the printer. A little too convenient if you ask me."

Chief Johnson leaned in and steepled his fingers. "C'mon, lemme have it."

Huxley switched to an image of their wedding. The bride was in a stunning mermaid-fitted dress that flared out at the bottom, and he wore a dark brown and gold suit. It was an earthy wedding with a beautiful mountain range in the back that didn't look like California. The bouquet was comprised of wildflowers that matched the simple natural theme. The groom seemed to be a lot harder to read than the bride. He looked happy, but she wore a seriousness that seemed off on a day that should've been her moment to shine.

"She don't look too happy," Nazario said.

"Maybe she's camera shy?" Wilson said.

"Bet it's a cultural thing. Y'all know my ex is from the Philippines, and when was the last time you seen her smile?" the chief asked and proceeded to answer the rhetorical question. "Neva, eva, eva."

Nazario didn't want to be the asshole who threw out her opinion. As the saying went, everyone had one, so she decided to keep her mouth shut. But her gut was telling her that something was off about the perfect couple. If, indeed, Cheonsa Soo-Min sent the harassing emails to her ex-husband, then why did she look so miserable at her own wedding? Wouldn't she be over the moon? Shouldn't she be? Nazario wasn't an expert on relationships anyhow, though she was pretty damn good at her job. Her detective radar was flying into the red flags zone.

"According to Colonel Winslow—"

"Wait a sec, can't just show a lovely pic like that without letting us know where that wedding was," Wilson interrupted conversationally like he had a knack for doing.

"Colorado Springs—he was stationed out there in Fort Carson for about a year. Same year they were married, he deployed. Around 2018. Left her alone in Colorado Springs,"

Huxley said. Then he added for clarity, "No family. No friends. Nothing."

"What about her parents?" Nazario said.

"Killed in an airplane crash during her last year in grad school. Got her MBA at twenty-nine in 2017 from UCCS."

"University of Colorado, Colorado Springs is a decent school," Chief Johnson said. "Nice hiking trails and beautiful out there during the summer. Hate all the snow, though."

"Gonna get you to ski on the bunny slope if it's the last thing I do," Nazario chided. Everyone knew Chief Johnson was terrified of skiing, afraid he'd break his legs or fatally slam into a tree.

"Would rather sit in the lodge drinking hot cocoa and watch all the other dummies on two sticks sliding down the mountain in below zero temps." Chief widened his eyes and laughed.

"So, that's how they met then? She enrolls in an MBA program at UCCS, graduates in 2017, her parents pass away in a plane crash, and she gets married in '18?" Wilson recited.

"Correct," Huxley said.

"And who was driving the plane?"

"Han-Joon Soo Min and Jisoo Soo-Min—her mother and father—were both perfume chemists and owned a fragrance store called *Scents of Han*. Sold everything that smelled good: candles, oils, perfume, lotions, handmade air fresheners. Her father, Han-Joon, had his pilot's license. Owned one of them Cessna 172 Skyhawks. I call it the death plane 'cause even I get scared to ride in one of them single engines. Can feel every bump and dip."

"Big baby," Nazario said.

"Sure am," Huxley said. "I hate them single engines."

"No different than riding a roller coaster," Wilson said.

"Except, oh, dying if it crashes into the mountain like they did?" Huxley said.

"Okay, okay, okay," Chief Johnson refocused the conversation. "Let's say Cheonsa Soo-Min had cold feet on her wedding day about becoming Mrs. Winslow. Or—or—like I said, it could come down to cultural differences. But here's what I really think went down. It's as simple as the grieving process. She was upset her parents were buried in some graveyard instead of being at the wedding. Upset that her daddy wasn't able to walk her down the aisle."

"Yeah, okay, I can see it now," Nazario admitted after learning about the fatal airplane crash. Chief Johnson's theory made a lot of sense. "They get married in 2018 after she graduates, and she most likely would have to forfeit her career to move around with the guy. You said he deployed right when they got married?"

"He literally deployed two days after the wedding," Huxley said. "They get hazardous duty pay on top of getting paid a lot more claiming their spouse. So, they chose to get married right before the deployment."

"Then five years later, he files?" Nazario said.

"Pretty much. Citing irreconcilable differences. And that's where we are today," Huxley changed the slide on his computer, and the overhead projector displayed what would be the start of dozens upon dozens of email exchanges. "We don't have time to read all of these, but my team did read them—exactly two hundred and thirty-five emails. We didn't skim. Read every damn one. They're all the same. Cheonsa, wanting Merrick back, wouldn't take no for an answer. He filed a military protection order and a civilian permanent protection order restraining Cheonsa Soo-Min from stalking or harassing him in any way."

"Lemme guess, she didn't stay away," Wilson said.

"Which is why those two greenies were at her house. They had a warrant for her arrest, might've said something stupid the way greenies do—we know how that ended. The shell casings found at the home are a match to the gun registered in her name. Now we have an opportunity: the colonel is in Clovis visiting his parents. He's about to be stationed overseas and will be a lot harder to track down. The good thing about Clovis is that Cheonsa's parents had also lived up there, too. They had that in common. If we can take a road trip, I think it'll be a great opportunity. We can interview the colonel, see what he knows about his missing ex-wife—who just so happens to be on the FBI's regional fugitive list—and get a read on his parents. Be surprised how much you can learn from in-laws," Huxley said.

"Well, what're we waiting for? Y'all need to hit the road, like, now," Chief Johnson said.

———

Clovis was more than a four-hour drive from Los Angeles—up the 5 and the 99 freeways—and the best way to investigate the case. It was a sensitive matter that couldn't be discussed over video. The last time Nazario was up in Clovis, there wasn't much around. Now, the city—once known for farming—was bustling with activity and great places to eat, nearly unrecognizable after years of urban revitalization.

"When there's a Whole Foods, Starbucks, and Trader Joe's on every dang corner, ya know the government put a shit ton of moolah to build the city up," Wilson joked.

"Yeah, no kidding." Nazario watched the new Clovis replace the memories of the sleepy town she'd remembered. Glass-fronted boutiques with chic mannequins, tech shops showcasing the latest gadgets, and artisanal coffee spots lined the streets. High-end restaurants like The Annex Kitchen, renowned for its authentic Italian cuisine, now dotted the city's landscape. Newly established vibrant eateries, such as Papi's

Mex Grill—famous for its brunch and happy hour—and Saizon, celebrated for its innovative Mexican dishes, showcased the growing diversity of the local food scene.

"I could almost live out here," Huxley said. "Whaddaya say, Honey Pie?"

"Wouldn't be the worst place in the world," Nazario told Huxley. "But, if ya don't stop calling me that godawful nickname, I'll put you in a flying armbar faster than you can speak two syllables."

Wilson snorted a loud chuckle from his belly while Huxley offered an amused grin. "Oh, the pains of being in love with a woman who can challenge the legend Bruce Lee himself. Think we should spar sometime—make it a date night activity."

"How romantic," Nazario added dryly.

They pulled up to a large two-story home that, while nice, was remarkably like the rest of the homes in the cul-de-sac. They each had the same tract housing unoriginality, but they were nice, nonetheless. And in California, this ordinary abode was still around 3000 sq ft. For the Golden State, that kind of coveted real estate was worth more than half a mil—which was not nothing.

Nazario had long resigned herself to a lifetime of renting—homeownership was a distant luxury on an LAPD detective's salary. She was worth more dead than alive, not to mention police officers had pretty good pensions and retirement plans. Anaya Nazario wasn't the kind to need saving, so she dug her heels in for as long as she could, evading every invitation from Blake Huxley to move in. She realized it made zero sense for them to be throwing cash away, paying twice on rent and mortgage when they could be saving and helping co-parent Ariabella together.

Damn, she had a human to take care of now. She still couldn't believe it—a human that needed clothes, food, shelter, a car eventually, and funds for college. If there was nothing else that could sober a recovering alcoholic like Nazario faster than the speed of sound, it was being a first-time parent. For once in her life, she finally felt grown up. Before having her child, all she ever thought about was herself. Admittedly, Nazario was a selfish bitch. But now, whenever she was away from her daughter, worry consumed her like a riptide pulling her underwater.

Caught up in her thoughts, Nazario snapped to attention after Wilson had called her name for the third time. "You alright?" Wilson put a hand on her shoulder.

"Fine, just ... well, just thinking about Ariabella."

"Maybe we tell Johnson to put someone else on this?" Huxley suggested.

She blew out a breath. Reluctant, she said, "No ... no way am I gonna do that. Never turned away a case in my entire twenty-year career on the force. Not fixing to do that now." Her tough demands and high expectations of herself often weighed heavily, and guilt struck the moment the words escaped her mouth. Still, she pushed past the maternal remorse clawing at her heart and was the first to approach the door, the two men trailing behind her.

When the door swung open, a tall man in civilian clothes stood before them—unassuming, with an easy, everyman charm. He lacked Huxley's muscular build and handsome, untamed edge, but there was something about him. His clean-cut, charming exterior carried a certain presence and, beneath it, a commanding aura that was impossible to ignore.

"Well, hi there," he smiled politely.

"Colonel Merrick Winslow?" Wilson asked cautiously.

"In the flesh—Chief Johnson told me you'd be stopping by. Come in, come in, come in. Y'all brought your appetites, I hope? I was about to light up the barbecue."

Nazario shifted her weight from foot to foot. Merrick's slate blue eyes floated to the men first before landing on her last with an unreadable expression she couldn't quite place. The rich aroma of marinated meat wafted through the house, a sharp contrast to the balmy SoCal evening. The velvety tone of Frank Sinatra hummed through the living room. An elderly couple that resembled their son sat on the couch sipping white wine— well, at least it was her least favorite booze of choice.

Red was her flavor, not the white crap.

But, as a wino, she'd drink hand sanitizer if she could. Although Nazario hadn't relapsed since before having her daughter, she was always aware of that itch she couldn't quite scratch. It was there, flooding her tongue with a craving that never fully faded, making her mouth water. The parents stood up and greeted them at the door.

"Come on in. We always welcome our brothers in blue, and we always cook enough for the whole block!" said the man, whom Nazario suspected was Jean Winslow, a proud Military Dad sporting a red MAGA hat.

"Papa Winslow?" Nazario smiled, sticking out her hand.

"That'd be me," he said with genial enthusiasm, giving her a firm handshake. He pointed to his wife. "And this is Mama Winslow, Mavis Lou."

The American flag fluttered proudly outside, its colors vivid against the porch backdrop, while Sean Hannity's voice boomed from the seventy-inch flatscreen inside. Fox News blared on, her least favorite host ranted on with his usual bravado—*a right-wing mouthpiece.* She grimaced. Nazario cruised on neutral when it came to politics, finding enough fault on both sides. Staying bipartisan as a detective came in handy during times like this. As pleasantries continued in this ideal Americana household, Merrick strode across the room, widening the space between himself and his guests. From the other side, his indigo eyes locked onto hers—his smile, gone.

A cold chill rippled through her body as a foreboding dread punched her in the gut. Something about Colonel Merrick Winslow screamed calculated control, and she was determined to answer the call.

NINE
THE SERPENT'S SHIELD

VON SCHLANGE CONFRONTED her business partner with steely resolve. The one thing she'd learned in getting to know him—Damião resisted change like an oak resisted the wind. Explaining the significance of modifying how he addressed her was an intimate matter—profoundly personal, akin to the sacredness of one's pronouns.

"I don't understand the need for the change?" Damião protested. "Why now?"

"Let's get the elephant out of the room, shall we? When I first met you on the airplane, did you recognize me? Zeus?"

Damião glanced out at the large lobby window, pouring natural light through. The sound of plantation workers busily sorting the coffee beans and grading them based on size, weight, and quality penetrated the thin walls. Coffee beans cascaded into the hickory barrels, clanking like rain on tin as workers rotated the beans. It was the soothing blend of wooden creaks magnifying an earthy rhythm of the plantation that jettisoned her mind to a tranquil place stress couldn't breach.

Now, they were arguing about something that might seem irrelevant to someone else but meant everything to her. Damião picked up his fresh cup of Brazilian coffee straight from the Rio Verde Coffee Plantations they could see from the front office window. He took a slow sip, unable to answer her question.

"You had to have recognized us."

Damião exhaled loudly and at last nodded once. "When I saw the news coverage, I collapsed in my living room, and I just ... I cried. I couldn't believe I'd been responsible for Dr. Wilder Friedrich's death. The Wilder who had so much fight and strength within her. The woman I'd grown to ... grown to have *sentimentos fortes*."

"And I had strong feelings for you."

"Had or have?"

"I'm not the one to be put on the spot. I told you before, and I'll tell you again—I'm not the type you bring home to Mom and Dad," Von said.

"I thought you were dead. Thought you'd ... you'd killed yourself like they said. It was all over the bloody news. I couldn't sleep. I couldn't eat. I blamed myself. I still blame myself for your ... for this transformation. This *mudar*."

"Interesting how the Portuguese word for change sounds so much like murder," Von said dryly. "Speaking of—that human filth—those Aryan assholes gutted me like a pig. Murdered the child that I was meant to have, and killed Sammy. I don't have my little sister anymore. I don't have a child that should've been seven by now. I don't have the working parts that made me a woman. I'll never know what it's like to feel a baby kick and grow inside me. Regardless, Damião, whatever they did and what you couldn't prevent during surgery—none of that was your fault. You saved my life, and for that, I'm grateful, but I'll tell you what I told my fiancé: I don't owe you a relationship I can't give. Don't owe any man my heart, my soul. That piece of me is mine to give and mine to keep."

Damião's shoulders slumped. "Understood: Wilder Agatha

Friedrich. Dr. Agatha Jones. Von Schlange. Whatever you wish to call yourself—*Eu amo tudo em você*," he said, setting his coffee cup down on the flat of the bay window's ledge. As if she didn't understand his professed love for her, he repeated in English. "I love all of you. And my love is mine to give, too. It's not something I'm ashamed of. It's not something I can control—that you can control. Wish it were as simple as a light switch."

"I'd very much like to keep business as business, and that's what this conversation should be focused on."

"So, you'd like me to call you Von from now on. Okay, Von, but I'm not so sure we should be hiring Cheonsa Soo-Min. Want to talk business? I'm part owner, and I say no."

"Then hire your own marketing professional. She'll work for me. There's a reason why she came to Brazil."

"Yes, precisely," Damião challenged, "perhaps the same reason you're here. Look, I'm not trying to tell you no—"

"You just did—your love confession's one thing. Your control over my business affairs is a whole other matter. One that's not yours. You don't want to work with Ms. Soo-Min, fine. I'm hiring her for my animal clinic. It's the reason I prefer four-legged fur clients—I can handle dog shit, but what I can't handle is the human kind."

Damião's face flushed the color of a Barbados cherry. They rarely argued. But then again, unlike her ex-fiancé, who had a knack for wanting to address everything straight away, Damião's one weakness was loathing confrontation. Her business partner was a tad too passive, which perhaps explained how they'd managed to go two years in Rio without so much as a toilet paper over-or-under tiff.

He was a voracious carnivore, and she, a vegan. Yet, like her relationship with her beloved dog, they made it work. This was their first-ever argument, the first time she'd seen him this animated.

"I thought you'd died once. I went to your bloody funeral, for Christ's sake. The last thing I want is to have to bury you again, and this time for good. You may think you have nine lives, Von, but this isn't the U.S. The people out here are a thousand times more ruthless. We have drug lords that make Compton look like Disneyland. On top of that, this Cheonsa Soo-Min is running in here, dragging along her demons and bringing them with her. We don't know—you have no idea who you're up against."

"I've got a wooden cross and holy water. I'll be fine."

"This isn't a joke."

"And I'm not laughing. I appreciate your concern, but Zeus and I—we don't back down from a fight. She can be spooked for a number of reasons. Maybe it's a simple explanation, but if it's something a lot bigger—"

"What if you get involved in something that's way over your head? Then what? I have to sit through another ..." his voice hitched, "another goddamn funeral? This time, this time with your cold dead body in the casket?"

"You have my word—you won't be dragged into anything. That I promise you."

"You can't possibly promise that!" he exploded. Von raised a brow, and Zeus stood at attention. "You have no idea what you're walking into—none at all!"

He took large, angry strides, walking his coffee over to their kitchen adjacent to the break room, and dropped his mug with a loud CLANK. It was not quite hard enough to break the mug, but hard enough to make Zeus snarl. The highly intelligent canine didn't care for violence of any kind, not unless they were defending an innocent life, and although he trusted Damião, Zeus could turn on a human because he understood that humans could turn on them.

Two weeks later, Cheonsa Soo-Min started at the clinic, and everything about her screamed fear. Even her walk seemed to carry deliberate hesitation, as if she were trying to be careful not to wake a sleeping baby.

"Feel free to bring your lunch. We've got a full fridge. Stock it with water and juices—Brazilian brands I think you'll appreciate—that is, if you're not too picky."

"I'm Korean—I eat just about anything," Cheonsa said, laughing for the first time. Her face lit up briefly, and for a second, Von saw a glimpse of what her new anxious employee could be. What she was before, whatever stole the light away from inside her that once made her shine brighter. Von had to wonder if she also held the same dimness. She knew her poker face was virtually unreadable, but when others stared deep into her eyes, could they see the missing spark that had been snatched away from her? The veterinarian never let people get close enough to find out, not even Damião.

As her new marketing director chortled, Von noticed her smooth skin like ivory silk without a sign of a wrinkle. Korean genetics that many Anglos would kill for, especially Katrine Adele Friedrich—her vain, famous psychologist and best-selling self-help author mother, who wrote about trauma but couldn't stop her own two daughters from encountering the worst monsters in human form. A pang, sharp as a Brazilian machete, drove into her gut.

The pain was as intense as being sliced open every time she thought of the price of her own survival. No contact. No closure. Just the last conversation with her parents in their home—days before Von and Zeus plunged off the edge of Point Fermin Cliffs. It was a cliff jump no one was expected to survive, let alone a petite five-foot-tall woman and her aging German Shepherd. Now, Von wondered what close call Cheonsa had faced. Von watched Cheonsa's eyes, rich coffee-brown, glinting with doe-like innocence.

Oh, Sammy...

A brief montage of her baby sister swept through her mind. Being twelve years old and cradling the squirmy little pink human against her chest with ten little fingers and ten little toes. The way Sammy cooed and blinked up at her, smiling as the infant recognized big sissy's voice. Being twelve when Samantha Friedrich was born made her a dozen years older and much more protective. When Sammy took her first steps, tottering from foot to foot, Von stood beside her parents. The three of them were in a straight line, laughing together—a rare Friedrich occasion. Her father, Dr. Anton Jörg Friedrich, one of the world's leading brain surgeons, was known as much for his brilliant surgical skills as for being a colossal asshole.

Her father loved to push competition on Von growing up. She had to be in all the school clubs and sports. Sometimes, she did it for her own interests, but most of the time, it was to make her father happy. He was harder on her than he ever was with Sammy and even scoffed at the idea of veterinarian school.

"Fiddling around with animals? That's no doctor—that's a dog walker," her father had scoffed, his words both devastating and demeaning after she told him she wouldn't follow in his footsteps to become a neurologist. But Dr. Katrine Friedrich would always step in with her two-cents psychology crap. It was almost worse to hear her mother treat the family like one of her mental health clients than to put up with her father's arrogant *everyone's beneath me* attitude.

So, the moment Sammy was born, her father wasted no time turning that relationship into a constant competition among the three.

"Anton, dear, let's not spoil the moment. I'm sure Wilder

wants to enjoy being a big sister without you turning whoever Sammy walks up to into one of your silly contests."

"A healthy little competition won't kill anyone," the neurosurgeon told his wife.

"It's okay, Mama," Von reassured, accepting her father's challenge. "Let's see which of us Sammy will go to first."

"Twenty dollars at the Arcade," Anton challenged his eldest child.

"Thirty," she shot back.

"And if you lose?"

"I'll mow the front lawn for a week."

"Deal!" Her father raised a silver brow and narrowed his eyes. "She's walking to me."

"We'll see about that—old man!"

Her mother glanced at their exchange and shook her head, a light chuckle escaping.

"The two of you are more alike than you know."

The echoes of the past returned to her, a time when there were blissful memories of her nuclear family. It was the times when Sammy was an infant and through her toddler years that were Von's favorite. It was a time she could remember her father being less of an asshole and the most jubilant she'd ever recalled. Once Sammy began to wobble, she walked uneasily across their large living room and right toward her big sissy.

Ever since she was born, Von and Sammy had been attached at the hip. She'd never known that kind of unconditional, all-consuming love until her sister was born.

Sammy, with her sun-kissed skin, light freckles that sprinkled her nose and cheeks during the summer months, and hair that transformed into golden fairy strands streaked by long days lying out on the beach. Von missed her laughter and youthful Liv Tyler innocence, which made her both sweet and an easy target. Pain surged in every cell, pumping her heart, forcing her hands into clenched fists. Von would do anything, even forfeit her own life, before allowing anyone else to be victimized.

Something about Cheonsa Soo-Min radiated the same purity and virtue Sammy had shown, that of a child who needed protection. Since their first heated argument, Damião had perfected the art of stonewalling, elevating his passivity to a new level of infuriating.

"Eventually, your silent treatment will tire you out," she'd told him that morning.

"And eventually, your savior complex is going to get someone killed."

Not *is going to*, Von thought, but *already has*.

For once, Von had no answer for Damião. She couldn't deny what he claimed—the truth was inescapable. If not for Von's lethal string of revenge slayings a couple of years ago, Sammy would be alive. There wouldn't have been a funeral for Dr. Wilder Friedrich, and she wouldn't be on the run, juggling an arsenal of fake identities: names, passports, birth certificates, social security numbers, and more. Changing one's identity wasn't as easy as the movies made it look. Lies took a lot of planning and mental choreography, not to mention memory. It was easy to slip up and forget, especially as the lies started to snowball and get bigger and bigger.

They walked through the bright office with large, customized windows to bring in natural sunlight. From nearly every window, the Rio Verde Coffee Plantations could be seen. The soothing sounds of workers drifted into the room, from harvesting ripe coffee cherries to sorting them out by removing the unripe ones. But it was the pulping process that Von could relate to, the removal of the outer skin and pulp of the cherry to get to the coffee bean. The shedding of skin like a snake. While her Brazilian clients knew her as Dr. Agatha Jones, she needed to shed her old self to reach Von Schlange. And she wondered, as she escorted Cheonsa Soo-Min from room to room—was her timid new hire here to shed her old self as well?

She refocused her spinning thoughts on the new hire orientation.

"The animal clinic doesn't have as many employees as the general clinic—the human side, but I'm okay with that. Damião currently has around five nurses and a secretary at the front, so seven, including him. Back here, it's just me and Beatriz Mendonça—she's my vet assistant and front-desk secretary. She helps around a lot. You'll meet her, she'll be arriving later. Her son has a dental appointment."

"Sounds like you run a tight operation," Cheonsa finally said, the words coming out in that same soft voice of hers, one that matched the hesitation in her walk.

"We get a lot done, the two of us." Von paused before rooms A and B, gesturing: "There are two rooms for our animal friends. I treat everything—domestic animals like dogs, cats, rabbits, and other small mammals. Your common pets. Before moving to Brazil, that's all I really treated, but I've moved on to livestock, too, like large agricultural."

"You mean like cattle, pigs, goats, sheep, horses—that sort of thing?"

"Yes, exactly."

"What about wildlife?"

"Brazil has a broad range of native species. I've seen macaws, toucans, turtles, and reptiles—snakes are my favorite. Plus, there are various monkey species since the Amazon forest is right here. I don't treat aquatic animals. When they come in, I refer them to a friend I know, a marine veterinarian."

"What about endangered species?"

Von liked the question. As quiet and timid as Cheonsa appeared, she had all the right questions, which spoke highly of her aptitude for being a fast learner and a good listener. "Yes,

I'm on the board of Carioca Conservation Society—it's an environmental conservation effort. We aim to preserve Rio's natural beauty and biodiversity amidst the push for urban development."

They walked into room A. It contained two large pictures on the walls, one listing dog breeds and one listing cat breeds. There was a computer, a sink, various cabinets with sterile equipment, and medical items, including latex gloves, medical gauze of multiple sizes, bandages, wraps for injuries or post-surgery care, and sutures for basic stitches. Two large lights hung above the metal table in the center of the room for operations. The room screamed of sterile, anti-bacterial cleaning agents, useful for removing odors such as animal urine and feces.

"This is Room A—where we do all of our surgeries. Room B is more for basic procedures: stitches, cyst removals, monitoring post-surgery care. Infections that need antibiotics, ear or eye issues—especially for our senior pets. Sadly, euthanasia, too. Things of that nature," Von explained.

Cheonsa looked around. "Everything looks so spotless. Smells so clean in here."

"We must keep everything up to code. The last thing we want is to get shut down. So, that's basically the layout. Without further delay, I'll show you to your office."

"My office?"

"Why, yes. You don't expect to sit out in the front, do you?" Von walked her to a mid-sized office overlooking the field of coffee cherries. "This is one of my favorite rooms. It's got the best view. Hope you like it, Marketing Director?"

"Marketing Director?"

"My mother—the psychologist—always said that one should never be threatened by people smarter than you or who have skills that you lack in any particular field. If anything, you want to surround yourself with people whose strengths improve your weaknesses. It's true—most men can't handle smart women, and many women become catty. People get their egos threatened. But I'm not threatened by your skills and education. I need you. Don't know anything about marketing, and that's why you're here. You're far too qualified for anything other than a director title and director pay."

"Really?"

"Really."

Von smiled as Cheonsa's eyes misted, taking in the room.

"Welcome aboard," Von said. "Whatever it is you've left behind in the U.S., I'm happy to be a part of this new chapter in your life."

Von and Cheonsa glanced out the window, watching the coffee cherries sway as their sweet, floral, berry-like aroma wafted through the open window. The natural, enticing scent. A prelude to a new beginning.

TEN

THE VICTIM'S NEW HOPE

CHEONSA SOO-MIN HADN'T EXPECTED to feel this happy since her divorce. For the first time in years, she was the driver behind the wheel, the player on the field—no longer the passenger, no longer sitting on the sidelines watching the game. She was finally in control, empowered. Von insisted that a part of Cheonsa's job was to tell her what to do and not do.

"If there's something wrong in how I'm promoting my business, then I want to hear it. Come to me with solutions. Ways we can grow the clinic."

"R-really?"

"Yes. Absolutely. Have any immediate thoughts? I realize that this is your first week."

"Well, my initial thoughts—the name out front simply says, 'The Clinic.' It's a bit too generic and doesn't immediately convey that it's a veterinary clinic. As for the signs depicting a human and an animal, I find them somewhat cheesy."

"I've always thought so, too. The whole thing was Damião's idea—preferred simplicity. Most locals find us, but I think we can be doing a better job at marketing. Any thoughts on what we do with our pre-existing name?"

Cheonsa had to pinch herself; her first week was off to an incredible start. Throughout her career, she had a history of working with male bosses who pretended her feedback didn't exist, only to present her ideas in board meetings as their own. She had also worked with women driven by jealousy and a sense of threat, smiling to her face while quietly finding ways to undermine her. But Von Schlange—Dr. Agatha Jones to her patients—was different. She genuinely valued Cheonsa's input, listening attentively to everything she said, creating a refreshing and nonthreatening work environment.

While a long way from the States, Cheonsa felt like she was growing, maturing into a better person, one that her parents would've been proud of—someone with a voice. Appa and Umma often scolded her, continuously on her to: "*Malhaebwa! Malhaebwa!*—Speak up! Speak up!"

As long as she could remember, shyness had claimed her tongue. Now, she was using her mind, thoughts, and opinions. Without fear. Without being silenced. Without retaliation. She'd tried on assertiveness for the first time in all her thirty-five years, and she found herself in love with the feeling.

"We should aim for a more … a more professional and inviting look," she said, trying on a tone that was fuller, more confident, and louder than her usual. "A look that communicates our focus on pet care. Perhaps incorporating a more descriptive name and modern, clean design elements would enhance our brand's appeal."

"Okay." Actively listening instead of dismissing her, Von nodded and met her eyes. "Since our name is generic, what should be the solution? I think Damião's pretty much set on The Clinic. It works for him."

Not allowing Damião's preference to derail her marketing plans for Von's side of the business, Cheonsa straightened her spine. "I have a solution for this."

"Good. Let's hear it."

"It's called brand segmentation. You can still be business partners, share the same building as you've been doing. Damião continues to have his space for the human side of things, and you have yours for the animal side, as you've been doing. Given that you're two different entities, why are you two still sharing the same name?"

"Good question. I dunno?" Von shrugged.

"We can rebrand your side, and that would include a new name and a new business sign out front. It would include a whole new website, social media accounts, everything. We can have your resume and picture on the web—"

"NO!" Von shouted, then cleared her throat as if she hadn't expected herself to have responded with such force. "Sorry, but I don't do pictures of any kind, and for the same reason that I'd imagine you'd want to avoid having your face plastered on a website or your name listed as an employee. Am I correct?"

Cheonsa paused for a beat, caught off-guard by Von's intuitive hunch that was spot on in a scary way. "So, you're ... hiding from something, too?"

"You can say that," Cheonsa's new boss said.

Cheonsa's gaze joined Von's as they both watched the plantation laborers help bring in a fresh batch of coffee cherries that needed to be processed. Under the scorching tropical sun, workers spread the coffee cherries on vast drying beds, turning them meticulously each day to ensure they evenly dried. Though she'd only lived in Brazil for a short month, she had already memorized the steps. The plantation workers left the air rich with fermented fruit and beans to soak in large vats, where days of fermentation worked their magic, breaking down the sticky mucilage.

As she watched the beans being washed and laid out to dry

and then hulled for roasting—her mind suddenly came up with the perfect name for Von's business.

"I've got it!" Cheonsa turned to Von, trying on her Portuguese, suggesting, "*Clínica Amigos Peludos!*"

Von rubbed the back of her German Shepherd, brows knit together in focused thought. Cheonsa had learned one thing: some people were easy to read, wore their hearts on their sleeves. Her boss wasn't one of them. It was next to impossible to decipher what was happening in the doctor's brain. The newfound confidence Cheonsa had worked so hard to rebuild inside began to crumble like a sandcastle hit by a tidal wave of rejection.

"You don't ... you don't like it?" The words shuffled out, child-like and small. If she could duck her head into her shell and never come out, she would.

"*Clínica Veterinária Amigos Peludos*—Whatdaya think, Zeus?" Von repeated in Portuguese and then switched to her dog's preferred language. "*Pelzige Freunde Tierklinik?*"

He barked once, and Von nodded.

"Is it stupid?"

"Furry Friends Animal Clinic," Von said with another look of seriousness.

"It's stupid." Cheonsa's shoulders sagged.

"It's perfect."

"I know it's stupid. I figured it was cute and—"

"It's p-e-r-f-e-c-t."

"It's what? Did you really just say it's perfect? Seriously?"

Von reached for her hand, squeezed it, and for reassurance—didn't let go.

"*Wanbyeoghan,*" Von repeated the word perfect in Korean. "Hopefully, you believe me in multiple languages. Google Translate included."

Cheonsa laughed, relief falling like gentle rain in a parched desert.

"You're hard to read, Dr. Von," Cheonsa said, then disclaimed. "Kinda mixed up your names. Hope Dr. Von is okay?"

"Just not in front of my patients. They all know me as Dr. Jones, and not many people I trust know me by Von Schlange. Don't want to confuse them. But, when we're solo—Von'll do, or Dr. Von—haven't ever been called that one before. Guess it does have a ring to it."

"You trust me? You just met me."

"If I didn't trust you, I wouldn't've hired you," Von said matter-of-factly. "Like I said, I got a knack for reading people. And I do trust your marketing expertise. I like how your mind works. I agree with the rebranding. *Clínica Veterinária Amigos Peludo*—Furry Friends Animal Clinic. It's great. Yes, to the new website. Yes, to the new sign out front."

"I like it, too. It's a perfect name for the animal clinic," Damião said in the doorway. "Hope the two of you will say yes to lunch on me?"

Von half-bowed, sweeping a hand to Cheonsa. "She's the boss. I'm always down for a lunch salad. A vegan diet always leaves you hungry. It's up to my marketing director."

Cheonsa blushed, tucking her hair behind her ears—something she did when nervous.

It was the first time she'd been put in any leadership position. Until now, she'd never really been given the alpha role or taken up that spot voluntarily. Eventually, people she'd meet, those more dominant, just knew she was easy to steer, like some dumb sheep. Cheonsa wasn't stupid. But it had been a lifelong battle for her—to speak up, to stand up for herself, to not let people walk over her, to raise her voice above a murmur.

As Von empowered her in a way no one had, her parents' unwavering bond came to mind.

Because Appa and Umma were so alike, they truly had a soul connection beyond their mutual careers as fragrance scientists. Her parents were embarrassingly gushy about their only child. Cheonsa's first memory was being five years old, hiding behind her parents' legs, plagued by the all-consuming spotlight that made her feel like she was burning alive. Now, as an adult, all she could focus on was the reality that she really didn't have any friends. The few friends she had prior to marrying Merrick were soon lost in the vast, uncharted world of 'out of touch' following their wedding.

"Well, what'll it be?" Von asked her, easing her mind out of the past. "Ever have Brazilian food? Forget Americanized shit. Nothing like the real thing. It almost makes me want to give up my vegan diet."

"Let's not get hasty." Damião grinned. "Aprazível's a great place for just about anyone. It has vegetarian and vegan options, but obviously, a very nice and tasty selection of classic Brazilian food, and they make an exception for Zeus since he's highly trained—so as long as we're sitting out on their porch."

Where were her parents' legs when she needed a good hiding place?

"S-sure." She fidgeted her fingers, social anxiety prickling. "I'd love to ... I've been wanting to try the food here."

"Well, okay then, looks like our lunch date's on," Von announced with a cheerful edge that belied her earlier poker face. Her boss was an enigma—one moment, it was like staring at a locked fortress, impossible to read. The next, she transformed completely—her demeanor light, almost whimsical, like sunlight breaking through dark clouds.

Maybe they were both harboring secrets, ones that kept a piece of their true selves away from the public eye. Maybe

Cheonsa had something in common with Von Schlange—they were both women with scars, women with a history that shaped them, and a future they were determined to seize.

Maybe, just maybe, behind Cheonsa's ever-present silence was a loud voice ready to shout.

ELEVEN
THE PERFECT FAMILY

JEAN WINSLOW and Mavis Lou Winslow never lost their smile or their neighborly Texan pleasantries. After being ushered in, they each took a seat in the large living room. A seventy-inch television was mounted on the wall, still blaring Fox News. Jean Winslow turned it down but didn't bother to change the channel, unapologetic.

"The election means everything to the American people." Jean Winslow pointed to the TV. "We're both from Texas—Trump land in those parts. But even here in Clovis, everyone wants change. With the inflation as high as it is, there's only one real choice."

"We're not here to talk politics," Nazario said directly.

"Not that we disagree with you, Papa J, not that we don't disagree with you," Wilson softened as he always did. "I recall when good ol' Don was in charge. Gas was as low as $1.77."

"On a national average, maybe," Huxley said, "but it certainly wasn't that low in Cali."

"But still, low as hell, and boy, do I miss those prices." Wilson turned his entire body toward Jean Winslow, engaging him fully as he spoke. Her partner's brown-nosing was as good as they came.

"And now it's the highest it's ever been. Everything's gone up. The Russians are running around doing whatever the hell they want. The Taliban wouldn't have attacked Israel if Trump were in office—" Jean Winslow ranted, hitting on a hot topic that couldn't be more divisive.

"Oh, and boy, what a mess we're in at the Gaza Strip," Wilson tsked. "Damned if you do and damned if you don't. A tragedy all around."

Nazario rolled her eyes, exchanging a knowing glance with Huxley, whose expression mirrored her own irritation. It was easy to rein her partner in, but a lot harder when the Colonel's father was so much more interested in making political small talk. Nazario had seen enough distraction methods not to get suckered into it.

"We're here for a little chat about a double homicide— involving two of our own," Nazario said. "Beat cops that were supposed to serve a restraining order got served a slug between the eyes instead."

Merrick tilted his head slightly, giving her an unreadable glance.

"Anyone care for a drink?" Mavis Lou interjected, clasping her hands. Her high-pitched voice carried a slight nasally country twang, making her the perfect grandmotherly host. "Got IPA—the good stuff, like Goose Island India Pale Ale—a large selection of wine, both red and white, some Texas sweet tea, and water in a bottle."

Nazario exhaled a loud breath, raking a hand down her face. Her palms went sweaty, and her heart began to sprint. Even now, after being sober since before Ariabella was born, her mouth salivated like she'd just finished a glass and wanted another. The cravings to relapse never went away. She'd even drink shitty white wine out of a box if she could. It was fixing to be a long meeting of constant redirection, including having to redirect her addiction.

"You said two blue?" Merrick finally broke his silence. "Whereabouts?"

"How long have you been divorced, Colonel?" Nazario asked instead.

"Would you care for some red wine before we begin?" he asked innocently.

Huxley carefully studied the Colonel before meeting Nazario's eyes. There was an unspoken understanding between the three of them, something that stirred an unsettling discomfort in her gut and made the father of her child feel uneasy.

Wilson was too busy jabbering away, keeping Mr. and Mrs. Winslow preoccupied.

She wondered how he knew she liked red wine. The words seemed deliberate.

"I'll pass on the red," she said.

"You sure?" Merrick said with a friendly grin. Nazario couldn't prove it yet, but his words dripped with calculated manipulation, a deliberate attempt to undermine her resolve and get her to relapse.

Huxley's voice carried a controlled, almost overly measured tone. "She's sure."

Wilson gave Merrick a cordial smile. "My partner—she don't drink. Waters all around will do just fine."

"Y'all say waters for everyone?" Mavis Lou said.

"Just for our three guests, dear," Jean Winslow told his wife.

Mavis Lou floated to the kitchen and returned with chilled bottles of water and glasses of ice for each of them. "I like my water nice and cold," she said.

Nazario waved her off. "No ice for me, thanks."

"Just the bottled water is fine," Huxley said.

"Hell, I like my water so cold it makes penguins jealous," Wilson said, making Mavis Lou and Jean Winslow laugh. "Ice, ice, baby."

Nazario opened her bottle, took a swig as if Mama was making her eat her liver and Brussels sprouts, then capped the water and set it down. She wasn't a water drinker. She was, however, an alcoholic who would prefer pounding booze instead of water any time and day of the week. The detective could already tell that if she didn't at least take a sip of the damn Dasani—she didn't want in the first place—they'd get offended. Wilson could sit around all day, shooting the shit. Texan MAGA Republicans. They were his kind of people. She just about had enough. The hell if they were sticking around for the barbecue and surface chatter.

They weren't wasting any more time—not if she had anything to say about it.

"Cheonsa Soo-Min," Nazario said, cutting out all the bullshit.

Huxley followed her lead. "What kind of problems have you been having with your ex-wife for you to need both a civilian restraining order and a military protection order?"

The air left the room. Mavis Lou shuffled quietly back to the kitchen to return the tray of unused mugs and dumped them in the sink. Ice clinked sharply against the stainless steel as Mavis Lou, not too gently, tossed the empty cups into the dishwasher.

Jean Winslow shifted his weight on the couch.

Mavis Lou sat next to her husband.

"She was a real nice girl," Jean Winslow started.

"At first," Mavis Lou added.

"At first," Jean Winslow echoed. "Poor thing, she just wouldn't take no for an answer."

Mavis Lou wrinkled her nose. "Couldn't hold down a job."

"That was a big issue," Jean Winslow said.

"It sure was—our Merrick was paying for everything. You'd think she'd be grateful, but she wasn't."

"Mavis Lou's right. She wasn't grateful in the least—always complaining about the Army life. You married a soldier—what in the hell do you expect? Typical entitled liberal."

"Spoiled is what she was. Spoiled rotten. Living off her parents' insurance money after they died in that plane crash. Don't need to work for her money. Expecting handouts. We didn't raise Merrick that way."

"No, we didn't." Jean Winslow crossed his arms. "He deployed multiple times, and all Cheonsa could do was bitch and moan. He was over there, could've been killed, risking his life so she could spend his money and keep crying about wanting to move back to Los Angeles because she was used to it."

"A military wife goes where her husband goes. You ain't supposed to get used to any one place—that's just how it is," Mavis Lou said.

"Go on and have a look at my emails," Jean Winslow said, getting up to grab his laptop. He handed it to Nazario. "Got them all in a folder."

"Appreciate the cooperation," Wilson said, wisely continuing to play the good cop.

Nazario and Huxley looked at the emails together. She tried her best not to show emotion, but the number of emails between Jean Winslow and his son was astounding. There were hundreds, even thousands, time-stamped throughout their marriage and into the divorce.

from: Jean Winslow <jwinslow@yahoo.com>
to: Col. Merrick Winslow<mwinslow@gmail.com>

date: October 2, 2020, 6:31 AM
subject: Lawyer Paid

Hi Merrick,

Hope you're doing well son. It's been hotter than usual in Clovis, especially for October. Your mom and I got the air conditioner fixed. Anyhow, I know this is hard, but it's the right decision. It's best for everyone. She's crazy and isn't right in the head. Cheonsa's making you look bad. You need a woman on your arm who understands the sacrifice it takes to be a proper Army wife. She's not cutting it, just like I told you she wouldn't when you married her. Hate to tell you I told you so, but I told you so.

I found you that lawyer and I paid her fees in full. You're welcome, son. Call me and let me know what she says. Don't let Cheonsa make you pay for her student loans or for anything else. She came into this marriage with nothing—she should leave with nothing.

Love,
Dad

from: Col. Merrick Winslow<mwinslow@gmail.com>
to: Jean Winslow <jwinslow@yahoo.com>
date: October 2, 2020, 6:31 AM
subject: Re: Lawyer Paid

Dad,

Sorry it's been so hot out there, but glad you fixed the AC. You know you didn't have to pay for the lawyer. I'll pay you back. I met with her, and she is certain we can see to it that Cheonsa doesn't get a cent. She's been calling me non-stop and emailing me. Can't take the hint or leave me alone.

Bracing myself for some "I'll kill myself" BS. What a fucking headache. She's dragging her feet and refusing to sign the divorce papers, thinking I'll reconcile and change my mind. Can't wait for this nightmare to be over.

Will call you tonight. Tell mom I'm okay.

Love,
Merrick

Nazario and Huxley read a few more—all of them were like this: Jean Winslow "guided" his son through nearly every aspect of his Army life, career, and marriage. It was admirable that he loved his son enough to be concerned about his professional and personal life, but this seemed to go way beyond parental duties.

Cheonsa Soo-Min wasn't just married to the colonel but to his parents, too.

"It's all there," Jean Winslow said proudly. "Got the paper trail. You can print it all out if you want. The lawyer's got all of it. Wasn't hard to get the protection order."

Nazario and Huxley exchanged a subtle look, one that didn't require words.

"You seem very concerned about your son, and we admire that," Wilson said, keeping his tone soft.

"We sure do," Huxley said. "Look, I'm a new parent myself, and I'd give up my life for my daughter."

"That said, if the two of you don't mind—we need to speak with the colonel alone," Nazario said.

"Why?" Jean Winslow frowned.

"We're real close," Mavis Lou said. "If not for our attendance at couples therapy, they would've divorced within the first year."

"Wait, you all went to couples therapy—like, *together?* You two and them two? Like with Cheonsa and your son?" Wilson asked.

"And what's wrong with that?" Jean Winslow said defensively. "Therapist said it was fine."

"She agreed with us when we petitioned. Finally understood that they could use the extra support. After all, military life ain't easy, especially with all the deployments. It ain't your typical civilian experience. It takes a whole village, and Cheonsa, well, the poor thing, didn't even have living parents. Hardly had any friends," Mavis Lou said.

"Anything you discuss with our son," Jean Winslow said, "you can discuss with us."

"Uh ... that's not true. Here's the thing. You two can leave so that we can talk to your adult son privately, or you both can stay, and we charge you with impeding an investigation," Nazario said, putting her foot down.

"We'll be issuing a subpoena for those emails, Papa J. They'll be coming in handy during discovery, so you are helping us to get to the bottom of this situation," Wilson said.

"If you're claiming our concern for our son's well-being is obstructing the investigation, then you're the hypocrite here. And now you want my computer? I'll just delete everything," Jean Winslow said with stubborn conviction.

"Here's what we're gonna do." Huxley took the laptop. "I'm

keeping this laptop because it's now become an exigent circumstance, and if the two of you refuse to allow us to speak with Merrick alone, we're arresting both of you. So, what's it gonna be?"

"Fuck you!" Jean Winslow shouted. "Get out of my house. You wanna speak to Merrick, you'll have to do it at the station on his terms."

"Excuse me?" Huxley stood to his feet. "Nice reversal. But we drove up here, took us four hours from Los Angeles to make it convenient for him."

"We didn't come here to arrest anyone, let alone a couple of seniors, but we'll do just that if you continue to be disruptive and refuse to allow your adult son—*a grown man*—to speak for himself," Nazario bit out.

"I said, get the fuck out of my house!" Jean Winslow, who was at least seventy-five, stood nose-to-nose with Huxley. "I know the law, and I know you can't be occupying my house without a warrant."

"C'mon, Jean," Mavis Lou warned in that syrupy voice of hers.

"Papa J, we don't need a warrant to talk with the colonel," Wilson said even-toned. "Interviews are a part of the investigation. We won't be rifling through nothing. Swear. All we need is to talk to the colonel in private. Promise it won't take up too much of your time. I know quality time with your son is very, very important. Especially with the military lifestyle. I know it's hard, since you don't know when he'll be stopping by for a visit. You don't know where in the world he'll be stationed next. That's gotta be tough, given how close y'all are."

Jean Winslow withdrew from the confrontation with Huxley, taking a step back.

The colonel looked amused—he got off on the attention. He hadn't so much as interjected a word to stop the situation from escalating. He strode casually to the fridge, took out a beer, and before he could open it, Mavis Lou snatched away the bottle.

"Oh, honey, I got that," she said. She wiped the condensation off the bottle with a napkin, opened it, and handed it to him.

Merrick thanked his mom and then turned to Jean Winslow. "Dad, it's fine."

Jean Winslow narrowed his eyes at Nazario and Huxley, then turned to Wilson. "Appreciate your support. I'd like to request that all communication go through you. Please return my laptop in one piece."

"I sure will, Papa J, I sure will."

"C'mon, Mavis Lou, let's go to lunch."

"You don't need to cancel the barbecue. We won't be long," Merrick said.

"It's alright, honey, we'll barbecue t'morrow. Take your time," Mavis Lou said.

"Don't answer if you don't feel comfortable, son," Jean Winslow advised, then pinned Nazario and Huxley with cold eyes. "We'll be contacting our attorney."

"You've every right to do so, Jean Winslow," Nazario said.

"Sorry about that," Merrick said, blowing out a long breath. "My ex-wife, she's put me through hell. My parents are a little overprotective."

They watched his parents leave. Merrick waved goodbye to his dad and blew a kiss to his mom, who, in turn, blew a kiss back. It must be their thing, Nazario thought. Merrick waited until his parents were completely out of the house and in their white Chevy Impala. They watched the car disappear down the street from the large living room window. His face transformed into a stern mask of authority; his eyes turned icy blue. The lines on his forehead deepened, and the frown around his lips set his jaw, erasing any trace of casual cordiality.

He turned to them, tone cold and edged with anger.

"Do we really have to talk about that bitch?"

Catching a glimpse of a dark truth lurking behind his calm façade, Nazario's heart raced. This perfect family image was a mask. There were secrets buried deep here, and she was determined to uncover them.

TWELVE
THE SERPENT'S AWAKENING

THE AIR CARRIED a medley of smoked churrasco, its sizzling skewers of grilled meat infused with an earthy charcoal scent—not entirely unpleasant to Von's vegan nose. The scents, amalgamated with a blend of spices, garlic, and a hint of lime juice, softened the carnivore dishes, making them less repulsive. The rich fragrance of feijoada filled the restaurant as waiters carried out steaming dishes of black beans simmering with sausage, ribs, and bacon. The hearty meals were plunked down before eager diners at an adjacent table, their anticipation almost palpable.

Von became used to the stench of meat but, even more, had to train herself not to overreact. As a veterinarian, her love for animals and ethical stance about their lives were the primary reason for her dietary choices—but health and environmental benefits played a part, too. Clean eating brought a sense of balance—lightness in the body, improved weight management, and better control over her health. She'd been thrust into surgical menopause, forced to endure it far too early after the night of the attack. There had been no defense against the armed men—not when it was just her and Zeus braving the icy winter night in Casper, Wyoming.

She brushed off the lingering shadows of the past as a familiar face across the room caught her attention with a wave. Eleutério Abraão stood out—a stout man with a light complexion, thick, dark eyebrows that framed his striking hazel eyes, and neatly cropped light brown hair. The personal trainer sat alone, wearing a fitted, breathable sports shirt he rarely went without. Aside from his well-built physique, there was a defined look about him, one that had a plethora of female clients begging to be his next client. Eleutério was the first natural bodybuilder and personal trainer she'd known to have a waiting list—almost all women—who'd be willing to pay just about anything to be seen at the gym pretending to be focused on their form instead of ogling the man's impressive biceps. He was big but not roid-big.

Having been a dedicated, all-natural weightlifter herself, Von knew the difference.

As inspiring as the fitness instructor was, Von had her beloved dog, and that was it. She worked alone, considered herself asexual, and not only was disinterested in relationships but had stringent rules when working out. The gym was her sacred space—a time to tune into Tool, Rage Against The Machine, and Nine Inch Nails, pop in her Bluetooth earbuds, and lift. It was her time to build strength. It was her time to concentrate on each muscle group like a sculptor fine-tuning their masterpiece.

It was her time to remember. Always remember. To never, ever forget.

It was her time to focus on the pain, the loss of her little sister, Sammy.

Back then, the Eleutério had asked Von if he could train her. She refused. The Brazilian Casanova wasn't used to hearing no. The rejection bruised his fragile ego—something Damião, among his few male clients, dismissed as nothing more than entitlement. Unlike Eleutério, Damião never made her feel awkward or threatened. He accepted her independence, strict vegan diet, and muscular physique. He loved her the way that she was. If only she could return his unrequited affections.

"You could've picked anyone else to be your personal trainer," Von said firmly. "I don't like him. Don't like the way he looks at me."

"Just ignore him," he'd told her.

"I do, but he still glares. Why do you need him to train you when you already know how to do everything?"

"Because he's my friend. A bit arrogant, sure."

"A bit? Your problem is that you're too nice." Von had laughed. "He's the most arrogant bodybuilder I'd ever met."

They ran into each other every day at the Iron Jungle Gym —*Ginásio Selva de Ferro.*

Every time she bumped into Eleutério, she could see his injured toxic masculinity written all over his face. See it in his tight smile and forced politeness. As if he was speaking with his narrowing eyes: How dare you reject my offer? Do you know who I am? Von Schlange didn't need some meathead with an ego to tell her how to train her body. If anything, she could teach him a lesson or two—and every other man who stopped to gawk —as she powered through a hundred pushups without breaking a sweat or pausing for water.

Damião called out, "*Como você tem estado?*"—asking his trainer how he'd been.

"*Bom!*" Eleutério exclaimed that he was good. Then gave Cheonsa a wink. "If you need a personal trainer, I'll give you my card."

Cheonsa blushed, as all the women did around the man.

"Eleutério Abraão." Damião turned to Cheonsa. "He's quite the popular personal trainer around here. A professional international bodybuilder. All natural. Has the kind of genetics most men would kill for."

"I'll move you to the top of my waitlist," Eleutério directed at Cheonsa. He sat close enough to their table to speak in a metered tone, and they could still hear him.

Cheonsa shifted in her seat, cheeks burning under the weight of Eleutério's arrogance. Von shot Damião a wordless, disapproving glare, narrowing her eyes.

"She'll be working out with me," Von said, giving Eleutério her gray, steely eyes, her first unspoken warning to him. "She's not interested."

Damião felt the need to apologize. "Sorry," he told her new marketing director.

Cheonsa's body went slack. "Thank you," she told Von, eyes growing moist. "That kind of guy ... he reminds me of my ex-husband. I didn't ... I didn't have a good experience. It was ... it still is a relationship that I seem to ... I can't escape. No matter where I move."

Von met Eleutério's eyes again as he sliced his knife into his bloody steak. It looked like he ordered the *Picanha*. It was a popular Brazilian steak often served medium-rare, not quite as rare as the trainer had requested. Von's stomach twisted, her fingers moving down the scar, following its length like a thread from her past—a thick keloid that refused to fade, a serpentine scar that carried the weight of memory. A flash of her on the ground with several men over her, pinning her down, returned. She was struggling but couldn't get them off. As Eleutério's knife sliced through his steak, the crimson piece met his wet mouth. Bloody juice slipped from his lips. She flinched as his blade no longer cut through meat but plunged into her abdomen, tearing through flesh, gutting her womb with surgical precision.

Von tore her eyes away, forcing deep breaths to steady

herself, anchoring her to the present. PTSD wasn't about memories slipping away, not like dementia or Alzheimer's—but the complete opposite—a relentless torment, vividly sharp, making her relive the pain in excruciating detail, over and over again.

Damião's warm hand went over hers, and he squeezed. "You okay?" he whispered, leaning in, concern etched in his mocha eyes.

Von snapped her gaze away from the grinning personal trainer. Something in that smile seemed to know what had happened to her.

"Did you tell him what had happened to me?" she pressed Damião.

Cheonsa's eyes anxiously ping-ponged between her and her business partner.

"I ... um ..."

"How could you?"

"I didn't go into the details."

"You told him about my attack?" Von bit out. "What happened to my body—it's my story to tell, not yours. Do you get that?"

Cheonsa looked like a turtle, shrinking her head into her shell.

"I'm ... I'm very sorry. You're right." Damião glanced at both of them. "Think maybe I should excuse myself. I'll take ... I'll take a taxi back."

"Yes, maybe you should," Von said.

Eleutério, having finished his tmeal, quickly paid for the check and then offered to drive Damião back home, *"Vou te levar para casa."*

Damião fanned his fingers across her dog's head, and Zeus quieted for the moment. "I have patient notes to input into the computer," he said, but the excuse sounded like a lie. The kind that escalated from the very tips of her toes, streaming upward to the top of her head, flooding her cheeks with heat. Her pulse revved, making her wish for jogging shoes to run off her frustration instead of sitting idle at a restaurant.

The moment Eleutério walked up, Zeus let out a low growl, his upper lip snarling, exposing sharp teeth. Since becoming an expat and moving to Rio De Janeiro, it had been the first time her dog showed displeasure for anyone in Brazil. So, it was curious to Von why he'd done so now. This wasn't their first time running into Eleutério, yet it was the first time that Zeus had regarded the personal trainer as someone he couldn't trust.

Anxiety on Cheonsa's face seemed to magnify with each passing disturbance as her eyes shifted worriedly to Zeus and then back up at Eleutério and Damião as the two men stopped by the table.

Eleutério handed her his business card. "Just in case you change your mind," he said, which earned him another growl from Zeus—this one deeper, more guttural, forcing Von to narrow her eyes at the personal trainer.

Cheonsa nodded mutely, glancing once at the business card before dropping it onto the table. Von picked it up and studied it. There was a picture of Eleutério's bronzed and waxed figure shining up on stage, slathered in body oil, strutting a front double bicep pose with arms flexed above his head to express definition.

"You should try competing," he told Von, sweeping his eyes across her defined biceps and chest that had once been flat but sculpted. Facial reconstruction and breast augmentation surgery to help her disappear hadn't stopped gym rats from nicknaming her "Bruce Lee" for her petite yet chiseled physique.

So many people had suggested she compete—mostly men—assuming her body was the only thing she was devoted to. Turning herself into a physically fit, muscular woman—with the strength to match—was rewarding. It felt empowering to weight train. To get stronger with each lift of iron. However, it never dampened the pain—the loss of being able to carry a child in her womb. Von returned Eleutério's amused grin: "Unlike you, my life doesn't revolve around the gym. The vet clinic that I run needs me."

"And as the doctor's new marketing director, she'll need me to stay focused, so I'll have to pass on your offer," Cheonsa braved, surprising the three of them. Eleutério, Von, and even Zeus glanced at her with curiosity.

Von smiled proudly. "Keep the card. Wouldn't want to waste paper."

She flicked the card back, and it hurled in the air, landing on the floor.

Cheonsa bent down to pick it up, against Von's protest: "Let that motherfucker pick it up himself."

But Von's too-nice marketing director handed it back to him anyway, her polite demeanor contrasting with the bite in Von's words.

Eleutério gripped Cheonsa's hand. *"Ele sabe que você está aqui."*

Cheonsa shivered, trying to yank her hand free from the man's firm hold as Eleutério held it for a beat too long. That hadn't alarmed Von as much as what had come out of the body-builder's mouth, which in Portuguese translated to English as, "He knows you're here."

Von rose to her feet, and Zeus followed, snarling louder this time.

"If you don't let go of my employee's hand, my dog'll chew a piece out of your juicy biceps like tearing into a rawhide," she warned.

"Hope he likes the taste of muscle. I've got plenty to go around." He finally let go of Cheonsa's hand, but her body trembled as though she was wearing cut-off shorts and a flimsy tank top in a snowstorm.

Damião, having walked ahead, saw the commotion from the doorway and called his fitness trainer's name. Her business partner knew better than to step in to save her like a damsel in distress, and that was partly what she liked about him. But his no-temper, aloof nature was a little too slow to react and a hell of a lot too self-controlled. Damião preferred to run from confrontations rather than face them head-on.

"What'd you mean 'He knows you're here.'" She stepped close enough to Eleutério's face that they were now attracting attention. Their waiter glanced over. Von smiled tightly and waved.

Eleutério apologized and assured the server in their native tongue that he was on his way out, "*Desculpe, estou indo embora.*"

"Who knows she's here?" Von said, for his ears only.

"And what'll you do?" he whispered, mouth still upturned in a provoking grin.

Cheonsa Soo-Min's eyes danced anxiously between them. "Dr. Jones," she said politely. She got points for addressing her with the right name in public. "Maybe we should cancel lunch."

"What will I do?" Von shot back, narrowing her eyes at him.

"Please, Dr. Jones," Cheonsa said.

"If she gets hurt in any way, shape, or form," Von said in Eleutério's ear, switching to Portuguese, a deadly warning that she'd end his life and the person who sent him. "*Eu vou matar você e o covarde que te enviou.*"

Eleutério's grin remained on his face. "You'll kill me? *Sério?* All five feet of you? You and your filthy mutt?" He returned low enough for her ears only, followed by a loud burst of laughter he couldn't contain. "You've no idea—*no fucking idea*—who I'm working with. You really should mind your own business and go back to playing doctor with your little pets."

"*Vamos.*" Damião nudged Eleutério and started for the exit, attempting to escape the heated exchange.

Men were weak—Von had learned—especially the ones that barked the most.

After fear-mongering tactics went dry, Eleutério joined Damião at the door, each tossing a wave behind their shoulders before strolling out of the restaurant.

Cheonsa's entire body slouched forward, face falling into her hands.

"Not gonna guilt or grill you. Not even gonna ask the million-dollar stupid question—like, what the hell just happened—but if there's something you needa tell me, now's a good time to do it. Trust, it sure is hard to give freely, but without it, Cheonsa Soo-Min, I can't help you."

A long pause stretched between them, but Von waited patiently as Cheonsa seemed to be at a loss for words. When the waiter returned, she ordered two coffees.

"*Dois cafés, por favor,*" she ordered for them.

"*Creme e açúcar?*"

"Hope you don't mind coffee? I take it black. You care for cream and sugar or that sweetener stuff?" Von asked Cheonsa, who nodded once.

The waiter returned with two coffees before Von could blink. The veterinarian and her new marketing director sipped in silence.

"They think I've been … stalking my ex-husband," she confessed, startling Von with the admission. "And killed two police officers."

"Might've or did?" Von said dryly. "I know what you didn't do. Didn't put that on your resume."

"According to the LAPD, I am a stalker who violated court

protection orders. They came by to arrest me with a warrant and everything. I had my gun out. All I was doing was trying to scare them. Needed to buy time to leave."

"Well, you're here, aren'tcha? Looks like you got away."

"Except I didn't."

"Didn't get away? You're in Brazil, Hon, not California."

"I didn't do anything. *I did not do anything.*" Cheonsa finally lifted her head. Tears began to crawl down her face. She reached for Von's hand and clasped it tight. "I swear it wasn't me."

"How come they think you did?"

"T-t-they don't ... they don't know who he really is. It's him. You won't understand. No one does. He is me. He's been me for years." She was shaking uncontrollably now. "I never stalked him, and I never killed anyone."

"Who is *he* supposed to be?"

"Colonel Merrick Winslow."

THIRTEEN

THE VICTIM'S NIGHTMARE

IT WAS the worst kind of nightmare—the kind where reality had a single, undeniable truth, yet only you and a manipulator knew it. And somehow, the world believed them. The world believed the liar. Cheonsa Soo-Min remembered the first two years post-divorce—when being single felt invasive, like loneliness had morphed into an uninvited guest.

Every day, the battle against memories haunted her. Waking up to half-eaten take-out food littered on the dining table she hadn't cleaned from the night prior and to the stench of dirty laundry heaped into piles all over her room. Shuffling into the kitchen groggy, having slept in too long. Waking up to silence instead of freshly brewed coffee felt like a small, piercing ache—a reminder of how empty mornings had become. Making coffee just for herself only deepened the hollow feeling, each step weighing heavier than it should.

"Why don't you get one of those coffee makers that you can schedule to start every morning?" her therapist had suggested.

"I hadn't thought of that," Cheonsa returned, eyes swollen from tears, crying into tissue paper that stacked up like fallen leaves in autumn.

"When was the last time you took a shower?"

Blowing her nose. "I dunno."

"You need to take care of yourself, Cheonsa. I'm trying to put this as kindly as I can, but I can smell you—"

"My parents studied scent for a living. I can smell myself."

She hated the way water felt. During that time, she'd gotten so used to wearing the same clothes throughout the day—never changing, never bathing or showering. She didn't wash her clothes, didn't even brush her teeth. She remembered the mustiness of her own body, the sour tang of unbrushed teeth, the stale reek of neglect.

Cheonsa hadn't cared about anything.

When the love of her life suddenly filed for divorce—left without a trace, emptied their bank accounts—she was devastated. None of it made any sense. They hadn't even discussed divorce. He'd smiled and made her ravioli with three-cheese marinara sauce just the way she liked it the night before, and the next day, he was gone. It wasn't so much the act of filing as it was the way he'd sprung it on her. It was cruel and inhuman. She spent the day driving around, looking for his truck, but couldn't find it anywhere. She called his number a dozen times, crying into the phone, begging him to take her back, asking him if there was something she'd done wrong.

She could fix it. She could change. She promised she would. *Just come back, and everything will be right again.* She was sorry that she got her MBA instead of pausing like he'd asked so they could have kids. She'd be a stay-at-home wife. She'd be a stay-at-home mother. Just come back, please—she promised she'd change. She'd give up her job for him. She was sorry she chose education instead of being a dutiful Army wife.

It was a tall order being an Army wife. It was likened to being a pastor's wife or the wife of the president. There were responsibilities, such as ensuring the other Army wives felt accepted and included. There were wifey events she was supposed to have organized. There were so many women better at this than her. There were so many perfect, doting military wives who moved around the country and the world with their husbands—*never ever complaining*. They smiled, posted pictures of their travels, and showed off their kids. They posted their excitement for moving to another city, another Army base, uprooting their lives, packing up their homes in neat, labeled boxes, quitting their jobs, saying goodbye, and making new friends to do it all over again.

Everyone was so much better at it than her. This was why he left. Regret hung heavy around her neck, drowning her in the ocean of "should haves." There were days she stayed glued to her laptop, studying for her classes—getting through her MBA program with little sleep and lots of coffee. All those days, she focused on her schoolwork. There wasn't a day she cooked. She was a decent housekeeper but a terrible cook. She preferred quick grab-and-go food that she could warm up in the microwave.

If only she'd taken classes for cooking instead.

If only she'd forfeited grad school for motherhood.

If only she'd rubbed elbows with her Army family.

If only she'd been the kind of officer's wife he could be proud of.

Instead, Cheonsa was selfish. All she thought about were her dreams of getting her MBA, and her love for marketing and business development. Her desire to make her parents proud, even if they weren't alive to witness it. She was horrible at military life. It took a certain kind of person to adapt and get used to all of the moves. It took a certain type of partner to dedicate their life to the way of the military. It killed her joy. It destroyed her happiness.

Her soul withered away into severe bouts of depression

every single time they had to pack up and go. Every single time Merrick deployed to Iraq or Afghanistan, he took a piece of her with him—a piece of her she couldn't get back. She tried to adjust. She went to therapy every single week. She dutifully used her finance and accounting skills to save every cent of his money instead of spending it the way other wives did. She never bought anything for herself, not even to get her nails or hair done.

Cheonsa thought she'd done the best that she could, but looking back after the divorce, she realized that her best was never going to be good enough. Little did she know, those two years—filled with pain and loss, endless wondering about what went wrong, and the slow, arduous journey of learning to live without him—would be remembered as years of peace. The time away from him opened her eyes and hardened her heart, turning pain into an opportunity for a new chance at a better life.

Fuck you, Merrick Winslow. I don't need you anymore— became her daily mantra.

Sadness and confusion had crystalized into bitter anger and a tenacious will.

She got a job as a marketing manager at a startup and went to every after-work mixer and team-building event. She loved their on-site group yoga and bring-your-pet-to-work options. When she didn't have a pet, her co-workers bought her a cute fish tank for her desk, accompanied by an active goldfish she named Buddy. For once in years, everything came together like lost currents merging in a stream, their separate paths uniting into a smooth, powerful flow.

She'd even started a steamy office romance with the hottest bachelor, who also happened to be her boss, which made their relationship that much more intense. Ethan Cole, the marketing director, was everything Merrick wasn't. He was laid back in his leadership style, not the alpha male or rigid military type, but an out-of-the-box thinker. He played the bass and guitar for fun at open mic nights around town.

Ethan's sun-kissed bronze skin from his daily dose of surfing, coupled with long, sandy, shaggy bangs that hung over his hazel eyes, gave him a relaxed beach vibe. With her heart guarded, she didn't quite express her feelings. Cheonsa had learned that love was far deeper than attraction, a good personality, and sex. Love meant a commitment, one that didn't abandon you. Love wasn't flippant breakups and cold divorces that came out of nowhere. This time around, she was looking for loyalty and wasn't in a rush to settle down again.

Cheonsa liked Ethan a lot but was happy taking things slow.

And then it began on a regular Monday morning, as she bounced into work, calling out to her marketing team and other employees. "Got Krispy Kreme, everyone. They're still nice and warm. If you've never had warm Krispy Kreme, you're missing out."

"You're awesome, Angel," her social media manager said, calling Cheonsa by the English translation of her Korean name. As members of her marketing team, along with IT and the business development departments, bustled into the kitchen, the rich aroma of freshly brewed coffee filled the air, mingling with happy groans of pleasure. Yet, amid the morning routine, Cheonsa had noticed one absence—Ethan.

He called for her, poking his head out of his office.

"Better come and get a glazed before they're all gone," she said.

"Hey." He made a motion with his hand. His face, serious. "Check it out."

"What is it?" She closed the door to his office and flushed. "You seriously want us to get naughty now? In your office? Kinda risky, don't you think?"

"Got this weird email," he said. "From some spoofer, some dummy account called foxtrothot121518@icloud.com."

"Did you say the numbers were 12, 15, 18?"

"Yeah."

"That was the day I got married."

"Maybe I shouldn't show this. Think it's a prank, Chee-Chee," Ethan warned, calling her by the affectionate nickname that only he could claim.

"Ethan, lemme see it."

"It's nothing. Never mind." He tried powering off his computer. "I wanna donut before those fat asses in the IT department eat them all."

"Lemme see the damn email." She glanced over his shoulder, snatching the mouse away from his hand and navigating to the screen before he could shut down his desktop.

Her mouth fell open, and she gasped.

There was a large picture of Merrick and his gorgeous new bride.

It wasn't that he'd moved on that shocked her silent.

"She looks just like you," Ethan admitted. "Don't that wedding dress look like the one we'd ceremoniously burned?"

It had been Ethan's idea to get rid of anything from the past in a bonfire ceremony that had been life-changing. Under the picture was a caption: Congratulations to the happy couple, Merrick and Vivian Winslow.

She had gorgeous Asian features that Cheonsa recognized as Korean, just like her.

Her hair was down and curled just like Cheonsa had worn hers. From her face to the figure-tight mermaid dress—complete with a train, laced and sequined like Cheonsa's—to the smaller details, like the flower tucked behind her right ear, the resemblance was uncanny. Everything was far too similar—this Vivian could be Cheonsa's stunt double.

With trembling hands, Cheonsa clicked on a close-up picture of the bride's hand.

"Oh my fucking God," the words fell out, too in shock to censor herself.

"There are a lot of rings that can look similar ... a lot of dresses that can look alike," Ethan said anxiously, trying to make her feel better.

"C'mon, Ethan."

"It's a prank."

"And if it's not?"

"Okay ... it's kind of ... it's a lot creepy." Ethan kissed her cheek. "Hey, I think you're the prettier version, and I like your name better. I mean, Vivian sounds like some grandma that spends her time at bingo or baking cookies all day."

None of Ethan's distraction techniques helped to ease the pain. Too focused on the pictures, she hadn't even read the email. There was one phrase, one phrase that she'd never forget.

Cheonsa Soo-Min was just the prototype.

It could've come from Vivian or maybe even Merrick's nosy parents, who had occupied every part of their marriage. Merrick's number one flaw, aside from being a toxic narcissist, was that he lacked the balls to stand up to his father. Jean Winslow had emailed his son no less than ten emails daily and had even picked out and paid for their divorce lawyer.

Not thinking anything of it, Ethan deleted the email rather than saving it—which ended up being a big mistake. It was the beginning of the stalking, the beginning of Merrick's harassment. He was allowed to move on, but Cheonsa couldn't, and he made sure of it.

A random phone call followed.

"Hey, it's me."

"W-w-what're you doing calling me."

"I'm happily married. I love my life."

"Why did you send my boss that email?"

"What do you mean?"

His voice sounded good despite the words that came out. The part of her that once longed to have him back was being pulled in again.

"You know what I mean." Cheonsa hugged herself. "What do you want?"

"Can you send me those videos?"

"What videos, Merrick?"

"The ones you used to send me when I was deployed."

"I'm not stripping for you," she returned, tone hushed despite being alone in her apartment. "It was something I did when I was your wife. I'm not your wife anymore. Ask Vivian."

"I'd like those videos so I can think about you when I'm out there."

"So, you're deploying again?"

"Yep. Vivian and I ... we got a fantastic sex life," he said, but his voice sounded like he was watching an uneventful golf game. "But I just can't come as good as I do with you. I liked coming hard, all over your body."

"You're sick, you know that? I'm hanging up."

"Lemme see your body again."

"Leave me alone. I don't know what you want, but you divorced me ... remember? You want something to masturbate to —ask your new wife."

Laughing, he tsked like she was pathetic.

"I wanna see your tits," Merrick demanded, laughter gone. His voice turned heavy and low, dripping with desire. "Show me your pussy. I'll pay you, so you don't have to work so hard. C'mon, it'll be easy money."

"I'm not your whore."

"Oh, but you can be my little whore. Does Ethan fuck you as good as I do? Is his cock as big as mine? Remember how you took it in your mouth. When I shoved it all the way down your throat, and you never once gagged the way Vivian does."

How did he know she was with Ethan? Cheonsa's voice trembled. "Leave me alone!"

She remembered hanging up, shaking and scared, hoping this was a one-time thing. But Colonel Merrick Winslow wasn't the type to be told no and wasn't going away, not when he had his mind set. It was a mixed bag of manipulation and psychological torment. He'd once been the love of her life who had allowed his parents to control and manage their relationship. Merrick had divorced her and apparently remarried a replica—Vivian, the better version of her.

The soft clinking of cutlery and the low hum of conversations filled the Aprazível. Its ambient hum of quiet clatter barely registered to Cheonsa. Her gaze fixed on the flickering candle between them. The dim lighting cast warm shadows across the intimate restaurant, where the scent of roasted garlic and fresh herbs mingled with the bitterness of her thoughts. Von leaned back in her chair, her fingers steepled, listening intently to Cheonsa's accounts of the dissolution of her marriage.

The Army officer at the center of it all had been the commanders' golden boy—disciplined, by the book, and decorated with honors. He was the kind of soldier who never missed a promotion, the poster child for military excellence. Yet behind the polished façade lay a man who had left destruction in his wake. Colonel Merrick Winslow was the perfect son, brother, soldier, and neighbor. Despite his two older sisters' jealousy over the attention he garnered from their parents, the Winslow clan was the epitome of the all-American family.

Cheonsa had no one to share any of this with, not until now.

"You didn't want the divorce?"

"No, I didn't. My parents were together until the very end. I wanted that for myself, and so when Merrick had me served, I was ... I was devastated. Crushed." Emotions wet her eyes, trickling down her cheeks. She wiped her face with the back of her hand. "My spirit and soul were broken."

"Sounds like you got sidelined."

"Had no idea. He wore that poker face of his. We didn't discuss divorce. He made me ravioli for dinner the night before, gave me a kiss on the cheek, and then the next day, I was served divorce papers."

"If I had to make a guess, it was a calculated move he was planning for a while."

"Well, you're right. It was a plan that included his father, no less—helping him pick out a lawyer and guide him all the way. It was the biggest betrayal ... ever. But then I moved on, got over it, or at least I tried to pick myself back up. Got a new job as a marketing manager at a great little start-up. Met Ethan on the job, and he was also great. He was so very different."

"Until?" Von questioned knowingly. "Wasn't just an email or a phone call, was it?"

Cheonsa blew out a breath. "He ... he wouldn't stop. It was insane. It was torturous. Eventually, Ethan's laid-back persona totally changed. I didn't blame him and still don't."

"What happened?" Von asked, then added. "Look, if it's too hard to talk about ... it's okay. I just ... I want to help, and I can't unless I know the full scoop."

"What happened? Only the single most humiliating thing that any woman could experience, like—ever."

Von reached out and clasped Cheonsa's hand. "It's okay. I know you don't know me very well yet, but I need you to believe me when I say this. As I tried to convey when we first met, Cheonsa, if someone is against you, trying to harm you in any way ... I'm the only person in Rio who you can trust. It's a bold statement, I know. And worse, I can't provide a lot of, how should I say this ... details. But from what I've been saying since day one, I'd like to help and can help. But I need to know what's going on."

The waiter came back with Brazilian cheese bread and set it before them.

"*Obrigada*," Von thanked the server.

"*Sem problemas*," they returned that it wasn't a problem.

Cheonsa waited until they were alone before swallowing a deep breath.

Von confessed, "*Pão de Queijo*—these addictive cheese breads are the thing I'd break my vegan diet for." Von apologized for the distraction and asked her to continue.

"I was at work, and that's when the video came through. It was sent to the entire staff. Ethan saw it. Everyone saw it, and it was sent from my work email account."

"Nudes?"

"Worse. Merrick and I ... having sex. Didn't know he ... recorded us. The camera, it was h-hidden in the c-c-closet." Cheonsa glanced down at the cheese bread, no longer desiring her favorite Brazilian dish. Her body, numb from that day of mortal humiliation.

"Holy shit." Von grabbed a cheese bread and took a bite, muffling, "It came from your work email?"

"Yes." She took a sip of her coffee instead. "I thought I was going to die. It was the single most mortifying experience. I even ... I took a few Ambien with wine, trying to kill myself. Only thing it did was knock me out and give me a hangover the next day. Apparently, I hadn't taken enough pills to do the trick."

"Oh, Cheonsa ... I'm so sorry. That's terrible. You sure it came from your email?"

Cheonsa nodded. "It had to be Merrick. He found a way to route it or something."

"But wouldn't it've shown his face?"

"The angle cut his face off. You could only see me." Shameful, quiet tears fell down her cheeks, voice cracking with pain. "I tried to explain the video, but it was unexplainable. I lost my job. I lost Ethan. I lost my dignity and the small amount of confidence I built up for myself."

"He was remarried, though?" Von looked confused. "He was the one who filed for divorce. Why do this? What would be the motive? Why try to ruin your life?"

"Apparently, I wasn't allowed to move on, but he was. His second marriage didn't last too long either. Couple of years later, he dumped her once he got bored with her like he did with me. That's when it ... that's when it all got worse."

"Why do you think the colonel—your ex-husband—would have anything to do with someone like Eleutério? How could the two possibly know one another?"

"Don't know. I just know that nothing's impossible with Merrick. He likes to be in control. He wanted to set me on the shelf when he was done with me, go do his thing, and then come back around and play with me at his will. It's not the kind of relationship I wanted."

"He asked you straight up for nudes?"

"Yes. Pictures and videos. Even said he'd send me money if I did."

"Did you save any of the correspondence?"

"Deleted most of them. I wasn't thinking several steps into the future. I didn't think to stockpile those disgusting emails. And his phone call—it wasn't recorded. Honestly, at the time, it was too triggering to save any of it. What was going through my head? Why should I keep something that was triggering?" Cheonsa dropped her head in her hands. The waiter came by and asked if they were still considering whether or not they wanted to move past coffees.

"You barely touched the cheese bread. Hungry anymore?"

"Not really."

Once they were alone, Von turned to her again. "You said something about two cops getting offed and that you had your gun, but it wasn't you. Getting the feeling you're feeding me bits and pieces of the story. What's the deal with the dead cops, and how does the colonel even know you're here?"

"Cops showed up at my house. Served me a restraining order. He had proof of a phone in my name texting him. Proof of emails, emails that were all in my name and were apparently sent to him. I've moved fifteen times since our divorce."

"And then what happened?"

"I panicked ... handcuffed them to the dining table, and in a rush, I left the gun behind. Had my bags packed, a one-way to Brazil. Was about to drive off when ... he pulled up. Next thing I know—"

Von interrupted her. "The fucker went in and shot them—with that gun of yours that you forgot, didn't he?"

Cheonsa stared down at her lap, shame hanging her head. She nodded once, then looked back up into Von's eyes. "Everywhere I go, Merrick ... he finds me."

FOURTEEN

THE UNTOUCHABLE PREDATOR

SHE COULD ONLY GO for so long before her body reminded her that she couldn't keep going without breaks. Detective Nazario's heart always ached whenever it was time to pump, picturing her tiny bundle of sweetness at home being watched by someone else instead of her mom. Huxley's mom helped when she could, but she had her own life—traveling, staying busy, enjoying her well-earned retirement. They needed consistency. That left them needing the sitter. Every time the detective imagined a stranger feeding Ariabella bottled breast milk, guilt crept in.

The insidious "bad mother" grew louder, curling around her thoughts with doubt.

Doubt had no place in Homicide. Doubt got more cops killed than the bad apples and planted negativity in society's mind. The scumbags of racism were out there, and Detective Nazario had known a few personally. It wasn't just modern racism but the good old-fashioned, in-your-face type. They were also the ones who gave her a hard time when she was coming up the ranks. The sexism was hard to dodge—even as a Nazario. Daughter of Lucas Nazario, the highest-ranking Puerto Rican cop in LAPD history. But there were plenty of good cops, too. The ones who hesitated, unwilling to fire their weapons, issuing countless warnings—and no longer alive today.

Doubt played with her focus, dragging her into a fog, at war with her love for the job and an even greater love for a brand-new human. The only thing she and the supervising special agent, Blake Huxley, did right. Ariabella was perfect in every single way. Before her birth, Anaya Nazario never cared how long she worked—skipping meals, running on coffee, replacing food with a bottle-of-wine-a-night habit. Now, she had to listen to her body for Ariabella's sake. And right now, her body betrayed her. The ache in her breast hit hard at the worst possible moment. She clenched her jaw against the guilt, forcing herself to focus. She didn't have time for this—not when she was about to question Winslow.

Her breasts were swollen and full. If she didn't pump straight away, mastitis would set in. The pain from having clogged milk ducts twice so far wasn't fun. They had just started questioning the colonel. Wrong timing for her body to crave her sweet little daughter. She missed her tiny fingers and toes, the way that Ariabella would snuggle close to her body.

Nazario felt chosen to be at the highest place in the ranks of any duty, and that was to protect a fragile, innocent being. Someone who relied upon her for everything, and now she was in Clovis, California, getting played by this smooth operator, this colonel with an impeccable military record, a veteran who should be honored for selflessly serving his country. The colonel's subtle, icy glare unsettled her in a way she couldn't quite name.

"Can we pivot for just a bit—talk a little more about your second marriage? Vivian, right? Is there a reason that ended in a divorce as well?" Wilson started.

"Colonel Winslow, looks like you filed for divorce from your first wife, Cheonsa Soo-Min. According to the County Clerk's Office, you equally filed for divorce against Vivian, your second wife, right? Irreconcilable differences, just like your first go-around. Can we talk a little about Vivian? Did she behave the same way Cheonsa did? Too clingy, or is this your pattern?" Huxley asked boldly, then gave Nazario a sideways glance. "Wilson and I have both been divorced. We know the pressure of the job, got our own hands-on experience when it comes to … patterns in relationships."

"Been divorced three times—hell, I know all about picking the same kinda woman that'll end up making me single," Wilson said. Nazario knew what her partner was doing, trying to rid the flush of anger from the colonel's cheeks with a little backpedaling. "It's like the DVs we get. Most times, them domestic violence situations end up the same. Pick the same person over and over, just a different face and a different name—same person with the same habits. Not always them angry boozer types, either. They can be anyone. Busy executives who don't got time for their wives. Chronic cheaters. Chronic addicts. Money's always the number one stressor. They divorce one, end up with another, and the same cycle continues. Rinse and repeat."

Colonel Winslow clamped his molars, forcing jaw muscles to flinch on command. His nostrils flared as he dragged in a sharp breath, chest expanding with rigid control. The tension rippled off him, but Nazario barely registered it as a dull ache swelled her chest, distracting her focus. A damp warmth spread across her chest, the wet sensation—the telltale signs of letdown —steering her eyes. She glanced down. Milk, meant for her daughter's hungry belly, bled through her shirt in two perfect circles. A badge of exhaustion. A walking headline: Busy. Lactating. Working Mom.

Now was a bad time to break up the macho man show. She

would much prefer to be home with her daughter than deal with a blatant narcissist who was too good for his ex-wives or whose ex-wives were unceremoniously terminated like two shunned soldiers dishonorably discharged.

"You don't gotta answer that, son." Jean returned, storming back into his house with Mavis Lou hot on his trail. It seemed these helicopter parents must've set a world record for the fastest lunch break in history, racing home to rescue their grown-ass son.

"It's called permissible deception. They're allowed to say whatever they want to get you to confess to something you didn't do," Mavis Lou bit out. "What on God's Earth does either of—those women—have to do with anything? If anything, he's the victim. My son's the victim here."

"Thought we made it clear that we requested a private conversation?" Huxley said, pointing up to the corner ceiling of the living room. There was a small camera mounted there, watching them. A strange chill ran up Nazario's spine. It wasn't typical to have a camera in one's living room. The last house Nazario had been to with more cameras than a Las Vegas casino ended in a bloody homicide when a family member tried to escape their controlling home.

Huxley pointed to the camera. "Hope your entire home isn't outfitted with those cameras. A bit extra, wouldn't you say?"

"We've been burglarized before," Mavis Lou said, voice edged with frustration. "And ever since Cheonsa's been stalking our son, we've every right to protect our home—whether that means cameras, guns, or whatever the hell it takes to keep us safe."

Shit, this was going to get nuclear, but if she didn't pump soon, she was going to explode like an over-pressurized reactor. Nazario pinched her shirt, trying to dry the milk ready to explode out of her like a broken hose.

She elbowed Huxley and leaned into his ear. "I need to pump. I can't wait. We've got a four-hour drive, and there's no way I can stand that long."

Huxley dragged a hand down his face. "Is there a private room we can use?"

Nazario didn't need him to ask for her. "I had a baby four months ago."

"Oh, you're breastfeeding?" Mavis Lou said, suddenly less upset.

"Why don't we all take a break for now?" Wilson injected.

"I thought the detective was the only one that needs the break?" Merrick modeled a cordial smile. "If ya'll drove four hours to have us this little chat, then let's finish what we started. Get'er done."

"I'll go get the pump," Wilson offered and was outside getting her pump out of the trunk before she could bark at him that she could get the contraption herself.

The over-protective colonel's father added his own parental sentiments, "As the in-laws, we've got plenty to say about that—*myeonuri-nyeon*—you know what that means? It's the only Korean word I know. Bitch daughter-in-law. She nearly ruined my son's life as crazy as she was," said Jean.

"As crazy as she is, Honey. Present tense," Mavis Lou corrected.

"As crazy as she still is—is right!" Jean grew louder. "We been there through it all. Son, why doncha take Detective Nazario to the spare bedroom. It's our turn to answer questions."

Huxley watched with cautious eyes as Merrick walked up. While he was at least four inches taller than the colonel and a hell of a lot more muscular, there was something in the way Colonel Merrick Winslow carried himself. He had an air about him that Nazario couldn't quite place. While he called himself the victim, having divorced two wives for reasons that were as simple as differences made her pause. It hadn't been for infidelity or anything more serious, though differences could certainly be serious.

She felt Huxley's hand on the small of her back. "You good?" he whispered all but two words. And although her on-and-off-again beau had barely made it to move-in levels, thanks to her utter fear of commitment, evident concern seemed to sweep across her baby daddy's face. It was the shine of apprehension in his eyes, how he studied the colonel with the same suspicion her cop instincts had also been alerted to.

Similar to how lawyers analyzed legal loopholes and crafted arguments to sway a jury, those in law had what Nazario's father had called his 'antennas.' Her dad often studied a room like he was fishing out the bad guy. Daddy's eyes always scanned the area no matter where they went—a restaurant, one of her taekwondo tournaments, grocery shopping, or at a neighbor's barbecue.

"Looking for bad guys?" she'd ask him.

"Can't help it, *mija*. My antennas are always up," he'd say.

Only when he was off work and in the safety of his home would those feelers retract. Just like her father, Huxley wore the same concern. Albeit subtle, it was noticeable to her. Small things she appreciated now. Knowing Blake Huxley—and Blake Huxley knowing her. The small gestures. The flickers of worry that didn't need drama. Not grand speeches, but the unsaid things. The silence between them, full of what no language could name. Love was more an accumulation of all the little things—the shared moments, the long hours, their careers—which solidified an unspoken commonality between them, one that was hard for civilian, non-law partners to "get."

And now, the child—part him, part her—a sweet, tiny human—their daughter, whom they loved more than anything.

Ariabella was their big-little miracle, given that they were both in their mid-forties when they conceived. It was a surprise that shocked them both, a surprise that brought them together.

Huxley nudged her, snapping her back to the meeting. Wilson strode in, handing her the oversized tote bag containing the breast pump.

"I'm good," she said under her breath.

"Sure?" Huxley kept a hushed tone. "We can find another place."

"Don't needa worry, no cameras in the guest bedroom," Merrick said. He had a charming disposition, hardly dangerous. Maybe it was her kidnapping during the Bridge Killer case—the bodies of undocumented immigrants found beneath L.A.'s bridges—that made her paranoid. Or maybe the birth of their daughter had done the same to Huxley.

She thanked Wilson and watched him sit with Jean Winslow and Mavis Lou, both leaning in, ready to bash their daughter-in-law. Interrogations were often difficult, but there were two kinds of people: the streetwise who clammed up and refused to talk, and those who were ready to tell you everything. Most expected law enforcement to prefer those who over-shared, but running their mouths often convoluted things, made it hard to get to the truth. The yappers were notorious for talking themselves into a corner, tripping up with all the varying versions of their story. Nazario hated having to wade through bullshit and truth to figure out one from the other. Wilson, on the other hand, could sit down for as long as it took, butter up the chatterboxes, and eventually get down to the real story.

That was what made them a good tag team—where she was weak, he was strong, and vice versa. Huxley was a lot like her: they both had the patience of a caffeinated squirrel, always on the move and easily agitated. Their alpha personalities sometimes made her and Huxley clash. Though they'd both had their egos checked since their daughter's arrival.

At least the silent ones were smart enough to shut their mouths and let their attorney do all the talking. Huxley joined Wilson, squeezing Nazario's hand before she left to pump. This wasn't ideal. It was the first week back to work from maternity leave, and already she was struggling to manage the balance.

Merrick whistled an unfamiliar tune as she walked quietly next to him.

"My daughter never got to breastfeed," he said conversationally. "Vivian was too old to carry, had a weak lining. Would've killed her if the baby kicked."

"Didn't know you had a child. Adoption or surrogacy?" Nazario wondered if she'd squeeze anything useful out of the colonel.

"Surrogacy—and expensive as fuck."

"What matters is that you have your daughter. I also have a little girl. They're quite special."

"Hope's mostly with her mother. Vivian turned into the Ice Queen after she was born. All she wanted was that baby," he said, resentment in his tone. They stopped at the last room on the left.

"Bet she's the best part of the relationship. The silver lining."

"Don't know if I would've done it had I had the chance to do it all over again," he bit out, the words stinging Nazario's heart. She couldn't imagine resenting her child in the same way. There was a discernible edge of selfishness, a 'she ruined my life' tone.

"Do you get a chance to spend time with her?"

"When I can. You know, I move around a lot—wherever they station me, gotta go. So, I see Hope when I'm able. For now, until I retire. We've got joint custody. But she's with her mother."

"Did Cheonsa want children?"

"She wanted babies more than anything, but I couldn't picture having kids with someone so unstable."

For the second time—as a working mother, and as someone whose life had been changed by her precious daughter, a gift—Nazario felt his bitter words stab at her maternal side. She imagined the pain Cheonsa must've gone through—wanting to be a mother more than anything and being denied that by her husband.

"The kids or no kids subject is quite a big one. The two of you didn't discuss it before you got married?"

"I thought I could have kids with her then, but I changed my mind." He shrugged like he was talking about a dish he wanted to send back at a restaurant—swap it out for something else. The way he spoke, it almost sounded cruel. Like he wanted to punish Cheonsa. Nazario's antennas were up way high and buzzing like crazy. But she didn't have enough proof of whatever it was that she was picking up on.

"So, how'd you break it to her? Tell her that the one thing she wanted more than anything, you didn't want anymore?"

"Just like I told you," he said, quoting, "I can't for the life of me picture having kids with you. I can't picture moving around with you, dealing with you and your little mini-mes." He laughed inappropriately. Nazario was seeing Merrick's darker side. Was this his true self? She didn't know but was determined to do her damnedest to find out.

"Kind of harsh," Nazario said as Merrick took out a set of keys and unlocked the door. "The door locks from the outside? You have ... locks like this on every door in the house? Who's got the keys?" For a minute, it didn't seem like he heard her question.

Then, Nazario saw it—bars on the windows. A cold knot tightened in her stomach.

"She cried those ugly tears, but I'd rather be straight to the point than fill her up with false hope," he said matter-of-factly. Nazario disagreed. There was a way to say something, and the way he went about it was all kinds of wrong. It was callous and hurtful. There was an evenness about him, an indifference she'd only seen in sociopaths.

He pushed the door open after unlocking it. "My parents and I have the keys."

"Why do you have bars on the windows?"

"We've had our house broken into before. I worry for my parents."

Why not just use an alarm, she wanted to say, but instead asked, "Did Cheonsa live here for a spell with you?"

"We were here for about a year to save up money."

"Did she have a copy of those keys?"

"Hell no," Colonel Merrick bellowed another raucous laughter. "One thing I learned about the military and running my operations is that you have to stay creative to keep them in line."

"Are you talking about your men or your ex-wives?"

The colonel gritted his teeth, a vein bulging across his forehead. "I like your spunk, Detective. It's ... *cute.*"

The hairs on the back of her neck stood on end. "You're not going to lock me in, too, are you?" Nazario's heart raced despite her attempt at jest in her delivery.

"Now, why would I do that?" He winked at her, then nodded to her tote bag. "Take all the time you need."

She entered the room and tried to lock it—but there was no way to lock it from the inside. This wasn't normal. Nazario glanced around, studying it from all angles. It was a basic setup —a queen-sized bed and generic, low-cost motel artwork hanging on the walls, forgettable and uninspired. She tested the knob, double-checking to see if it was unlocked, and it was. Relief swept through her until she glanced closer at the back of the teal-colored door. There were nail marks. Nazario ran her fingers over them, lingering as she pulled out her cell phone and snapped a few pictures.

Had someone been held there against their will?

Nazario suddenly no longer felt safe. She wanted to leave, but if she didn't pump now, she'd surely get mastitis again. There could be a reasonable explanation for the marks on the door, she thought, trying to soothe her cop brain and dispel any worry. Closing the window drapes, she took her shirt off. Her breasts were sore and engorged with milk. Unsnapping the back of her bra, a faint *creak, creak, creak* sounded from somewhere. Nazario instinctively placed her arms around her breasts and looked around. The ceilings. The bookshelf. The desk. She'd recognize some hidden cameras, but nowadays, they could look like a pen on a desk, and you'd never know it was a camera. It was impossible to know if she was being watched, though something inside her felt like there were eyes on her, eyes from somewhere.

Exhaling, she quickly dropped her bra and attached the suction cups. She made sure the bottles were screwed on correctly, so they could collect her milk. As soon as the pump started going, she closed her eyes briefly and exhaled a sigh of relief. The milk immediately started filling up both bottles. The machine's suction sounds made her feel like a cow on some farm attached to an automatic milking system.

Earlier this week, Nazario had left her pump at home and had to express her milk manually into her empty decaf coffee cup. She wasn't used to this motherhood thing, unaccustomed to being unable to go a few hours without pumping. Part of her understood why some women decided to skip breastfeeding altogether. There was the old culture that shamed women into not breastfeeding, but it was a woman's right to choose whether or not to breastfeed or feed their child formula.

*Creak, creak, creak...*she heard it again. She wasn't hearing things. The sound was palpable. Swiveling her head around, Nazario tried to find the location of the sound, but it was hard to detect.

She glanced at her watch. Twenty minutes later, both bottles were full to the top.

Creak, creak, creak ...

Nazario turned off the machine and glanced around. The sound stopped. Nazario dismissed it, figuring it was likely the machine. She detached the suction cups and screwed the cap on both of the bottles. She massaged her naked breasts, now reduced in size but still tender to touch. Tucking her milk back in the bag, the sound came again and louder this time.

Creak, creak, creak ... "Oh yeah." *Creak, creak, creak ...* "Fuck yeah."

The voice was low but recognizable. A slippery, disgusting squeaky sound, the kind you'd hear when someone was fucking or masturbating.

"Merrick? Son, come back down here for a second," Jean shouted, rising toward the second floor where she was ... where he was.

Nazario's heart slammed against her chest. Covering her breasts, she got up and looked closer at the walls. There it was, small but there. A tiny hole she hadn't noticed at first on the opposing wall—positioned directly in front of her, a perfect vantage point to showcase her naked breasts.

A shadowy eye, glinting with a hint of blue, locked onto her for a fleeting second before vanishing. Nazario quickly covered her breasts and glanced back into the peephole. Merrick was nude from the waist down, wiping residue of ejaculation from his filthy dick with a towel.

"Sorry, Dad, work call," Merrick lied with convincing fabrication. "Captain Miller from ops. Had dinner here, remember? Needed last-minute details for a training exercise."

Merrick glanced back at the peephole one last time, grinned, and then strutted out of the room, whistling that unfamiliar tune with an air of unassailable confidence—as if he were untouchable, the world bending to his will.

FIFTEEN

THE SERPENT'S CONSTRICTION

VON SCHLANGE WAS ENAMORED with the Avenida Niemeyer, a coastal road framed by lush hillsides and a biodiverse ecosystem rich with plant life—the jabuticaba, known for its grape-like fruit, and native trees like the pau-brasil, famous for their historic redwood.

But it was the ecological balance that supported a wide range of life and caught her interest as an animal lover. This was what made driving up the coastline of the Mata Atlântica (Atlantic Forest), home to endemic species of animals and plants, so special to her. It was the reason she moved to Brazil and what made the veterinarian in Von Schlange fall in love with the area.

Coastal wildlife wasn't limited to seagulls and frigate birds—reptiles and small mammals also made their home there, many of which she'd studied. The destination's allure lay in stunning Atlantic views, golden beaches like the Praia do Vidigal and Praia de São Conrado, and the dramatic cliffs of Avenida Niemeyer that dropped to over 100 meters. Though picturesque, the windy road made Von nervous, as it was notorious for accidents, including a deadly 2019 landslide that struck a traveling bus, killing two passengers.

Everyone in Rio De Janeiro knew of the gorgeous but deadly coastal road that had been shut down on numerous occasions. Now, yellow and black crime tape roped off the area. The *polícia militar* were in blue and black uniforms. In Brazil, the military police handled everything from petty crimes to homicide and even vehicle accidents. One officer spread out cones before them to block off the road. Traffic had come to a dead stop. While Von had heard all about this road and had driven it dozens of times, she preferred side streets, even if it took her longer to return home. Because she was driving Cheonsa home, Von thought to do the whole tourist thing, and boy, did they enter a trap. No one was moving, and all the cars lined up behind them had cut their engines off to preserve gas.

They were lucky to be in the first car, with front-row seats to all the action. Out of morbid curiosity, Von wondered if there were dead bodies. There was only one emergency responder, given that she'd spotted the *Serviço de Atendimento Móvel de Urgência*—Brazil's version of an ambulance service. The SAMU white van and the *polícia* cruisers were the only vehicles before them.

For a brief moment, Von could feel the cool wind whipping against her face, her thighs burning with each lunge forward, voices shouting after her as she and Zeus sprinted toward Point Fermin Cliff. The night swirling all around her as they dove off the cliff, the air catching beneath her open arms, and for an elongated few seconds, she was flying, free-falling toward emancipation from a litany of deaths caused by her very own hands, murders she never once lost sleep over and never would.

She would never forget hitting the water hard, sinking beneath its inky abyss, swallowing salty ocean, and feeling her body respond to the years of training. Weight training at the gym to prepare every muscle, swimming laps until she got her timing down and swimmer's strength up. Sinking herself under the water and holding her breath over and over until her lungs withstood five minutes without breathing. The average person could only do one to two minutes, while the world record holder, Budimir Šobat, achieved a whopping twenty-four minutes.

Whoever had driven off the cliff on Avenida Niemeyer was undoubtedly deceased. However, the paramedics were hoisting someone on the stretcher, picking them up from the side of the road. It looked like they'd jumped out of their vehicle before it went off the cliff.

Von's phone chimed—WhatsApp. *BlackDragon6.*

He always found her, always knew her every move.

Jefferson Pierce was the only hacker who had more aliases than she did. He sometimes went by Ace, other times Black-Dragon6. Von was certain he had many more aliases, depending on the chat room he was in. Despite having a lucrative job working for the FBI as an informant, Jefferson kept his vows to her—he'd never rat her out. He had embedded himself into her electronics, a ghost in the machine she never tried to exorcise. Instead of resisting, she embraced his unnerving talent—how he could track anyone, slip past firewalls like they were paper, and unearth secrets meant to stay buried. He had saved her life more times than she could count. Without him, she wouldn't be breathing—as he wouldn't be if she hadn't saved him from the Aryan Brotherhood. Maybe that's why he felt indebted to her.

Her breath hitched as she glanced down at the screen, grip tightening.

BlackDragon6: *Found something on Merrick Winslow that you and your new marketing director might find quite useful.*

She looked down to find a screenshot of an encrypted text message between the colonel and the personal trainer.

Winslow: *It's time to send that message to my ex-wifey. Get rid of the doctor.*

Eleutério: *Which one? Should I send you the surveillance pics of them that the PI took and all their info?*

Winslow: *No! Don't know what they look like. Don't want to. If this ever comes back, I need plausible deniability. I'm going off your intel—I trust you will get this right for the amount of cash I paid you. Start with Lover Boy. Then that vet, whoever the hell she is. Faces don't matter. Just make them disappear.*

Cheonsa screamed, startling Zeus, who'd been sitting quietly in the back seat. "He's doing this! It's Merrick, I know it!"

Denial began to flood her senses, pulse speeding out of control. Von could hardly breathe as her eyes returned to take a closer look. Eleutério was in a neck brace, being rolled into the back of the SAMU. Words left her. The entire world stopped as Von lost her breath. Her fingers white-knuckled the steering wheel, teeth clenching until she swore she'd crack her molars.

"Please let him be alive," Von begged quietly to herself through an unsteady breath.

"Oh my God. Oh my God. Damião ... he's down there." Cheonsa said the dreaded words that she could not say. "He's down there, and it's all my fault. Merrick did this. Eleutério said ... he said that he knew I was here." Cheonsa's head fell in her hands, and she sobbed uncontrollably, her body trembling, gripped by the kind of fear that no woman should ever have to live with, that no woman should be subjected to by some fucked up ex-husband on a power trip. Von knew very little about the perpetrator or the full story except for the bits and pieces that Cheonsa Soo-Min had shared.

Von was a killer. But her murdering days were behind her. It had to be behind her, but the rage was blistering inside. Her eyes burned with dryness, begging for moisture. She hadn't even realized that she'd been staring straight ahead the entire time without so much as blinking once. In a zone. A deadly zone. One that could not believe, would not believe that Damião was gone. Her Damião. The man she wouldn't allow herself to get close to. The man whom she'd found herself daydreaming about, fantasizing about what it would be like if she only permitted herself to feel—to be touched, held, kissed passionately, made love to. The trauma of the vicious, nearly fatal attack and emergency surgery that left her barren had never quite healed. It left her wanting neither a man, woman, nor any romantic relationship.

Now, Von would have to kiss Damião in her dreams.

Now, Von would have to see his kind smile in memory.

Now, Von would have to hire a new doctor to replace him.

Damião Sequeira had saved her life. Like Sammy, her beloved little sister, Damião Sequeira, was irreplaceable. For the second time in her life since Samantha's brutal murder, Von Schlange prayed to a God she no longer believed in. Prayed to a God that her business partner, her friend, the man who loved her, would be, by sheer miracle, alive. Because if he was dead and if it wasn't an accident, Von prayed to a God she hoped was real to stop her from doing what was in her nature, raging through her veins, reawakening the darkness.

If her sweet, kind, generous Damião was no longer with her, not even God herself could stop what she would do to her new targets, her new prey. Even if it meant getting caught, even if it meant going to prison for the rest of her life—Von knew that the Brazilian police weren't like the Americans. They'd hardly blink at this "accident" and call her a lunatic for blaming an upstanding citizen, one known by the Rio de Janeiro community, such as Eleutério. But worse, what would they say if she brought up some Army Colonel with wild claims of his connection to some car wreck that was a homicide?

No one would do anything, just like the men who got away with Sammy's murder, the men who got away with nearly killing her and murdering her unborn child. Left to the law, left to the detectives and the police—they'd get away with it. They always did. No, Von wouldn't allow it. So, she begged and pleaded as her heart sped so fast that she felt like she was going to vomit, hoping Dr. Damião Sequeira was still alive.

People waiting behind them started stepping out of their vehicles, some honking their horns impatiently. Von's mouth went dry, though the palms of her hands moistened with tension. Cheonsa's tears were unstoppable, an avalanche that turned the young woman inconsolable. While everyone experienced their emotions differently, Von had never seen a reaction quite like it. It wasn't the kind of response you'd get from someone guilty of committing a crime. Rather, it was the response of someone living in mortal fear.

"You're gonna need to calm down," Von said eventually. "I'm gonna need you to answer some questions. Can you do that?"

Cheonsa's body was still convulsing, head buried in her hands.

"He won't s-s-stop. He'll never l-l-leave me alone until I'm d-d-dead." The words came out muffled through choked sobs.

"I'm not gonna let that happen. Now, why do you think your ex-husband has connections here in Brazil? What's he after?"

She lifted her head, her face a mess of snot and tears, eyes swollen and puffy. Von took out a travel-sized tissue and handed it to her. Cheonsa blew her nose and wiped her wet eyes.

"He's Colonel Merrick Winslow. He's all about manipulation and control. He wanted me to beg him not to divorce me, which is what I did, and then the moment I moved on, he came back. I told him to l-l-leave me a-a-alone. He hasn't stopped. He won't s-s-stop," Cheonsa said, then warned. "Now ... now he'll come after you."

"Why?"

"Why do you think? For hiring me. For giving me a new life, a fresh start. I told you ... I told you I didn't want you to get involved, told you and Dr. Sequeira, and now ... now he's ... he's ... oh God!"

Just as the EMTs loaded the surviving victim—Eleutério was rushed out of there—the red glare from the sirens and their haunting music blared through the night. The nightmare Von had been dreading unfolded, completing Cheonsa's unfinished sentence. The prediction was no longer a what-if. *The polícia militar* used a pulley system to rappel down two of their more agile members.

"Wait here. Be right back," Von instructed Cheonsa, who nodded, still quivering from the latest turn of events. This devastating wreck was no longer some random accident. It was a whole other toxic mystery—one that involved her new employee, and because Von had hired her, it had now cost a life. She still couldn't believe it, struggling to reconcile death with Dr. Damião Sequeira's name, unable to say them in the same breath. It was a breath she held as she stood back—yet close enough to lean forward and peek over the cliff.

"*Pronto!*" one of them shouted up from below.

"*Vamos começar a puxar,*" said the police officer with the captain's insignia of three gold bars on his uniform, exuding an air of authority that left no doubt he was in charge. Just as the captain affirmed, a cohort of *polícia* and emergency medical technicians began to pull the ropes, hoisting the two officers who had secured the body up. Their faces grim but determined, they strained under the weight of pulling three grown men up from the three-hundred-foot drop below.

An officer tethered to the body looked defeated. "*O passageiro não está respirando.*"

Von heard what they said in Portuguese, but her mind refused to let go of hope. *No, no, no ... he has to be breathing. We have to do CPR!* She wouldn't give up, not until she saw him herself. Not until they did everything humanly possible to save him.

Von rushed over and didn't hesitate for a second. She stacked herself behind the last man and used her well-defined biceps and upper body strength to give the team the extra force they needed to safely retrieve the men.

"*Puxe agore!*" With the crisis consuming them all, Von ordered the men to pull now, and without a second glance in her direction, they obeyed immediately. Grunts from strain echoed into the night.

Panicked, Von sized up the situation—three men, including Damião, each around 180. They struggled to hoist him to safety, and even with her jumping in to help, they were well over 540 pounds, dangling over a 300-foot drop off the Avenida Niemeyer cliffs. This was going to be a fight.

Internal heat from her surgical menopause made her body perspire, sweat trickling down her six-pack and neck that bulged with mean veins. Her thighs constricted as she dug her heels into the earth, tightened her grip on the rope, and leaned back. Although at five feet even, Von wasn't what most would categorize as petite. Not with her chiseled physique, equal parts muscular and athletic.

"*Mais, mais, mais! Empurrar!*" shouted the captain to pull more.

Her quads and hamstrings shook from the strain of weight, biceps, and triceps fiery from the relentless effort of hauling three bodies up against gravity. For a moment, she was transported back to the hospital room, fingers feeling dozens of stitches that snaked up her abdomen. Her entire stomach region felt like it was ablaze. Still, it was Damião's kind eyes, his gentle hand resting on hers, and his reassuring smile that kept her going after the total hysterectomy that took away her chance to conceive a child she desperately wanted.

Her fingers gripped tighter around the rope, and with everything inside her, Von pulled the men up with the help of the others. It was this final push that brought the men up at last. Their hands clasped desperately at the cliff's edge. She could see arms and the tops of their heads. But it was when she saw Damião's limp, bloody body that the pain in her heart became a chainsaw, ripping her in half. It was the kind of agony that had shattered her the moment Sammy was brutally murdered by the savage Aryan Brotherhood.

Nothing eased the pain, but one thing came close—killing the bastard who'd taken her beloved Sammy, stolen her innocence, and shattered her life. Her little sister was murdered in retaliation for the men Von had snuffed out from the Brotherhood sex ring. Yes, payback was common in the criminal underworld. They wanted to hurt her, steal away the one joy that made life worth living—her baby sister, twelve years younger, who'd been kidnapped at sixteen, used in the illegal sex ring, and rescued at eighteen. But the light in Sammy's eyes was gone, replaced with a hollow, cold, hard edge that Von didn't understand back then. Not until she was attacked herself by the same men who'd escaped lengthy prison sentences.

Yes, Von knew all about payback. Since the death of Sammy, nothing was ever the same. And now, that same pain was like a butcher knife hacking into her soul, devastating any semblance of the normalcy she'd tried to build. Damião knew she'd faked her own death, but didn't quite know the details involved in her act of vengeance that had claimed the lives of eight men.

One by one, she found them.

One by one, she stalked them.

One by one, she killed them.

Had Von let the law handle things the legal way, Sammy would still be alive, and Von would have a living, breathing child instead of a buried one.

Now, on the precipice of this cliff in Brazil, the police tried to pull her away, but Von dropped to her knees and lifted Damião's head in her lap. His chest had been ripped open with a jagged shard of metal from the wreckage. Ebony brows were bloodied, glasses fractured but still on his face.

"Do you really need that strap?" Von remembered asking.

Damião laughed and told her something that hit her in a painfully ironic way.

"I can do sprints, and my glasses never come off. I'm telling you, if I fell hundreds of feet, they would still be on my face."

"Well, let's not try and prove that theory correct," Von had countered.

Damião had been correct. He'd even been right about his apprehension in hiring Cheonsa Soo-Min. It was too late. Von wasn't turning her back on her new employee now. But Damião had been concerned about the possibility of an external threat that Cheonsa unwittingly invited. She'd do anything to hear his voice one last time, with her again. Von ran a hand along his cheek. He looked like he was sleeping. She put her forehead on his, and a guttural sob came tearing out.

"*Afaste-se do corpo*," said the captain, repeated in heavy accented English. "I said, step away from de body. *Isso é uma—* it's an investigation, *senhora*."

Von gathered herself just as she felt a gentle arm around her shoulder. Cheonsa had gotten out of the vehicle. Her face, wet with remorse, told the story without words. Von thought she would be upset with her, but instead, there was an intense need to protect her.

They rose together and stepped back, watching the Brazilian medical technicians and the *polícia militar* hoist Damião's broken body, heart no longer beating, lungs vacant of all signs of breath. Von clenched her fists, inhaled deeply through her nose, and a rage she hadn't felt since Sammy's murder returned.

Whoever did this would pay in a slow and painful way. Whoever did this would not see her coming. Whoever did this would have to answer to the Serpent Woman, for she wouldn't stop until she had them trapped—slowly constricting their every move like a snake crushing its prey before swallowing them whole, leaving no trace behind.

SIXTEEN

THE RETURN HOME

RIO DE JANEIRO, Brazil, no longer held the allure of a fresh start. What had once masked the weight of the past with its vibrant rhythm and fleeting sense of renewal now felt hollow, the charm eroded by time and reality. Although Cheonsa Soo-Min had only been in the Land of Samba for just a little over a month, it already felt like she'd been there for years. Running from her former life had accomplished nothing, and it was foolish to think Merrick wouldn't find her.

It had been a week since the vehicular homicide that the *polícia militar* were calling "an accident," but she and her inked veterinarian boss knew the truth. Eleutério had been hired by the colonel to kill Dr. Damião Sequeira—jealousy that she had survived him, rebuilt herself, and didn't shatter the way he'd hoped after the divorce. How dare she get a good job, turn her life around, and thrive without being under the colonel's controlling thumb?

She remembered their conversation as if it had just happened—all of the times she fought for independence, all of the times she tried to make their marriage work. Cheonsa searched for a place where she truly belonged, tried to contribute to their savings to have something of her own. To hold on to a piece of herself before it withered away completely. Echoes from the past refused to let her forget. Their voices—his and hers—still in her mind, recycled conversations looping in a vicious cycle.

"I'd like to get a job on base," she'd once suggested.

"And do what?" Merrick scoffed. "Don't think it's a good idea."

"Why not? I can, I dunno ... work at the commissary or in one of the offices. Don't mind doing reception work or work as a check-out clerk. Maybe I can eventually work my way up to doing something with my MBA. Everyone needs marketing—"

"You've been let go from how many jobs?"

"Because we were moving, Merrick."

"You're not going to work on base when I'm deploying."

"I don't understand what you're so worked up about. It'll be fine—"

"They talk. You get in there, and they'll all start yapping and gossiping. I got a reputation to uphold, and I won't have you on post, sitting around with a bunch of nosy nellies starting a bunch of shit, or worse, some horny grunt comes around you and tries to start up an affair. Drag my good name through the mud. Not happening."

"You don't trust me?"

"I don't trust *them*."

"I want to work, Merrick, and you're not going to stop me."

"Fine. Go ahead and apply, sweetheart," he said, giving her a kiss. For a moment, joy raced through her. He brushed his fingers across the back of her cheek and then whispered in her ear. "No one'll hire you. I'll make sure of it."

Joy crumbled under the weight of her husband's grip. Then,

without warning, he walked away on his own terms, severing their vows, leaving her blindsided—no warning, no balance, no chance to prepare. The freedom she should've embraced when served with divorce felt like a cruel maneuver, a mockery of liberation. And just when she'd finally started living her life, living without him, Colonel Merrick Winslow returned to reclaim her soul.

Returning to stalk. Returning to instill fear. Returning to torment her.

The voice of the news broadcaster cut through the memories, anchoring her back to the present. It had been a week since she saw Von, overwhelmed by the guilt of what she'd done, that Cheonsa had brought this upon the clinic and the people who ran it.

Von had only texted once earlier in the week, and when Cheonsa told her boss that she needed time and space, it was a relief when Von had granted her request. After years of being controlled, it felt nice to ask for space and be given just that. BBC World News burst through the small living room with a familiar voice that infested her personal space, infested the sliver of freedom and happiness she had left.

"In today's special report on counter-terrorism task forces and concerns over the global implications of ongoing conflicts, BBC World News has delved into the escalating tensions not only between Ukraine and Russia, but also the enduring struggles between Israel and Hamas and the volatile situation in Gaza. As part of our investigation into how these global conflicts impact security strategies, we had the privilege of speaking with Colonel Merrick Winslow from the United States via satellite. Here's what he had to say about the current state of global security and the challenges faced by military operations around the world."

The screen cut from the news anchor to that familiar, sandy blond hair, soft blue eyes, and deceitful boyish charm. Cheonsa could hardly move, hardly breathe, pulse quickening. She wanted to turn off the television but knew she couldn't. Merrick held her again—frozen, powerless, his.

"Thank you for having me. In the complex theater of international relations, the current conflicts in Ukraine and the persistent clashes between Israel and Hamas highlight the fragile balance of global power. I mean, the situation in Gaza presents a multifaceted challenge that tests strategic capacities. Our main focus is to safeguard our interests and to secure high-value targets. It's crucial to understand that the dynamics of global unrest can influence operational effectiveness far beyond traditional borders."

Colonel Merrick Winslow stood resolute, his Army green uniform exuding an air of unyielding authority. The jacket, perfectly tailored to his frame, bore the silver stars of his rank, gleaming with a gold brilliance. His polished black nameplate glinted under the light, bearing the last name she once proudly carried. It now knifed at her insides, the blade twisting in her gut. The uniform was meticulously arranged with service ribbons, each a tribute to his storied career. His uniform was both a symbol of power and discipline.

As the camera focused on him, Merrick paused, his hand moving deliberately to adjust the watch. The metal band and stark, functional face ticked with a menacing rhythm. He adjusted his watch with practiced precision, a deliberate gesture carrying an unspoken weight. Was he trying to tell Cheonsa that her time was running out?

"For those who might believe they can operate unobserved, I'll make myself very clear: our intelligence and surveillance capacities are extensive," Merrick continued, looking right into the camera, right at her. "Even when one thinks they've moved beyond the reach of their previous engagement, the shadows of conflict often extend further than anticipated."

Cheonsa remembered the time Merrick gave her permission to have a drink with her friends alone without his company. But when he showed up and sat at the bar, watching her from a distance, gone was her 'girl's night out.' When it was time for her to leave, she knew. Merrick caught her eyes from across the bar, adjusting his watch the way he did now. Trying to be casual, she told her friends she had enough to drink and left, trying not to look suspicious. Her husband, fast on her heels, followed her home in his car.

Her ex-husband's voice went on with ominous innuendos. "In times of global instability, miscalculations can have significant consequences. It should stand as a reminder that with every secure perimeter, the potential for threat remains ever present." Merrick paused for effect and leaned into the camera. "So, to those who think distance grants safety: understand this—there is no sanctuary when it comes to security. There is no true refuge, only a temporary ceasefire. One can run and play games of cat and mouse, but understand this: our reach is as expansive as the conflicts that are redefining the global landscape. There's no sanctuary from the relentless pursuits that cross borders and find you wherever you try to hide."

Tears streamed down Cheonsa's face, as her body trembled with each veiled threat.

"We thank you for your time, Colonel Winslow, and for your service," beamed the news broadcaster. "I always like to leave my interviews on a fun note. I know with your job, you travel quite a bit. Any vacation plans? What's your next destination spot for pleasure and not for work."

Merrick laughed, and for a fleeting moment, it felt as though he were right there with her before the reality of who he truly was set in. Before all of the lies, gaslighting, and manipulation.

Some days, she wished she were naïve, wished she had never uncovered his darkness, wished she had dared to have been the one to have filed for divorce. Even if he was the one to leave on his terms, he'd returned on his terms as well. Cheonsa had no say. Cheonsa wasn't allowed to have a voice. Cheonsa wasn't allowed to be autonomous. She was meant to sit on a shelf and collect dust. Meant to wait around for him. To leave her as he wished. To leave her as he pleased, to indulge in other women at his whim, and then come back to her whenever he chose, picking her back up, brushing her off, and claiming her again.

She used to love his laughter, loved the way it lit up his face, exposed his straight white teeth, the way his eyes squinted into crescent moons of joy. Their joy. Their wedded bliss and happiness. Her handsome uniformed man, how she proudly stood next to him, unable to fathom a day without him, a world without her officer ...

"Merrick ... Merrick. Open the door. Open this door, please. It's been five days," Cheonsa remembered telling him. Whenever she made a mistake, which was often, she'd have to be locked in the bedroom until she behaved, and she promised she would. She promised she'd be a better wife. She didn't mean to burn the rice. She didn't mean to make the other Army wives snicker behind her back, embarrass him before his subordinates, make him look bad to the Army because she forgot to attend a meeting or didn't talk to the other Army wives long enough. Maintaining such high standards was hard, but she promised to change. Promised to be better this time.

"You know I love you, sweetheart," Merrick said after leaving her locked in the bedroom for a whole week. She was allowed to eat once a day. Food he'd give her. High proteins and veggies. A 500-calorie-a-day diet for as long as she was in the bedroom. She'd gained weight and didn't lose it fast enough.

She should've gone on longer runs. She should've avoided eating dessert. It was all her fault.

"This is for your own good. Make you better. You understand, right?"

"Yes. I'm sorry."

"Sorry for what? Don't hear that you learned. Be specific, or you're going back in."

"I'm sorry I gained weight. I'm fat, and I embarrassed you in front of your soldiers. I know I should be an example for the other Army wives, and I failed at my duty."

"The door is locked from the outside for a reason. It's a lesson in discipline. To make you stronger. Mental toughness training. My parents did it for me, and I can't thank them enough. It taught me lessons that made me who I am today. Do you understand?"

"Yes, yes, of course." She knew what he was referring to. Each of the bedrooms in his parent's house locked from the outside. So, at any time, one could be locked inside with no way out. There were bars on the windows to prevent escape. When they lived out of the Airstream, those were glorious days until he decided to buy a real home, and Merrick fashioned it with the same prison-like setup.

"You know what to do. Take your clothes off and step on the scale."

She stripped down and weighed herself before him, like she did once a day.

Before the confinement, she was five-two and 145 lbs. After the seven-day lock-in, the digital scale began calculating. Her heart raced. She hoped she'd lost the weight. Finally, it clocked her in at 133 lbs.

"I'm sorry," she pleaded, voice trembling as she tried to inject reason into her words. "I'll run every morning to get down to 120, I promise. I don't want to go back in. Please, Merrick. I'm sorry."

He roped his arms around her and kissed her tenderly on the forehead. "Think you can get down to 120 by the end of next week? Gotta drop it before the military ball."

"Yes. Yes, I promise. I'll start running and get back on my sixteen-hour fasts."

"You see. Sometimes, tough love works." He held her face. "Now, what do you say?"

"Thank you. Thank you for putting me in the discipline room," she said, like all the times before. "I promise to never disappoint you again."

Her mind scrambled back from what once was, as the harshness of the truth set in. It felt surreal—this was the man she envisioned forever with, the man who, in the beginning, seemed incapable of fault. A charismatic Army officer, now standing on television briefing the world, the kind of man she would've proudly shared this very moment with—if only she hadn't come to realize he was a psychopath.

"Oh, I always have plans," Merrick answered the BBC journalist, voice cracking through horrible memories she'd wished would stay forgotten and buried. Shame filled every cell of her body. The kind of shame that came with knowing others would soon start asking questions like:

How could an MBA graduate like you allow such abuse?

Why couldn't you stand up for yourself and leave him?

Why did you stay for so long in an abusive relationship?

How come you didn't tell someone what he was doing?

They weren't in her situation. They weren't in her shoes. They didn't know the kind of reverse psychology, mind-fucking Merrick was so good at. He never hit her. He never even raised his voice. He had her convinced his methods were normal. He had her convinced that his ideas were superior. Everything he did was out of love and for her own good.

"Well, Colonel, let's hear of those big plans of yours," the journalists said with a hint of intrigue. "Given you work so hard for your country—surely you find time to enjoy life as well?"

"I'm involved in a significant investigation, assisting the LAPD with a critical case," he said, his smile broad and flawless. "But, once I wrap things up, I'm really looking forward to my big trip—heading to Rio de Janeiro, Brazil."

SEVENTEEN

THE SECRET BETWEEN THEM

DETECTIVE ANAYA NAZARIO had often wondered what it was like for sexual assault victims, but now she had something of an understanding. She had never felt so defiled, yet she was caught in a dilemma in terms of what to do in such an awkward situation. Nazario recalled her father's response when she asked him what the number one rule was for being an undercover Gang and Narco detective.

"I want to be a cop like you, Daddy. Please tell me."

"I'd prefer that you don't do what I do. Your mother will have a fit if you do."

"I don't care what she thinks. This is what I want to do," Nazario remembered her eighteen-year-old self saying, just before her father was murdered while working undercover. "So, what's the most important rule of the job?"

"Well, if I'm not going to change your mind—"

"You're not, so tell me."

Daddy laughed and gave her hand as squeeze before growing serious. "Since you're not going to leave this alone ... whatever happens, you never ever break your cover. This is true, *mija,* even when you're not working undercover. When you're investigating a case or someone for that matter, never let your perp know what you know. Always, always keep your cards close. Just like poker."

Daddy was an excellent poker player and a damn good cop.

"I'm just telling you straight. It's not this romantic notion you got in your head, Anaya. Being a bad cop is easy. Being a good one is hard. You always stay on the right side of the law. Never cave to them power trips. Too many dummies out there make the good cops look like shit because it's easy to cave to the pressure. It's easy to cave to the stress. This isn't a job you clock out of. You'll always have your antenna's up, even when you're off duty. You'll never be able to relax at a barbecue, never will be able to see your friends the same. You'll always be scouting locations for the bad guy. It's no way to live, *mija*. I'm telling you, it's not easy. The pay isn't even that good for what we do. All the risks that are involved. All the haters who can't stand cops. It's not some glamorous job. The moment you put that uniform on, you've got a sworn duty to uphold the law instead of letting the power get to your head."

Daddy often told her stories of the bad seeds in the force, but he always kept his head down, always did the right thing, and never got trapped on the wrong side of leadership. Before she became a cop, she never understood how someone could abuse their badge. But since being on the force for more than twenty years, she got how it could happen.

Temptations to dip into the drug bins that had been seized. Temptations to pay off criminals and collaborate behind closed doors. Temptations to beat assailants who had been resisting arrest. Temptations to abuse racial profiling and become a racist yourself. She'd even seen BIPOC police officers turn against their own. After all, when on the force, there was only one color —that color was blue. But Nazario had sworn an oath to her father's legacy. She swore an oath to the civilians she served.

She swore an oath that she'd never allow her moral compass to be diminished by the temptation to do the wrong thing.

This was a turning moment for her. The woman inside her wanted to scream and shout at the top of her lungs, get in the face of Colonel Merrick Winslow, confront him for being what he stood accused of—a sexual deviant, a fucking peeping pervert. It was clear that the colonel caved into the wrong side of the law. Like police, Winslow had a duty to uphold as an Army Officer—honor, integrity, the oath he swore—and he had broken that trust. Yes, the woman inside wanted to get in his face and tell everyone what happened. But the colonel was far too smart to do something if he knew he wouldn't get away with it. He'd only feign innocence and, like all other guilty sons of bitches: deny, deny, deny.

Not only would he deny everything, but he would go as far as suing the LAPD for harassment and liable. While liable cases were hard to prove, Jean Winslow and Mavis Lou Winslow had the money and too much time on their retired hands. They'd drag Nazario through the courts. Regardless of whether she was the victim, Nazario had to consider the charges against Cheonsa Soo-Min. Winslow's ex-wife was facing a murder charge for the deaths of two rookie police officers who had come to arrest her in her home. She was supposedly guilty of breaking not only her civilian restraining order, but the military protection order the colonel had against her. Criminal stalking charges and now murder on her rap sheet weren't light offenses. But Nazario's gut instinct had to wonder—without physical proof yet—who was really the murderer? Who was really the stalker?

In civilian laymen's terms, Colonel Merrick Winslow was the bad guy. Her cop antenna had picked that up from the moment she laid eyes on the army officer. To prove her case, she had to keep what had occurred in the bedroom their little secret. She had to let Winslow believe she was afraid of him, afraid to speak up, afraid to do the right thing, afraid to turn him in, afraid of the implications that it could have on her career. Nazario wasn't afraid of nobody. But this was one of those poker moments where she had no choice but to wait to fill Wilson and Huxley in when they were long gone.

A part of her wanted to keep it to herself, but she'd never kept anything from Wilson or her baby's daddy. So, upon re-entering the meeting, Nazario smiled casually at Jean Winslow and Mavis Lou Winslow.

"Everything turn out okay?" Mavis Lou said, nodding to her tote bag that carried her breast pump and milk. "Need to put the milk in the fridge, so it doesn't spoil?"

"I'm alright. We won't be much longer."

Huxley leaned in close, his breath warm against her ear. "You don't look too good. Are we sure we're good?"

"We'll talk later," she returned for his ears only. Huxley glanced briefly at Colonel Winslow, and the men exchanged a strange glance. It was almost as if the officer was taunting Huxley without having to say a word, telling him with his eyes— *I saw your woman's tits, and I liked it so much that I came hard. My dick wanted her. What're you going to do about it?* Nazario inhaled through her nose, filled her lungs to capacity, and exhaled slowly through her mouth. She'd interviewed plenty of guilty assholes and learned how to keep her mind sharp, locked against the games they tried to play.

But she did view the colonel differently. She saw him for what he was, his true colors. That defiled feeling never left her, but she never let it show, coasting on neutral, emotions in check. There was one good thing about Winslow's little whack-job slip-up. She now had something to go off of, something to investigate further. Had he been a good boy, she wouldn't have known where to look and who to look into. She'd have continued to see Cheonsa Soo-Min as a crazy ex-wife and a cop killer—a criminal stalker on the run, evading the law.

Thank you, you filthy piece of shit, she thought as she gave Winslow a tight smile.

"Heard you're fixing to take a well-deserved trip to Rio de Janeiro. That was some speech you gave to folks over at the BBC, by the way," Wilson said conversationally. "Don't think I ever been to Brazil. The one country I been meaning to visit."

Jean Winslow and Mavis Lou Winslow looked at their son with pride. "He deserves it, the hell that crazy Korean put him through. Need to lock her up," Jean Winslow said.

"And throw away the key," finished Mavis Lou.

"Any other reason why for Brazil? Anything we don't know about?" Huxley asked.

"What kind of question's that?" Jean Winslow jumped in to defend his son. "I don't like where this is going. Questioning our son, who deserves the country's respect, deserves your respect. He did nothing but love that girl, and she clung on like a damn octopus. Wouldn't sign the divorce papers for a year. Dragged the whole thing out in court. Wouldn't leave him be. Criminal stalking is serious."

"Y'all been here long enough. So, if y'all are done grilling our boy, think your time here's up." Mavis Lou stormed to the door, opened it, and waited for them to leave.

"They're just being thorough," Merrick told his protective parents. "We can sit here all day long, and I'll answer a hundred more questions. Don't got anything to hide. Only thing in Brazil is the sunshine and *Praia do Abricó*, my favorite beach where I don't have to wear a thing."

He gave Nazario a sideways glance followed by a knowing, sheepish grin. Their little secret didn't go past Huxley, who narrowed his eyes at Merrick—those FBI feelers of his, akin to her cop antennas, picking up a warning signal. Wilson watched the exchange, giving Nazario a quick look. Nazario felt relieved to know that she didn't have to say a word about what had occurred while she was pumping. Merrick's creep vibe was something others in law enforcement instinctively sensed.

"Think they'd ban me from *Praia do Abricó*." Wilson chuckled. "Never will attend a nude beach unless I plan on scaring everyone away. Already scared off my last date. Lost a lot of weight, need that skin surgery. Hell, need a whole lot of plastic surgery, and even then, don't think I got the guts to let everything hang out there for all to see."

Nazario cut in, "If you've turned over everything you've got on your ex-wife—"

"I have, and my parents have, too. You've got the emails she sent me, all them text messages to me and my parents. If that's not enough, don't know what else you need?" the colonel said.

"The LAPD told us that the ballistics report came back, and those cops were shot with our ex-daughter-in-law's very own gun. What else do you want? Everything points to her, and y'all should be doing something about it," Jean Winslow lectured.

"You subpoenaed our phone records and got whatcha needed. What else you want?" Mavis Lou grilled. "That Cheonsa's crazier than a rodeo clown at a bullfight. Our son has every right to vacation wherever the hell he wants and without you people giving him the third degree."

"Merrick's not a suspect, is he?" Jean Winslow stood to his feet and stormed to the door, where his wife was waiting for them to get the hell out of their home.

Wilson kept his composure. "Well, no, he's not—"

"Then your time here's up. We'd like to pop open a case of beers, watch the news, and have us a barbecue in peace. Don't always get to see Merrick due to his job. We at least deserve to enjoy his presence without y'all spoiling quality family time," Jean Winslow said.

Then the colonel said the magic words every detective hated to hear, a legal warning that shut their interrogation down right then and there. "Not answering any more questions without my lawyer present."

Not always, but lawyering up screamed of guilt, and they all knew it.

Huxley grabbed Nazario's tote bag and carried it for her as the three of them saw themselves out of the Winslow home. A lingering air of suspicious hostility and defensiveness did not escape their notice.

———

"What do you mean there was a lock on the outside of the door?" Huxley said when they were in the car. He didn't waste any time asking her about the breast-pumping situation. Nazario underestimated his hunch.

"What makes you think anything went down?" Nazario said.

"'Cause I know you," Huxley said.

"Also thought it was strange that Colonel Winslow was gone within the same time frame. Didn't come down right away. Was gone almost as long as you were," Wilson said, keeping his eyes trained on the road as he drove.

Nazario had begun with the lock on the outside of the doors when explaining what she'd seen. She thought it was peculiar, but didn't know how to bring up the little secret only she and Merrick shared. It was something she almost didn't want to tell them. Maybe it was a woman thing. Maybe it was the discomfort of exposing something so intimate. Maybe it was the same reason why rape victims struggle to share being victimized with close friends and loved ones. In the retelling, there was a sense of being re-victimized, a sense of nakedness and vulnerability that was hard to hide and escape.

Shame. Humiliation. Embarrassment. They enveloped the incident like a shroud. But she knew she couldn't bear the weight alone. Not just because she and Detective Isaac Wilson, partners for twenty years, kept no secrets from each other—the reason ran much deeper.

Nor was it because she was the type to hide things from Huxley. The colonel's sexually deviant behavior might have something to do with the case, and not telling them what had occurred could put an innocent person in prison. Nazario couldn't live with that.

"He was ... he was watching me."

"He was *what?*" the words shot out of Huxley's mouth.

"Whaddya mean? You saying the colonel was ... er ... spying?" Wilson prodded gently.

"Yeah," Nazario finally said and told them what had occurred, leaving nothing out.

"That sick fuck!" Huxley was livid. "We need to report his ass to CID."

"What kinda man spanks his monkey to a woman pumping Mommy juice?" Wilson said.

"The kind that shouldn't be an officer. The kind that should be immediately discharged from his command!" Huxley snarled.

"The Department of Army Criminal Investigation Division will only complicate matters," Nazario reasoned, staying level-headed, knowing Huxley would react this way. She wasn't letting that perv Merrick get under her skin. "As much as I'd like to chop his filthy dick off, I think we can use this ... little episode to our advantage."

"We can't let this go unreported," Huxley seethed, adding,

"gotta at least fill Chief Johnson in on it, and the bureau, too. Maybe even go all the way up to Deputy Frost."

"Something tells me my partner's fixing to say no," Wilson said. "C'mon, Nazario, cough it up. Whatcha plotting in that big brain of yours?"

Nazario was silent for a ten count, then went with her hunch. "I dunno, but something tells me that Cheonsa Soo-Min isn't our perp."

"Got a shit pile of evidence we can't ignore, Honey-Pie," Huxley countered, his annoying nickname earning him a sideways glance. "But, if we're looking in the wrong direction, which way should we go with this?"

"I can't prove it yet, but all that 'evidence' painting the ex-wife as a stalker? Feels totally manufactured. If you ask me where we should focus—my gut says it all points to Colonel Merrick Winslow."

EIGHTEEN

THE LAST FLIGHT

"WHAT DO you mean I can't see him? My name is Dr. Agatha Jones, I'm a veterinarian, and he was my business partner. *A Clínica and Clínica Veterinária Amigos Peludos*—it's the only dual family medicine and animal clinic in Rio. You must've heard of it. I have a right to see him," Von argued in English with the *Técnico de Necrotério*.

The paunchy morgue technician, face set in a serious expression, peeled off his latex gloves and threw them in the trash. He dropped his N95 mask to his chin. "*Não*," he shot her down again. Bored eyes, fatigued from having to repeat the same line, glared at her. "*Somente família*."

"But I am practically family."

"*Parceiro de negócios*," he corrected her, "*não é o mesmo*."

"Please. *Cinco minutos*."

"I said business partner is not ze same. I'll not lose my job breaking ze rules. You'll have to speak with ze *Instituto Médico Legal*. IML must give you special permission. You can say your goodbyes at ze funeral if his *família* approves. It was *um acidente,* and nothing you say to him can bring him back,

Doutora Jones. Even if you go to IML, zis will take a very long time. By zen, he will be buried. *Desculpe,*" the morgue technician apologized one last time. "I know zis is not what you want to hear. His *família* has already come by to identify him. You can't just show up at ze morgue to see ze body. Even in America, I'm certain ze rules are ze same. Now, I must get back to work."

Her iPhone chimed with a text message. It was from Beatriz, her front office receptionist.

The morgue technician looked down at her phone and then returned to her.

"And it looks like you must get back to work, *também,*" he said, then bid her a good day in Portuguese. "*Adeus, tenha um bom dia.*"

Von stormed off, slamming a palm hard against the entrance door, causing nearby morgue technicians and personnel to murmur in their native tongue. It was true. There wasn't much she could do. Saying goodbye to a corpse made little logical sense, even when she'd hear grieving, devoted pet owners wanting to hold their dead pooch. But it was the only way the human mind could somehow find the strength to let go. Perhaps seeing the bluish-gray body in rigor mortis, its stiff, cold flesh, finally made it real.

Though, in her mind, she expected to greet Damião at the office. They'd chat about their day, swapping gossip over any unusual patients. More often than not, she claimed the prize for the most interesting stories—especially when it involved the quirks of die-hard animal lovers.

She waited until she was in her Jeep before breaking down, sobbing into her hands. A wave of sadness swept over her, breaking through the steel chambers where she kept it all locked away. Streams of pain wet her face. Zeus, sitting shotgun, leaned over and licked her cheeks. He was unaccustomed to seeing her this way. The last time Von wept was when Sammy was murdered. The hard truth was that Von didn't even know her own emotions as well as she thought. Her heart betrayed her, exposing the soft underbelly of her fears, vulnerable and raw.

Her phone chimed again. Von wiped her eyes and looked at the screen.

Beatriz: *Cheonsa came in to look for you. She asked me to tell you to check your email. She looked very upset. She said she was leaving.*

Von logged into her ProtonMail account. She used it for its end-to-end encryption, trusting that no one except the intended recipient could intercept or read her messages. The security it provided was unmatched. ProtonMail stored everything encrypted, even on their servers, so not even the company could access her data. Equipped with zero-access encryption and Swiss privacy laws, Von knew her emails were as secure as possible.

She also appreciated ProtonMail's ability to send self-destructing emails, which allowed her to control how long a message existed before vanishing permanently from both her and the recipient's inbox. The interface was simple, but the power behind it was formidable. She could even send anonymous emails without worrying about invasive ads or data tracking. For someone like her—on the run and living in the shadows —ProtonMail's secured layers were more than a convenience. They were her lifeline.

from: Cheonsa Soo-Min <csoomin@gmail.com>
to: Dr. Agatha Jones <ajones@protonmail.com>
date: May 28, 2024, 4:58 AM
subject: Coming 2 Brazil

Von, I'm so sorry for everything. All of this is my fault. I knew I shouldn't have involved you and the clinic, and now someone's dead because of me. Below is the link to yesterday's news conference on BBC. Can't believe it, but Merrick is coming to Brazil. Don't know how he found me. But he has. And he won't stop. He'll never leave me alone. They think I killed 2 police officers. They think I'm stalking him. He manufactured all this evidence on me. No one believes me. The cops don't believe me. He's even found ways to send himself text messages from my number!

Sorry to have to leave like this. I wanted to work for you. I love Brazil. I wanted a new life and thought I finally had it. There's no way I can stay here now, not when he's coming here. Please don't come for me. Please move on with your life ... I'm begging you to stay out of this. Don't get involved. You don't know Colonel Merrick Winslow. You don't know who you're up against. They'll always protect him, cover for him. That's how the military works. Someone has to practically end up dead before they do anything.

There's no protection for stalking victims.
If something happens to me—it was Merrick.

~Cheonsa

———

Von didn't have time to second-guess her plans. She asked Beatriz to cancel future appointments and paid her wages for a full year, opting to temporarily shut the clinic down. Damião's death gave her the perfect excuse to close up shop, and with Von owning the building, she didn't have to worry about paying rent or finding tenants to fill the space.

"I really liked working for you, *Doutora* Jones," Beatriz sniffled. "Will the clinic re-open in the future?"

"I enjoyed having you at the clinic. It's an unfortunate situation with Dr. Sequeira's ... fatal accident. Right now, I need time to re-assess the business." Which was partly true. "I'll stay in touch and promise that you'll be rehired when and if we do re-open. That's if you're not already working elsewhere."

Beatriz pulled her in for a fierce hug. She kissed Zeus on his head and thanked Von again for the generous advanced year's salary. At home, Von opened WhatsApp on her mobile, knowing only one person could help her find where Cheonsa Soo-Min was heading. She had to get to her before *he* could. Even if the colonel claimed he was heading to Brazil, it could've been a ruse to scare Cheonsa out of hiding and have her flying back to the States.

The former Marine sniper was the only friend she could say she had other than Damião and Zeus. She had a hard time trusting people, but knew Jefferson would be key in helping her get to Cheonsa and Colonel Merrick Winslow.

WhatsApp was her safest option for chatting with the hacker due to its privacy encryption capabilities. Though Meta still collected user data, Von made sure to trigger the conversations to vanish mode, which allowed the messages to disappear after they'd been viewed. Tapping on the app, Von searched for her only contact and typed the message.

Von: *Need a big favor. I should let this one go, but I can't. Afraid Cheonsa will end up dead if I don't intervene. Need your help.*

She glanced down at the message, a finger hovering over the delete button.

Before she could change her mind, Von sent the text. There was no other person as good at finding anyone, hacking anyone's emails, embedding himself on computers, and performing all kinds of digital trickery that had been impressive enough to land him a job with the feds instead of jail time. When her phone chimed, her pulse forgot its rhythm. Jefferson Pierce responded as though he'd been expecting her.

BlackDragon6: *Was that screenshot useful? How's Brazil, by the way? You successfully disappeared off the face of this earth. You know you're a wanted fugitive, right? Coming back to the States and out of retirement is dangerous—a stupid suicidal risk.*

Von didn't even bother asking how Jefferson knew her whereabouts.

Von: *I know what's at stake.*

BlackDragon6: *Playing savior can get you caught and locked up this time, V. But I'm a sucker for a challenge. The colonel got to him, didn't he? How'd he do it?*

Von: *Car accident. Jumped out before it went over the cliff.*

BlackDragon6: *That Army bitch. A Marine would've done it themselves.*

Von: *His ex-wife was in Brazil working for us. Winslow made this BBC interview with a cryptic message. Like he was talking straight to her. Sending you the link.*

Von sent the video interview to her hacker buddy and waited for a response.

BlackDragon6: *Don't know much about this Colonel Merrick Winslow dipshit, but I know one thing. They—the DOJ machine is fixing to cover for the guy. Ya know that, right?*

Von: *His wife - Cheonsa Soo-Min. Think she took a flight back to the States. Need her location. Need to track the colonel's every move.*

BlackDragon6: *I'm on it. If he's been stalking her, it's about power and control with them officer types. Will let you know where she's at, but I can't promise he won't get to her first.*

Von: *Find out where she is. Need to find her. Got a real bad feeling.*

BlackDragon6: *Will do my best, but she might be walking into a trap. As far as the colonel is concerned, I'll find out when he eats, sleeps, and takes a shit.*

Von: *Need her location ASAP.*

BlackDragon6: *Gimme 24 hrs.*

NINETEEN
THE STATES OF ESCAPE

CHEONSA SOO-MIN KNEW BETTER than to return to her remote rental home in Topanga Canyon, as it had been a murder scene and likely taped shut. They'd be looking for her there. She was a wanted cop-killer, a wanted aggravated stalker. Through the airport and the fourteen-hour flight back to California, Cheonsa wore her disguise: a dark blond wig and sunglasses. Her skin was fair enough to look believably Caucasian, hiding her Korean eyes behind her black-tinted Ray-Bans.

Not having anywhere to go, she checked into a Marriott Bonvoy. It was a hotel she and Merrick frequented during their courtship. While a nagging voice inside told her she should pick another hotel, the Bonvoy held too many good memories. It was the place she retreated to after the divorce, a refuge where she clung to the remnants of a life that had slipped through her fingers. The Marriott Bonvoy became more than just a hotel—it was a fragile link to the past, a space where she could pretend, for a moment, that things hadn't fallen apart.

When Merrick had deployed to Afghanistan, she stayed there, curling up in his unwashed shirts as faint traces of his cologne cleaved to the fabric. His bittersweet presence, like a ghost in the room. It was her way of holding onto him, even though the distance between them felt insurmountable. As she checked into the hotel, even without his shirt to cling to, it felt like he was just away again, deployed to the Middle East.

She imagined he could walk through those doors any minute, as he had so many times before. It was hard to fathom how she could treasure memories of a man who was now hell-bent on destroying her. Merrick wasn't just stalking her; he was tormenting her, framing her for the murders of two cops, and making her look like the crazed ex-wife unable to let go. And yet, it wasn't even about getting back together. Colonel Merrick Winslow didn't want her. He didn't want anyone else to have her either. It was control—twisted, sick control—keeping her in the grip while pretending she no longer existed to him, expunged from his life but never truly free from his reach.

To him, she was like an old photograph—kept in a dusty drawer, forgotten until it suited him to remember. He never cared enough to cherish it but couldn't bring himself to throw it away, either. She was a remnant of something he no longer valued, though he still needed her there, silently trapped in the past, unable to move forward. He didn't care about her life, only that she remained in the miserable orbit of his power, a constant reminder that no matter how far she tried to run, he could still crush her whenever he pleased.

Cheonsa unpacked her luggage and put her clothes away in the bedroom dresser. It was a nice-sized room with a king-sized bed, full kitchen, refrigerator, stove, and a television in the living room and one in the bedroom. She looked around, feeling imme-diately at home as she glanced out the fourth-floor window with the view of the outdoor heated pool and Jacuzzi. Her mind drifted to Brazil, back to the coffee fields that stretched for miles, carpeting the rolling hills of Rio de Janeiro with a sea of deep green. She missed watching the workers move along the rows with practiced dedication, plucking ripe coffee cherries from the bushes.

But the beauty of Brazil was a shattered memory, tainted by fear. Anxiety turned Cheonsa's stomach. Her thoughts lingered on Von, her mind spinning with worry, hoping her former boss wouldn't come looking for her. It was difficult to forget that BBC news conference where her ex announced he would soon be vacationing in Brazil. Glancing down at the pool, Cheonsa watched steam curl from its surface, rising in delicate tendrils. The heat wavered in the air, a mirage effect, beckoning her. Its whispering warmth invited her to embrace its depths. The Marriott Bonvoy was the only hotel in the area with a heated pool, one of her favorite perks of staying there.

Cheonsa donned her simple black one-piece swimsuit, taking off her blond wig, relieving her itchy scalp. Swallowing a breath, her shaky hand pressed the elevator as it slowly descended to the first floor. In the lobby, the receptionist gave her a friendly smile. Cheonsa glanced nervously away, somehow feeling vulnerable without her disguise to cloak her. She should've worn the sunglasses but left them upstairs, given how the night was clocking out the sun, though it lingered like a worker refusing to leave on time, casting its final rays before disappearing for good.

A couple in their late fifties sat kissing in the Jacuzzi. Cheonsa found herself writing their story. They probably were high school sweethearts, the kind that was for real from the moment they said, "I do." Maybe they had two beautiful kids that made all their friends jealous because their parents were not only still married but still madly in love with one another. It was the kind of mature love that everyone wanted for themselves. The kind of understanding and companionship that never grew old. Slipping into the pool, she could see herself in the Jacuzzi with Merrick when they started dating. The way he looked at her with lust and carnal desire. How he kissed her like it was his last day with her before a deployment.

She thought she had the kind of love her parents had, but she was wrong.

Cheonsa dunked her head under the water, exhaling all the air in her lungs as she sank to the bottom, waiting until her body begged for breath. She opened her eyes and screamed, swallowed by the water, suffocating in the silence, tears blending into its currents. When her body couldn't take much more, she swam to the surface and inhaled a long-needed breath. It was a gorgeous night. The water hugged her body. Sleep would elude her, thanks to a cocktail of jetlag and stress. Her anxiety had multiplied, paranoia an obvious side effect of having to pick up and flee a place that had quickly become her home.

Swimming laps always helped her fall asleep, so she started with alternating side strokes from one end of the pool to the other. The warmth of the water soothed her aching limbs, stiff from the long flight that had reignited a lingering lower lumbar strain from years of packing up and moving from place to place. Her unused muscles burned in a good way, thigh muscles constricted with every kick, biceps, and triceps begging her to stop. But she continued pushing forward, pushing her body to swim faster, images of the devastating car crash fresh in her mind. Seeing the Brazilian medics roping Dr. Sequeira's body up as they hoisted the corpse up from off the cliff.

Digging deep into that place of never quit, Cheonsa challenged herself not to give up despite every fiber in her wanting to throw in the towel and stop. She forced herself to fight through the burn. She swam hard and fast, lap after lap, until Cheonsa counted to ten. Pausing at last, she gasped for air, exhilarated with renewed fatigue that beckoned her to the king-sized bed.

All she wanted to do was sleep. Sleep without an alarm jolting her awake. Sleep to escape the despair, the fear, the gnawing hopelessness. She wished sleep could erase her real-life nightmare, that when she awoke, Merrick would be gone, vanished from her life like a bad dream. Maybe he'd find someone else to torment, remarry yet again, and leave her alone —leave her to finally breathe.

She padded up the stairs, a towel loosely draped around her damp body, water still dripping from her hair. As she opened the door to her room, her breath caught—terror clutched at her chest. Rose petals, a trail of crimson, started at the entryway, leading her to the bed. Her pulse quickened. She followed them reluctantly, her footsteps slow and heavy. When she reached the bed, her stomach dropped—a sea of roses covered the sheets, an opened bottle of red wine stood next to the two glasses on the nightstand.

Fear surged through her, and a tremor coursed down her spine. She turned swiftly, her heart pounding in her throat. Merrick had found her. Cheonsa's skin prickled with the icy grip of dread, clutching the towel closer to her chest, a flimsy shield that wouldn't protect her from him.

"Hello, darling, I've missed you." Merrick sauntered out of the bathroom.

"H-h-how'd you get in here?"

"You still love me. It's very sweet of you to've picked our hotel."

"I need you to leave. I'm calling the cops."

He grabbed the phone cord and ripped it from the wall, his grip tightening around her cell phone, which had been forgotten in the hotel room.

"Call the cops, and you'll be the one in cuffs. You're an international fugitive. There's an Interpol notice out on you," he said, stepping toward her with slow, deliberate intent.

"You ... you killed the doctor."

"The *Avenida Niemeyer* is dangerous to drive for those not paying attention," Merrick began, inching even closer. She fumbled back on wobbly legs until her back was pressed against the wall, trapping her there before him. "There were five thousand three hundred and thirty-two deaths ... oops, correction, five thousand three hundred and thirty-three since 2019 on that windy road. It's a death trap."

He fanned the back of his fingers along her cheek.

"W-w-what do you want from me?" Silent tears trickled down her face.

"Should've never ignored me, Cheonsa." His teeth clenched. "No one ignores me."

"I moved on. You got the divorce you wanted. I am not your property. Please, please ... just leave me alone."

Cheonsa drove her knee hard into his groin, forcing him to double over in pain. Seizing the moment, she freed herself, slipping out from under him as he clutched his knees, muttering curses through gritted teeth. With Merrick blocking the door, Cheonsa ran into the bedroom, slamming the door shut. Her ex-husband recovered quickly, and before she could lock it, he kicked the door open. She screamed, crying out for help, stumbling backward as Merrick lunged for her, toppling her to the bed.

Merrick grabbed a pillow and slammed it down over her face with unrelenting force, her voice muffled under the weight. She struggled wildly, her limbs thrashing in desperation as air became a distant memory. Her lungs burned, but the panic that surged through her began to slow, her body giving in to the inevitable. Just thirty minutes ago, she had been in the hotel pool, floating beneath the surface, holding her breath as the water hugged her. She remembered the calm that had washed over her then, how the coolness had offered a brief escape.

But now, it was no escape—just a death sentence.

Her pulse faded, slowing until she was barely aware of the cold barrel pressed against her temple. He was close, whispering something she couldn't hear. Then she saw them—Umma and Appa, her parents waiting for her. They stood in a garden of wildflowers, smiling, bathed in bright sunlight. She wanted to go to them, feel their warmth. As the pressure of the gun increased and Merrick lifted the pillow, Cheonsa closed her eyes. *I'll sleep now ... forever.*

Her final thought slipped away into darkness.

The shot rang out, but she was already gone.

TWENTY

THE WEIGHT OF DOUBT

BEING AWAY from her baby girl for just a few short hours had felt like eternal hell. Nazario hadn't realized how inadequate four months of maternity leave would be until she returned to active duty. While she could've asked for more time off, the workaholic in her warred with this new maternal side, the part of her that longed to hold her daughter close, feel her suckle on her breasts.

Nazario cradled her sweet little miracle against her chest as Ariabella greedily fed from her. All the while, she could not get what Merrick had done out of her mind. He had defiled the very thing that was most sacred between mother and child. Defiled the moment, replacing it now with his peeping eyes, his filthy cock in his hand, perverting the one pure thing—nursing an innocent human with nourishment no man-made formula could deliver.

Huxley sat beside her and their daughter on the couch and put an arm around her, stroking his fingers through Ariabella's curls. Nazario had been more silent than usual, and it didn't take much effort to figure out why. Huxley knew her better than she knew herself, which was why he didn't press her to delve deeper into the shocking event. He was good about following her lead in terms of what she was comfortable sharing. She appreciated his gentle nature and willingness to give her space when needed. His empathy for their demanding job and hands-on approach with their daughter surprised Nazario.

She didn't know she could grow to love him more until they both matured as adults once their daughter came into their lives. Being a first-time parent often changed people, and not always in positive ways. Nazario had seen this first-hand. She'd witnessed child abuse: neglect, emotional abuse, psychological abuse, and physical. Sometimes, the unseen scars cut the deepest. Parenthood was an incredible responsibility, one that meant she was accountable for potentially damaging a soul for the rest of their lives. Damaged adults carried a damaged inner child, one that never healed no matter how much time had passed and how much therapy one had.

Nazario hadn't known what to expect once Ariabella was born. A part of her feared she would suck at being a mother, that Huxley would suck at being a father, that parenthood would put a wedge between them. But just the opposite had occurred. Huxley never had to be asked to do anything. He took on laundry duty. Made her breakfast in bed. Cooked dinners since she was constantly setting off the smoke alarm because she burned everything to the point to where even the fire extinguisher started giving her the side-eye.

He took turns helping with every two-hour feeding so she could sleep. Huxley became a master diaper changer, never once gagging at poopy diapers. He stocked the fridge, went on late-night craving runs without complaining, and massaged her aching feet after a long day. And when Nazario couldn't sleep, he would stroke her back with a gentle, feathery touch until she drifted off. He was a good guy before parenthood but transformed into a better man after their daughter was born. She was his queen. Ariabella, his little princess.

Nazario couldn't have asked for a better partner to do life with. All the years she'd spent pushing him away had only solidified the love she had for him now, solidified the oath she vowed to her little family unit, that she'd never dare do anything to sabotage something so special that it only comes around once in a lifetime. Given how in tune Huxley was with her needs, the way he loved her with not only words but action, it was apparent that the violation the colonel had achieved without recourse hadn't affected only her.

They were a unit, and it happened to *them*.

One look from Huxley was like he was looking into her soul. He knew that Merrick had tried to take something from her, violate her body with this one disgusting masturbatory act. They often worked with rape victims, and while this was nowhere near in comparison to something so heinous, the internal emotional resonance was the same, felt the same.

Huxley leaned in and kissed the top of Nazario's head.

"You okay, Anaya?" he whispered.

She sighed, switching their daughter to the other breast engorged with milk.

Quiet but firm. "The colonel thinks he can get away with anything. He's been empowered for too long."

"I know what kind of man he is, but how're you feeling—like really feeling?"

"The truth?"

"Only if you wanna talk about it."

"I feel dirty. Stripped of something pure." Pausing for a ten count. "The way he looked at me, like he was daring me to say something to someone, like he knew he could spew whatever lie out of his mouth: deny, deny, and deny some more."

Lifting her chin, he looked in her eyes. "I'd like to beat the shit out of him." His jaw tightened. "I'm so angry. Want you to know how I feel, too. Need you to know just how livid I am over this. We're not letting him get away with this, Anaya. That I promise you. Just don't want this to come between us, don't want what he did to ... to be the reason you push me away again."

She cupped his face, bringing him close, kissing his lips while they cradled their daughter. Their tongues swam in a sweet, tender dance, a renewed longing that surprised her as a surge of electric desire charged between them. He returned her kiss with fierce, raw conviction. She needed him to understand that she would never allow her fear of intimacy—something that had haunted her since her father's murder—be the reason their fragile family unraveled. It was a fate too common for sexual assault survivors, their trauma seeping into future relationships, blurring the line between past and present pain. Victims struggled to separate the two, and even the kindest men, like Blake Huxley, could become shadowed by the face of the abuser.

But Anaya Nazario was resolute. She would not let Colonel Merrick Winslow's twisted actions taint what she and Huxley had built. His toxicity would not poison their future, as she would fight like hell to keep it that way.

The sound of Ariabella's tiny snore made them both smile as their lips parted. Desire rose in their cheeks. Nazario watched as Huxley gently placed their daughter in the crib, her little face peaceful against the soft mattress. The bubblegum-pink walls with the flower decals she'd meticulously placed along them seemed to bloom in the soft glow of the nightlight, casting delicate shadows that danced across the room.

It was a space that exuded warmth, a stark contrast to the cold realities of their job outside. The mobile above the crib turned slowly, its pastel butterflies and stars swaying lazily, a lullaby without sound. The faint memory of her daughter wrapped around her, a comfort she desperately needed. Nazario's gaze drifted to the plush toys on the shelf, standing sentinel over Ariabella as she slept. This room—this tiny, perfect world—was her daughter's sanctuary, a place untouched by the violence and darkness that Nazario faced every day.

She wished, for a fleeting moment, that she could stay in this bubble of calm, safe from the looming typhoon of life as a homicide detective. But there was always another case, another threat. Now, Colonel Merrick Winslow was on their radar—along with Cheonsa Soo-Min, who they believed was the true victim, despite whatever so-called evidence the colonel had against her—even if it was her gun that had killed two police officers.

Her eyes lingered on her daughter's peaceful form, promising herself, as she had many times before, that no matter what chaos awaited her, this room—and the little girl within it—would always remain her haven. Huxley put an arm around her, and they watched their child's chest rise and fall, amazed that they became parents in their forties with their rainbow baby. The stir of passion from their kiss lingered. Nazario realized that they hadn't made love since Ariabella was born. Desire urged them out of their sleeping child's bedroom and into their own.

Nazario held his face in her hands, pushing her tongue into his mouth, hungrily drinking from him. He moaned as she yanked his shirt off him, and he hoisted her shirt over her head. The rest of their clothes came off in a hurried scramble. Nazario pushed Huxley to the bed. He fell on his back, raising a wicked brow. She wanted to show him that she wouldn't let what happened at the Winslow home interfere with their relationship, spoil what they had.

She crawled on top of him and seized his lips. His hands cupped her tender breasts, and hers held the hardness of his need in her hand. "I love you, Blake," she said against parted lips, "nothing and no one's coming between us. I'll never push you away ever again."

His mouth found her neck, then down toward her breasts, kissing the flat of her belly. She balanced herself on him, holding onto the headboard. He lowered himself until she was straddling his face. His tongue entered her wet crown, drinking from her nectar. She arched her back, fingers gripping the headboard. When she couldn't take much more, her mouth reclaimed his, slipping his shaft inside her. She rode him with slow, deliberate strokes, savoring every deep thrust, intoxicated by the sound of him whispering his love for her in her ears. His hands clutched her hips, moving her faster, the tempo heightening their united climax that came out in a muffled scream, both trying not to wake the baby.

Leaving him inside her, she dropped against him. Both panting for breath, hearts speeding to the all-consuming pleasure rippling like aftershocks from an earthquake. He put a large muscular arm around her back and held her close to him, kissing her sweaty temples.

"You're the love of my life," he finally said, ice-blue eyes looking at her with tenderness.

A slow smile curved her lips. "You've always had my heart." Her voice softened and with eyes glinting. "But you'll have to share it with Ariabella."

"I didn't want to push you ... not after the baby, and everything else we've been through," Huxley said, voice low but steady. "But trust me, Anaya, we'll get to the bottom of this. That bastard isn't slipping away. I don't care what rank he holds —he's not untouchable."

"Something tells me we'll be facing an uphill battle. Red tape and cover-ups."

Nazario's phone buzzed, followed almost immediately by

Huxley's. They smiled knowingly before Huxley quipped, "Wanna bet this is one of those 'drop everything' calls?"

"If it is, no way the babysitter's coming this late," Nazario muttered, thinking about her best friend. "Auntie Gus might bail us out—Captain Humphrey's always up for a favor. Besides, her wife still owes me for orchestrating that rainbow-infused wedding of theirs."

Their phones rang again, breaking the quiet that had settled between them. Nazario sighed softly, slipping on her robe as the cool fabric brushed against her warm skin. She glanced over at Huxley, who was already reaching for his phone, his muscles still tense from their recent intimacy. Without a word, they both picked up their devices, the persistent ringing pulling them back into the world, momentarily settling aside the connection they'd just shared.

She overheard Huxley asking Deputy Frost how he was doing before refocusing her ears on her caller. Huxley's supervisor was calling him, so that meant it was serious. Likewise, her own boss was probably calling for the same reason.

Chief Johnson on the other line. "Hope I didn't wake you."

"Just put Ariabella to bed. What's up, sir?"

Letting out a long sigh. "We found Cheonsa Soo-Min. We'll need you and your beau at the Marriott Bonvoy in Torrance, STAT. Detective Wilson's already on his way."

"The three of us for an arrest? Isn't that patrol's job?"

"For the DB."

"Dead body? What? Hold up, hold up. You saying—"

"Our chief suspect is dead," he said, weariness in his tone.

Nazario glanced at Huxley as he muttered, "Shit."

They exchanged a wide-eyed glance, having been both briefed on their deceased.

She raked a hand through her hair. "Homicide?"

"Apparent suicide, but we won't know until y'all investigate. Scene's still hot."

"I think this points to the colonel, sir."

"That's quite an accusation, Nazario. Best be careful who we point the finger at."

Nazario quickly told Chief Johnson what had gone down at Jean Winslow and Mavis Lou Winslow's home, including the suspicious doors that locked from the outside to prevent guests from leaving the room. As Huxley hung up his call and got dressed, he gave her a sympathetic look, listening in on her conversation with the chief.

Chief Johnson's voice came through heated. "Hold up—you sayin' this man was spyin' on you? While you were pumpin'? Sick mothafucka." A pause, then a sharp exhale. "That's some twisted-ass shit right there. And he what, just stood there after, like it ain't nothin'?"

"Like he was invincible, sir."

Another pause, then, "Nah, this dude think he slick, huh? We gon' handle it, Nazario. Ain't nobody gettin' away with treating my detective like that on my watch, you hear? We gon' get that fool, and he ain't gon' see it comin'. They callin' it a suicide, but now that you told me this shit—look extra close, Detective. Look for signs it might've been a homicide."

"That was my plan, sir," she assured. "We'll be leaving in five."

"And, hey, Nazario?"

"Yes, sir?"

"I'm real sorry you had to go through that."

"I'm sorrier that we couldn't get to Cheonsa Soo-Min first, sir."

Nazario ended the call, assuring Chief Johnson they'd bring him and Deputy Frost up to speed on everything they would uncover. As she set the phone down, Huxley was already dialing Gus. After a quick exchange, her best friend agreed to come over and watch Ariabella while they made their way to the Marriott in Torrance.

The moment the call ended, Huxley turned to her, pulling her into his arms. His hold was solid. Comforting. He swayed, breath warm against her neck as he rocked her back and forth—each movement grounding her, easing the weight of the conversation she didn't want to have.

"Something tells me this was no suicide," Huxley whispered.

"Something tells me the same thing," Nazario returned.

Cupping her face in his hands. "Hey ... you okay?"

She nodded, but the tears came streaming anyway, hot and relentless, tracing a path down her cheeks in silent defeat. Huxley's thumbs swept them away with tender care. His confident and unwavering voice echoed Chief Johnson's promise.

"We're gonna find him, Nazario. We're gonna get him."

But doubt gnawed at her insides, twisting her stomach. One problem. They honestly didn't have enough on Winslow to bring him in or charge him with anything—*not yet*. The law loomed like an unscalable wall, and they were armed with nothing but scraps. Still, a quiet fire ignited in her chest, determination burning in the back of her throat, pulse thrumming with fury.

It was an uphill battle, but one she had no intention of losing.

TWENTY-ONE

THE FATAL DOSE

VON SCHLANGE STOOD before the mirror, eyes tracing the scattered disguises before her. She reached for the sleek, jet-black wig, feeling the silken weight of human hair slip through her fingers. It was long, almost silky, cascading down to the middle of her back, blending seamlessly with the shadows that clung to the corners of the room.

The wig was only the beginning, but the small details—the subtle shift of her eyes, the curve of her fuller lips—completed her metamorphosis into someone entirely unrecognizable. With practiced precision, she placed the dark contact lenses, hiding cold grey eyes behind a warm, deceptive gaze. The conversion was striking—she was someone else now, the woman she needed to be. No one would recognize her like this. All of her tattoos, from those on her neck, scalp, and forearms, were cloaked with Dermablend, a thick, skin-colored cream designed to cover ink.

Von tilted her head, gaze scrutinizing the reflection in the mirror. The makeup was flawless, but it was the dramatic work beneath the surface—the cosmetic procedures—that trans-formed her. Thanks to the meticulously placed Botox injections, her once-thin lips were fuller. But the real change was the brow lift she'd undergone a year ago, shortly after arriving in Brazil. It gave her eyes a slight, feline slant that completely altered her expression. Cheek implants further enhanced the effect, sculpting her face into the high, sharp cheekbones she had always craved.

Her once modest breasts, a mere flat expanse of muscle, had been augmented to a size C, finalizing the renovation from the austere Dr. Wilder Agatha Friedrich to someone entirely new. Damião had been against it all—the surgeries, the extreme changes, the loss of her old self—but even he had understood why it had to be done. In her line of work, blending in was not an option. She needed to disappear, to become unrecognizable. She'd succeeded beautifully.

Von tilted her head slightly, assessing the final effect. Every feature had to tell a different story, every nuance a layer of her new identity. The contacts softened her gaze, making her appear more human—approachable, even. But beneath the façade, a hint of satisfaction flickered in her altered eyes. Convincing, yes. But more importantly, undetectable. Zeus tilted his head, giving her a sideways look, whining his concern.

"It's okay," she assured him it was temporary in the only language her dog understood—German. "*Es ist vorübergehend.*"

When she stepped out, leaving Zeus behind, he barked his protest.

She had to visit Eleutério at the public *Hospital Municipal Souza Aguiar* without her four-legged sidekick. "*Ich komme wieder.*" She scratched the back of his ear. "I'll be back."

Von slipped into a loosely fitted black dress that came to her knees, paired with a matching Stella McCartney faux leather crossbody purse and heels. Courtesy of Jefferson Pierce, the ex-Marine, she not only tracked down the hospital where Eleutério Abraão was recovering but also uncovered the room number and name of the relative they were expecting to visit. Today,

Von was Luana Abraão, his cousin. The resemblance wasn't quite exact. However, the illusion was more than convincing with the long black wig, bronzed spray-on tan, iconic Brazilian Colcci sunglasses, and polished dress.

———

The public hospital buzzed with chaotic energy, a steady hum of voices rising over the clatter of stretchers and the occasional intercom calling out instructions to hurried doctors. Natural sunlight streamed through tall, smudged windows at *Hospital Municipal Souza Aguiar,* casting shadows across the linoleum floors. The air was equal parts antiseptic and humid, marking another typical Brazilian afternoon.

Von's high heels clicked sharply against the floor as she made her way through the crowded hallway, the rhythmic staccato cutting through the noise. Nurses rushed past, murmuring hurried instructions to one another, while patients sat slumped in plastic chairs, their tired faces turned toward flickering TVs mounted on the walls.

Approaching the client service desk, her reflection briefly caught the sunlight bouncing off the polished surfaces. The receptionist behind the counter lifted her eyes, expression a merger of forced politeness and exhaustion. Already handling someone on the phone, her free hand reached toward Von with a clipboard, ready for the subsequent inquiry.

"*Bom dia,*" Von said, her voice crisp above the din. "*Eleutério Abraão por favor, sou primo dele—Luana Abraão.*" The name rolled off her tongue with the familiarity of someone used to entering doors. In her introduction, she informed the hospital help desk clerk that she was there for Eleutério and that she was his cousin. Her confident casualness—a deliberate effort to appear convincing. Eyes red from too many hours behind the desk at *Souza Aguiar*, the receptionist provided a quick nod and slid a form toward her, barely lifting her gaze before answering the next call.

"*Quarto 412?*" Von queried, hoping Jefferson Pierce wasn't wrong.

"*Sim,*" the clerk confirmed. "*Querto 412.*" After receiving directions from the clerk, Von rode the elevators up to the fourth floor, stopping first at the restroom two doors down from 412. She strode toward one of the stalls, locked it behind her, dug into her purse, and took out a small vial. Von crouched in the cramped bathroom stall, her fingers steady as she carefully drew the potassium chloride (KCI) from the small vial into the syringe. She knew the dose had to be precise—too much and suspicion might arise during the autopsy. The solution was potent, however, with each milliliter carrying 4 mEq of potassium. Just 25 milliliters, equivalent to 100 mEq of the concentrated liquid, could silently stop a heart, disrupting its electrical signals, mimicking a natural heart attack.

She watched the syringe fill, the clear liquid rising slowly, knowing that once she injected 100 mEq of potassium chloride into Eleutério's bloodstream, it would be more than enough to end the bastard's life without a trace. Who needed a hot shot of heroin, a cocktail of slow poisons like antifreeze, when you had something so simple, fast-acting, and untraceable as potassium chloride? The chemical compound, also known as KCI, was primarily used in her clinic for the hard choice of having to euthanize sick or elderly pets. Though in small doses, she'd also administered potassium chloride as an electrolyte supplement for animals suffering from hypokalemia.

Looking over the injection, she capped the needle and gently placed it in her purse. During days like these, it helped being a veterinarian and having some formal medical training. Today, however, she'd be ridding the world of not a beloved pet but rather a shit-bag who didn't deserve to live. She promised Cheonsa Soo-Min and swore on Dr. Damião Sequeira's life that Eleutério wouldn't get away with it. The sooner she finished him off, the sooner she could board her one-way flight to Los Angeles, California, where Cheonsa was hiding, according to her hacker friend—and where Colonel Merrick Winslow waited.

Glancing in the mirror, she refreshed her lipstick, adjusted the wig, and click-clacked her way to room 412, hoping to catch Eleutério before the hospital staff could release him from their care. When she arrived, Von peeked through the small window on the door. Perfect timing. He was lying on the hospital bed, awake and watching something on TV mounted on the wall. When she walked through the door, eyes still on the Brazilian programming, Eleutério told his cousin that she was early, "*Luana, você chegou cedo.*"

Answering in English. "I think I'm right on time."

Voice sounding familiar, Eleutério jolted in bed, head in a neck brace. He winced, turning to look at her, eyes widening.

"Who are you? How did you get in here?"

"Look very closely."

Eleutério studied her for a beat before recognition finally seemed to sweep across his face. He grinned at her with delight. "Sorry about your *business partner. Avenida Niemeyer* road is very dangerous, especially at night."

Taking slow steps toward his hospital bed. "Lucky for you that you survived," she began, then had to ask. "How did the colonel get you involved?"

"*Quem?*" he asked, playing dumb.

"Stop playing stupid." She leaned in, face inches from his. "You know who—the man who paid you to kill him."

Nervous, he adjusted himself, eyes darting wildly around the room, glancing at a remote-like device with a button to call the nurse. It was lying on a table with a tray of dishes from his late dinner. Before he could rise to his feet, she got to him first, standing next to him.

"I'm ... I'm calling the nurse."

"You'll do no such thing."

With her back to the camera perched in the corner of the room, Von angled herself, making sure she stayed out of the lens's view. Her fingers quickly found the brachial plexus tie-in just below Eleutério's shoulder, pressing hard into the nerve cluster. His eyes grew large as his arm went limp from the pressure point technique she'd learned in Dim Mak, a martial arts class she took that was also known as "the touch of death," which emphasized pressure points in order to incapacitate an opponent. Arm dangling uselessly to his side, Von seized the moment, discreetly slipping the syringe from her purse, keeping her body shielded from the hospital camera's watchful lens. In one smooth, concealed motion, she plunged the needle into his powerless arm, injecting the fatal dose of potassium chloride, heart racing with anticipation.

She knew that in a few short minutes, Eleutério's bloodstream would turn hyperkalemic from the excess KCl, leading to a disruption of heart functions, including bradycardia—or slowing of the heart rate in conjunction with arrhythmias—irregular heartbeats followed by cardiac arrest, muscle paralysis, and finally, death. Von could already see the changes beginning to ripple through his body. Eleutério's face twitched, his breathing uneven as his muscles jerked in faint spasms. Once flushed, his skin paled as life slowly drained from him.

His chest heaved in uneven jerks, the erratic rhythm of his heart betraying itself in the subtle clench and release of his fists. Eyes, once alert, now flickered with confusion as they began to lose focus, pupils narrowing, searching for breath that wouldn't come. The subtle tremor in his fingers grew more violent, and then suddenly, his body went still—too still. His lips parted in a silent gasp, and Von knew the end was closing in as his heart staggered toward a final, fatal pause.

Von leaned in and whispered in his ear. "Rot in hell, you son of a bitch."

Before the EKG monitor could shriek its conclusive warning, Von Schlange quietly slipped away from his room. A satisfied smirk tugged at her lips as she whistled a cheerful tune.

———

Von donned the same disguise, erasing any trace of who she was. Once kept at jaw length, her natural blond hair was dyed 'Midnight Rebel' black, with part of her scalp shaved to reveal the serpent tattoo beneath. Though the long black wig now concealed it, all of her tattoos were camouflaged with Dermablend. She dressed for comfort on the long, 12–15-hour flight to Los Angeles, wearing skinny jeans and a fitted top that flattered her new curves. It was the kind of outfit she would never dare normally wear—except Luana Abraão would.

Her black Dr. Martens combat boots worked perfectly with her ensemble, but it was her tight red, low-cut V-neck, long-sleeved cotton shirt that had several men straining their necks to gawk as she sauntered down the aisle, playing her part. Von found seat 22A just a few rows ahead. Zeus trailed behind her, sporting his service dog vest. He lay at her feet, stretched out comfortably on the floor. Von had bought two tickets to keep 22B beside her empty, giving her dog plenty of space to stretch in front of both seats.

Von's phone chimed, and she glanced down, noticing that she had a missed message on WhatsApp. Nervous adrenaline soured her stomach. Jefferson Pierce wouldn't be DMing unless it was necessary. Her finger hovered over the app, hesitating, wondering if she should wait until she made it to Los Angeles to check. When impatience won the battle, Von tapped her phone quickly, but the weak signal caused frustrating delays. The app struggled to load, and the lag was driving her mad.

"Good evening, ladies and gentlemen. Welcome to flight 137 to sunny Los Angeles. We'll be departing shortly, so please ensure all carry-on items are securely stowed in the overhead bins or under your seat in front of you. We also ask that you switch off all electronic devices or set them to airplane mode. For your safety, please keep your seatbelts fastened. You may remove them once the seatbelt sign is off. We will be serving beverages and meals shortly. Thank you, and we hope you enjoy the flight."

The flight attendant then repeated the announcement in Portuguese.

Von glanced down at her phone. "C'mon ... c'mon," she muttered anxiously.

Finally, the message she'd been waiting for populated. Her heart raced as she read the DM.

BlackDragon6: *Good news and bad news. Good news: Found Colonel Merrick Winslow and Cheonsa Soo-Min. Bad news: Cheonsa's dead. LAPD's calling it a suicide. Think the colonel got to her. Sorry, Von.*

Jefferson then texted her the address to the colonel's location.

"*Senhora, vou preciscar que desligue o seu cellular,*" the flight attendant said.

Von stared at her cell phone, the screen dark and lifeless. The weight of the command to power it down now felt suffocating, as if she'd severed the last fragile thread tying her to Cheonsa. She obeyed, tense fingers pressing the button until the screen blinked out. Silence swallowed her—a crushing void that threatened to pull her under.

She was too late.

Reality slammed into her chest with the brutal force of a freight train, her soul splintering. Cheonsa was gone. All the whispered promises of saving her new friend before it was too late now mocked her mercilessly. Her breath hitched, heart thundered with the clawing grief, but no tears came—only the empty ache of failure. Whether Cheonsa's death was by her own hand or staged didn't matter. There was only one person responsible—the relentless ex-husband Cheonsa had spent years fleeing, the same man who had driven her late marketing director into hiding.

Von had sworn to protect her. Promised she'd help Cheonsa start a new life. But promises didn't stop bullets. Didn't save Damião. Didn't matter in the end. Another vow. Another failure.

Only vengeance remained now—a burning, steadfast force consuming everything.

The devastation surged through her veins, turning to ice, hardening into something toxic and dangerous as her pulse quickened, not with sorrow but with fiery vengeance. There would be no forgiveness for this, no mercy. Cheonsa Soo-Min's death would be answered. As the plane taxied off the runway, a calm fury settled into her bones. If she couldn't save Cheonsa, then she'd make him pay.

Colonel Merrick Winslow had no idea what he had unleashed.

TWENTY-TWO
THE EARLY GRAVE

THE STENCH of rigor mortis hit Nazario's nose, an odor she was all too familiar with—but since the birth of her daughter, death's lingering scent seemed to amplify. She pulled the top of her shirt over her nose. Meanwhile, Detective Wilson noisily munched on a carrot, never minding the reek of a corpse and earning him a sidelong glance from both her and Huxley. Her partner never let decomposition get in the way of stuffing his face with something.

"Hey, Bugs Bunny—mind putting away the carrots?" Huxley snipped.

"Eh, what's up, Doc? You'd rather I chomp on a greasy burrito?"

"We'd rather you not eat at a crime scene with a DB," Nazario countered.

"Oh, you two are so squirmy," Wilson stuffed the small Ziplock baggie of baby carrots inside his blazer pocket. "The dead don't mind if I enjoy a healthy snack."

The two familiar SID leads approached them. The Scientific Investigation Division was notoriously late. However,

Chuck Whittier and Ellen Yang, donning their hazmat suits and N95 masks, were early for once.

"Whittier, Yang, nice to see you here," Huxley said. "What're we looking at?"

"Dusted for fingerprints, didn't find any," Whittier said.

Yang jumped in. "With the position of the gun and the entry wound, it was looking like a suicide—"

"I'm feeling a 'but' coming on?" Wilson arched a brow.

Yang nodded. "But when we sprayed in the bathroom with Luminol, the sink lit up."

"Hard for Cheonsa Soo-Min to wash her hands after she's dead," Nazario mused.

"Bathtub lit up too. Around the handles, showerhead, and drain," Whittier said.

"Crime photographer just left," Yang added, "snapped the pics. Full shots of the scene, the weapon, the blood splatter, and all the luminol stuff."

"What's the status on those crime scene photos?" Nazario asked.

"Said they should be uploaded into VeriPic within the hour. They should be live in the system in ten," Wittier said.

"And close-ups of the wrist bruising and defense wounds?" Huxley asked.

"Affirmative," Yang piped in. "Marked as priority. I'll flag them in VeriPic when I get back to the office."

"Everything's locked, and chain-of-custody will be logged in real-time." Whittier squared his shoulders. "No one's tampering with this evidence."

Nazario shot him a quick nod of approval. "Send us the link as soon as it's in."

"If luminol picked up blood in the sink and bathtub, then our perp washed up after," Huxley said.

"That's what we're thinking," Yang added. "Also thought it

strange—her hands smelled like soap. Tooth-picked under the nails for DNA. Bagged it. But it's like her hands were washed post-mortem."

"Broken nails and scratches on the back of her hands," Whittier said.

"Defense wounds," Nazario said decidedly.

"That's our guess," Whittier said.

"Our part's done. Evidence will be sent to the lab. Hopefully, we get some DNA under the nails, but we highly doubt it."

"Good work," Nazario said. As both Whittier and Yang left the scene, the coroner's van pulled up. "Better get to the body before they take it away."

They followed a delicate trail of rose petals, a path of velvet crimson that sprinkled under their feet and seemed to intertwine with the rot of death—a bitter contrast that reeked of cruel irony, leading them to the body. Cheonsa Soo-Min was a grayish-blue. Even beneath latex gloves, her skin was cold, body stiff. Eyes a shade of milky-death. Bruises marked her wrists—the size of large fingers. Huxley took a gloved hand and lightly placed it where the finger marks were. They were not quite a match, as Huxley, being six-four, had large hands. But Wilson, being six feet, took his turn after Huxley. The marks were a closer match to his hands.

"How tall's Colonel Winslow?" Huxley asked.

"Around six feet," Nazario answered.

"How tall're you, Wilson?" Huxley asked.

"Six-even," Wilson said.

Nazario felt sick to her stomach, the same twisty, sour feeling that came over her when she saw that eyeball staring through the peephole in the wall.

"We're gonna have to fight like hell to make sure she isn't

put in the suicide box," Nazario finally said after a long drag of air.

"Think the chief is going to give us shit? Johnson trusts us," Wilson said. "The marks on her wrists look like she was held down at some point. We all see it. No suicide victim I've ever seen had defense wounds and hand marks around their wrists like this."

"He's not who I'm worried about," Nazario said.

"Will do what I can to make sure the bureau's on our side on this as a suspected homicide," Huxley said.

"Bigger concern is that if it gets out who we think was involved, someone way high up the ladder's gonna bury this as a 10-56, cover up for that asshole." Nazario pulled out her phone and tapped voice memo. "Single gunshot wound to the left temple—initially staged as a suicide. But defensive wounds and bruising around the wrists suggest otherwise. This is homicide. Get Colonel Winslow in for questioning."

She ended the recording just as the coroner approached, tailed by a young assistant.

They combed through the room one last time, searching for anything SID might have overlooked, but it was clear the forensic team had been thorough. Every trace of evidence had already been bagged and tagged.

"Whittier and Yang did a good job," Nazario said.

"They even took the trash," Wilson said, pointing to the bathroom. "Don't know if they'll find anything in it, though. If the colonel's our guy, he'd be stupid to throw anything away with his DNA on it."

"How're we looking?" the coroner asked, having patiently waited with their assistant at the door. "Okay if we grab the body, or y'all need more time with her?"

"Well, guys? We done yet, so I can go back to eating my rabbit food?" Wilson turned to Nazario and Huxley.

Nazario and Huxley shot Wilson a glare. "We're done here," Nazario told the coroner, the weight of the investigation pressing down on her shoulders. This was just the beginning, and they all knew it. As they stepped outside, a black sedan sat idling. A bald man wearing dark shades and stern features stared at them.

"Can we help you?" Huxley called out.

Wordless, he rolled up the limo-tinted windows and sped off.

"Anyone catch the license plate?" Nazario said.

"Shit!" Huxley snatched out his phone, tried to snap a picture, but it was too late.

"Something tells me the colonel's got eyes on us," Wilson said.

———

Chief Johnson leaned back in his chair, fingertips pressed together in a thoughtful pyramid. His long silence was more of a statement, though Nazario knew a lecture was about to break the tense quiet.

Huxley, Nazario, and Wilson exchanged looks of anticipation, the kind of knowing they had gained from having worked with the chief for a decade and a half.

"Y'all realize who you're accusing, right? Colonel Winslow got mighty powerful friends in D.C. We're talking way high up the chain. Before you start hauling him in for questioning, make damn sure the evidence is bulletproof. That's if you even have anything," Chief Johnson warned. "'Cause the way it's looking, it's nothing but circumstantial—which means you got jack shit other than accusing a military officer, a veteran who served his country, an American hero of murdering his ex-wife—an ex-wife that he divorced, not the other way around."

"We got hand marks around her wrists. Defense wounds. The bureau's got me on this case because of the sensitive matter involving a colonel," Huxley said. "We realize who we're talking about here, but we all saw it, sir. We were all there. This isn't a 10-56."

"Nope. It's no suicide, Chief Johnson." Wilson blew out a large breath. "It's homicide."

"Handprints around the wrists—so what? Could've happened before she killed herself. A scratch here and there. A broken nail. Could've broken the nail gardening. Scratched her hands trimming the rose bush. SID's got no fingerprints at the scene, no DNA, most likely." Turning to Nazario. "Even your claims that he was looking in on you while you were pumping your milk. Your word against his."

"She wasn't lying." The words shot out of Huxley's mouth with a force that Nazario didn't expect.

"Mind your tone, Huxley," Chief Johnson warned.

"She wasn't lying—*sir*." Huxley gritted out. "The fucking pervert was watching from the other room, violating your detective—the mother of my child. Jacking off while we were downstairs interviewing his parents. Then, washes his hands and walks out like nothing happened. The balls on the guy are bigger than his ego. He thinks he can get away with anything."

"He really did have a smug look on his face like he was untouchable," Wilson said. "My partner deserves to have it reported. It's sexual assault."

"It's voyeurism and invasion of privacy at the most. I'm not even sure if the courts would classify spying and spanking your monkey as criminal voyeurism," Chief Johnson said. "Look, I'm not calling anyone a liar—and I'm sorry, Nazario, I really am. But I'm not so sure the LAPD or even the FBI should be chasing this one down the road."

"What would you have us do? Ignore all the signs? Just let it go?" Nazario countered.

"I'm saying that if y'all misstep, they're going after your jobs and after mine. Guaranteed. And the powers that be will take it a step further and make sure none of us work in law enforcement ever again. Now, I didn't bust my ass as a black man, struggling my way up the ranks, only to risk it going after someone like Winslow. One wrong move is all that it takes. I'll be damned before I get caught up in something that could yank that all away."

"No one's losing their jobs," Huxley said.

"Don't know that, Huxley. I done seen it all." Johnson swiveled his chair until his back was to them. Pensive silence lingered as he stared out his office window. After a long beat, Chief Johnson, still facing away, began to speak. It was a story neither Nazario nor Wilson had ever heard. Nazario doubted Huxley even knew it. "Chief Walt McGrath was damn good at his job, but he was ... he was by the book. Old-school, with a twenty-year reputation as the no-nonsense type. The kind that had integrity. He was good. Church-goer kind of good. Dug around and fired a bunch of dirty cops. Your father, Nazario— you know he and I were partners for a long time. This case made Lucas decide to jump off homicide and join Gang and Narco. Wish he'd stayed on. Maybe he'd still be alive today."

Nazario glanced at her father's wedding ring, which had been on Huxley's left hand since the necklace broke. While they weren't Mr. and Mrs., the gesture was meant to be temporary, but Huxley had never taken it off, and she never asked for it back. Whenever she saw it on Huxley's hand, it felt like her father's spirit was with her, their daughter, protecting their little family trio. She drew in a shaky breath, and Huxley gave her a subtle smile, an understood acknowledgment that he'd helped solve her father's cold case. He'd been murdered while working undercover dealing with dangerous gangs. But it wasn't a gang member that killed him—Madison Vanwell, his jealous lover, couldn't take having Daddy's baby without a commitment. Daddy would never leave Nazario's mother.

"Thought the rumor mill circulated that Chief McGrath went rogue?" Wilson said.

"Heard the same thing," Nazario said.

"That's the story that was released to the public." Chief Johnson steepled his fingers behind his head, lifting his face to the ceiling. "Nate Corbin, he was a powerful and very influential tech mogul. Everyone knew him as this generous philanthropist. But he had close ties to the political elites. A whistleblower turned up dead. Lucas and I—we uncovered an underground ring. Corbin was trafficking information, manipulating high-stakes financial markets using illegal methods."

Wilson whistled. "I remember that vaguely. That wasn't what was reported, though?"

"Corbin had friends in the media—city council members, district attorneys, hell, even state senators. People tried to warn Chief McGrath, but he didn't listen. All them dirty cops, some with a history of violence, targeting minorities at traffic stops. Well, y'all know, the bad apples give good cops a bad name. McGrath was trying to 'drain the swamp' as Trump puts it. But when they were fired, guess who they went to when we were trying to shake Corbin down?"

"They went to Corbin, didn't they?" Nazario said.

Johnson adjusted his seat and turned to face them. "Every single one of them. So, not only did Corbin have the media, the lawyers, the politicians—he had all the disgruntled cops, too. Racist fuckers that put us through hell—your father, a Puerto Rican, and me, the only Black officer at the time. McGrath stood up for us, stood up for the people in Los Angeles, the minorities that got beat on and pulled over—sometimes for no reason. He cleaned up our department. But sometimes ... sometimes, there are people you don't want to mess with. Corbin was that guy."

Chief Johnson stared down his ebony fingers, thoughtful contemplation muting him temporarily. He looked up, eyes shiny with emotion. He swallowed a breath.

"Chief McGrath was an outstanding leader. He was the best of the best. He didn't deserve to go out the way he did. He lost his badge, forced to retire in shame and disgrace. Despite all the shit, McGrath had one wish before he was leaving the job he loved, a job he was damn good at—he thought about me. He told the department he would retire on the condition that they put the first black man as Chief of Homicide. He went to bat for Lucas, too." Johnson gave Nazario his eyes. "Your father and I became better under McGrath's leadership. We learned everything. We learned the difference between integrity and those that let the power of the badge go to their heads."

Silence fell between them like an anchor, sinking them to the bottom of an ocean of moral conflict—caught between the weight of doing what was right and the pull of what felt necessary.

"It's our job to investigate. Make a professional judgment based on the crime scene. Whittier, Yang—all of us are calling it in as a homicide, and if Colonel Winslow's a suspect, we gotta bring him in. We must interview him," Nazario said.

"I'm with Nazario on this one," Wilson said. "Let us bring him in, have us a friendly chat."

"We can't let the guy just walk. Someone's dead. A young, innocent woman who had her whole life ahead of her—" Huxley began.

Chief Johnson cut him off. "Not so innocent, since she was wanted for murdering two of our blue."

"Regardless, this isn't a 10-56, sir. If the colonel's a suspect, we have to pursue it," Huxley said. "We're not letting the bastard intimidate us."

Chief Johnson pinched the bridge of his nose.

"McGrath would've been proud of all of you. But I don't want any of us to become targets. We can't approach Winslow the same way we do the others. Understood? Need a whole different approach. If he's calculated, powerful—we gotta be steps ahead of him," said the chief.

"That's why you got me on the team." Wilson smiled widely. "Don't worry, sir. We won't give him the impression that he's a suspect. Flattery, charm, smooth talk—it's my specialty."

"I'm putting my trust in the three of you because you're the best we've got and that's why the Bureau's asked me to put you on our team again, Huxley," Johnson said. "Keep me posted when he comes in and remember we can't keep him—"

"We know, we know, we know." Nazario threw her hands in the air. "Of course, we're not holding him without evidence."

Chief Johnson nodded reluctantly. "Alright, then. Dismissed."

As they turned to leave, Johnson's voice carried after them with weighted suspicion.

"One more thing," Johnson said, leaning forward. "If Winslow really sent himself all them text messages and emails so he could frame Cheonsa Soo-Min, make her look like the stalker when it was him the whole time, then who the hell knows what the man's capable of? Don't know if this old cop brain of mine is throwing up the red flags. Don't know jack about this Army officer, but I sure seen plenty like him out there —guys like Harvey Weinstein, Epstein, Cosby, R. Kelly, Kevin Spacey, and now even Diddy. There are more out there, too many to count. Powerful men, thinking they can get away with vile, predatory behavior, take advantage of their positions to target innocent victims. Most of them got away with it for years, decades even. How many haven't been caught? The Nate Corbins of the world not only walked free but ruined the life of an upstanding police officer—destroyed his reputation, ended his marriage. Drove Chief McGrath to take his own life."

Chief Johnson stood up slowly, eyes heavy with the weight of the conversation, and walked over to a framed photograph on the wall. The picture, a bit faded with age, bared a moment frozen in time—a backyard barbecue, sun setting in the background, casting a golden hue over the three men. In the center stood the late Chief McGrath, his broad smile genuine, a beer raised in casual toast. To his right, Johnson himself—much younger then—wearing the look of a man who still believed the world could be fixed. And then next to him, Lucas Nazario, Nazario's father, laughing, spirits lighter and less jaded. The camaraderie between them was palpable, a snapshot of better days before the betrayals, the disgrace, and the losses. The kind of bond forged not just in the station, but in the trenches of their shared battles.

A finger traced the frame's edge, a shadow of sadness flickering in the chief's eyes.

"If our gut is telling us something's up with Winslow, we're gonna need a whole lot more than instinctual hearsay and speculation. Better gimme cold, hard facts. Concrete proof—and if you can *not* deliver—then we'll be staying far away from Colonel Merrick Winslow."

Nazario wanted nothing more than to believe that fear hadn't pierced her veins. She wanted to believe she was strong enough to face whatever lay ahead, that Winslow was just another suspect, another case, someone who couldn't have set up his ex-wife to be a stalker only to do the very thing he'd accused her of. When she first took on the case, she'd wanted to believe the colonel had integrity. But like most of humanity with multi-dimensions, the colonel was more than just a veteran and

American hero—he was a filthy scumbag that got off on spying, violating boundaries. A man who'd already proven his depravity. And if he was capable of that, he was more than capable of killing Cheonsa Soo-Min.

She wanted to believe her instincts weren't screaming at her to be careful, to tread lightly. She wanted to believe this wasn't personal, that it didn't hit too close to home. She wanted to believe the badge still meant something—that justice wasn't blind to power or privilege.

But deep down, she knew better.

However, she was Lucas Nazario's daughter—the man who instilled integrity, discipline, and moral conviction. Somewhere out there was the truth waiting to be uncovered. And if Winslow had to be brought in under the pretense of informing him about the supposed suicide of his ex-wife, then so be it. Regardless of how dangerous the path became, Detective Anaya Nazario would find out what really happened—no matter the cost.

TWENTY-THREE

THE PERFECT TRAP

THE BRIGADIER LOUNGE buzzed with life—a pulsating hub of off-duty soldiers and high-ranking officers from all military branches, each chasing their rare moments of freedom. While the nearest base, Los Angeles Air Force Base (LAAFB) in El Segundo, was just a short drive from Manhattan Beach, the bar had a reputation that stretched far beyond its geographical reach.

Despite not being close to sprawling military installations, The Brigadier Lounge had become a magnet for service members from all over the country. Nestled in the heart of Manhattan Beach, the lounge offered an unadulterated mix of exclusivity and proximity, a quick twenty-five-minute drive north of Torrance, just six miles from the Marriott Bonvoy, where Cheonsa Soo-Min had been murdered.

Inside, the air was a mélange of whiskey, wafting cigar smoke, and leather. The deep thrum of techno music reverberated through the nightclub, its bassline syncing with the strobe lights that cloaked the room with alternating flashes of red, white, and blue—an unspoken nod to the military's patriotic roots. A mix of brass, uniformed soldiers, and off-duty grunts in jeans downed drinks. Laughter and the low hum of conversation punctuated the atmosphere.

Polished wood and metal accents transformed the lounge into a sleek, unique design that screamed of modern luxury fit for those wishing to indulge in secluded private booths and overpriced cocktails, which mirrored its clientele. Beneath an array of gleaming military insignias, the bartenders moved with swift precision, mixing and serving drinks to thirsty patrons. Women of all ages and backgrounds mingled through the lounge effortlessly, their upscale attire a tribute to the exclusive venue. Dressed to impress, every female attendee had donned fitted attire that accentuated their God-given curves.

In a club full of glamorous women, Von Schlange had made sure she stood out, commanding the room's attention with deliberate ease. Her long, dark, wavy wig cascaded down her back, while her toned legs were accentuated by towering heels that clicked sharply with each confident step. The black leather dress clung to her body like a second skin, its shine catching the strobe light with each sway of her hips. But it was the plunging neckline that dipped low enough to reveal augmented, voluptuous breasts that caused nearly every man to gawk.

Before stopping by the club, Von had visited a medical spa where she received injections to make her lips fuller. They complimented the other aesthetic surgeries she'd already undergone, especially the brow lift, which sharpened her already striking features, giving her eyes that sleek feline allure. Every man followed her with their stares—*I'd like to fuck you*—projected without shame, as if she were a prize to claim. Each lingering look fed a fire within her. The reaction was exactly the kind she'd engineered—seduction, control, power. Like a predator in a den of prey, she moved with deliberation, fully aware of the effect she had and ready to use it to her advantage.

Von ignored the gawking men drooling after her.

She was here for one man: Colonel Merrick Winslow.

Scanning the crowded nightclub, she feared it would be difficult to find the colonel. Luck was on her side when she spotted him sitting at the bar chatting with another man who could've been a fellow officer or a soldier. It was hard to determine as they were both in civilian clothes. If she had to make an educated guess, most likely, it was an officer, as high-ranking officers ordinarily hung out with their own.

The moment Von approached the bar, both men stopped talking and pivoted her way.

Von lifted her gaze, her long fake lashes fluttering as she locked eyes with the colonel. A flirtatious smile curled the corners of her lips. In an act of chivalry, the colonel stood and gestured to his barstool.

"Why doncha take my seat, sweetheart," he said, giving her a once over like a starved lion who hadn't caught prey to devour for days.

"That's so kind of you." She slid into the seat, crossed her legs—her tight skirt hiking up her thighs. The colonel's friend nodded at the two of them, taking the hint.

"Take my spot, brother. Got an early morning." The man gave the colonel a quick slap on the back. "Catcha later, Merrick."

"See you this weekend at Red Hawk Range. And don't forget to bring your Glock 19," the colonel said.

Von turned to the bartender, trying to flag him down. The colonel waited until his buddy left before redirecting his attention to her. He leaned in, speaking in her ear, cutting through the noisy bar.

"Whatever you're drinking, it's on me," he said, running a finger up her leg.

Von watched his finger, allowing him to touch her, to think

he was in control. She tilted her head, eyeing him with a playful smirk. "What do you think I want?"

His gaze never left hers. "You look like someone who enjoys something ... strong, with a bite."

A slow smile spread across Von's lips, eyes narrowing in a calculated, sultry regard.

"Interesting guess. I like my drinks the way I like my company ... hard with a complex, layered flavor."

She mirrored him, running her own finger up the inner part of his thighs, pausing just before his bulging manhood, showing beneath his fitted jeans. "Negroni," she said, trapping her plump Botoxed bottom lip beneath her teeth. "And make it strong, wouldya?"

"Bold choice," he commended, clearly intrigued. He flagged the bartender and ordered a Dirty Martini and her Negroni. "So, what should I call you?"

The bartender swiftly returned, setting the drinks before them.

"Luana." She swirled the deep red liquid. "And what should I call you other than ... sexy?"

She plucked the olive, speared on a silver cocktail pick, resting atop his Dirty Martini. With a teasing smile, she twirled her tongue around the oval green olive before sucking it in her mouth. His blue eyes rested on her lips. She took a sip of her Negroni, the sharp bitterness of the Campari hitting her tongue first, followed by the sweet warmth of the vermouth. The gin cut through, crisp and herbal, a perfect reflection of the game she was playing—smooth, yet with an edge sharp enough to draw blood.

He chuckled, his fingers tracing the edge of his glass. "Colonel Merrick Winslow," he said, "but you can call me Merrick."

"A colonel, huh? Oh, how I love a man in uniform."

"What brings you in here today on a Thursday night? It's surprising to see someone like you in here alone. There must be a lucky man in your life?"

She shrugged, taking another sip of her cocktail. "And there must be a lucky woman in yours."

"Divorced twice and happily single—you?"

"Never married and happily single," she said. "What're you doing down here in Manhattan Beach? Don't think there's an army base here."

"Stationed at Fort Irwin, about 150 miles northeast of here in the Mohave Desert. I oversee the training exercises there. We run realistic war simulations, focused on tactical skills, leadership development, and readiness for deployment—that sort of thing," he explained. "Family's up north in Clovis. I paid a visit to my folks. Here on R&R. Staying at the Shade Hotel right here in Manhattan Beach. How about you?"

"Just here for one thing." Her eyes glimmered, a knowing look flashing across her face. "To get exactly what I came for."

Merrick smirked. "Maybe I can help with that. Why don't I take you out tomorrow?"

"I don't do dates."

"What *do* you do?"

She swallowed the last of her drink. "I'd like to do you."

"How I love a direct woman who knows what she wants." Merrick stepped closer, chest a breath from hers. "Your place or mine?"

She grabbed his shirt, pressing him hard against her lips in a tongueless kiss, surprising the army officer. "Yours," she said against his lips.

"Now?"

"Why delay?"

Merrick cocked a brow. He closed out the tab and took the opportunity to write an address to his hotel on a napkin.

"Don't keep me waiting," Merrick said, flashing her a cocky grin before turning to leave.

Von's gaze followed him as he walked out, her expression unreadable, but inside, satisfaction curled through her. The moment he stepped out the door, her mind was already calculating the next move. Perfect. The first step had been executed. Now Merrick was hooked—exactly where she needed him. This was only the beginning.

Soon enough, he wouldn't even realize he was walking right into her trap.

———

The Shade Hotel stood as a monolith of modern architecture: its boxy exterior a prime example of minimalist design. Towering against the Manhattan Beach city skyline, the luxury boutique hotel was a seamless blend of matte-black panels and reflective glass, absorbing and distorting the surrounding lights into a mosaic of shadows and brilliance. Neon signage subtly illuminated the entrance, casting a cool blue hue that contrasted with the warm, bustling streets below.

Unlike traditional hotels that were adorned with ornate details, the Shade Hotel exuded an air of enigmatic sophistication. Its sharp lines and geometric precision gave it a fortress-like presence, suggesting exclusivity. The entrance was flanked by sleek, automated doors that slid open silently, revealing a beautiful lobby. High ceilings supported exposed steel beams, their industrial aesthetic softened by ambient lighting that cast a gentle glow on the polished floors.

Art installations—abstract sculptures and avant-garde paintings—were strategically placed throughout the hotel, each piece carefully curated to evoke a sense of wonder and intellectual engagement. These works went beyond decoration; they held a deeper significance. Their abstract forms and bold use of color invited guests to pause, reflect, and draw their own meaning, often provoking thoughtful dialogue. The placement of these installations in key areas of the hotel, such as near seating areas or in traditional spaces, created moments of contemplation and emotional response, enhancing the overall atmosphere of sophistication and mystery.

As Von approached the front desk, her heels echoed softly against the marble, each step a deliberate move toward her objective. The concierge, impeccably dressed in a tailored suit, greeted her with a practiced smile that didn't quite reach his eyes. His demeanor was professional yet distant, embodying the hotel's ethos. She couldn't shake the feeling that the Shade Hotel was more than just a place to stay—it was a nexus of power and intrigue. The very air seemed to buzz with wealth. As she handed over Merrick's name and room number, the weight of responsibility settled firmly on her shoulders.

Heart pounding against her chest, Von did her best to keep calm, play the part.

Today, she was Luana—not Dr. Wilder Agatha Friedrich, her birth name, not Dr. Agatha Jones, and certainly not Von Schlange. Each identity had its time and purpose. But today required a different face, a different mask, and Luana was the one who fit.

The concierge got on the phone and dialed. "Colonel Winslow, there's a Ms. Luana down here at the lobby. I wanted to double-check if you are indeed expecting her, sir?" He nodded once. "Thank you, sir. I'll send her up."

"Everything alright?" Von asked patiently.

"Of course, ma'am. We just need to verify all guests who aren't registered with us. Nothing personal—it's standard policy." The concierge modeled a polite smile. "Third floor, penthouse suite 301."

"Thank you," she said and walked to the gleaming elevator. Inside, her reflection stared back from the polished steel walls.

The cool hum of the elevator was the only sound as it whisked her up to the third floor, where the hotel's most exclusive room awaited. The sprinting rhythm of her heart was steady—today, Luana would do whatever she must to hook the colonel in her carnal grip. She had done this before, played this game more than she could count. But this moment, in the penthouse suite, was the first time with Colonel Merrick Winslow.

She stepped into a quiet, plush hallway as the doors slid open with a soft chime. The dim lighting, crafted for intimacy, gave the illusion of safety. It was the calm before the storm. The thick carpet muffled her steps as she moved toward the penthouse door. Room 301—subtle yet still bearing a faint mark of elegance. Reaching the suite, she knocked on the door once. Merrick didn't keep her waiting, opening the door right away.

"Thought you'd get cold feet."

"I'm a woman of my word."

Inside, the penthouse suite redefined luxury. Spacious and airy, the opulent room boasted floor-to-ceiling windows framing the sweeping night skyline. The soft, ambient glow of the city lights reflected off the distant ocean gave off a shimmering silver hue that swept the room. Below, Manhattan Beach stretched, its darkened shoreline kissed by the sea's quiet pulse, cast a tranquil backdrop that contrasted their simmering tension. The scent of expensive cologne wafted in the air, blending with the furnishing's understated tone. A California King bed, dressed in crisp white linens, faced a wall-mounted flat-screen TV. The muted news played quietly in the background, its soft glow not disturbing the tranquil ambiance.

Colonel Merrick Winslow stood near the wet bar, pouring himself a drink. His broad back was to her, but he didn't need to look. She could sense his awareness, his calculated calm. The man was too careful for his own good, but not careful enough. She was in his room after all, and after only knowing him over a short drink at a bar.

"Luana," her new identity fell off his lips. "You're quite a surprise."

"What surprises you about me?"

"A sexy single woman like you would not want to have a dinner date before coming up to my hotel room."

"Why not skip dinner and get to dessert?" she cooed.

He chuckled softly, swirling his whiskey before taking a slow sip. "I've got quite the selection—bourbon, scotch, vodka, gin, a nice selection of wines, or even a cold beer if that's more of your speed. Name your poison."

Von tilted her head, considering his offer for a moment, planning her words carefully. A faint smile played across her lips as she met his gaze. "Surprise me," she said, her tone light but measured. "I like a drink that tells me something about the person pouring it." She moved a little closer, bridging the space between them. "Let's see what you think suits me."

He smirked, reaching for a bottle of Cabernet Sauvignon, its dark richness reflecting in the soft glow of the room. The deep red wine swirled into the glass as he poured, filling it halfway. He handed it to her, his gaze steady.

"Full-bodied and intense." There was a hint of amusement in his voice. "Figured you'd appreciate something with character."

Von had never been a drinker, but Luana was, and to play the role, she'd have to set aside her teetotaler ways—no matter how much it went against her nature. At five feet even and a solid hundred and fifteen pounds of muscle toned from years of weightlifting, Von had little experience with alcohol. But she was no stranger to meticulous preparation. Using her Luana Abraão alias, she'd written herself a prescription for Naltrexone, the drug that would dull the effects of alcohol in her system. Luana's identity was foolproof, complete with all the right paperwork—driver's license, passport, birth certificate.

Under this guise, Von looked nothing like her true self: blond, gray eyes, tattoos covering her scalp, forearms, and neck. Taking the max dose of Naltrexone allowed her to down as many drinks as necessary to keep the charade without feeling the effects. She could sip drink after drink, her mind sharp, her body unaffected—ready to seduce the colonel without ever losing control. As Merrick gazed at her with glossy, bedroom eyes, she pressed her body firmly against his, her hand finding his cock, hard beneath his jeans. She kissed him fiercely, slipping her tongue into his mouth as they tangled in a lustful, primal dance.

After a breathless pause, Merrick's hand slid down her back, his fingers grazing her skin through the thin faux-leather cocktail dress. He cupped her ass, grip tightening as he pulled her closer, their bodies flush against each other, heat radiating between them. Her breath hitched as his fingers pressed deeper, possessive and hungry. Her hands roamed over his chest, while his other hand found her waist, guiding her hips to meet his in a slow, deliberate grind.

Von moaned softly, forcing herself to feign desire—how tempting it was to kill him now, but that would be far too easy. This was about control, about feeding his ego and slowly unraveling him. She had to disarm Colonel Merrick Winslow. She had to disarm him emotionally, dismantle him mentally, and gather every piece of information she could before breaking him entirely. Only then, when he was a shell, would Von finally slay his last breath—after he'd already lost everything that mattered.

Merrick's hold wasn't just firm—it was painfully tight, fingers digging into her flesh with a force that stung her skin. It wasn't just a possessive grip but a display of dominance he thought he had. The pressure of his hand made it clear he wasn't about to let go easily, as if his strength alone could bind her to him. Every second of his unrelenting hold only fueled her simmering anger. She thought about Cheonsa Soo-Min, recalled the fear in her eyes. When Jefferson Pierce relayed that the media was speculating her death had been a suicide, Von knew the colonel had gotten to her first.

"Hold that thought and pour yourself another drink while I hit the bathroom," Merrick said, though it was more of an order, not a suggestion. He gave her ass one last firm squeeze, again, a little too roughly. Oh, if he wanted rough sex, Luana would give him just what he wanted.

The moment he was out of sight, she snatched his glass of whisky.

This was her chance, her chance to get the colonel drunk faster.

Moving with swift precision, she reached into her purse and pulled out a small Ziplock bag crushed with Valium. While she wasn't an MD, her veterinarian training knew just how much of any given drug would be needed for animals—and Merrick was an animal—not worthy of being called a man. She carefully dumped the Valium into the whisky and twirled it, making sure the powerful drug had completely dissolved in the dark liquid. She knew what would happen once he returned. The Valium would work in concert with the alcohol already in his system. At first, he'd feel relaxed—more at ease, more susceptible. But soon, the drug would deepen its hold, amplify the effects of the whisky. His muscles would slacken, growing sluggish, while his thoughts would grow hazy.

Medically, she understood what was about to happen—the depressant effects of both the Valium and the alcohol would decelerate his central nervous system. Disorienting him. Making the colonel more vulnerable. He wouldn't be able to refrain from drinking more, from losing control of the situation entirely. She didn't need to cause a blackout or even paralysis—*not yet*. Just get Merrick drunk, faster. Satisfied, she did as she was directed and poured herself another glass of wine, taking a slow sip as she leaned back in her chair, waiting.

The bathroom door opened, and she heard Merrick's footsteps returning, his familiar swagger still intact—for now. He reappeared, grinning cocky and smug as before. "Miss me?" he teased, heading straight for his drink. He raised it to his lips without hesitation, downing a large gulp.

A seductive smile spread across her lips. "We're not nearly drunk enough. How about a couple more drinks before I get naked and fuck you like you deserve." She leaned in and, with her tongue, licked his ear. "I like it rough. I want it hard."

Merrick's lips curled into a predatory grin. "When I take control, there's no going back."

"And what if I want to be dominated?" she dared him.

"Let's see if you really want what you're asking for." He finished his whisky.

She topped off his drink. "I won't just break you. I'll make you *want* to be broken."

"Bold words," he slurred, his body slackening, the glass wavering in his hand.

"I'll make sure you remember this moment," she said, watching as the Valium took hold, confusion flickering across his face, the brief tension in his jaw giving way to the drug's pull.

Von's smile deepened. The game was hers now.

TWENTY-FOUR
THE PREDATOR'S PATH

DETECTIVE ANAYA NAZARIO had been waiting all week for a list of names she doubted the feds could even pull together. Colonel Winslow's ex-girlfriends and second wife weren't just challenging to find—they were buried under layers of silence, intimidation, and most likely, bribes. These women knew better than to leave a trail, and the ones who did were probably too terrified to talk.

Nazario drummed her fingers on the desk, the rhythmic tapping barely keeping time with the dull throbbing in her skull. She sipped lukewarm coffee, grimacing as the bitterness coated her tongue. With a sigh, she popped two extra-strength Tylenol, praying they'd do more than just take the edge off her pounding headache. The clock on the wall ticked away the minutes as she stared at the empty inbox on her laptop, hoping that somewhere, buried in those shadows, one of Winslow's ghosts would finally speak.

At seven in the evening, it was time to head home. Nazario's breasts ached, full of milk, as her daughter's needs tugged at her, their bodies perfectly in sync with Ariabella's feeding schedule. Wilson approached her office and rapped lightly on the door.

"Can't keep that baby waiting, Nazario." Wilson strode in and plopped down on the chair facing her desk. "You look like you're in pain. Headache still bothering you?"

"Yeah." She opened and closed her mouth, massaging her jaw like a rusted hinge in urgent need of oil. "TMJ's back full force—I've already ground through several nightguards."

"This isn't gonna help. But I got nada. No luck on my end. Can't even find his living second ex-wife. She's not on any of them social networks. I mean, shit, even my gramps—he's on Facebook. Bet the grinding would ease a bit if we could only find someone willing to talk."

"If we can't catch a lead, Chief Johnson'll close us down so fast, we won't even have time to blink." Nazario rooted through her desk, found the Advil. Two pills down, chased with cold, bitter coffee. She plunked the bottle beside the half-empty Tylenol and met her partner's weary eyes.

"Take too much, and it'll kill your liver," Wilson warned. "Knew someone once that got fatty liver disease from downing Tylenol every day. True story. Go home to that sweet little girl. If you haven't pumped yet, that headache could be from waiting too long. Would hate to see you getting mastitis for a third time."

It had slipped her mind how mastitis affected her body. It caused fever, cold chills, headaches, body aches. It totally sucked. But she knew what was causing the migraine—stress. Stress from attempting to investigate a high-profile officer whose record was ironclad. He was charismatic, articulate, and confident, with a boy-next-door appeal that made him even more likable. The military loved him. His superiors couldn't stop praising him, not only for his leadership skills but also for his impressive number of deployments to the Middle East.

"The Tylenol or Advil should help with the mastitis, but you're right. I gotta get home. I'm about to burst and spray this place down with breast milk."

Wilson let out a hearty chuckle that shook his whole body. "Tell your man to step up the efforts, get us a lead on the colonel's love life."

"He's playing stay-at-home dad tonight."

"Actually, I got called in a few hours ago on an urgent matter. Captain Gus and her wife are watching our princess," Huxley's voice boomed as he walked up. "Sorry, I didn't text you."

"What would be so urgent on your day off?" Nazario said.

"Yeah, Daddy," Wilson said with a playful grin, "what could possibly tear you away from that gorgeous little girl?"

Huxley closed Nazario's office door and took the seat next to Wilson.

"One of those things we couldn't talk about over the phone," Huxley said.

"It's like that, huh?" Wilson raised a brow.

Huxley handed Nazario a manila envelope. "You never know who's listening in."

"What's this?" Nazario took the envelope and slowly opened it up.

"What you've been wanting."

"No ... really?" Nazario carefully pulled out a stack of photographs and papers.

The photos looked to be recent, clearly taken during covert surveillance. As Nazario flipped through them, her breath caught. The first picture showed a woman with dark hair and Asian features—Winslow's second ex-wife. She looked eerily like Cheonsa Soo-Min, as though she could pass as her sister, her Korean heritage strikingly apparent. Nazario's pulse quickened, unsettled by the resemblance.

The other two photos featured women of different ethnicities, each striking in their own way. One, with sharp cheekbones and caramel skin, could have passed as a Latina; the other had darker skin and soft curls framing her face. All three women were united by one commonality—they had been close to Winslow, and now each was in hiding.

"They've done a good job staying off the grid," Huxley said. "Cyber Crime Analyst traced them through scattered social media breadcrumbs and public records, but it took some digging."

Nazario nodded, scanning the paperwork and then handing them to Wilson.

"Damn, the colonel's got game. They look like models," Wilson said.

The paperwork contained each woman's last known location, aliases, digital footprints—what little there was—all laid out in meticulous detail.

"They're good at hiding, but no one's invisible," Huxley said.

"I was starting to lose hope," Nazario said. "Good work, and thanks for keeping your thumb on the cyber team."

"If the records were public, why couldn't we find them?" Wilson asked.

"Correction—they *were* public. I thought you two would find this interesting. Each of their records had been sealed through the courts. Even the basic things like divorce, marriage, financial records, previous place of employment, and their mailing address," Huxley explained.

"How'd you unseal them?" Nazario glanced up and gave Wilson the remaining paperwork in her hands.

"Deputy Frost, he had pull with some judge who owed him a favor," Huxley said.

Nazario watched as Wilson flipped through the photos and paperwork she handed him, his expression growing more intent with each flip of the page. Her mind wasn't on the contents of the envelope, though. It was on Deputy Frost and the Serpent

Woman case. She could still remember the press conferences, the strained smiles, and the carefully worded statements. Frost had been meticulous about protecting Von Schlange's identity, not out of concern for the investigation's integrity but to shield the FBI from the shame of their failures.

They hadn't caught the men on Von's list—men who thought their power made them invincible. The bureau had fumbled, letting those monsters slip through their fingers. Though the Serpent Woman had stepped up to finish the job, her involvement complicated matters. Frost had covered their tracks, distorting the truth—smoke, and mirrors to preserve the agency's image. He'd kept the real story under wraps, spinning a web of half-truths to the media, all to hide the bureau's glaring mistakes. As Wilson continued to read through the paperwork, Nazario's mind already began piecing together the larger picture. Winslow's second ex-wife's uncanny resemblance to Cheonsa Soo-Min wasn't just a coincidence—it couldn't be. Nazario couldn't shake the feeling that this was all connected, like a thread being pulled through everything, like one tangled knot that she was desperate to unravel.

"Way to pull through, Huxley, way to pull through." Wilson bumped fists with Huxley, then turned to her. "Why don't I do you one and contact his ex-wife and the other two girlfriends while you run home, Nazario? Empty the tanks before you get sick."

Cold chills started to settle in despite having taken Tylenol and Advil, a sign that she had mastitis for a third time, thanks to her lack of keeping up with a strict breast pumping schedule. Nazario was too into her work, too focused at times to take breaks, and while that made her a damn good detective, it was also her weakness. She often prioritized work over her health, something she was aware of—like her alcohol addiction, Nazario was a workaholic.

"You alright, Anaya?" Worry etched Huxley's face.

"Mastitis again. Got the cold chills coming on. Tylenol and Advil haven't kicked in quite yet. Head feels like it's in a vice grip."

"I'll start making the calls, see if my charm works its magic. You head home, partner, take care of yourself and that sweet baby," Wilson said.

"Hope you don't mind, but I reached out to each of them. Ex-girlfriends haven't returned my calls or emails. But Vivian, Winslow's second ex-wife, was cooperative. Just got off the phone with her. It wasn't easy to convince her, claimed she has a busy schedule. Vivian's willing to talk today in two hours. Gave me a hard deadline," Huxley explained. "If you're not feeling well—"

"There's no way I'm missing the interview," Nazario said with stubborn conviction.

"We can handle it, Nazario. Would hate to see you get worse," Wilson insisted.

"Where's the location?" Nazario asked, ignoring all concerns for her well-being.

Huxley blew out a breath. The two knew her too well. There was no changing her mind, no matter how achy she felt. "Pasadena—an hour or so away."

"Oh, more than that with traffic," Nazario reasoned. "At least an hour and a half. I won't have time to go home and feed Ariabella."

"Anaya, I really wish you'd take tonight off—" Huxley began.

Nazario pinned her baby daddy with her eyes. "Blake, I'm going, and that's that."

"No sense in trying to steer a stubborn bull," Wilson said. "No way in hell is Nazario gonna sit this one out."

Nazario opened her "mom drawer" and pulled out her breast pump. "I'll be ready in fifteen."

"That's our cue." Wilson nudged Huxley, who stood with his hands on his hips, breath coming out in short huffs. "We'll wait in the Tahoe."

———

Nazario felt a hundred times better after pumping. The cold chills dissipated, as did the massive breast swelling. Having drained the milk and stored it away in her mini fridge in her office, the headache vanished, but the tension between her and Huxley did not.

"I'd really wish you'd take better care of yourself," Huxley finally said, cutting through the strain that filled the SUV. "Being at home with our daughter wouldn't be so bad, would it?"

"I feel fine. Much better after pumping, actually. And I could say the same thing to you—you could be home with Ariabella. Just because I'm a woman doesn't mean I should be the one taking more time off. You barely took any paternity time. Why don't you go home and watch her?"

"This isn't a gender issue I'm talking about. It's about your health. You're pushing yourself too hard, and I'm worried about you. All I'm saying is that it wouldn't be a bad thing if you took more time off."

"How is it not about our roles, Blake? You're saying I'm the one who should stay home like a dutiful, barefoot woman. Would you say the same thing to a man if they had a headache?"

"No, because they don't have breasts engorged with milk that needs to be pumped every three hours, or they get mastitis for a third time."

"Alright, kids, now that's enough—the both of you," Wilson

said over his shoulder, keeping his eyes on the road as he drove. "I've got the solution. It's real simple. Add a few timers on, set yourself up with alarms, remind yourself when you've gotta pump. That way, you don't work through the day and forget."

Nazario and Huxley exchanged glances, acknowledging Wilson's simple, logical solution.

"Now, this was all unplanned, from my understanding. So, it's an adjustment for both of you. I'm not a parent, but I can imagine it's a big adjustment. Gotta remember that you're on the same team. You each love that little girl—she's lucky to have two amazing parents in her life," Wilson's voice took on a soothing, familiar tone, the same one that often broke through with the tough interviewees Nazario couldn't crack. In their fifteen years as partners, he had mastered the art of negotiations and interrogations, using a human touch and empathy that disarmed even the most hardened criminals.

As Nazario and Huxley remained silent, like scolded kids awaiting their punishment in the principal's office, Wilson carried on, "You two can alternate taking time off. That way, she has one of you at home. Switch your days off if you must. I'll help when I can. Heard Auntie Gus and her wife are great with your little girl. But there's no need to fight about it. You love each other. You love your princess. It's gonna take time management, staying flexible, and working together is all."

Nazario turned to Huxley, who sat quietly in the passenger seat, his brows furrowed in worry. She placed her hand gently on his shoulder. He hesitated for a moment, then put his hand on top of hers, giving it a gentle squeeze.

"I know you're just worried," she said softly, meeting his eyes. "And I get it. I do. But pushing myself doesn't mean I'm neglecting Ariabella. I'm trying to balance everything, just like you are."

Huxley's jaw tightened, and he let out a long breath,

rubbing his thumb over her hand. "I just don't want you to burn out. You're doing so much, and I feel like I'm not pulling my weight."

She shook her head. "This isn't about pulling weight. It's about partnership. I know you care, and I care, too. I just ... I don't want it to feel like my place is only at home because I'm her mom. We both have demanding jobs, and we both love her. We can make this work—and like Wilson said—together."

Huxley's lips curved into a tired smile. "I didn't mean it like that. You're right. It's not about you taking more time off just because you're her mom. It's about making sure neither of us is stretched too thin. I was scared you were pushing yourself too hard."

Nazario's grip tightened on his hand. "We'll figure it out. Maybe Wilson's right—we can take turns. It doesn't have to fall on just one of us."

Huxley kissed the back of her hand, the tension between them easing. "We always make it work. I'm sorry if I was—I dunno—overprotective of you, I guess. I love you, and we all know you don't always put yourself first."

"I love you, too, Blake. I do. And I promise to be better, okay?"

Their hands remained clasped, the truce lightening the air between them—understanding not only the challenges of law enforcement work, but also the even more demanding job of being new parents to a tiny, helpless human who relied on them completely.

"Now that's the spirit," Wilson boomed with a hearty laugh, adding levity to the stressful conversation. "Leave it to me. I'll set the timers on your phone so you never skip on your breast pumping schedule."

Nazario jabbed back. "I knew you were good for something."

Before she knew it, their conversation had made the drive feel quicker than expected. They cruised the 210 freeway, and at eight at night, the usual gridlock had finally eased, allowing them to pick up speed. The distant glow of the city lights faded behind them as they neared Vivian's home in Pasadena. Eager to dig deeper into Vivian's past, Nazario hoped Winslow's second ex-wife could shed light on anything that might reveal new insights into the army officer's shadowy life.

They pulled up to a two-story Craftsman nestled on a tree-lined Pasadena street, its stylish façade by a low stone wall that lent the house an air of unpretentious charm. A wide porch stretched across the front, supported by sturdy columns. Large windows glowed with soft light, casting a welcoming glow illuminating the night. An immaculate garden with lush green hedges and hydrangea bushes decorated the lawn. The home must've been easily appraised at two million, especially in California, where the prices of homes were virtually unaffordable.

Wilson whistled as they walked up to the front door. "Wonder if Vivian got a fat spousal support check," he quipped, eyeing the sleek cobblestone driveway that led to the detached garden, its doors painted bright yellow.

"It almost looks too perfect. Something feels off about it," Huxley said.

Nazario knew what he meant. The house had a well-kept, beautiful façade, though as they stepped closer, the air seemed still, a little too quiet for a neighborhood like this. Even the evening breeze that whispered through the nearby tree felt unnatural, as if it hadn't passed through this place in years, carrying with it an unsettling sense of abandonment. There were no children playing or parents tidying up the yard, no signs of life coming home from a late dinner or gathering. Yet, the home was spotlessly maintained, the front lawn pristine, as though the owner craved an almost obsessive sense of order and control.

"This fits a type of psychological profile I've seen repeatedly." Nazario studied the manicured lawn, her eyes narrowing. "Someone who needs control—structure. When everything on the outside is this flawless, it's usually because they're trying to keep something from unraveling on the inside. But to keep this case from folding, we best give the chief something more than a hunch. Let's see if Vivian will open up to us."

As they knocked, Nazario prayed Vivian held the key to Winslow's secrets.

TWENTY-FIVE
THE DEADLY SEDUCTION

COLONEL MERRICK WINSLOW had downed four glasses of whisky, drunk but not too intoxicated that he'd pass out. Von needed him drunk, but still lucid—just enough to lower his guard without losing his senses. It took a carefully designed cocktail of Jameson and Valium to strike the perfect balance.

"Think I didn't eat enough," Merrick slurred, pushing to his feet. He swayed, stumbling against the edge of the coffee table with a dull thud, his shins colliding with the wood. He winced, laughing it off with a sloppy grin. Von was at his side in an instant, her arm slipping under his to stabilize him, though careful not to help too much.

"Let's get you to bed," she purred, coaxing him toward the main bedroom.

Merrick leaned on her as they moved, their steps awkward and unsteady, his weight bearing down with each faltering shuffle. Adrenaline charged through her veins as her premeditated plans unfolded with unnerving ease. Once they reached the room, he collapsed onto the bed, eyes glassy but still attentive.

Von smiled at him, her expression feigning the innocence of a docile woman—something she certainly wasn't but knew how to play well. Batting her false eyelashes, she spoke with a soft, teasing lilt, "Maybe I should let you sleep it off." Her voice was light, almost playful, cloaking her devious nature. Von was a pragmatist, immune to the myth of goodness—convinced fairness was no match for evil. No, the only way to fight evil was to wield evil itself. She walked out to the living room and grabbed her purse.

"Hey," he hollered, "party's just gettin' started."

She returned to the room and plunked her purse onto the nightstand. Everything she needed was inside, tailored for this exciting night with the colonel.

She sat back down on the bed, and he pulled her close to him with a rough grip. But Von, ever calculating, leaned into the seduction, letting him believe he had the upper hand. Her hands found his clothes—off with his shirt, off with his jeans, stripping him of his underwear until he was lying there naked on the bed. Merrick grinned lazily, sloppy, filthy hands groping her breasts, fingers rubbing between her thighs. She stepped back until his hands fell away.

"Hold that thought," she whispered, and when he wasn't looking, she retrieved handcuffs from her purse. Merrick barely noticed the cold steel locking around his wrist until the first cuff clicked into place. His drunken grin faltered momentarily, confusion clouding his glossy eyes as Von smoothly pulled his other arm toward the headboard, securing it with the second cuff.

"Wait, what's this ...?" he slurred, tugging weakly at the restraints.

Von Schlange wasn't the type to use handcuffs in the bedroom. While she leaned toward asexuality, she preferred her encounters raw and organic, driven by natural chemistry and desire. But tonight wasn't about intimacy or lust. The colonel was only the second person she had ever cuffed. Her first?

Darren Fischer—a man she had bound to his bed before setting him ablaze, leaving nothing but ashes in her wake.

But Merrick was different. She couldn't afford mistakes, not this time. Von wasn't just a dangerous woman operating in the shadows but an international fugitive, with Interpol's eyes on her. A Red Notice had been issued—an international alert for law enforcement across borders to track her down. It wasn't an arrest warrant, but it might as well have been. It meant she could be detained and extradited at a moment's notice if she slipped up. Every move now carried greater risk, with nations working together to bring her in.

Von had evaded capture so far, sliding through the cracks in the system by camouflaging herself in the underworld of other countries—Brazil and plastic surgery had helped her survive without recognition. But she knew her time was running thin. Powerful and well-connected, the colonel's disappearance could draw even more unwanted attention. However, having him bound and vulnerable was necessary for this dangerous game, one Von had no intention of losing.

She moved to the edge of the bed, having an unexpected treat for the colonel.

"Whaddaya got up your sleeve?" he asked, arms limp.

Von danced with slow, deliberate grace designed to captivate Winslow's fading awareness. So much so that he barely acknowledged the handcuffs. Groggy from the Valium and whiskey she had slipped him earlier, his eyes struggled to focus, but the sight of her sultry body swaying in front of him seemed to pull him back from the haze.

Her hips rolled in an unhurried, hypnotic rhythm, hands trailing sensually over her body. As she began to peel away her black dress, she smiled down at him, her lips curving in wicked amusement. Inch by inch, the dress slid off, revealing the scarlet negligee underneath. The lace webbed across her chest, barely containing her augmented breasts, the neckline plunging to expose just enough to make him strain against the handcuffs for a closer look. The sheer fabric clung to her six-pack, low-key lighting accentuating the definition in her muscles, the hem brushing against her upper thighs.

Winslow's eyes narrowed. "You're full of surprises," he slurred, voice thick with wooziness but spiked with desire. Von tossed the dress aside, standing before him in nothing but the crimson lingerie, moving slow and predatory as she crawled onto the bed. She hovered just above him, eyes gleaming with intent as she imagined his blurred vision, desperate to follow her every move, powerless to resist despite the fog clouding his mind.

Von straddled Merrick, her blood-red negligee hugging her body in all the right places, the lace teasingly framing her exposed skin. She moved with resolve, sliding him inside her crotchless panties, her hips grinding down with rough, deliberate strides. Every motion was designed to rouse, command attention, and break his will. The bed creaked beneath them, her rhythm relentless, as she claimed him in ways that left no room for resistance.

His breath came in sharp hisses, the sound satisfying her. She could feel the tension in his body, the sluggishness of the drug and booze dulling his mind, making him more pliable, easier to control. Wrists strained against the cuffs, but the metallic clinks only added to her sense of dominance.

"Slow down," he muttered, lethargic and weak. But she barely acknowledged him. Instead, she quickened her pace, hips driving down harder, more forceful, savoring the way his body jolted beneath her. She was in complete control, and his feeble protests only fueled her.

Without warning, she slapped him hard across the face, the sound sharp in the dimly lit room. His head snapped to the side, and his breath came in broken gasps. Leaning in close, breath hot against his ear, she warned, "You're mine now."

Von watched him carefully, her lips curving into a satisfied grin as his body stiffened in response. Between his groans and the way his muscles tensed beneath her—it was all proof of the power she now held. She reveled in it, her control absolute, and she continued to move, each rough stride pushing him further into submission. The flicker of helplessness in his eyes thrilled her. Colonel Merrick Winslow, once so powerful and untouchable, was now bound and vulnerable beneath her, his groggy mind and body no match for her calculated, animalistic rhythm.

Merrick's body tightened beneath her with every demanding thrust. He was so close—she knew it from his ragged breath, body trembling under her command. His climax was inevitable, teetering right at the edge. And just as he was about to come, she got off him.

His body jerked against the handcuffs, and a raw, frustrated growl escaped his throat. She could see the anger flash across his face, his eyes wide with disbelief, chest heaving from her sudden denial.

"You bitch," he spat, voice dripping with venom. His wrists strained against the cuffs, drawing blood. "What the hell kind of game are you playing?"

Von struck his face even harder for a second time, the force snapping his head to the side as the sharp crack echoed through the hotel suite. His cheeks were the color of a bad sunburn. His face twisted, his true dark side coming out.

"Uncuff me now! You have no idea what I'm capable of. You're going to pay, you fucking cunt!" he screamed.

Without a word, she calmly put her clothes back on and crossed the room, picking up her discarded bag and slinging it over her shoulder. Without so much as a second glance, she strode toward the door.

"Luana!" he barked, but she ignored him. "You fucking bitch! Let me go. That's an order!"

She returned to his side with duct tape, sealed his mouth shut, and then duct-taped his ankles. If the asshole screamed for too long, someone might call the cops, and Von couldn't have that.

She fished her phone from her purse, eyes glinting as she aimed the camera.

"Say cheese!" she said with mocking glee. Merrick thrashed, his muffled screams choked by the duct tape as he jerked against the handcuffs, cutting deeper into his bleeding wrists. She snapped a few shots, each one an image that could shatter his career if they ever reached the military brass. Oh, this was far more satisfying than killing him right away, she thought as Von savored the thrill of his helplessness.

Satisfied, she opened the door and glanced back. A cold smile curled her lips.

"Enjoy the rest of your night, Colonel," she said evenly and then stepped out, shutting the door behind her, leaving him handcuffed to the bed, alone and powerless.

————

Von moved swiftly into the penthouse's living room, her gaze darting over every surface as she searched for anything—anything at all—that might reveal the colonel's true nature, anything that could expose him beyond his current state, naked and bound to the bed.

Spotting his laptop on the computer desk, Von moved toward it, only to find it locked as anticipated. If anyone could crack the code, though, it was Jefferson Pierce. The former marine turned hacker could crack anything—how he did it, Von had no idea—nor did she care to find out. All she needed was the access he could provide.

Resting at the foot of the desk, she noticed a laptop bag. The moment she unzipped it, a thick folder slid out, flaring her curiosity. Inside, she found printouts of email exchanges between Colonel Merrick Winslow and Cheonsa Soo-Min. At first glance, they painted Cheonsa as the obsessive stalker, with her supposed messages pleading, demanding, even threatening. Yet, as Von read on, the tone didn't align at all with the Cheonsa she remembered. It was as though someone was trying too hard to mimic her voice.

Von's eyes lingered over one email, where "Cheonsa" seemed to alternate between anger and desperation that felt forced. Cheonsa's real messages had always been clear, grounded—even in brief exchanges, she'd conveyed calm. Here, though, her words were extremely erratic, almost scripted to paint a picture of obsession and instability. Then Von noticed something peculiar. She turned one of the printouts over and squinted at the faint details in the header metadata still visible on the copy.

The emails claimed to be from Cheonsa, but the IP address logged at the top was the same across several of the messages from "her"—and it traced back to a location far from where Cheonsa lived or worked. With growing suspicion, Von jotted down the IP address and checked it against the original IP of Winslow's replies. Identical. Both geolocating signals traced back to a familiar address: Winslow's office. He'd been fabricating emails from Cheonsa to himself. Von flipped through more messages, noticing the time-stamps. The emails claiming to be from Cheonsa often arrived in seconds or minutes before Winslow's responses, all during times when Cheonsa was known to be at work or out of town.

This was a setup, and Winslow was the puppet master.

Digging further into the folder, Von discovered a note scrawled in Winslow's handwriting. It cataloged a series of aliases and encrypted email accounts—each tied to a specific burner phone number or VPN proxy address. The list extended to multiple social media handles, each with its own login details and backup codes, meticulously written down to avoid any slip-ups. This wasn't just a reminder but a blueprint for sustained deception, a web of digital identities Winslow had used to orchestrate his scheme and harass Cheonsa while masking his real identity.

Beneath the folder lay dozens of surveillance photos of Cheonsa. Each was timestamped in the corner with digital precision, showing her daily life in eerie detail: picking out produce at a grocery store, waiting at the pharmacy, browsing a bookstore, strolling through her neighborhood. Winslow's notes on the back of each photo were chillingly clinical—location coordinates, time of day, her actions cataloged and analyzed. One picture taken from an angle outside her rental home's window showed her undressing and slipping into her pajamas, clearly intended to invade her most private moments.

In one of the laptop case's pockets, Von's fingers brushed against a burner phone. When she powered it on, she found an entire trail of messages from a number labeled "Cheonsa." The texts were unhinged, filled with desperation and aggression—but the timestamps and message frequencies were peculiar. A quick scroll through the sent messages revealed both sides of the conversation: Winslow had been messaging himself, crafting dialogue that framed Cheonsa as his relentless stalker. There were even GPS records embedded in the metadata, with notes indicating fake locations he attributed to Cheonsa, further building his fabricated story.

With every piece of concrete evidence, the extent of Winslow's obsession and deception grew more horrifying. From his meticulous data logs, burner phone interactions, and precise digital trail, he'd clearly left nothing to chance. This wasn't just a collection of records; it was a damning case file, one that would crumble his reputation if it ever saw the light of day. Von slipped the burner phone back and closed the laptop case, her pulse steady. She now held everything needed to unmask the colonel's twisted game.

Technically, Von had enough on the colonel and didn't need the laptop. The evidence in the folder was damning, but she knew better than to take any chances. If this went to court, a sharp defense lawyer could argue that the printed emails, IP addresses, and logs were fabricated or doctored—especially without direct access to the original digital data. To counter that, she needed the raw evidence straight from the source. That's where the FBI's Operational Technology Division (OTD) would come in, particularly their Computer Analysis and Response Team (CART). CART specialists had the training and forensic tools to analyze digital devices down to the metadata. With the laptop in hand, they could trace the IP addresses, verify email timestamps, and uncover embedded geolocation data. CART could often recover deleted information and reconstruct digital footprints, a skill honed from years of handling everything from cybercrime to counterterrorism cases.

Von knew CART's digital forensics could expose far more than the printouts in the folder. By diving into the laptop's hard drive, the team could examine Winslow's email accounts, aliases, and hidden social media handles in real-time, pulling up unaltered records of his communications and interactions. They'd be able to confirm if the incriminating IP addresses matched Winslow's network locations, whether from his office or home. The burner phone might also contain data traces that would link back to Winslow's laptop, creating a digital trail that even the most skilled hacker would struggle to refute.

With both the printed records and the laptop's digital files, the FBI would be able to piece together the timeline and prove that Winslow had been stalking and manipulating her. Everything he did was driven by self-interest alone. The evidence was nearly impossible to undermine—so solid that all the legal maneuvering and denial could not wash away the truth.

Von checked on the colonel, who suddenly grew quiet. She checked his pulse—he was asleep, the Valium and whiskey finally kicking in. Von took a wet towel and wiped him down, making sure she left no trace of her DNA anywhere on him or in the room. Satisfied, Von returned to the living room and dropped into the chair before the colonel's laptop. It was the final nail in Winslow's coffin—now she just needed his password. She pulled out her phone and launched WhatsApp to text the only person she could trust.

She typed quickly, her fingers tapping the screen with a sense of urgency.

Von: *Got my hands on Winslow's laptop. It's locked, but I'll need to get in. Any chance you can help?*

A minute later, Jefferson's reply appeared. Damn, he was fast.

Jefferson: *Sure thing. I'll need the laptop to unlock it—unless it's a MacBook. They're easier to work around.*

Von: *MacBook. I can meet you to give it to you.*

She was already mentally mapping the quickest route to get to the hacker when Jefferson's next message stopped her.

Jefferson: *Don't worry about it. Don't need the laptop.*

Five minutes later, a string of potential codes came in.

Jefferson: *Try these: 4829, 5624, 0913, 1745, 2368*

Von's fingers hesitated over the keyboard just as Jefferson sent another message.

Jefferson: *If those don't work, let me know. And remember, it could also require a longer sequence or even a phrase—some users set up 6 or even 8 digits, most use numerical passwords.*

Von: *You're amazing. I owe you one.*

Von took a deep breath, fingers ready over the MacBook's keyboard. Each code Jefferson had sent was exactly what she needed to bypass the laptop security—now, all she needed was the right digit to get inside. Von entered each code, her fingers quick but steady, her anticipation growing with each failed attempt. 4829 ... no luck. 5624 ... still nothing. 0913, 1745, 2368—nothing worked. She let out a frustrated sigh, tapping back into WhatsApp.

Von: *None of them worked. Any other ideas?*

Within moments, Jefferson responded.

Jefferson: *Alright, try this:* 112990

She took a breath, typed in the new code, and hit "Enter." This time, the screen unlocked, the MacBook's desktop loading before her eyes.

Von: *I'm in! How'd you figure that one out?*

Jefferson: *It was Cheonsa Soo-Min's birthdate. He probably thought it'd be the last code anyone would guess. Too personal, too obvious.*

A chill ran down Von's spine. Winslow's control ran deeper than she'd anticipated, his obsession sickeningly personal. She quickly typed the password into the notes on her iPhone, knowing she'd need it later, and shut the laptop. She didn't have time to root around in the computer now. Von glanced around the room one last time, feeling a sudden urgency to leave. Winslow's dark world was bleeding into hers, and every instinct told her to get out. As she turned toward the door, her phone buzzed with a new message from Jefferson.

Jefferson: *Be careful, Von. You've just opened one hell of a door.*

Without another glance, Von slipped the laptop back into the case. Taking it with her, she exited quietly, her mind racing. This was just the beginning, and she knew it. Whatever Winslow had hidden, she was about to unravel, one secret at a time. But the real question coiled in her mind like a serpent ready to strike—should she let the law sink its teeth into him, trusting that justice would hold firm, or would he slip through, freed by some silver-tongued lawyer who could twist the truth into shadows of doubt? Winslow could walk away unscathed, free to hunt again, his venom spreading to new victims.

Or, perhaps, she could return to the Shade Hotel and deliver the reckoning he could never escape—the final hand that would silence his darkness once and for all.

TWENTY-SIX
THE END OF JUSTICE

VIVIAN KWON MET them at the door, her hand gently resting on the shoulder of Hope Winslow, a bright-eyed three-year-old who seemed like her mother's reflection captured in a smaller frame. Hope's dark, almond-shaped eyes glimmered with the same quiet intensity as Vivian's, a softness wrapped in unspoken strength. She anchored herself to Vivian's side, her gaze shifting with shy curiosity.

From the shape of her cheeks to how her mouth turned up in the hint of a smile, it was as if Hope had borrowed every line and hue from her mother, leaving only traces of her father's presence like faint brushstrokes in a completed painting. Vivian gave them a polite smile, turned to her daughter, and suggested, "Sweetie, how about you go play with your doll house?"

A middle-aged woman came up behind Hope. "How about we play for a bit, and then we can practice writing your name?" she said, ushering the little girl away.

"Thank you, Janice." Vivian smiled, then turned to them, explaining, "My nanny. With my nursing job, I tend to work sixteen-hour shifts. I can't imagine working as a single mom without her."

Vivian's voice, high-pitched and slightly nasally, floated to Nazario's ears with disarming warmth, every syllable feather-like, almost brushing against the edge of a melodic whine. There was a delicate politeness embedded in her tone, like a songbird's gentle trill, brightening the air around her. Each word was wrapped in softness, as if her voice itself was trying to cushion even the roughest edges of conversation. Nazario found herself marveling at the effect. It was a voice you couldn't help but feel safe around, one that turned greetings into gestures of kindness.

"I most likely will need to get a nanny myself for my daughter," Nazario said. "My best friend steps up when she can, but since we're both in law enforcement, we have demanding jobs and schedules."

"It's hard to hand them over to strangers, but with the right person, they can become the family you've always wanted," Vivian said with a bright smile.

Nazario couldn't fathom why Colonel Merrick Winslow would ever divorce someone with such a gentle spirit. Vivian seemed to effortlessly radiate thoughtfulness, every gesture and tone reflecting a warmth that made her home feel immediately welcoming, like stepping into a sunlit room. It was hard to picture her with anyone who didn't cherish that lightness, let alone a man like Winslow, whose rough edges and calculated manner seemed worlds away from Vivian's almost ethereal presence. Nazario couldn't shake the thought—what had possessed Winslow to leave a woman who felt like a balm to everyone around her?

"LAPD, right?" Vivian turned to Nazario. "Detective Anaya Nazario and ...?" She paused, looking to Wilson and Huxley, a soft line of bewilderment furrowing her brow.

"Sorry if we've bombarded you and pulled you away from your cute little daughter. I'm Detective Isaac Wilson, Detective Nazario's partner."

"And I'm Supervising Special Agent Blake Huxley—"

Vivian rested a manicured hand on her chest. "Oh my ... FB ... FBI?"

Huxley nodded. "Blame the miscommunication on me," he said. "Coming off paternity leave—new dad brain's still in effect. Should've told you that the visit would include more than just the detectives. The FBI put me on this case because of the ... sensitive nature. And military ties."

"It's no bother—none at all." Vivian smiled politely, then cleared her throat, eyes darting to the floor. "I ... I didn't want to do the interview. Not at first. But then I ... I thought about Hope, thought about the kind of role model and mother she needs. I realized, well, I realized that I have to do the right thing even if it's reliving old trauma."

She gestured for them to come in.

Nazario was the first to step into the home. "Truly appreciate your help," she said.

Huxley and Wilson followed behind. The two-story home was as graceful and composed as its owner. Moonlight poured in through the large windows, casting a soft, serene glow. The living room featured pale, upholstered furniture arranged in an open and airy layout.

A handcrafted oak coffee table held a vase of fresh lilies and a neat stack of books. Shelves along one wall displayed family photos, ceramics, and polished sculptures. The soft floral scent lingered, subtle but memorable. Vivian's presence was reflected in the muted tones—creams, grays, and soft blues—infusing the space with calm.

Nazario sank into a Tiffany-blue recliner. Huxley and Wilson took the nearby dove-gray couch, its pillows perfectly arranged. Huxley leaned back, hands on his knees, while Wilson sat forward, quietly admiring the room.

Nazario felt a surprised sense of tranquility wash over her.

Nazario's eyes wandered and then settled on the wall-mounted waterfall. It featured a sleek tempered glass panel framed in brushed stainless steel, with water cascading down its surface in a continuous, gentle flow. Soft LED lights illuminated the falling water, a glow that danced across the room. The soothing sound of the water added a tranquil ambiance, blending harmoniously with the home's décor. The elegant piece served as a visual focal point, contributing to the calming atmosphere.

Wilson glanced around, taking in the polished décor and the light trickle of the waterfall fountain on the wall. He leaned back on the couch, one arm casually draped along the top edge, his posture relaxed but watchful. "Feels like I'm at a spa. Do we get cucumber water with this interrogation, or is that extra?" he quipped with a grin.

Nazario suppressed a smile while Huxley looked amused.

"I do love cucumbers and lemon in my water. Anyone thirsty?"

Wilson and Huxley both shook their heads. "I'm okay, thanks for the offer," Nazario added.

Vivian sat down on the empty lounger opposite Nazario.

"There's no easy way to start, so we're just gonna jump right in," Nazario said. "As we explained over the phone, we're here to discuss Colonel Merrick Winslow."

The smile on Vivian's lips faded into a flat, pressed line. The shine in her eyes dulled as she glanced out the large living room window, watching a small goldfinch resting on a branch, wishing she could be that bird and fly far away from a meeting about her ex-husband.

"It took me a very long time to heal," she said, voice strained. "Merrick's the last person I want to talk about."

Wilson started, adopting his best negotiator's tone. "Ms. Kwon—"

"Please, Vivian will do."

"Pardon my formality. Vivian—we know this is a tough subject, so we appreciate anything you can give us, anything that can help us with our case."

The whistling sound of a tea kettle blurted through the tense atmosphere just in time. Vivian excused herself, voice as faint as the smile she forced back on her lips.

"Anyone care for tea—green tea or chamomile?" she asked, delaying the way a politician would during a difficult interview.

"Not much of a tea drinker," Huxley said.

"I'm good," Nazario added.

"No thanks, Vivian," Wilson called out. "Take your time. We're in no rush."

Vivian doctored up the tea, complete with honey, then sat back down, careful not to spill the hot liquid. Tendrils of heat unfurled like ghost ribbons spiraling up from the teacup. Her fingers clung to it as though anchoring herself against a chill or an unsteady hand. She lifted her gaze, letting it hide beneath the veil of her lashes.

"When I first met Merrick, he was the most romantic person I'd ever met. He did everything big. It wasn't just a dozen roses, but three dozen. I couldn't believe it. When we made love, he'd place rose petals everywhere. I felt like the luckiest woman alive. He would write these love letters, emails that took my breath away. It made me feel special, like I was his sole support system while he was deployed. We dated briefly before he had to leave for Afghanistan. The handsome officer in uniform. So well-spoken. Charismatic. And well read. Cultured, having traveled the world. Educated. Someone with the best taste in food, a palate for good wine. He wasn't the contemporary books type. He read all the classics and could quote verses from memory. Every day, it was like living in a dream." Vivian sighed, staring out the living room window, the memories of her past lingering like shadows she couldn't shake. "Sandy blond hair. Blue eyes. A smile and a boyish charm—everything about him swept me off my feet. For my birthday, he gifted me these gorgeous two-carat diamond earrings."

"Well, fantastic." Wilson let out a light chuckle. "The kind of guy that leaves the rest of us regular folks in the dust."

Nazario brought her ankles together, a gesture of composure as she struggled to banish the image of Colonel Merrick Winslow, pants down, leering at her breast-pumping like he was watching a peep show. "So, he was easy to love?"

Huxley's sidelong glance suggested he could see Nazario's efforts to keep it professional.

"Very much so—at first, anyway."

Huxley leaned in. "Don't mean to sour the romantic image you've painted, but from my experience in psychological profiling—this stage is called love bombing. It's quite common in the first stages of a manipulative relationship. Usually, the love bomber is a narcissist. Okay. Someone who enjoys control. Someone obviously charming. The relationship often happens real fast. Dependency builds through this intense shower of affection. It causes the victim to become addicted to it. Love bombers make their partners dependent on their validation."

"Then isolation tends to happen soon after," Nazario came in. "Isolate their partner from friends, family. I would imagine that's easy to do when you're a military wife. You move wherever they're deployed or stationed. Harder to prove that way. Not saying that all military men or women are manipulative narcissists. But Vivian—we met him. Spoke to him along with Jean and Mavis Lou."

"Oh gawd." Vivian rolled her eyes to the ceiling, pinching the bridge of her nose. "Ever heard of in-laws from hell?"

"Divorced a few times over here—so, yes and yes on the in-law's front," Wilson said. "But you'll have to excuse my perplexity, Ms. Kwon—sorry, Vivian. Been doing this a real long time. We all have. Each of us, we're good judge of character. Reading people, well, it's our thing. We might've only known you for—" Checking his watch. "An hour or so. But pardon my language— you're way too damn nice, beautiful, and polite. You're a great mother. Empathetic. Not trying to make gender general- izations—"

"I know what you mean," Vivian said, smiling warmly. "I'm not offended."

Wilson put a gentle hand on Vivian's shoulder. "Don't need to've known you all my life to get that vibe from you. So, what in the world would Jean Winslow and Mavis Lou have to complain about?"

"They were constantly in Merrick's ear. Wasn't just married to him, but to his parents. Tried to talk to him about it, but it always led to an unwinnable argument. Nothing I did was good enough. No matter how good of an Army wife I tried to be, I wasn't perfect enough. But that wasn't even the worst of it."

The three of them exchanged a curious look.

"Vivian, was there anything dangerous about your ex- husband? Anything he did that was ... out of the ordinary?" Huxley asked.

Nazario raised a brow and leaned forward, her gaze sharp. "Maybe the rooms that locked from the outside? The ones in Jean Winslow and Mavis Lou's home?"

Vivian's face twisted, an expression caught between dread and resignation. She looked away, fingers twining together as though bracing against a long-buried memory. "I didn't ... I didn't know anyone else knew about those doors," she whis- pered, her voice barely audible, thick with apprehension. "Mer- rick... he had this way of controlling everything. It started small, you know? Quiet reminders, gentle reprimands. But if I ever crossed some invisible line, he'd ... lock me in. Hours would pass, sometimes a whole night trapped in a room he'd secured from the outside."

"And Merrick was the only one with keys—my guess," Nazario said.

Vivian nodded. "At first, I thought it was strange to have our rooms locked from the outside," Vivian began, her voice wavering. "But Merrick insisted it was just a safety measure—something about protecting us, securing the house. I didn't push back because he had this way of making everything sound—I dunno—reasonable, normal? He had me convinced that it was what I needed, what we needed. I thought it was strange he delayed having me meet his parents. Kept asking. Thought it was a little different that he had picked out the house and outfitted it with those locks before we were even engaged."

"So, he didn't ask for your input? Picking out a house—it's a joint decision and a big one at that," Wilson said.

"It started with our dates," Vivian murmured, a hint of regret coloring her words. "Merrick would pick the restaurant, even down to the type of food we'd eat. Chinese instead of Mexican, Thai instead of Indian. I didn't question it at first—just thought he was being thoughtful. Making all the plans. But looking back … I realize now that I never had a say. He used to pick out what dish I should order. Picked out the wine that would pair with the food. Honestly, I was flattered. Figured he was well traveled, had good—no—great taste. It helped when I hadn't been to the restaurant and didn't know what was good. So, I didn't think anything of it. He showered me with all kinds of gifts. As I've said, initially, it was romantic. Then, he surprised me with the biggest gift—a house. In his name, not in mine. All of the furniture was already chosen. The colors on the walls. Hardwood floors instead of carpet. Even the art. Everything was pre-selected by him. Mind you, it was a beautiful house. The décor was gorgeous. So perfect. I was in love with him, and I trusted him. Trusted that he did these things out of pure intent. He loved me. He was helping me—making the hard decisions so I didn't have to."

Vivian paused, staring out the living room windows again as if the glass might offer some escape. Nazario watched her, feeling a surge of incredulity that she struggled to suppress. How could Vivian have trusted Merrick for so long? She exchanged a quick glance with Huxley and Wilson, catching the same mix of disbelief in their eyes. When Vivian finally turned to face them, Nazario tried to soften her gaze, not wanting to add to the shame that had already flickered across Vivian's face.

Nazario felt the need to repeat what Vivian said, "He surprised you with the house before proposing, and you hadn't even met his parents yet?"

Just saying it out loud sounded strange. Nazario had to be certain she didn't accidentally get the events and timeline wrong.

"It was a little unconventional." Vivian took a deep breath, gaze distant. "But then, when I finally met his parents, I noticed what you did. All of their rooms—their doors were locked from the outside like it was part of how they lived. I figured it was maybe a family habit or some outdated precaution they'd never bothered to change. But the more time I spent there, the more it felt—I dunno—intentional."

She shivered slightly, her hands tightening into fists. "Merrick's father, Jean Winslow, he'd walk by the doors, sometimes pausing just long enough to check the locks, like he needed to make sure they were always secure. And Merrick? He'd stand there watching like he was ... proud. Like it was a skill he'd inherited, something he'd been raised to believe in. It was unsettling, but I brushed it off, thinking I was just being paranoid."

"Did they ... ever lock you in?" Nazario asked.

"We were not allowed to sleep in the same bedroom. Every night, before bed, Jean would lock the door. At first, I thought it was meant to keep Merrick out. Only Merrick and Jean Winslow had the key. No explanation. I was stuck, waiting in the morning. The room they'd put me in had no bathroom. I'd have to make sure I didn't drink anything before bed, worried that I'd ... that I'd have an accident. Sometimes, Merrick would let himself in my room. We'd have sex, and then after ... he'd lock me back in again until morning." Tears filled her eyes. "I kept telling myself it was just his way of showing he cared. Maybe this was what love looked like. I ignored that voice in the back of my mind, the one whispering that he saw me as his property. I buried it, told myself I was overthinking, that real love sometimes meant giving up a bit of ... a bit of freedom."

"And you still said yes when he proposed?" Huxley frowned, his anger barely contained. Nazario could see the same fury simmering in his eyes, the same fire she'd seen when she'd told him about Merrick, spying on her while she was breast pumping.

She shut her eyes, regret etching her face. "He had every-thing planned—the dress, the wedding, every last detail chosen for me. When he proposed, I ... I couldn't say no. I was caught up in that twisted kind of love, the kind that keeps you tethered to your abuser. By the time I finally understood what those locks represented, I was already in too deep to escape."

Nazario and Huxley exchanged a tense look. Pieces of Vivian's story were connecting in ways they hadn't expected. Wilson, who'd been listening, let out a whistle, shaking his head in disbelief. "Shit. Locked doors on the outside," he said, "that's not a family quirk—that's a damn prison."

"Ever seen his first wife, Cheonsa Soo-Min?" Nazario pulled her phone out.

"N-n-no. He made me promise him that I would leave it

behind us, made me promise that I wouldn't look her up on social."

Nazario handed Vivian her phone. It was a picture of Cheonsa and Merrick's wedding.

"She looks exactly like me." Vivian's breath hitched. "And that wedding dress—it's almost identical to the one I wore."

"If you zoom in on her hand, the wedding ring looks the same, too," Nazario said.

Huxley crossed his arms. "This isn't unusual for someone like Winslow. Psychologically, he's likely driven by unresolved attachment issues or narcissistic traits. Marrying a woman who resembles his first wife isn't just coincidence—it's a way for him to recreate and control a relationship he perceives as idealized. By choosing a similar-looking dress and ring, he's essentially rewriting his past, constructing a new version of what he thinks a 'perfect' marriage should look like, only this time with total control over every detail."

Nazario nodded and chimed in, "Supervising Special Agent Huxley is right. In his mind, his wife isn't a person with her own identity—she's a reflection of what he wants, a way to fill that psychological void without any of the complications of a real relationship. The matching dress and ring reinforces that image, keeping her trapped in the role he's constructed for her, a role she never asked for. And anyone who deviates from that role ... well, they don't last long in his life."

"That's why he filed for divorce from Cheonsa Soo-Min and why he filed for divorce with you," Wilson said. "You probably started gaining autonomy. I'm sure things changed after the two of you had Hope. Is there a reason why you had the baby, knowing things weren't right?"

Vivian sighed. "I always wanted a child but couldn't carry because my endometrial lining was too thin. So, we spent a whole lot of money on a surrogate. Honestly, I was hoping that having a child, that it would—"

"Save the marriage?" Nazario rubbed her chin.

"Yes." Vivian's shoulders slumped. "He only grew more jealous of my connection with Hope. She changed my entire life and was the best thing that could've ever happened to me."

"For a man like Winslow, someone narcissistic and controlling, having a child—especially one who brings you joy and a sense of independence—would be unbearable." Huxley crossed his arms. "In his mind, you're supposed to orbit around him, to reflect whatever role he's assigned to you. Looks like the moment Hope came into the picture, his influence over you started to fade. That connection you had with your daughter is something he couldn't control or compete with, and it disrupted the power he thought he held over you."

"Just had a baby myself, so I know it's a team effort," Nazario said, smiling at Huxley. "It takes both parents, fully committed without letting jealousy or competition get in the way. In a healthy relationship, there's always enough love to go around. But in an unhealthy one ... a baby can't fix what's broken. If anything, it can make the cracks even deeper."

"I think it's time I reach out to Cheonsa Soo-Min," Vivian said. "Maybe it can help us both to heal, to gain some sort of closure because when Merrick filed for divorce out of the blue— it was a mind fuck. I went through so many emotions. Confusion. Denial. I blamed myself. Begged him to stay in the marriage for Hope—even though deep inside, I knew he was doing me a favor."

Nazario exchanged a knowing look with Wilson and Huxley, reading the silent question in their eyes—who would be the one to break it to Vivian that any chance of a meeting with Cheonsa was now impossible.

"Don't think you'll be meeting Cheonsa anytime soon, Ms. Kwon," Wilson started.

"And why not? Merrick isn't in control of my life anymore. I worked hard through years of therapy to undo what he did, to regain my confidence, get my life back—"

Nazario didn't waste time. "Cheonsa's dead, Vivian. Someone wanted to make it look like a suicide, but we have reason to believe that it was a homicide."

The air seemed to rush out from Vivian's lungs in a sharp gasp. "It was him—I know it," she said, her voice cracking, barely holding back the tears. "But if you think he'll spend even one day behind bars, you're wrong. Merrick and his parents, they've got judges, lawyers, cops—all in their pocket. They'll cover for him, no matter what."

Nazario watched as Vivian's entire body shook, her face crumpling as she buried it in her hands, grief spilling out in waves she could no longer contain. Though she and Cheonsa had been strangers, Nazario sensed an invisible thread connecting them—a bond of shared pain forged by one man: Colonel Merrick Winslow. It was a connection neither woman had asked for, but one that now left Vivian shattered, haunted by the thought that it could just as easily have been her. Only another ex-wife of Winslow could truly grasp the relentless weight of Cheonsa's death—and the futility of challenging a man fortified by powerful allies, unbreakable in the eyes of the law.

TWENTY-SEVEN

TWILIGHT OF THE SERPENT

VON SCHLANGE HAD AMASSED every piece of ammunition she needed to annihilate Colonel Merrick Winslow's carefully constructed façade. The evidence, from his secret escapades to his web of manipulation and lies, was a wrecking ball poised to demolish his life. Still, an unshakeable unease clung to her life like Cheonsa's ghost trailing her step, whispering doubts she couldn't silence.

She scrolled through the pictures once again—Winslow sprawled on the bed, naked and bound, a grotesque portrait of vulnerability that made her lips curl into a satisfied grin. But it wasn't those images that carried true weight. Rather, it was the thread of exchanges between Winslow and his ex-wife. He'd constructed a house of mirrors reflecting nothing but distortion and deceit, which framed Cheonsa Soo-Min as an unhinged criminal stalker. That was the bulletproof vest of her case—the damning evidence that could obliterate him in the eyes of any jury.

All she had to do was hit send. One email to the proper chain of command, and Winslow's world would collapse in on itself like a sandcastle swallowed up by the tide. She could walk away, leave it in the hands of authorities, and wash the stink of him off her soul. So why couldn't she do it? Von's grip tightened on her phone, her knuckles turning white. The thought of letting the system handle him felt like a bad joke. She despised the law—an intricate game played by judges, lawyers, and cops who all too often bent the rules to serve their own interests.

And the military? Even worse.

They would shield their own, burying his sins under a mountain of red tape and medals. No, Winslow wasn't going to receive justice if left to them. Not after the conversation she'd had with Jefferson Pierce over WhatsApp—a conversation that only deepened her distrust.

Von: *Need to know who's investigating this and get their email.*

BlackDragon6: *If you plan to send it to them, it might not do you any good.*

Von: *Why? Who is it?*

BlackDragon6: *Who do you think? Cheonsa's death was within LAPD jurisdiction.*

Von: *Detective Nazario & Detective Wilson? Supervising Special Agent Blake Huxley is on it, too, isn't he?*

BlackDragon6: *Yep—don't have doubts they'd want to put this guy away, but I found out a few more things about the colonel.*

Von: *Other than he's a POS murderer and master manipulator? A fucking alpha male controlling narcissist?*

BlackDragon6: *He's got everyone in his back pocket. Like everyone. People way up in the chain: top military, all the judges, JAG, CID, lawyers. Everyone—even the president of the U.S. of fucking A. No way this dude's going to prison. Guarantee: even if they put him away, he'd get pardoned. Bet money on it!*

Von: *Fuck!!*

BlackDragon6: *Do what you want with that. Sending you*

Detective Nazario's email address. Don't forget to use Proton-Mail encryption self-destructing email.

Von: *Got it.*

BlackDragon6: *You know my vote—I'd say add him to your list of accomplishments.*

Von Schlange understood the weight behind the phrase "list of accomplishments." It was a euphemism, a polite veneer over something far darker. For her, it translated to one thing: adding Colonel Merrick Winslow's name to her hit list. Another name etched into the grim ledger of men she had ended—a tally she carried not as a burden but as a medal of honor. Each kill was a notch carved by vengeance, a thirst for the blood of those who deserved it.

BlackDragon6's words refused to leave her. A glaring truth remained: power protected its own, and that was the truth. How could Von rely on a system as corrupt as the man she wanted to destroy? Her fingers hovered over her laptop's keyboard. The send button loomed like a trigger, daring her to pull it. If she sent the evidence, she would be putting her faith in a flawed machine. But if she kept it and acted now, she'd make sure Winslow paid—not with a slap on the wrist, but with every ounce of pain he deserved.

Her breath came in slow, measured pulls, at war with the dilemma. To trust or to destroy? To hand him over or bury him herself? The law was supposed to be the sword of justice, but to Von, it was a blunt instrument controlled by blind fools. No, Colonel Winslow deserved sharper punishment. For an hour, she had only considered two options until it hit her—there was a third option.

Von logged into her ProtonMail account using a secure connection routed through multiple layers of anonymity. She spent hours preparing, needing the guarantee that every digital footprint would vanish before it could be traced. First, she connected her laptop to a high-security VPN, masking her IP address and rerouting her activity through several international servers. Next, she fired up Tails, an amnesic operating system that left no trace of her activity once the session ended. For good measure, her laptop's MAC address had been spoofed to ensure even the hardware signature couldn't be linked back to her.

The encrypted email was a digital espionage masterpiece that gave her great pride. She composed it directly within ProtonMail's interface, automatically encrypting the message end-to-end. The recipient: Detective Anaya Nazario. It was an obsession, the way Von had spent more than a year studying Detective Anaya Nazario's investigative style since their first encounter. Back then, Nazario had been assigned to track her down, determined to stop Von's calculated spree of executions against men connected to a sprawling illegal sex ring and the white supremacist network of the Aryan Nation Brotherhood.

During all that time, Von had watched Nazario from a distance, scrutinizing each move she made. She observed how the detective pieced together evidence with surgical precision, doggedly pursuing leads even when they seemed like dead ends, and how she defied bureaucratic red tape that usually crippled others in law enforcement. But not the detective. Anaya Nazario wasn't just thorough—she was relentless, and that made her dangerous.

Von had needed to stay one step ahead, and understanding Nazario's methods had been her lifeline. She'd learned to predict the detective's moves, to counteract her strategies before they could close in. But now, with Winslow in her crosshairs, Von saw a new use for that knowledge. This time, she wasn't out-maneuvering Nazario—she was leveraging her. The detective's persistence and integrity would serve Von's cause, whether Nazario knew it or not.

Von knew the detective's email was likely monitored, but

she was still the best way to get evidence into the right hands. And the email was damning: a dossier of photos, chat logs, and forged transactions that showed Colonel Merrick Winslow's true self. But Von wasn't about to leave her fate to chance. In order to obscure the origin further, she accessed ProtonMail over Tor Browser, layering additional built-in security. This made it impossible to trace her IP address, as it became a randomized series of nodes around the globe, each wiping its hands clean of her activity.

The last step was setting the email to self-destruct. Proton-Mail allowed her to flag time-sensitive messages and, therefore, configure them to erase after fifteen minutes of opening. This would give the detective enough time to download the files, while the encryption ensured the message remained untampered and untraceable to Von—unless someone had the decryption key. And she wasn't about to share that with anyone.

Von took a deep breath, the cursor hovering over the button. The email was an untraceable digital bullet aimed straight at Winslow's engineered veneer. Once she clicked send, the email would leave no digital breadcrumbs to lead anyone back to her. It was the kind of perfection only paranoia could build.

The button clicked.

And just like that, the evidence was on its way. Within moments, Von wiped her laptop's drive clean, her heart hammering as she shut it down. Somewhere out there, Nazario would open her inbox to find the truth Von had delivered—truth that couldn't be traced, undone, or ignored. This had been part one of Plan C, the crowning result of Von's methodical planning. Initially, Plan A had seemed straightforward: email the evidence and let the system dismantle Colonel Merrick Winslow's life piece by piece. Plan B, on the other hand, was visceral and final—kill the colonel and eliminate him as a threat entirely. For hours, she wavered between the two, the scales tipping back and forth as she debated the risks and rewards of each.

But then, a third option had crystallized, sharp and undeniable in its brilliance. Plan C wasn't about choosing—it was about doing both. She would deliver the evidence to the authorities, ensuring his name and reputation were dragged through the mud. And then, when the fallout began, she would deliver her form of justice—a reckoning far beyond the reach of any courtroom, as brutal and unflinching as the truth itself. It wasn't just justice. It was poetry. Plan C was more than vengeance—it was a safeguard against the Colonel's unyielding grasp on power. Winslow wasn't just a man with influence; he symbolized the system's worst failures.

After texting with Jefferson Pierce over WhatsApp, Von had done her research, and everything he mentioned was laid bare for public consumption on Google. Images of Winslow proudly standing shoulder to shoulder with the president, a polished smile plastered across his face as they posed together on the White House lawn—photos of him at galas, surrounded by judges and high-profile lawyers raising glasses with politicians. Colonel Merrick Winslow's network was a who's who of insider powerbrokers, a fortress of heavyweight influence and privilege that could shield him from any consequence.

It was sickening how he could paint himself as a patriot, a hero, while the truth of his vile actions remained buried beneath his accolades. Von knew his connections ran deeper than the pictures suggested. These weren't just acquaintances—they were allies, people who would go to extraordinary lengths to protect him. If the case even reached court, they'd ensure it never saw the light of day. If he were convicted, his sentence would vanish with a presidential pen stroke. The military would lionize him, covering up his crimes under the guise of honor and sacrifice, perhaps even reframing his actions as PTSD symptoms from deployments—a tragic byproduct of his service rather than the calculated cruelty they truly were.

To them, he wasn't a predator—he was above reproach.

It would be another cover-up, another chapter in the long, infuriating book of men like him evading justice. Von couldn't stomach it. Plan C ensured that he wouldn't just lose everything he had built—it would strip away everything he was, leaving no room for redemption, no chance of escape. After sending the email to Detective Nazario, Von turned her attention to what came next, her hand firm as she reached for the tools she needed.

———

The room was dark except for the soft glow of a desk lamp, long shadows across the walls cast from its amber light. Von Schlange sat at the desk in her hotel room, her faux-leather black medical bag open like a predator's maw. Von never owned leather due to her vegan lifestyle. Zeus sat patiently at her feet. Like her faithful fur partner, the bag had been her companion for years— back when her work had been innocent. Or at least noble. It carried the faint scent of antiseptics, layered with the lingering musk of stables, kennels, and the quiet hum of her old vet clinic, a connection stretching from Casper, Wyoming, to Rio de Janeiro, Brazil.

Nestled inside was a MOSLA Insulin Cooler Travel Case. Compact and efficient, its ice packs ensured the temperature-sensitive contents remained potent. She opened the black bag with practiced ease, fingers brushing over the cooler's smooth surface as she unzipped it. Inside, among the chilled compartments, rested the vial. Her movements were steady, deliberate, as she retrieved it. Succinylcholine chloride. The label was worn, but the name and expiration date remained legible.

Expiring in one year, it was a tool of precision—a weapon disguised as medicine.

She held it to the light, tilting the glass just enough to catch the liquid's clarity. It looked harmless, even delicate, but she knew better. In less than a minute, it would strip a body of its will, silencing muscles, leaving the heart to hammer against the prison of a conscious mind. Like venom from a serpent's bite, the paralysis would strike and spread, coiling through the body. Von selected a syringe from the sterile pack, the faint crinkle of plastic unnervingly loud in the stillness. She slid the needle in the vial's rubber stopper, the motion smooth, almost reverent. Her hands worked with a memory of their own, the muscle memory of a healer. Once, she'd used this drug to calm frantic horses, immobilize dogs too large or too strong to restrain. Back then, it had been an act of mercy. Now, it was something else entirely.

The syringe filled slowly, the plunger drawing back like a taut bow string. The liquid was clear, innocuous, but Von knew its dangerous potency. Succinylcholine didn't kill with a bang or a flash. It was quiet, insidious. It didn't stop the heart—it left it beating while the body suffocated in betrayal. The victim's brain would stay alert, aware of every agonizing second. She flicked the syringe, watching a fine spray bead from the needle's tip. A smirk tugged at her lips—a wisp of satisfaction drifted across her expression. The dosage had to be perfect. Too little, and Colonel Merrick Winslow might survive long enough to fight back. Too much, and he might slip into a painless oblivion before he truly understood the weight of his sins.

Von wasn't here to grant mercy.

Sliding the syringe into the insulated compartment of the MOSLA Insulin Cooler Travel Case, Von secured it with an elastic loop. The bag had once carried syringes into stables, onto farms, to panicked calls from clients in the dead of night. Now, it would accompany her into a different kind of night, one far darker. Across the hotel room, Von's image gazed back at her from the wall-mounted mirror. The woman she saw was unrecognizable—cheekbones sharper, gray eyes, cold as steel. She'd traded her scalpel for a blade, her syringe for poison. But hadn't this been inevitable? She told herself this was justice.

Merrick's crimes deserved no less than the deliberate agony he had inflicted on others.

Von grabbed her long, dark wig and secured her natural blond hair beneath a wig cap. She carefully inserted the brown contacts over her striking gray eyes, blinking until they settled. A glance in the mirror confirmed it—her true identity was again thoroughly concealed beneath the disguise. It wasn't the colonel she feared recognizing her true self—her precautions were purely strategic. Hotel security cameras were a different threat entirely. She couldn't risk her face being flagged, not with the LAPD, particularly Detective Nazario, and INTERPOL hunting her for the string of murders tied to her name. Von Schlange wasn't just a fugitive; she was a globally wanted serial killer.

Zeus, however, had no disguise. Detective Nazario and her team would undoubtedly recognize him, a detail that should have given Von pause. She considered leaving him behind in the hotel room but dismissed the thought. Zeus had an uncanny ability to sense the good from the bad, and she was certain he'd relish the spectacle—watching yet another man meet the end he so thoroughly deserved.

Von snapped the bag shut with a metallic click, and Zeus leaped up. "*Lass uns gehen,*" she ordered—"Let's go."

The weight of the medical bag was comforting, grounding. She turned off the light, leaving the room in darkness. The bag swung at her side as she and Zeus stepped into the night. It wasn't the healer's bag anymore. It was an executioner's toolkit.

———

As the door swung open, Colonel Merrick Winslow jolted against the handcuffs that secured him to the bedpost. His wrists were lacerated and bloody. For a brief moment, she considered the risk. Could someone at the hotel have noticed something amiss? A colleague stopping by, an employee remembering a passing detail? He'd been clearly trying to escape but had failed. Merrick's eyes widened at the sight of Zeus—a massive, one-hundred-pound German Shepherd, easily the largest and most muscular Von had ever owned or trained.

Merrick attempted a scream that was muted by the duct tape covering his mouth. Zeus's ears shot up, a deep growl rumbling from his throat as his lips curled back, revealing sharp, glistening teeth. Von ambled toward the bed, gripping her medical bag as Zeus marched next to her, keeping time with her steps like a loyal guard. Once next to the bed, Von—not so gently—ripped the duct tape off, taking a layer of epidermis with it before yanking the gag from the colonel's mouth. It didn't take him long before he launched into her.

As soon as the gag came off, Winslow's jaw tightened, his words spilling out with a razor's edge.

"You fucking cunt," he said, cold as stone, words barely above a growl. "You think this ends me? I know people—real power. They'll erase you before you even see it coming. You don't even know who you've crossed." He leaned forward, the bloody handcuffs biting into his wrists like hungry jaws, each movement reopening the raw grooves carved by his unrelenting struggle. "You can't keep me here. One way or the other, I'll get out—I always do. And when I do, I promise you, you stupid bitch—when I'm done, there won't be enough of you left to bury."

Von remained silent, letting him rant, empty words wasted

on borrowed time. This was his last rite, whether he knew it or not. Without hesitation, she unzipped the medical bag, pulled out the syringe prepped with Succinylcholine chloride, and lifted it to the light. A quick flick of her finger sent ripples through the liquid, the faint sound cutting through the stillness like a countdown.

"W-w-what's that? What the hell is that?" Merrick's arms flexed as he yanked hard against his restraints. His legs started to buck, though, with them bound at the ankles, it hardly helped his cause. There was no way he was getting free no matter what he tried.

"*Hol seine Beine.*" Von signaled Zeus to get his legs.

Zeus leaped on the bed, sinking his teeth into the colonel's ankles.

Merrick cried out, desperate to kick her dog off. But it was no use. Once Zeus clamped down, pain surged across the colonel's face. He twisted in agony as he yelled, "Get this fucking mutt off me! Do you hear me? Get him off!"

He thrashed his legs, but Zeus's jaws held firm, locked like cement hardening under the blistering Arizona sun. As her dog's teeth sank deeper, Von imagined beautiful, sharp waves of pain rushing through his body as his muscles seized and spasmed uncontrollably. Von capitalized on the moment as his body went rigid, Merrick's struggles giving way to a brief, vulnerable stillness brought on by bodily torment.

"Unfortunately for you, this won't act quickly," she said, finally breaking her silence as her fingers found a thick pulsing vein in his left arm. With the steady, expert hand of a veterinarian, Von punctured his skin and pressed the plunger, injecting him with the solution. Her voice dropped to an icy calm as she added, "You'll have plenty of time to regret your choices."

"*Loslassen,*" Von said, and Zeus obeyed, letting go of Merrick's ankles.

The Succinylcholine chloride coursed through his veins, and Von could almost imagine the burn, like liquid fire igniting every nerve, trapping him in his own body. Von knew precisely what was happening—her veterinary training had taught her how the drug paralyzed every voluntary muscle, leaving its victim fully conscious but utterly helpless. He was a prisoner in his own body. Limbs jerked, and his muscles convulsed violently before surrendering to the inevitable stillness.

Von's eyes fell on the nightstand, and she noticed it had been left half open. Inside, she could see what looked like a military-grade combat knife. The blade was sharp, faintly gleaming under the dim light. She picked it up, feeling its weight, the serrated edges cold against her fingers.

"Yours, I assume." Her voice was as still as a windless lake.

His nostrils flared as he fought for each breath, tears trailing from the corners of his wide eyes and commingling with mucus from his nose.

Von took her time, enjoying the panic in his eyes. "You locked your women in, I'm sure," she continued, thoughtfully. "Why else would you have doors that lock from the outside? Here's what I think. They were locked in and made your sex slaves. Prisoners. For you to do what you wished. How does it feel to be imprisoned in your own body?"

His chest heaved in a frantic bid for air, but the paralysis moved quickly, suffocating him from the inside out. The colonel's eyes locked with Von's, wide with silent terror—bloodshot and desperate, begging for mercy she would never give. His throat gurgled, lips trembling in a futile attempt to scream, but the room stayed eerily quiet, save for the faint rasp of his dying breath.

She lowered the blade, her hands as unshakeable as her father's—Von, after all, was Dr. Anton Jörg Friedrich's daughter. The world-renowned neurosurgeon had passed down more than just his genes. He had instilled in Von a stubborn focus, a surgeon's ability to separate emotion from action. The knife slid into Merrick's flesh, deliberate and deep enough to ignite pain, deep enough to ensure he would bleed out slowly. His eyes bulged in silent agony, the only part of him that could still move. His pupils dilated, darting wildly between the knife and her face, a trapped animal silently begging for leniency he knew wouldn't come. Sweat glistened on his brow, mingling with the crimson stream seeping from the fresh wound.

His face was a mask of panic—of helplessness.

Von's expression never wavered as she carved with the blade, following a deliberate path down his torso. The S took shape, starting at his chest and ending at the soft, vulnerable flesh of his lower abdomen. It was her signature, the same mark etched into her body—a keloid scar stretching from her diaphragm to her pubic line, created by men like him. Men who stole her ability to conceive. Killed the child growing in her womb. Men who gutted her and left her to die in the cold Casper, Wyoming, snow.

A scar of valor, a scar that signified survival and trans-formation.

The blood welled and pooled beneath the blade, a single crimson statement as she signed her name into his flesh. When she finally straightened, she stared into his terrified eyes and didn't look away, her gaze steady as she watched with grim focus as her victim's body succumbed to the drug, to the wound on his belly carved by his own blade.

Von pulled out another syringe of Succinylcholine chloride. If she gave it to him, he'd die quicker, die of a heart attack, or she could let him bleed out, which would take much longer. The colonel's face was a mélange of pain and self-pity.

"Heart attack or slow bleed—what's your preference?" she

asked, her tone light and casual, like a waiter offering the evening special.

He lay there, fully conscious, his body locked in paralysis from the drug, yet acutely aware of the blood draining from his wounds. His eyes flickered toward the syringe in her hand, the faintest twitch in his pupils betraying a silent answer—or maybe a desperate plea. Should she grant him his wish? Let him have his heart attack?

Von's gaze lingered on him for a moment, calculating. The thought that he might survive, that hotel staff might stumble upon him and save him, tightened her resolve. She reached for the syringe again. She had dosed him just enough to immobilize, not to kill—but that wouldn't do. Not for him.

"This is just insurance. In case someone finds you before you bleed out." She drove the needle into his vein once more, injecting the second dose of Succinylcholine chloride. This time, it was a fatal dose. It would paralyze his diaphragm entirely, stop his heart, and induce a myocardial infarction. She watched as the subtle flickers of life faded from his eyes. "Consider this my final act of courtesy on behalf of Cheonsa Soo-Min."

A spark of recognition swept across his face, eyes growing wide.

She glanced at her watch—midnight. The twilight hour, a time caught between one day's end and the birth of another, felt like destiny. This was the colonel's twilight, the final descent before the serpent delivered its venom. It was the purest moment to seal his fate—the inescapable karma he had carved with his own hands.

TWENTY-EIGHT

THE SERPENT'S TRUTH

DETECTIVE ANAYA NAZARIO hadn't checked her emails in a week, which was why she was the queen of email hoarding. Her inbox had gotten out of control, especially since the birth of her daughter. There were thousands of emails in her work account, and because LAPD was a government agency, they weren't just protected by government-level security—she couldn't delete them.

Her personal Gmail account was a whole lot worse. Between her primary account, social, and promotions tabs—the digital hoarding had reached unmanageable levels. So, she finally took the afternoon while Ariabella was napping to delete a bunch of junk to clear up her personal account. At least ten thousand sales, social alerts, and WordPress blog posts from those she followed were sent to the trash folder. Seeing her inbox clear of clutter felt freeing.

"You look like you've got one of your migraines again." Huxley kissed her cheek. "You doing okay?"

"Tackling my inbox," Nazario groaned. "It's an absolute digital nightmare. Just finished deleting thousands of emails, and now my Gmail account is nice and empty."

"Ah ... that's why I delete them on a daily."

"I envy your discipline."

"And now, to check my dreaded work account." Nazario let her head hang forward and then feigned a dramatic attempt to bang it on the keyboard, but without making contact. Huxley laughed, his hands kneading the knots in her shoulder.

"You're so dramatic," he teased, rubbing at the tension he found there.

"You would be, too, if you were about to face this inbox," she shot back, her voice heavy with exaggerated misery.

"You'll survive."

"Barely," she grumbled, earning another laugh.

"Well, now's the perfect time with baby girl asleep. How about a fresh cup of coffee?"

"Please."

"On it." He plunked another kiss on the top of her head. "Lemme know if there's anything of interest."

"Oh, I seriously doubt it. Chief Johnson doesn't do email. He prefers in-person meetings—he's old-school that way. Hell, most of what I receive are LAPD announcements, employee training stuff, newsletters, or political government shit I could care less about."

Nazario stifled a yawn as she opened a new browser tab and logged into her secure work email, exhaustion settling deep in her bones. She, Wilson, and Huxley had spent hours the previous night poring over case files, cross-referencing intel from their interview with Vivian Kwon, and chasing fragments of evidence that refused to connect. There were gaps in the time-line that gnawed at her focus, making her feel like she was running out of time—and options.

All of it was made worse by a call they'd received from Jean Winslow. He hadn't even let her answer with a proper announcement of her name and title. "Detective Nazario—

better stand down and leave my son alone, or I swear to God I will have your badge, your partner's badge, and Agent Huxley's career. I'll end each of you. My son's a veteran. A respected member of our community. He's served his country, and all for y'all to try and take him down in this witch-hunt."

It was beyond frustrating. She wasn't one to let threats prevent her from doing her job, but it was unnerving how involved the colonel's parents were in his life. It made her wonder what lengths they'd go to cover up for their son if, indeed, he was liable for much more. Had he been the one stalking Cheonsa Soo-Min and not the other way around? Worse, had he been somehow responsible for Cheonsa's death? Vivian had warned them about the family's connections and the extent they'd go to ensure none of Winslow's transgressions were made public. What made it worse was that, legally, they didn't have a case.

Vivian's testimony, while compelling, wasn't enough to tie Winslow to anything concrete. Without physical evidence or corroborating witnesses, Kwon's statements were just hearsay—a skilled defense lawyer would dismantle it in court without breaking a sweat. In legal terms, they had no probable cause, let alone enough to secure a conviction. To bring Winslow down, they needed more than an ex-wife's accusations. They needed hard evidence—a smoking gun, a paper trail, or a credible witness willing to testify. Nazario had her hunch, had her gut, and first-hand experience with the colonel. Still, she couldn't even get him on charges of peeping on her without proof. It would be her word against his. By the time she brought it up to the law, his family would've spackled plaster over it and covered it up.

For now, Winslow was untouchable—and a night of chasing dead ends—drained every ounce of energy from her body. It didn't help that Ariabella had woken up at 3 a.m. for a feeding, leaving Nazario to juggle the delicate balance of motherhood and the unrelenting demands of her investigation. She rubbed her temples, her mind circling back to the Bureau's procedural frameworks: pattern analysis, victimology, and geo-profiling. The pieces were scattered like a puzzle—she just needed the key to make them fit.

As her inbox loaded, she braced herself, dreading the mountain of unread messages waiting for her. Her gaze skimmed over subject lines until one stopped her cold. Nazario's heart slammed in her chest, and her gut twisted in that knowing way. She hadn't even clicked on it before she called out, trying not to be too loud, afraid she'd wake their daughter. "Blake, you better come here. I think we got something."

Huxley returned with coffee, set it before her, and leaned in, reading over her shoulder.

Subject: Special Delivery: The Colonel's Twilight

Detective Nazario,

In the attached file, you'll find everything you need to expose the truth about our Colonel Merrick Winslow—his crimes, his victims, and now his reckoning. But first, take a good look at him.

The only question is, can you find him before his twilight truly ends?

Here's a hint: He's hiding in the shade, but there's no escape from the light.

~V

Embedded in the body of the email was a picture large

enough to fill their screen. Colonel Merrick Winslow was naked, wrists bloodied and handcuffed to the bed, ankles bound together by duct tape. His face was turned to the side, mouth sealed shut with silver tape. The camera captured him mid-breath, frozen in a grotesque portrait of vulnerability—of helplessness.

Huxley swiped a hand down his face and slumped in a chair beside her. "Why does this all look very familiar?"

One name came to mind, a name that burst from her lips. "Darren Fischer," she said, then added, "The handcuffs are the same, bindings around the ankles."

"All we're missing is the fire that turned him into burnt toast."

"Wait—I still have our folder on her, the one with those post-surgery images." Nazario navigated away from her email and opened a folder titled *Serpent Woman*. She clicked through the old news articles, the weight of each headline dragging her deeper into the past.

"Veterinarian Left for Dead: Miracle Survival of Dr. Wilder Agatha Friedrich, Casper's Beloved Animal Doctor," read one. The story unfolded in stark, brutal detail. The veterinarian had been viciously attacked by a group of men affiliated with the Aryan Nation. The assault came after one of them had been released from prison on good behavior. Authorities called it a ruthless act of revenge—retribution for Wilder's younger sister, Samantha, who had testified against the men in an illegal sex ring before being murdered by them. Wilder's then-fiancé had also been targeted and gravely injured in the same attack. Though he survived, their relationship did not.

The men had cut Wilder open and left her to die in the unforgiving cold. Temperatures had plummeted to a bone-chilling -20°F that night, a deadly chill that could freeze exposed skin in minutes. Her abdomen had been slashed open, forcing an emergency hysterectomy to save her life. Wilder had been pregnant at the time, making the brutality of the attack even more devastating. If not for her loyal German Shepherd, Zeus, she would have frozen in the snow. The dog had shielded her with his own body, applying enough pressure to slow the bleeding until help arrived.

Nazario's breath hitched as she switched to the next file. It was a photograph sent to her by a detective friend in Casper. The image snapped her into silence—a snowy landscape stained red, Zeus lying protectively over Dr. Friedrich's crumbled form, his fur matted with her blood. The stark contrast of the crimson against the white snow burned into Nazario's mind like a violent painting she couldn't unsee. Her throat tightened as she clicked to the next image. It was a hospital photo, a candid shot taken post-surgery. Dr. Friedrich lay pale and gaunt in her hospital bed, her sunken cheeks barely masking the determination in her eyes. Her gown was pulled up to reveal a thick maroon keloid scar in the shape of an S etched down the length of her abdomen—a cruel imitation of a snake. It was hauntingly similar to the one carved into Merrick's body.

Nazario sat back in her chair. The images swam in her mind. Blood on the snow. The lifeless stillness of Wyoming's winter. Zeus's unwavering loyalty. And finally, the brutality— the precision—that tied everything together. She met Huxley's eyes, and they lulled in confused silence. She could hear him thinking, mirroring the thoughts still whirling in her own head.

"Never thought we'd ever hear from her again," Nazario finally said, breaking the silence.

"She took a big risk," Huxley said, "coming out of retirement. Thing is, how in the world is she connected to Colonel Winslow?"

"Maybe there's something in the folder." Nazario and

Huxley returned their attention to her laptop. She downloaded the zip file and waited for it to load.

"Can't wait to see how much research she put in."

"Judging by the file size, guessing it's as thorough as anything you'd find at the Bureau."

"Hell, probably more so."

"She should hang up her veterinarian hat and work for the FBI," Nazario said.

"Or get hired to be a professional hit-woman, and speaking of—we better call Wilson and rope Deputy Frost and Chief Johnson in stat. If we don't get to the colonel quickly, we'll never hear the end of it from Jean Winslow and Mavis Lou. Their only son gets murdered because we didn't take him down when we should've?"

"You know we didn't have enough on him to hold him," Nazario reasoned. "But I bet we do now."

"Von Schlange had to have known Cheonsa Soo-Min," Huxley said.

"It's downloaded!" Nazario announced, her voice taut as she opened the zip folder. She double-checked that all the files were downloaded—confirmed. But when she went back to her inbox, the email was gone. "It took fifteen minutes for it to download and fifteen to self-destruct. Must've been sent by one of those encrypted email services that allow their clients to set these expiration timers on their emails."

"Good thing you downloaded it right away," Huxley said, leaning in closer, his presence brimming with tension. The screen displayed multiple subfolders: Phone Records, Surveillance, Emails, Metadata, and, finally, Court Documents.

"This is everything we've been missing," Huxley muttered, his tone a blend of amazement and unease.

Nazario clicked the Phone Records first. The files revealed organized logs, a meticulous record kept with each entry timestamped and cross-referenced with ownership data. One record stood out: a burner phone registered under Cheonsa Soo-Min's name.

"This number," Nazario said, pointing at the screen. "Von must've found a way to trace it. It was purchased in cash two weeks before Winslow claimed Cheonsa started harassing him. And here—" She opened a transcript of texts. "Winslow used it to text himself, fabricating threats."

Text Message Transcript:

Winslow (to his primary number): *You'll regret this, Merrick. We're meant to be together.*

Winslow (replying to himself): *Please accept the divorce, Cheonsa. Leave me alone. You need to get yourself some help.*

"The timestamps align perfectly with the days he filed his complaints," Huxley said. "This guy set her up down to the minute."

Nazario opened emails next. A flood of messages appeared on the screen, seemingly sent between Cheonsa and the colonel.

"Same story here," Nazario murmured. "These emails make it look like she was obsessed, but Von must've found a way to hack his account and pull up the metadata. Both accounts—Cheonsa's and Winslow's—were accessed from his own IP address."

Huxley shook his head. "He wasn't just texting himself. He was emailing himself, too. Building a case out of thin air. But why?"

"He divorced her when he wanted and came back when he felt like it, like she was some toy to put on a shelf, to take down and play with when he felt like it. She probably rejected him at first, which made him angry. How dare she move on? How dare she survive the divorce? How dare she reject him? That had to be the reason."

A click brought them to Surveillance. Nazario pressed play

on one of the videos, showing Winslow leaving his house late at night. He glanced over his shoulder as though he was concerned that someone was following him.

"Wait," Huxley said, pausing the video. "Look here."

He pointed to the reflection in a nearby car window. The angle showed Winslow glancing up at the camera mounted in front of his house.

"This is staged," Huxley muttered. "He wanted it to look like Cheonsa was stalking him. He didn't just manipulate the system—he created his own evidence."

Nazario nodded grimly and moved to the Metadata folder. Inside were documents and spreadsheets generated by Von's hacker, showing data extraction from Winslow's own devices.

"Here," she said, finger tracing the screen. "This spreadsheet links Winslow's personal laptop to the fake accounts he created under Cheonsa's name."

The entries revealed activity logs: more fake text messages, fabricated emails, and even a trail of internet searches about stalking laws and restraining orders.

"This ties him to everything," Huxley said, his voice sharp. "Our Serpent Woman left no stone unturned."

They opened the court documents last, finding scanned copies of Winslow's affidavits—submitted to support restraining orders against Cheonsa. "Look at this," Nazario said, pointing to a highlighted section. "Merrick claimed she sent threatening emails on this date—but the metadata proves those emails came from his device."

"Perjury," Huxley said, his jaw tightening. "This guy lied under oath and used the courts to destroy her."

Nazario scrolled through more files: a bank statement showing Winslow had purchased the burner phone, timestamps matching fabricated threats, and a final document that made her breath hitch—a hacker memo from Winslow's lawyer.

Internal Memo: Ensure all documentation presents Cheonsa as unstable. Leveraging her history of anxiety to build credibility for Merrick's claims.

Nazario sat back, her mind buzzing with weight insurmountable new evidence weighing her down. Von hadn't just sent them a case file—she dismantled Winslow's entire narrative. But Nazario couldn't ignore the message behind the delivery: Von didn't trust the system to act. She had handed them the truth and dared them to do something about it.

She read the last line once more, this time out loud. "The only question is, can you find him before his twilight truly ends? Here's a hint: He's hiding in the shade, but there's no escape from the light."

"Hiding in the shade ... hiding in the shade." Huxley scratched his chin. Ariabella began crying in the other room. "That phrase sticks out."

Nazario got up. Huxley put a hand on her shoulder.

"I got her," he said, and strode off to get their daughter. He returned with her, bouncing their little girl in his arms. He handed Ariabella to Nazario. "Think she wants to eat."

"Hey, sweet pea," she whispered, her voice soft as she cradled Ariabella close. The baby's tiny mouth opened and searched instinctively, mouthing the air in a clear sign of hunger. Nazario guided her to her breast, and her daughter latched on eagerly, nursing with a fierceness that spoke of pure need and trust.

The sacred bond, this untainted connection between mother and child, should have felt like a refuge. Instead, it was shadowed by the intrusive memory of Colonel Merrick Winslow. He sullied something precious, warping what should have been a moment of innocence into something vile. Her thoughts dragged her back to Clovis—the hum of the pump, quiet privacy meant only for her to store milk for her baby. And then, the colonel's eyes, watching her from the other side through a peephole in the wall, turning it into a grotesque violation of something so intimate. The memory was a stain she couldn't wash away, no matter how hard she clung to the purity of the present moment.

Nazario forced her mind to return to their ultimate goal—finding the colonel before it was too late. Huxley took over her laptop and began navigating back to the email. He zoomed in on the picture of Winslow, sprawled naked and handcuffed to the bed.

"I think I see something," Nazario said, then instructed. "The nightstand—there's a coffee cup on it. Isn't that the name of the hotel on the front? Can you move in closer?"

Huxley narrowed in on the coffee cup. "Bingo. Shade hotel."

"It makes sense. Hiding in the shade, but there's no escape from the light. Meaning she's exposed him. If he's at the Shade Hotel, we had better get there before anyone else. No sense in getting patrol involved or the Bureau," Nazario said, texting their babysitter, Elena Cruz, when she couldn't get hold of her best friend, Gus. "Strange, Gus always picks up my calls, especially during off hours. Phone's going straight to voicemail."

"Maybe she's working late," Huxley reasoned, then returned to the images. "Von didn't just expose him—she cut him up real good. Those lacerations look deep. Von didn't just send this for fun. That hint about him bleeding out? If we don't get to him first, either he's dead, or someone else cleans up before we can pin any of this on him."

Nazario switched Ariabella to her other breast, and the baby latched on and continued to hungrily drink her dinner. Thoughts tumbled over each other like dominoes falling in chaotic succession, one triggering the next before the last had even settled. "Elena's ten minutes away. If patrol or the Bureau shows up—and they're somehow paid off by the colonel, fuck—the evidence could disappear faster than it came in. Winslow's got allies everywhere—enough to make sure this never sees the light of day."

"Exactly." Huxley brushed his fingers across Ariabella's cheek. "If patrol or the Bureau shows up first, this turns into a circus. Evidence gets mishandled, or worse, buried. Those friends Merrick has in high places—they wouldn't think twice about scrubbing his name clean before we can even connect the dots."

"And let's not forget Von's been one step ahead of everyone." With her free hand, Nazario double-checked that the zip folder was saved on her laptop. She powered down the computer with a sharp click, the screen's glow fading like the last ember of a dying fire. The unrelenting pressure built in her chest, pressing on her as she crossed the room. Her steps were measured but deliberate, as if the floor itself might give way beneath her.

Still cradling her daughter, she sank into the couch, its cushions swallowing her like a tide pulling her under, offering no relief—only stillness. Huxley trailed after her, silent but solid. He was her lighthouse in the distance. He settled next to her, the sofa groaning under their weight.

"If we don't control this from the start, someone else will, and I don't trust anyone else to play this straight. I don't know who in the Bureau has been paid off, nor do you. You know as well as I do there are dirty agents and dirty cops," Huxley said.

Nazario nodded, her jaw set. "If he dies before we arrive, at least we'll have a clean chain of custody for everything Von sent us. But if someone else gets there first, this entire operation can fall apart. We're not letting that happen."

Nazario sat on the edge of the couch, holding their baby as the soft suckling sounds filled the tense silence. She adjusted the blanket over her shoulder, her mind mentally scrolling through all the evidence Von had sent. It felt like a ticking bomb—each minute they waited, threatening to blow the case wide open, or bury it forever.

Huxley pushed up from the couch and glanced out the living room windows. "The sitter should be here any second."

Despite the warmth of her daughter nestled against her, a current of urgency prickled at the edges of Nazario's focus, her heartbeat quickening in tandem with the ticking clock in her mind. She kissed Ariabella's tiny forehead, the baby's sigh easing tension as another grew inside her. Her breasts, now empty from the feeding, ached faintly. At least she was done—one less tether holding Nazario back.

"She's here," Huxley said, adrenaline threading his voice low to avoid waking the baby.

As the headlights of Elena Cruz's vehicle finally cut across the driveway, Nazario exhaled sharply, a mix of relief and dread flooding her system.

It was time.

TWENTY-NINE
THE COST OF LOYALTY

DETECTIVE NAZARIO and Supervising Special Agent Blake Huxley were delayed in arriving at the crime scene, having to wait for their babysitter. Elena Cruz had been ten minutes late, but given the last-minute emergency call, they were grateful their sitter was available on such short notice and had a flexible schedule.

When they'd interviewed Elena for the position, there were other nannies and caregivers with more impressive resumes. But they needed someone who could be on-call, someone who was able to drop everything and watch Ariabella at the eleventh hour. Elena Cruz was the daughter of dreamers, immigrants who'd left Guatemala's green hills to become part of the diversity of Los Angeles's melting pot of cultures. From the instant that she met Elena, Nazario figured her new babysitter had gotten her nurturing side from her mother, who was also a nanny, and her drive from her father, who opened his own auto body shop.

Her father managed to fund Elena's bachelor's and master's degrees in early education. As a biracial Puerto Rican detective who had busted her ass to climb up the ranks of LAPD—a ladder that was more of a boy's club—Nazario admired Elena's drive to become a teacher. It was a calling she approached with the same resolve that Nazario herself relied on as a detective. Hiring Elana had given Nazario a small semblance of peace, one that was rare in her line of work. But that peace was a distant thought as she pulled into the lot of the Shade Hotel.

To her surprise, her partner—who ordinarily always arrived on scene with a bag of something to eat, regardless of the presence of a rotting corpse—was already hovering over the bed, hands covered in latex gloves and carrying a notepad and pen, old-school style. Out of habit or stubbornness, Wilson preferred to write out his notes instead of typing them on his mobile, and, most of all, he hated using the voice recorder app like the green Gen Z cops fresh out of the academy.

While Nazario had gone digital—Wilson was stuck in his ways.

One thing hadn't changed: he'd arrived ahead of them, punctual and prepared. Just as they had planned and wanted, there were no patrol cars outside—no crime scene tape to draw attention. Judging by the faint odor of rigor mortis, the scene was still hot, and the body not cold enough. Blood leaked down the sides of the colonel's body, pooling around his obliques, though it wasn't a significant amount.

"Not enough blood for a bleed out, and he doesn't stink too bad," Nazario started, "so it looks like COD is something else— maybe in his bloodstream."

"You read my mind," Wilson said. "Decomp hasn't kicked in quite yet. Must've been a fresh kill."

"We believe it's our girl," Huxley said, specifying in German, "*Die Schlangenfrau.*"

"Die—what?" Wilson frowned. "English, Huxley. Don't know what the hell you just said."

"The Serpent Woman—Von Schlange—it's what she goes

by," Nazario said. "You know, that case you sat out when you had your heart attack."

"Ah ... that fun femme fatale case that had you and Huxley flying and driving all over the country." Wilson chuckled. "I missed a good one, held up in the hospital."

"The only case I couldn't close," Nazario said, frustration edging her tone.

"Can't win 'em all, Nazario. Jumped over them cliffs? Where was that?" Wilson snapped his finger. Nazario could hear him thinking, trying to recall the location.

"Point Fermin Cliffs," Huxley said, filling in the blank space left in Wilson's mind.

"Yeah, that's right—Long Beach," Wilson said. "The LAPD and the Bureau, didn't they call it in as a 10-56?"

"They never found the body," Nazario and Huxley said in unison. Their gaze met, a flicker of grim amusement passing between them before they returned to the corpse.

"It was deemed a suicide, but according to her parents, Dr. Wilder Friedrich, AKA Von Schlange, was a highly skilled cliff jumper." Nazario leaned in and started examining the corpse from the head down. Dried blood crusted around his wrists, lacerated from a futile struggle to be freed of the cuffs.

"And that dog of hers had been cliff jumping since he was a pup," Huxley said.

Wilson whistled. "I really missed a good case, almost croaking of a fat man's death."

Hands protected by nitrile gloves, Nazario knelt next to the lifeless body of Colonel Merrick Winslow. Other than the dull hum of the air conditioning, the hotel room was too quiet. Her eyes scanned to his neck. "Well, he wasn't choked out." Blood splatter speckled the floor, trailing off the sides of the body, suggesting a methodical, tidy incision. It didn't give off the pattern that would assume crime of passion, which was a lot messier, more chaotic.

The edges of the cut were sharp and deliberate and looked to be left by seasoned hands.

Hands accustomed to surgery—Von Schlange's.

Nazario wanted to deny she'd failed—failed to close *The Serpent Woman* case, failed to reach the colonel before his final breath. She wanted to deny Von Schlange was still alive, that the one case left unresolved had returned to haunt her. It was more than the email, which proved she was alive. This latest DB was her handiwork.

Wilson shuffled in his coat pocket and took out a baggie of broccoli. "So, you think it's her? That Serpent Woman?" The words muffled between crunches. "The one who took a hundred-foot dive off the Point Fermin cliffs with her dog and vanished into thin air?"

"Was wondering when you'd bring those out," Huxley said. Nazario was wrong to think Wilson would go a case without snacking on a homicide scene.

Her partner's words slipped past her ears as Nazario's focus was deadlocked at the point of incision. The nineteenth letter in the alphabet carved into Colonel Winslow's abdomen was the smooth work of someone who'd studied enough anatomy to know precisely how deep to puncture the epidermis. She adjusted her phone and took a series of photos, moving from wide shots to tight close-ups, documenting the details before anyone else could trample onto the scene. Once the call went out, the floodgates would open: the forensics team from SID (Scientific Investigation Division), CID (Army Criminal Investigation Division)—and maybe even more agents from the FBI, especially given the high-profile nature of the colonel.

Nazario knew the second she called this in, her small team of three would lose control. It was partly why they'd added

Blake Huxley to certain LAPD homicide cases. He could keep the Bureau informed while aiding in detailed research. He'd transitioned from cold cases to supervising in the BAU (Behavioral Analysis Unit), applying his expertise in behavioral-based investigations, offender profiling, motive analysis, and pattern recognition to past homicides. The supervising agent was also able to pull up the NCIC (National Crime Information Center) —a national database of crimes across the country: sex offenders, personal crimes, gang affiliations, and even general property damage like fires and more. Her baby daddy's involvement in Nazario's cases had transformed from initial annoyance to earned appreciation.

Regardless of Huxley's pull with the FBI—the Army brass would still demand jurisdiction. Military protocol would surely take over and harm any chances they had of catching Von Schlange off-guard, evaporating everything under a mountain of red tape. Huxley was kneeling on the other side of the body, his head angled for a better look. "Clean cut. No jagged edges. She knew how deep to go without hitting anything vital."

Nazario nodded. "That's her style. Controlled. Precise. And if she's indeed alive—she's escalated." She shifted her attention to the colonel's lower body, her eyes scanning for anything out of place. Her gaze stopped at his ankle. Two puncture wounds stood out against the pale skin, evenly spaced and unmistakable. Bite marks. Her breath caught. She leaned in closer, squinting to confirm.

"Shit," she muttered.

Wilson tilted his head, following her line of sight. "What? Gonna share with the class, or are you keeping secrets from us, lowly males?"

Nazario gestured with her gloved hand. "Look at the ankle. Those aren't just marks. That's a dog bite."

Huxley pressed in closer, brows furrowing, examining the wound. "Of course it is."

Nazario straightened, peeling off one glove with a sharp snap. "The email wasn't faked—it was definitely sent by Von Schlange."

Wilson's expression was a collage of disbelief and unease. "So let me get this straight. She jumps off a cliff with a German Shepherd. They both survive and now he's her muscle?"

"He's always been her reinforcer." Nazario shot him a look. "Zeus isn't just a dog. He's trained. Loyal. Based on the bite marks—Zeus is alive, and so is his handler."

Huxley reached for a penlight and shone it over the bite marks, leaning closer without touching skin. "The wounds are fresh. Could've happened within a couple of hours. The dog was used to subdue him. We already suspected this wasn't random, but now we have confirmation. Pictures in the email alone wouldn't have been enough concrete evidence."

Nazario gestured to Huxley. "We'll confirm it. Have forensics swab the wound for saliva. If Zeus left DNA, we'll have physical proof she's not just back—she's bold enough to make it personal."

"Then she must've known Cheonsa Soo-Min," Huxley said.

Wilson broke the silence. "So, I guess we're chasing after Von and her dog."

Nazario's expression hardened. "We've been chasing her. But now we know who's doing the hunting." She stood and snapped off her second glove. "We're done here. Let's get forensics and the coroner out. And put out a notice: anyone who sees a German Shepherd in the area with its handler, we want to know—stat."

Huxley nodded, voice grim. "You think anyone's going to make that connection?"

Nazario's lips pressed into a thin line. "Like I said—Zeus isn't just any dog, and Von isn't just any killer."

"Well, should we call it in?" Wilson asked, wagging his iPhone in the air.

"Better call Chief Johnson, first," Nazario instructed.

"On it." Wilson flipped through his contacts, dialed, and put the chief on speakerphone.

"Is this good news or bad news?" Chief Johnson said.

"Depends on what you consider bad news, sir."

"Oh boy, c'mon—give it to me."

"Good news is that we found Colonel Merrick Winslow. Bad news—she got to him first."

"She?"

"Our cliff jumper's alive and well, and so is her dog, apparently."

"You're kidding me? Dr. Wilder Friedrich?"

"Yep—Von Schlange—that fun case I missed while I was laid up in the hospital and almost went out John Candy style," Wilson said, dating himself. Nazario had forgotten the late comedian had died of a massive heart attack in his sleep at just forty-three years young.

"Not funny, Wilson," Chief scolded. "What's the COD?"

"We don't know, but we got here before anyone else did."

Nazario added her analysis, "I was kinda skeptical that she was still alive at first, even after she sent us some damning evidence. But this scene has her signature all over it. And those emails involved a shit ton of research, which is also Von's style. It essentially proves the colonel was framing Cheonsa Soo-Min for everything. The two cops who were shot with her gun and all the other stuff with the stalking. He was basically texting and emailing himself. We think he became obsessed with her when she rejected his advances—wanting to rekindle things after he'd left her high and dry and filed for divorce. Think he didn't like to take no for an answer and—"

"He killed her, didn't he?"

"We believe so, sir."

"Supervising Special Agent Huxley there, or is he on baby duty?"

"Yep, I'm here, Chief," Huxley replied like a student answering roll call. "Looked through all the files. Could've put him behind bars for a long time."

"So, why kill him?"

Nazario stepped in. "We interviewed his second wife, Vivian Kwon, and from everything she told us, the man had serious connections. The kind that would likely bury the whole fucking case. He wouldn't have served a day locked up. Our girl knew this, and, well, she took matters into her own hands—as is her MO."

"Shit. Wonder where she's been hiding?"

"Out of the country, I'm sure," Huxley told the chief.

"What's your speculation on the COD?"

"Well, he was naked and handcuffed to the bed like Darren Fischer, only this time, she didn't set him on fire," Nazario said dryly. "Left a signature on the body, though."

"Signature?"

"A big ol' S running down the length of his body," Wilson said.

"Did he bleed out then?"

"Doesn't look like it, sir. Bled some, but not nearly enough to be the cause of death," she reasoned. "No strangulation marks around the throat. Figure, whatever did him in might be in his bloodstream. Our Serpent Woman is a veterinarian by trade and would know what to inject to kill him. A blood panel and toxicology report should give us more info."

"Better call SID, the crime scene photographer, and the

coroner—get them all out to gather evidence. Doubt we'll find any prints, but worth trying," Chief said. "Good work, you guys, and smart call to get there before anyone else. Send me everything she sent you—think I gotta plan."

"What're you fixing to do with it, sir?" Huxley asked.

"Let's just say that if Colonel Merrick Winslow thought he could get away with what he did—well, every newspaper in the country'll be running his dark side by the morning. Anonymous source, of course. Won't be tracing it back to us," Chief Johnson said.

"Gonna make Jean Winslow and Mavis Lou Winslow real, *real* mad," Wilson said.

"Let them try suing every newspaper in the country—burn their money covering up for a cop killer, stalker, and ex-wife murderer."

They wrapped up the call, and before long, everyone was present—the science investigative division began dusting for prints and using luminol, but it didn't tell them anything. There was no blood anywhere, not even in the bathroom sink where Von might've washed up. The only blood was what had leaked from the carving on his abdomen. So, it was clear he wasn't killed somewhere else and then brought to the bed. He was likely killed right there on it. The crime scene photographer snapped pictures after SID had completed their findings.

Once the coroner, Dr. Santiago Cruz, and his assistant showed up, Nazario could tell that he had a hunch by the expression on his face.

The three of them waited with bated breath as the coroner touched the colonel's palms and then rubbed his gloved index and thumb together. "Clammy palms and the bluish tint to his skin—seen this hundreds of times. It's my belief that he died of a heart attack, but a tox and blood panel would certainly let us know. I'll also be able to make a clear determination once I open him up and take a peek at his heart," Dr. Reyes said.

"Dr. Reyes, could something've," Nazario began thoughtfully, "induced a heart attack?"

"Oh, definitely—a host of substances, when they're injected, could instigate a heart attack. Potassium chloride disrupts the heart's electrical signals, leading to cardiac arrest. Adrenaline or epinephrine in high doses can overstimulate the heart. This is especially true if the vic already had underlying conditions. I mean, even an overdose of insulin could cause severe hypoglycemia, putting a fatal strain on the heart."

Dr. Reyes paused, adjusting his gloves.

"Calcium chloride wreaks havoc by throwing off the heart's rhythm, and digitalis—"

"The digit—what?" Wilson's face screwed into confusion.

"The Latin root word—*digitus*—where we get the word finger. Digitoxins come from plants and can be used to improve heart conditions. But, in high doses, they can be toxic. Trigger a fatal arrhythmia."

"Thanks for the lesson, Dr. Reyes. Learned something new," Wilson said.

Huxley nodded, impressed. "No kidding."

"Cocaine or methamphetamine, when injected, can cause vasospasms or arterial blockages, which also can lead to a heart attack. You get my point. Toxic substances like certain pesticides or nerve agents can mimic a cardiac event." Reyes adjusted his glasses. "As I stated, I'll need to see the condition of the heart and the toxicology results. At first glance, I think it was a heart attack. What prompted it? We'll know soon enough, but there's no shortage of possibilities."

Wilson blanched. "Holy Moly—that is a lot of possibilities. I had me a heart attack last year, and all I had to do was stuff my face."

"Oh, I heard." Dr. Reyes, familiar with the team from working every homicide scene alongside them, gave Wilson a thorough once-over. "It looks like you've lost a lot of weight, Detective Wilson. That's definitely a good start."

"Looks like we're done here," Nazario said just as her phone rang sharply. She fished it out of her pocket and frowned at the Private Number flashing on the screen.

Wilson's tone turned cautious. "Who is it?"

Holding up a hand to silence her partner, she answered, "Detective Nazario."

"This is Dr. Patel from Cedars-Sinai Trauma and Emergency Unit," a clipped, urgent voice came through. "You're listed as Captain Augusta Humphrey's emergency contact." A beat of tense silence threatened to swallow Nazario whole. "She's been admitted—gravely injured. Don't know what your schedule looks like, Detective, but it's wise that you come sooner than later."

A wave of vertigo sent the room spinning, her knees buckled beneath her. She stumbled as if the ground itself had shifted, threatening to upend the very foundation of her life. Gus, Huxley, and Nazario had met in grad school at George Washington University—bonded by a shared obsession with criminology that had held strong for more than two decades.

Gripping the phone, Nazario forgot to breathe, chest constricting for air as she demanded to know, "How'd it happen?"

Huxley and Wilson's eyes never left hers. "Gunshot wound," the doctor started. "It is ... I'm sorry to tell you this, but it's critical. You might want to get here as soon as you can. Her wife, Quinn, she's been asking for you."

"Be there in fifteen." Anxious, shaky fingers cut the call. Her eyes met Wilson's concern and Huxley's sharp focus—both locked on her.

Huxley went first. "What's wrong, Anaya?"

"It's Gus." She could hardly speak, voice hoarse with emotion. "She's ... she's at the trauma unit at Cedars, gunshot wound. It's serious."

"Shit." Wilson dug in his pocket for his keys. "I'll follow you there—how bad we talking?"

Nazario couldn't speak. The awful news hit her chest with the force of a Mack Truck. Before she could answer, her phone buzzed again. Chief Johnson's name glowed on the screen, and a flood of renewed dread swamped her veins—a toxic cocktail of adrenaline and fear.

"Did Dr. Patel call you," Chief Johnson's voice began, shaky. "About Gus?"

"Just got off the phone with him." Tears blurred her vision.

"It's bad." Chief Johnson warned. "Gus was putting the pieces together on Jaxon Ryker, doing a deep dive into his operations. This guy was into all sorts of shit—counterfeit drugs, ties to some major players—but Ryker diversifies his criminality. Goes far beyond gang activity. He was branching out."

Nazario frowned, clenching the phone. "Don't know him. What does this all mean?"

"There's been a series of homicides—executions, really—tied to folks who were formerly associated with his ops or about to talk," Johnson explained. "We weren't sure they were connected at first. Narco flagged them, but since they're murders, they're falling into your lap now."

Nazario's heart sank. "So, Ryker has a hit list?"

"Unfortunately—yes," Johnson said. "Gus and her team noticed the patterns. Quinn was even digging into some of it for her story. Gus is out—these murders are officially yours."

"It makes Quinn a target now." Nazario's mind was already running through scenarios.

"We're surprised Quinn's alive and Gus is hanging on. All

of the vics were clean hits—single gunshots, no mess. One guy got torched in a car. Professional work. They were former crew members that Ryker perceived showed disloyalty or rivals who might've known too much. Gus was undercover, and once they found out she was a narc—well, you know the rest."

Nazario exhaled sharply. "How many cases are we looking at?"

"Three so far, but there could be more," Johnson said. "I'll send you the files. We didn't have enough to link them prior. But now that we know Ryker's cleaning house—we got motive. This is personal. Gus was about to blow the lid off his whole operation."

"And Quinn? Is she safe at the hospital alone?"

"Got officers there watching her, but if Ryker knows how close she was to cracking this, she's a target, too. Gus was keeping it tight, didn't want to compromise the case. She was planning to loop you in once she had concrete evidence linking the homicides to Ryker."

Nazario's jaws tightened, the weight of it all sinking into her soul. "I need everything we have on those murders—case files, forensics, all of it. If there's a connection, we'll find it."

"Already in motion," Johnson assured her. "But we must be careful. Ryker is as dangerous as they come. He has eyes and ears everywhere. The feds want Huxley to assist you."

Nazario paused to fill Huxley in on what Johnson had said, then turned the phone toward him so he could address the chief directly.

"Of course," Huxley said, catching the tail end of the conversation. "But what do you mean dangerous, sir? You realize 'dangerous' is a broad term. It can mean anything."

"Let's just say he's big on loyalty. Anyone who doesn't toe the line—former allies, informants, law enforcement. They get marked." The chief paused for a beat. "They wind up left barely breathing or not breathing at all."

Nazario made eye contact with Huxley and Wilson. "The three of us—we can handle it," she replied firmly. "We're heading to the hospital now."

"I'll meet you there," Johnson said, then added his apology as if it was his fault, "Sorry, wished we had a break between Winslow's case and Ryker's. Need to get on this before it escalates."

As she ended the call, Huxley tore out of the hospital driveway with Wilson close behind. Chief Johnson's words played on a loop, sharpening her unease. Her best friend lay in critical condition, and a dangerous criminal was prepared to execute anyone who got in his way. They had just zipped one predator into a body bag—an unexpected death. But now, a new threat loomed. Jaxon Ryker was still out there, more ruthless, more dangerous. And if they didn't stop him soon, the next body wouldn't be a surprise.

It would be a message.

THIRTY
THE SERPENT'S WARNING

VON SCHLANGE'S carry-on had enough clothes to last just a few days, mostly outfits that her Luana Abraão alias would wear and a mid-sized bag of dog food for Zeus, who wore his blue service dog vest today. From her Colcci sunglasses and long, realistic, wavy brunette wig made of human hair to her fitted V-neck black top, skinny jeans, and Steve Madden platform wedges, Von looked every bit the part—ready for her one-way flight to Rio de Janeiro.

She and Zeus were about to leave their hotel room to wait outside for their Uber when a message came through on Whats-App. Her heart sank, chest tightening with dread. She was certain nothing good could come of the message. Hesitating to look, Von quickly considered her two choices: head to the Los Angeles International Airport and pretend she didn't see the message or find out what Jefferson Pierce had to say. The hacker wouldn't bother to send her a message, not when he knew she was about to leave. Pierce and only Pierce knew her location and her next move. No way he'd message her at such a critical time—when she had to escape the U.S. unmolested—unless it were abso-fucking-lutely necessary.

Despite her nerves being on edge and heart thrusting at frenetic speeds, Von's hands, like her famous neurosurgeon father's, never shook. With a steady finger, she finally opened the app, unable to shake the dark shadow of trepidation that refused to leave her gut.

BlackDragon6: *Can't leave yet. Got a new threat. It's Detective Nazario's baby. She's in danger—her babysitter, too.*

Von: *Fuck. Who? Connected to Colonel Merrick Winslow?*

BlackDragon6: *No connection to the colonel. Someone else. Name's Jaxon Ryker. Real bad dude. Runs illegal drugs and a gang network. Takes out people that turn on him. You recall Captain Augusta Humphrey of Gang and Narco? Goes by Gus?*

Von thought for a moment, then remembered Sammy, her sister. She was saved from an illegal sex ring by Gus. If it hadn't been for the captain, Sammy would've been dead long before. Sadly, Von couldn't save her little sister and, instead, inadvertently led her into the hands of killers out for revenge. During the time Von was trying to take down members of the Aryan Nation who had attacked her and left her for dead, they found out that Von was targeting them. In retaliation, the Schultz brothers—key enforcers in Jerry Bell's Aryan crew—had brutally murdered Sammy, leaving her body to freeze in the icy winter near Boston Harbor.

Von had taken out the Schultz brothers and Jerry Bell while saving Detective Nazario, who'd been pregnant at the time. Supervising Special Agent Blake Huxley was also present at the abandoned factory near Point Fermin Cliffs in Long Beach, but neither wore Kevlar. Von recalled the weight of her father's bulletproof vest as she dove in front of the detective, shielding her from Bell's bullet before it struck Nazario's pregnant belly. Von managed to save the detective's life and the life of her unborn daughter before making a daring getaway, jumping off the cliffs and escaping to freedom without a trace except for an abandoned boat and her father's gun left behind. She didn't expect that she and Zeus would survive. But as the cold water hit her—blurring everything around her, swallowing her into the depths of the Pacific—she realized she had no choice but to fight. Her body wrestled with the tide, the water pulling her down, but she managed to break the surface—Zeus beside her.

They swam to the boat that was waiting for her, thanks to Jamal Wagner. JW was a former convict and influential leader of a predominant Black prison gang during his time in San Quinton. JW knew his rival, Jerry Bell, leader of the Aryan prison gang, from their time on the inside. He was more than happy to help her escape, so long as she kept her promise—eliminate the leader of the white supremacist gang. But now that Jerry Bell and the bastards who had killed her baby sister were dead—her past was crawling back up, breaking out of that dark room in her mind where she'd kept her sins locked.

Von snapped back to the present, returning from that dark, rainy night—the night she was sure would be her last day on Earth. She hadn't expected to rise to the surface, let alone swim to JW's six-seater Marex 375. She wasn't supposed to survive. Zeus wasn't supposed to survive. But they had—and she could've just left Cheonsa Soo-Min's ex-husband well enough alone. Left him to live his life, to continue to victimize more women, left him to escape justice, pull out all his contacts from his Rolodex, and avoid prison time.

But Von couldn't let it go, no matter how hard she tried. She couldn't let the colonel's paid enforcer—Eleutério Abraão, outrun his actions. Not after he'd taken the life of a kind, sweet man. Dr. Damião Sequeira didn't deserve to be caught in the crosshairs. He did nothing wrong. He wasn't even the one who hired Cheonsa—she did. Winslow hadn't only taken aim at his ex-wife, who was living her life happily without him. He had targeted those who were close to Cheonsa. Winslow should've had Eleutério kill Von.

Maybe she was meant to be next?

After all, she was the one who'd hired the new marketing director, but instead, an innocent man was murdered. She recalled her former business partner warning her about her new hire, concerned that the baggage Cheonsa came with sounded dangerous. Von didn't listen, and now Damião was dead. Cheonsa Soo-Min was dead. Sammy was dead. And now someone was threatening Nazario's child?

She didn't know anything about this Jaxon Ryker, but if he were anything like Colonel Merrick Winslow—he'd do anything to eliminate those who'd crossed him. Could she live with herself if something were to happen to an innocent baby? Could she live with herself if something were to happen to the babysitter?

Would the cops get to Nazario's home before she could?

And if they didn't, would another perpetrator slip through the law's grip, like so many she'd known? It happened with the Aryan Brotherhood members when all they did was serve time for dog fighting instead of the illegal sex ring because the witnesses were too afraid to speak up. Her first kill, Darren Fischer, had gotten out early on 'good behavior.' Now, if she stepped in to stop this new threat, there was a chance she'd get caught. But the alternative would mean that a baby would be kidnapped or, worse, sold on the black market.

Von felt the weight of responsibility clutching her lungs, squeezing the air from her chest. She had enough self-awareness to be in tune with her strengths and weaknesses. Von could hear Dr. Katrine Adele Friedrich, her mother, the famed psychologist, in her mind.

"You're a murderer, sweetheart," Katrine would say. *"One with a savior complex."*

Another message came through via WhatsApp, trying to pull her deeper into the darkness where she played judge, jury, and executioner. Yes, Von Schlange was a serial killer, but she also had a code. The one thing she despised more than men who preyed on vulnerable women was the exploitation of children—an act that crossed every boundary of morality and humanity.

She glanced down at the message.

BlackDragon6: *911 response times have been delayed lately. The cops won't get there fast enough, and even if they do, Ryker's men will be heavily armed. They'll take out the police before they even have a chance. You're the only one who can reach Nazario's home in time.*

Von: *Well, shit—don't have a gun, just Zeus.*

BlackDragon6: *You've never needed a gun in all the other situations. You'll need to rely on instincts. Save the baby and the babysitter.*

Von: *Why're you trusting me? You're still doing ops for the FBI—why not tell them?*

BlackDragon6: *Because I trust you to act fast, and I don't trust everyone in the Bureau. Ryker's got deep pockets like Winslow. He's bought people off before, and I don't know how far his influence goes. If I report this through official channels, it might tip him off. You're the only one I can count on to handle this without compromise.*

Von: *How do you even know Ryker's heading to the detective's home—if not already there?*

BlackDragon6: *I intercepted chatter on an encrypted channel Ryker's crew uses—mentions of Nazario's address and something about "retrieving the package." Cross-referenced it with a recent GPS ping from one of their burner phones heading in her direction. They're not there yet, but they're moving fast. You've got a narrow window to get there first.*

Von: *Was just heading to the airport. What if we're caught?*

BlackDragon6: *You can't let this one go, Von. It ain't your style.*

Von: *What're you talking about? I'm an international fugitive!*

BlackDragon6: *The FBI is desperate to stop Jaxon Ryker. They're running out of options, and you're their best shot.*

Von: *And you think they'll just let me waltz in and start working with them? It worked for you because you're a hacker. I've killed people—lots of people. Big difference.*

BlackDragon6: *Maybe not. But listen, desperate people make desperate deals. Just don't get caught before you make yours. Go —now!*

Von erased her WhatsApp history and logged out in a hurry.

She clicked her tongue and ordered Zeus to *"Lass uns gehen."* Her faithful dog sprang to his feet, followed her out the door and into the waiting Uber.

"Um ... I don't take dogs in my—"

"You do now." Von handed him a Benjamin Franklin. The apprehensive Uber driver stared at the cash for a beat before taking the money without further complaint. "We're no longer heading to the airport," Von said, giving him Huxley's Brentwood home address. An address committed to memory—along with other details: the SSA, his live-in detective girlfriend, and the mother of his child.

At Von's request, the driver eased his car to a stop several houses down. Grateful that the night veiled their presence, she and Zeus padded down the alley behind the agent's home, their steps muted against the lightless paved road. The air held the fragrance of damp earth from the light sprinkle. While it hadn't rained hard, the sparse shower wet the ground beneath them. Not wanting to leave a trail of muddy shoes and paw prints, Von guided Zeus through the darkness, moving like phantoms until the back entrance to the house emerged.

The house light glowed warmly against the dark, the cheerful tune of Frozen drifting from the television and past her ears. Crouching at the back door, she snapped on disposable Microflex gloves and worked the tension wrench she brought as she inserted the lockpick into the doorknob's keyhole. *Bingo!* The faint click of success rose above the melody of "Let It Go" just as she and Zeus slipped inside, careful not to utter a sound.

With Elena Cruz's back to her, Von seized the opportunity to peek over the young sitter's shoulder. She was slipping into sleep, eyes heavy with fatigue, the baby monitor resting next to her on the sofa. Von touched a finger to her lips—*shhh*, she silently told Zeus as she lifted a baby blanket draped over the living room's lounger and put it to her dog's nose. It only took a simple motion for her smart canine to follow the scent up the stairs with his handler closely behind.

Using his strong senses, Zeus quickly found the baby's room. Ariabella was sound asleep, chest rising and falling as a light rasp of her breath escaped her pouty lips, and the cutest little snore Von had ever heard came from her button nose. She resembled the detective with dark ringlets framing her apple face, long, dark lashes, and a full, rosy mouth slightly parted in sleep. A delicate waft of baby powder teased Von's senses as the distinct new-baby scent stirred an ache that coiled deep in her abdomen, an ache that came and went but never truly healed. Drifting hands wandered to the ridges of her maroon keloid scar, tracing that sinuous reminder etched along the length of her belly, a belly that would never feel a baby kick, never carry, never grow a tiny human.

Eyes wide open, the memories returned as if she was sitting in the front row of a stage play, seeing her body pinned down, the cold blade of the knife biting through her flesh, the feel of blood siphoning from her body, weakening her pulse with each crimson rivulet that stained the freezing snow beneath her naked body. As she looked down at the child swaddled in serene new life, raw pain rose again, one that refused to heal with time.

Motherhood was all she'd ever wanted.

Maybe someday she could adopt. Maybe someday she could explore other types of treatments, such as surrogacy. Sammy had begged Von to use her eggs, begged to let her be a surrogate. Though, the calling to seek revenge outweighed her maternal desires. Each life she'd taken came rushing back, every snatch of humanity stolen by her own hands—yet a small, stable voice whispered to her soul.

How can you expect to care for a new life if you take others?

Perhaps someone like her didn't deserve motherhood. Perhaps her calling was far greater—to protect those who deserved to live a full, long life. Perhaps her calling was to protect this sweet, precious little human, protect the detective's future—even if that meant ending her own. It was the most self-less thing she could do, and in her heart, Von knew that it wasn't just the right decision but the only one she could live with. Then suddenly, a low growl curled in Zeus's throat, a warning as his sensitive ears heard the ascending footsteps before she had. Quickly plucking the sleeping baby from her crib, Von carefully moved little Ariabella into the closet, placing her on a bed of towels and then closing the closet door without a creak.

Zeus hid behind the crib and Von behind the door. If it opened, she'd be tucked in the corner, out of line of sight. Her fingers skimmed the edge of the changing table, searching for anything she could use as a weapon. The baby monitor was too light. There were no wooden toys or glass bottles within reach. By the time the intruder stepped inside, she was out of time.

A tall man, easily over six feet, with a soft, beer-belly midsection, stepped into the nursery. Heavy, black boots—likely steeled-toed and capable of crushing Zeus along with her petite five-foot frame—pounded the wood beneath them. His crooked nose hinted at an old break, while his prominent cheekbones and sallow skin magnified the coldness in his beady, unfeeling eyes as they scanned the room like a vulture searching for its next meal.

He closed the space between the door and the crib in two wide steps. Large hands tore the cover off and then snatched the mattress out, throwing it on the floor. The angry stranger kicked the crib so hard that a chunk of the wood broke off.

"The fucking baby ain't here," he screeched, "Jax ain't gonna be happy."

Von's pulse quickened as a small newborn whimper escaped from the baby. Just as the henchman strode to the closet, Zeus sprang out from behind the crib and planted himself in front of the closet door, lips curling back in a lethal snarl, sharp teeth bared. The man narrowed his eyes at her German Shepherd, deliberately reaching for a gun tucked in a holster. Von looked closer. It was a black regulation holster, scuffed about the edges and it bore the stamp of department-issued gear. But what gave away his identity was the grip of the Glock, which also appeared to be standard issue. No mistaking it.

He pointed the gun at Zeus, cocking the trigger back, taking a step closer to the closet. And then she saw a chain about his neck and a flash of silver from his badge hanging loosely. Dressed in civilian clothes, with a police radio clipped to his belt, the cop wasn't there to save the baby—he was here to take her. No way was he undercover. Zeus snarled. Von knew her dog wouldn't if the guy were one of the good ones.

A dirty cop.

Colonel Merrick Winslow had his sins locked up tight, hidden behind the polished image of a man who'd played by the rules. At least until she sent his secrets over to Nazario. Jaxon

Ryker, though? Different story. A known criminal, a man with an empire. Winslow had the rank to move pieces on the board. Ryker had the muscle to take what he wanted.

They were two sides of the same filthy coin.

Von quickly yanked on latex gloves she always carried in her pocket.

Before the dirty cop could pull the trigger, Zeus used the power of his back legs to spring up in the air and disarm the man with a single bite. His gun clanked to the floor, bouncing off the wood with a noisy clatter. Von dove for it, as Zeus's teeth sunk deeper, drawing blood. The attacker stumbled back as the rush of pain surged across his wincing face. The crooked cop gripped Zeus's head, ready to snap his neck. Von seized her chance, fingers closing around the cop's gun that had fallen to the floor.

Von aimed the FN 509 MRD-LE, 9mm semi-automatic, a weapon she'd learned had been issued to the LAPD as of December 2024, replacing their older Smith & Wesson, Beretta, and Glock 22—the new FN 509 had better features such as a flat-faced trigger and sported a 17-round magazine capacity. The flat-faced trigger gave cops the advantage of offering consistent finger placement, allowing their fingers to rest naturally anywhere along the trigger face. It also provided better leverage so that the shooter could have a consistent, repeatable trigger press no matter the size of the person's hand, improving control over the weapon and assisting in faster follow-up shots.

Von hated guns, though she quickly researched what types were issued to cops—just to stay a step ahead and for moments like this, when she had to figure out how to handle one on short notice. Luckily, last month, she took private lessons from a marksman who trained her how to use a variety of popular handguns, from what the average gun owner purchased to all the top models given to police officers. Impressively predictable every time, the flat-face trigger broke clean at 90 degrees—that's why she trusted herself with it. Having trained extensively on the FN 509 MRD-LE, Von knew the weapon like her own hands. A gun like this didn't misfire—it did what you told it to do, nothing more, nothing less.

The Los Angeles Police Department called the 509 a much-needed upgrade, but from her extensive investigation, the red-dot optic gave the handler an edge. The tritium sights, embedded on the front and rear of the pistol, were made from tiny glass vials containing tritium, which produced a glowing green effect to aid the gun owner in lining up the shot. Setting her finger low, thanks to the flat trigger, gave her better leverage. Control. She set her feet in clock stance—twelve and three—dropping her weight forward. Face twisting with effort and fighting off the pain, the dirty cop's free hand squeezed even tighter around Zeus's neck, whose teeth were still buried in the man's wrist, blood filling her German Shepherd's mouth, streaming down the cop's forearm.

Before Zeus had his neck snapped, Von aimed the red dot at the center of his chest and pressed the trigger straight back. Fear flooded her—afraid that she might've hit Zeus. But the shot was clean and final. The FN did its job: straight to the heart. The cop's chest arched backward as if he'd been hit with one of those fifty-pound medicine balls, body folding like a bowstring. His knees shook, hand sliding away from Zeus's head. Her canine lurched free, and with the power of his one-hundred-pound muscular frame, Zeus jumped onto the body. Losing his footing, the dirty cop toppled backward like a felled tree, crashing hard enough to shake the ground beneath them.

"Ronnie! Ronnie, what's going on up there?" a man yelled from downstairs, voice edging with panic.

Von closed the distance between herself and the body in three steps. Thankful she'd put on gloves before she entered the home so as not to leave prints, she lifted the bloody badge from around his neck. Typically, a badge worn around the neck was just that—a shield, nothing more. But this one was different. The leather case had fallen open when he hit the ground, the thin chain tangled against his chest. Inside, alongside the gold LAPD badge, was his department-issued ID card. The name stared back at her: Officer Ronnie Salerno, Badge Number 50712. Despite his disguise in plain clothes, the officer didn't bother to hide his badge.

Ronnie began coughing up blood—breath shallow and almost gone.

The second man, likely another dirty cop, screamed, "Stay here, handcuffed, and shut your stupid mouth, or you'll get your brains blown out!"

Elena Cruz sobbed loud enough for her to hear from the upstairs nursery. Von sprinted to the closet and checked on the baby, who'd stopped crying. Cheeks were ruddy and still wet from tears, but the rise and fall of her little chest confirmed that Ariabella was okay. Von double-checked the baby's pulse—steady, normal. She breathed a deep sigh of relief. However, it didn't last long. The thud of charging footsteps grew louder, forcing her to shove the closet door shut in a hurry. One signal with her finger to Zeus, and he took his position next to her. This time, they didn't hide. With the door cracked closed, Von and her canine partner waited, facing the entryway.

The door swung open with a loud thud, shaking baby pictures on the walls. Yet the exhausted baby hadn't sounded awake.

The second man's voice came out frantic, "Ronnie, you alright?"

His eyes widened as he met the barrel of Ronnie's LAPD department-issued FN 509 MRD-LE, just as he pointed his own FN at Von. She knew immediately he was indeed another dirty cop. Von trained the red dot settling perfectly between his eyes—a small, unblinking point of precision. Steady and certain, the red dot hovered there like a crimson light of judgment, lingering for Von to make her final choice.

He pulled the trigger—but Von was faster. Her shot landed dead center. Bullseye.

His body crumpled in on itself, the momentum of the bullet snapping his head back. Pieces of skull and brain matter colored the eggshell walls like a Pollock painting. His gun arm jerked violently, the force sending his final shot to go wild. The bullet punched into the ceiling, tearing through drywall, chunks of it crashing to the floor around his lifeless form.

"Beschütze das Baby," she ordered Zeus. He did what he was told, waiting by the closet door to protect the baby.

Avoiding having to stare at the half-blown skull of the second cop, Von flopped the body over and found the badge in a leather case in the dead man's back pocket: Marcus Delgado, Badge Number 62189. She plunked his badge on his chest, then seized the keys to his handcuffs before charging downstairs to check on the babysitter. Elena Cruz was sobbing and shaking when Von approached her.

"Please don't kill me."

"I'm here to help you." Von uncuffed her. "Do you have your phone?"

"They threw it over near the front door."

Von found the sitter's phone and handed it to her. "Get out of here. Do not get the fucking LAPD involved. We don't know who's dirty or who's clean. It'll take you twenty minutes to get home. Wait five minutes into your drive before calling Detective Nazario. Tell her two dirty cops came in here trying to kidnap the baby. Tell them they were working for Jaxon Ryker. Can you remember that?"

"Jaxon Ryker. Two dirty cops. Baby almost kidnapped. Don't go to the LAPD," she said, words coming out in a staccato, anxious rhythm. "W-who are you? Who do I say is with the baby?"

Von tried her Spanish. *"La Mujer Serpiente mantiene a Ariabella a salvo,"* Von said, then asked her, "Did you get that?"

Tears continued to crawl down Elena's cheeks. Trembling hands wiped her eyes as she nodded, "The ... Serpent Woman is keeping Ariabella safe," she returned in English.

Von waited at the window, her breath fogging the glass as she watched Elena's taillights fade into the inky night. Once the babysitter was out of sight, she climbed the stairs slowly, heels clicking against the hardwood. Von had almost forgotten about the brown contacts and the long dark wig she hid beneath. The dramatic shift of her reflection was startling. Tonight, she was Luana Abraão—a name, a disguise, a lie. But underneath it all, she was still Von Schlange. Still the Serpent Woman. Still a killer.

Her Steve Madden platform wedges stepped around the two bodies as the air filled with the iron-heavy scent of blood. It clung to her, crawled under her skin. Zeus sat unmoved by the closet, body rigid, eyes locked on her as if asking what was next. Von knelt and scratched behind his ear. *"Guter Junge,"* she praised him in German, told him he was a good boy. She opened the closet door—and there was Ariabella, swaddled in a blanket. Stunned awake by the loud gunshots, she began to cry, face wet and ruddy. Von plucked the baby from her makeshift nest and held her close.

The infant stirred against her, then let out a louder wail. Von gathered Ariabella against her chest, the baby's tiny tears warm against her skin. She pressed a steady hand to the child's back, shushing her softly as she lowered into the rocking chair. When the baby began to calm against her, soothed by Von's caress, her heart fused with the little human in a way that wholly shattered her defenses—a bond she'd never thought she'd feel. Pure love. With each slow, deliberate motion, she rocked them both, her gaze fixed on the shadows gathering in the corners of the room.

She should have run. Every instinct screamed for her to get out—disappear before the cops, or worse, arrived. But instead, she held the delicate babe in her left arm, her right hand gripping the pistol. Even if more cops came, which side of the law would they be on? The clean ones, who'd haul her in by the book? Or the dirty ones, who'd kill her where she stood? But Von didn't move. She knew what staying meant—it would lead to her capture, the end of her freedom. Yet none of that mattered. Ensuring the baby's safety outweighed every selfish instinct she had left.

Von rocked slowly, her arms wrapped around the child. The house was silent now. The only sound was the faint ringing in her ears from the gunfire and the soft rhythm of Ariabella's breathing. It was steady, unbroken. Safe. Von leaned her head back, staring at the ceiling.

She'd made her choice.

There was no undoing it now.

THIRTY-ONE

THE ALLIANCE OF NECESSITY

DETECTIVE ANAYA NAZARIO sat beside her best friend's hospital bed, her shaky fingers clasping Gus's limp, cold hand. The rhythmic beeping of the monitors filled the room, a marked disparity to the heavy silence between breaths. Across from her, Quinn—Gus's wife—sat slumped in the chair, shoulders rounded by the unbearable weight of watching her partner fight for life. Three devastating, precise gunshots to the gut had left Gus teetering on the edge. The massive blood loss made every heartbeat a fragile miracle of survival.

Earlier, Chief Johnson had visited Gus, but once Nazario, Huxley, and Wilson showed, the doctor ordered someone to leave in order to reduce the number of bodies filling the small space. Post-COVID precautions required limited visitors at one time. She'd been waiting for Gus to awaken, though the doctor warned her not to get her hopes up. Nazario just wanted to hear Gus's voice again. Wanted the promise of a full recovery that the surgeon couldn't guarantee. While this wasn't the first time Gus had been shot, it was by far the worst.

The three bullets had torn through her abdomen, a dangerous area packed with vital organs and major blood vessels. The damage was catastrophic—beyond massive blood loss, the looming risk of infection from perforated intestines was what the medical staff was mainly concerned about. Nazario's best friend was no stranger to pain, but this time, survival felt like a cruel gamble against impossible odds. The doctor had assured them of the old generic term that things could've been much worse.

"It's a good thing we were able to retrieve the bullets. There are times, depending upon the location of the bullet, when we're unable to. In the case of Captain Humphrey, we were able to retrieve all three," the doctor had told them when they'd arrived two hours prior. "Our number one, most important goal was to stop the bleeding and prevent fatal blood loss. We achieved that, so the surgery was a success."

"What's her recovery time looking like?" Nazario asked the doctor.

"Presuming she lives. Not trying to sound grim, but there's always the possibility of post-surgery complications," warned the doctor grimly. A cold weight punched the air from Nazario's lungs, leaving her breathless, suffocating. "She'll be in ICU for at least another week. Recovery time can stretch anywhere between four to six weeks. As I told Chief Johnson of Homicide and Captain Gus's boss—Deputy Chief Drake of Gang and Narco—I'll not be advising her return to duty until, at the very least, the six-week mark and no sooner than that. Even if she can regain mobility, the captain underwent serious abdominal surgery. We need to ensure that there are zero complications with impacted organs."

Wilson whistled, and Nazario groaned. "Six weeks is an eternity in our line of work. Gus would want to get back to her case ASAP. Whether the doctor's like it or not."

"Yeah, Gus is not one to want to lay around for nearly two months," Huxley said.

"She'll be miserable if she can't return to work, stat," Quinn said, gripping her wife's hand.

"Oh, I know I was after my heart attack last year. Held up for three months. Wasn't able to return to work until I cleared ninety days. Ninety days of pure hell, going from eating pizza and In-N-Out to salads and a two-thousand-calorie diet. Went from sitting on my ass and stuffing my fat face with junk food to owning a Fitbit and going for walks." Wilson chuckled, patting his now-flat belly. "Finally, no more looking like I was more pregnant than Nazario was with Ariabella."

Nazario and Huxley tried to keep a straight face but failed miserably. Their smiles broke through almost in unison. Wilson always had a knack for easing tense situations. A quiet laugh escaped Huxley while Nazario shook her head in reluctant amusement.

"That heart attack might've been what saved your life, Detective Wilson," the doctor told her partner, then pivoted back to Gus, nodding at his patient. "Look, I know the captain's working an important case, and while I'm not privy to the details, judging by Chief Johnson and Deputy Chief Drake's response—I get that it's one of those once-in-a-career, critical assignments. However high-profile and whomever this criminal you're chasing might be, I know one thing—they weren't just aiming to injure. They were aiming to kill. These things happen. I get that it's a part of the job. What you all do is dangerous. I've patched up plenty of you blue folks over the years. Always the same—can't wait to get back to work, no matter what shape you're in. But it's also my job to ensure that my patient is fully healed before returning to duty," the doctor said. "Now, I'll let you visit for another half hour or so, but my patient needs rest. So, I kindly ask that you don't extend your stay for much longer than the allotted time."

When the doctor left to give them some alone time with

Gus, a spell of tense silence settled back in the hospital room. Gus finally stirred, and her eyes fluttered awake. A thin smile crossed her lips, even as she winced from the pain. She fixed them with her amber eyes. Quinn leaned in and kissed her on the lips. A low sob shook her shoulders as she buried her wet face in the crook of Gus's neck.

"I should never have told you about Jaxon Ryker. Never should've roped you into the story," Quinn wept. "When I heard that you were shot three times, I thought you were dead." Once she finally pulled away, her cheeks were damp, hands trembling against Gus's shoulder, as if letting go might mean losing her all over again. "Fought my way into your room, but they forced me out. There was so much blood. I totally freaked out. Screaming at the nurses and the doctors to save you. You were unconscious. Shit, I thought you'd never wake up."

Gus smiled at her wife, gently taking Quinn's hand from her shoulder and pressing her lips to the back of it. "You're good—damn good, one hell of a crime reporter," she started weakly. A laborious breath escaped her lungs, eyes blinking slow and drowsy. "If you hadn't ... broken the case, we—" Gus frowned as if trying to focus, her mind and body still returning from a brutal shooting and a lifesaving emergency surgery that had left her in critical condition. "Might've been too late. But Gang and Narco—that's my turf. I ... I would've found Ryker. They'd have sent me under ... undercover anyway. You know that babe."

"I know, but why do I feel like it's my fault?"

"It's not your fault, nothing you could've done to stop the hit," Nazario said.

"First time my cover's ever been blown." Sluggish eyes trailed to Nazario. Exhaustion twisted Gus's face. "Feels like I fucked it up. Like, I have no idea how Ryker knew that I was a cop. I'm always careful."

Quinn grew nervous. She slumped back in her chair and

buried her face in her hands. "It's my fault. They ... they followed me. They saw me with you."

"What?" Gus struggled to sit up. "Feels like my guts are on fucking fire."

"Sorry, I didn't tell you. I wanted to run the story so badly that I ... I ignored the photos."

"What photos?" Gus looked visibly pissed—anger and perplexity tightening her features.

"Maybe we should step out," Wilson added gently, "give you guys some privacy."

"Good call, think we should leave you two to talk alone," Nazario agreed.

"Yeah, we'll be outside if you need us." Huxley checked his watch. "Got about twenty minutes before the doctor kicks us out."

"We're family, and no one's leaving," Gus bit out between clenched teeth. "Chief Johnson and Deputy Chief Drake, the new head of Gang and Narco, will be putting y'all on this. We all need to hear this. Tell us, Quinn. What fucking photos?"

Quinn froze, her face paling as Gus's words hung heavy in the air. Her hands fumbled with the edge of her sleeve, avoiding Gus's scorching gaze. "I didn't know how to tell you," she said, her voice barely above a whisper.

Quinn always had a youthful look for someone in her thirties, but now, with her shoulders sagging and guilt making her seem small, to Nazario, her best friend's wife looked even younger—like a teenager caught lying to a parent, bracing for the fallout.

"We could always talk about everything and anything." The words were strained.

Nazario plucked a bottle of water from her hospital tray and put it to Gus's lips.

After a sip, with sheer will and stubborn conviction, she

continued, questioning her wife, "What've you been keeping from me, Quinn?"

Gus was livid. Beneath it, the sting of newlywed bliss colliding with reality.

"A couple of weeks ago, I got an envelope at the office. It had ... photos. Of us. Together. At home, out on a walk, little moments no one should've seen." She hesitated, rubbing her throat as though it was tightening. Tears brimmed in her eyes. "There was a note. It said if I ran the story on Ryker, they'd kill you. I wanted to bury it, to pull out. But the story was too big. The Los Angeles Sentinel has been hurting. Several times, we've been on the brink of bankruptcy. We needed this article. My boss ... she said if I didn't publish, I'd be fired."

Gus closed her eyes. "So, you chose your job over my life?"

"I'm not so sure it's that simple, Gus," Nazario defended.

"The fuck it isn't." Gus slammed the bed with a fist, only to wince from the pain.

Huxley grabbed Nazario's hand and squeezed, giving her silent support.

Quinn's voice broke as she looked up, pleading. "Baby, I thought I could handle it. Thought I could keep you safe, keep my job, and expose him. I didn't think they'd actually figure out who you were. I thought they were bluffing—"

"Bluffing?" Gus's eyes flew open, shooting daggers. A semblance of the old Gus—and her iron strength—was return-ing. "You're too naïve, Quinn. I've told you so many times. It could cost you, cost us. Jaxon Ryker's a shot caller, a goddamn crime lord. He's a heavyweight and one sophisticated gangster—he's as high up on the chain as they come!"

Quinn's hands fell limply to her sides, defeated. "I'm sorry. I can't change my decisions. I know that. I had no idea this would happen. It's all on me. I should've never run the story, but I was in a hard place. It made me angry that they were trying to blackmail me. The L.A. Sentinel needed this story."

"And I needed to *not* get fucking shot. Three fucking times. Now, I'm off the case for, what, at least a week—"

She hadn't heard her best friend use so many F-bombs in a hot minute. "Um," Nazario cleared her throat. "It's more like six."

"Six motherfucking weeks? Are you kidding me?" Gus looked like she was ready to punch a hole in the wall, muscular arms flexing, jaw muscles dancing as she ground her molars the way Nazario had seen when the captain was highly agitated and pissed off. Raw pain—both physical and now emotional—cut through Gus, sharp and undeniable.

"Doc said he's not releasing you back to duty until you've fully healed," Huxley reported. "Said it'll be six weeks at a minimum."

The room fell silent once again, tension thick enough to choke on. Nazario didn't need words to know Gus was on edge —her rigid posture, the sharpness in her eyes, and the anger no longer simmering beneath the surface but volcanic, ready to erupt.

Wilson offered a gentle reminder, one aimed at mediating the situation. "No one wins in a damned if you do, damned if you don't situation," he started, voice keeping calm. "Take it from someone who's been divorced more times than I'd like to admit—the two of you can get through this, and you will. Why do I think so? You're my favorite couple. You're meant for one another. Twin souls, as they say."

Nazario understood Wilson's point—Quinn might've made a grave mistake, but it was a difficult position to be in.

Quinn stood to her feet, wiping her face. "I love you, Gus, and I said I'm sorry, and I know that's not good enough." She tried on a brave smile that didn't quite reach her sad eyes. "If I had to do it all over again, I would've never published that stupid article. I can always get another job, but I can't replace you."

Gus said nothing, fury radiating from her like steam escaping a pressure cooker about to blow. Quinn grabbed her purse from the bedside table and dug her keys out, gripping them in her hand.

"Been here all day. Haven't showered or eaten anything. Need to go home, take a bubble bath, order Chinese. I'll come back tomorrow to check in on you," she said as Gus avoided her eyes, staring out the hospital window.

Nazario could see Gus's longing to escape, the longing to be anywhere but bedridden in a cold, sanitized hospital room. The detective recalled being in a similar situation when she had her knee crushed by a former UFC champion turned drug dealer. Despite having a full leg brace for three months, she didn't have to stay in the hospital for long and didn't require six weeks off duty. But she also empathized with the guilt her best friend's wife was experiencing. Feeling the weight of Quinn's turmoil, she pulled her into a reassuring embrace, offering comfort.

Quinn sobbed against Nazario's shoulders. "It'll be alright. It's done now. We can't change the past. Gus is alive. That's what matters now," Nazario consoled her.

Her best friend's wife nodded, wiping the wet from her face yet again, and then excused herself, leaving the room without so much as a glance back.

Nazario's phone rang. She looked down at the caller ID— Elena Cruz.

"It's the babysitter," she told Huxley. "Hi Elena, we're about to wrap up. Had to stop at the hospital to visit a friend. We'll be on our way—"

"Detective Nazario!" Elena's voice was tumbling out in a frantic rush. "Oh my God, you have to listen—"

"What is it?" Nazario shifted the phone to her ear. Huxley glared at her with concern.

"What's going on? Is everything okay?" He leaned in closer. Wilson furrowed his brows, while Gus's breathing became short and quick, worry etched across her face.

"Two cops, they came to the house. But they weren't on the level. They—they tried to take Ariabella. They were working for someone ... what's his name, what's his name Jake—no—Jaxon Ryker! That's it. I didn't know what to do. I thought they were going to kill me."

The world ground to a halt. Nazario's chest tightened, each breath a desperate fight for air. The tight panic squeezed around her lungs returned, constricting her breath. Gus had just been shot. No doubt Ryker's men were studying all of the captain's closest friends and loved ones long before the shooting, determined to make an example of anyone who crossed him. And Nazario, being Gus's best friend, made their hit list.

"Where's ... where's the baby now?" Nazario clutched at her chest.

"A woman—she showed up—told me not to go to the LAPD. She said ... she said they don't know who's dirty or clean there." Elena's voice hitched. "She called herself *La Mujer Serpiente*. She said she'd keep Ariabella safe, told me to ... to call you. She told me to leave. Afraid I'd get hurt. I'm on my way home, but ... Oh God, Detective, what's going on? Who are these people?"

"Listen to me. Do you think you're being followed?"

"N-no, I don't think so ... I was careful. This Serpent Woman ..." she continued, her voice stammering. "I think she ... think she took them both out. Heard two shots. Oh God ... this has never happened to me before. I'm scared. Sorry, I wanted to keep the baby safe. Had no idea this would happen."

Elena wasn't just crying; she was sobbing hysterically.

Nazario tried her level best to maintain calm despite frantic panic and adrenaline coursing through her body.

"Go home. Lock the doors. Don't talk to anyone. I'll see if I can get a squad car to make some rounds—"

"No!" She sobbed louder now. "What if they work for this Ryker guy?"

"Okay, okay. Go home and lock the doors. Call me if anything happens." Nazario cut the phone and addressed watchful eyes.

"What's wrong, Anaya? What happened?" Huxley gripped her shoulders.

"Jaxon Ryker—two of his men were at the house. They tried ... they tried to kidnap the baby," Nazario said. "Elena was at the house when the men barged in, but she wasn't alone. She had ... she had help."

"Shit!" Gus pounded a fist on the bed for a second time. "Where's the babysitter?"

"She was relieved by ... by someone we thought was dead," Nazario explained, thinking of Von Schlange. "But it gets worse. The men working for Ryker—they were both cops. Dirty."

Nazario tried to breathe, clutching her chest as a wave of panic seized her heart.

"Breathe through your nose. C'mon, breathe," Wilson coached gently. "Where's the baby now? Who's with the baby? Is the babysitter okay? Is she still there?"

"Babysitter is on her way home. Was told not to go to the PD because we don't know who's on Ryker's payroll," Nazario explained.

"So, the baby's alone? Who's with Ariabella?" Huxley was shaking.

"Von Schlange—she apparently killed both cops. She's ... she's with the baby now."

"The Serpent Woman? The one that was called in as a 10-56?" Gus looked stunned.

"She was a skilled cliff jumper—her and her dog. It was no suicide. They're alive," Nazario said. "What do we do? Did you know there were cops answering to Ryker, Gus?"

"No, I did not. The men who ambushed me were both wearing ski masks."

"So, they could've been cops?"

"I wouldn't put it past Jaxon Ryker. He's not some low-level thug. He's sophisticated, calculated, educated. The high-profile danger you don't see coming. Like tonight. Listen to me: do not involve patrol. Don't call it in. Not yet." Gus went rigid, eyes wide with alarm. "Elena's right—we don't know who's clean. Just get out of here. Now. Go to your baby. And call me the second you've got the 411."

Nazario swallowed the question burning in the back of her throat: *What the hell do we do about Von Schlange?* But it didn't matter—not now. There was only one priority: her baby, fragile and helpless, was in the hands of the Serpent Woman, the lethal and unpredictable serial killer, the child's unexpected protector.

THIRTY-TWO
THE BLACK NOVA

VON FOUND a bottle of breastmilk in the fridge downstairs and warmed it up in a warmer with the cute name Mom Cozy—a gadget designed to heat without risking the delicate nutrients. It took her a few fumbling minutes and a quick Google search to figure it out. Once the bottle was ready, she carried it up to the nursery on the second floor, settled in the rocking chair, and began swaying as she fed a very hungry Ariabella.

The baby's hunger was brief but urgent. Within minutes, she was drifting back to sleep, her tiny chest rising and falling against Von. She cradled the infant close with her left arm while her right gripped the FN 509 MRD-LE pistol. Her gaze darted to the windows and doors. Every little creak of the house sent her on edge, sharpening her focus. It was hell, not knowing whether someone else connected to Jaxon Ryker might burst through the doors and charge into the home—Von wasn't about to be caught off-guard.

Von knew she was probably in over her head, but she'd die to protect the child.

She could've been on a plane heading one-way to Rio de Janeiro, escape yet another two bodies tacked onto her kill list.

Von could've continued being Luana Abraão until she returned to Brazil, returned to her veterinarian clinic, returned to the culture she'd grown to love, and the best coffee anywhere in the world. But now, everything changed. While the baby snored softly, Von thought about her last WhatsApp exchange with BlackDragon6—Jefferson Pierce had given her a tip, told her what she needed to do in order to avoid prison time. Talking her way out of a jail cell didn't seem all that simple. Murder was still murder. If every parent of an abused child could go after the perpetrators and kill them without consequences, it would be a different world entirely—a world without law, without order. It would be a world where justice was twisted into personal vendettas, and chaos would reign as everyone took the law into their own hands.

No, the legal system wasn't built on an eye-for-an-eye philosophy.

However, Von had turned her own world into a passion for extinguishing those who had escaped justice and the law. She was a serial killer. The words echoed in her mind, foreign and surreal, as though they belonged to someone else's story, not her own. Just thinking about them felt like stepping outside of herself, like watching a stranger from afar—someone with her face, her hands, and her choices, however detached from the person she believed she was.

The realization didn't just creep in; it crashed over her, heavy and suffocating, as if the air itself had thickened with the weight of her truth. The label, ugly and inescapable, clung to her like a second skin—but unlike a snake that could shed its own, this one remained: uncomfortable, undeniable. Yet it had become a shield she carried with equal parts pride and defiance, a paradox she could neither escape nor deny.

There was a spell when she dreamed, a time when her mind and body would remind her of each killing, play it back to her as she slept. Only, Von never woke up in a cold sweat, never screamed out, never thrashed around in her sleep. Each and every time she had those vivid dreams, Von awoke pleased with herself. Pleased with the actions she took, pleased that all of her calculated preparations were from someone with a sound mind. Someone who would never claim insanity. Someone who was neither a sociopath nor a psychopath. Someone who was simply not going to allow evil to get away with evil. Someone who knew exactly what she was doing, knew exactly who was guilty, how to find them, and how to execute every last one.

Her only regret was that Sammy, her little sister, had been sacrificed.

The loss of her only sister had etched a scar that time could never erase. Now, the deaths of Cheonsa Soo-Min and Dr. Damião Sequeira added to that scar, building a callous over the pain and regret she would be forced to live with for the rest of her life. She didn't regret, however, being Ariabella's protector. There was no regret in ensuring that—whether Detective Nazario had been hunting Von or not—Nazario's child and the life of her sitter, Elena Cruz, remained safe.

The sound of the door slamming open jolted Von's heart, though she kept calm under the pressure, under the potential new threat. Rocking the chair back and forth with the sleeping babe in her arms, she racked the FN back, preparing to shoot at the incoming party that would come through the door.

Footsteps pounded up the stairs, the door slamming hard against the wall as it flew open. Just as she was ready to open fire, Detective Anaya Nazario and Supervising Special Agent Blake Huxley burst in with frantic shouts: "LAPD!" "FBI!" Both with weapons drawn, they came face-to-face with Luana Abraão. Confusion etched across their faces as they searched hers for any trace of the old Von Schlange. Their gaze shifted down to a growling Zeus, then back to her, before finally settling on their infant cradled in Von's arms.

The two were focused on her with parental fear, so much so that they hardly acknowledged the two bloody corpses of the dirty cops who had almost kidnapped their child. A pang struck Von's heart, sharp and unrelenting, as she drew the baby closer. It wasn't hers—she knew that—but for a fleeting second, she let herself pretend. The child she'd lost six years ago, ripped from her in the blood-soaked attack that nearly claimed her life, seemed to breathe in the soft rise and fall of the infant's chest. This is what it would feel like, she thought—what it should have felt like. To cradle a life so small yet infinite, to quiet their cries with whispered promises. To guard them against the world that felt colder with every breath. To know that terror didn't end when the fight did, but lived in the dark corners of a parent's heart, always whispering the same unthinkable fear: *What if I can't keep them safe?*

"Where's Von Schlange?" Keeping his weapon on her, Huxley's voice landed heavy, as if he'd slammed a fist on the table of her mind, pulling her back to the room.

Von lifted her hand, the one still holding the FN 509 MRD-LE. Nazario snatched the pistol from her hand, then said, "You had some work done. I almost didn't recognize you." Nazario squinted her eyes, scanning Von's face again before turning to Huxley with her observations. "Look at her eyes and jawline—contact lenses, a wig, but those eyes and the square jaw. It's her. Had work done to her lips, something with the forehead to make the eyebrows look higher, more arched. Breast augmentation, but those arms—I will never forget those muscular arms anywhere. Haven't met that many women, with the exception of Gus, with that type of weightlifting physique."

"Holy shit," Huxley said, stepping closer to Von, tilting his head as if to try and find a trace of what she'd once looked like. "That's a damn good disguise."

"She's fed. Just downed four ounces of breast milk. Used the warmer instead of the microwave, so to keep the nutrients of the breast milk intact," Von told them. "I'd prefer the two of you put your guns away. No need for more bloodshed today."

"Not a chance in hell." Huxley took a step even closer, his Glock 19 poised inches from Von's temple. He ordered her, "Hand Ariabella over to Detective Nazario. Do anything stupid, and I'll drop you with one clean shot."

Nazario slid her gun into the holsters strapped to her hip and moved toward the rocking chair with cautious intent, her gaze locked on Von like a lioness watching a threat near her cub. Tension seemed to radiate off the detective, the unspoken question hanging in the air: *Would Von make a move?* The child stirred slightly in Von's arms. Her small weight had grounded Von through the entire ordeal. She was an anchor to a sense of purpose that felt unshakeable—every action, every deadly decision, justified by the need to eliminate any threat to this child's life, even if it meant trading her freedom for a prison cell. She had protected the baby from monsters tonight, but knew Nazario wasn't looking at a hero—she was staring down a killer.

Von handed Nazario the sleeping baby, tears welling in the detective's eyes as relief swept through her. Nazario thanked her for keeping the baby safe, just as Supervising Special Agent Huxley advanced, handcuffs catching the light with an ominous glint. Von froze, her pulse thundering in her ears as her entire life unraveled before her eyes in a rapid, merciless reel. She knew her day would come, knew that this was her fate, and wondered if there were any words she could say that held the keys to her freedom. As if someone had read her mind, the door downstairs boomed open.

"Were you expecting someone?" Huxley bit out.

"No," Von said evenly.

Huxley didn't hesitate, barking, "Stay down!" to Nazario as he leveled his semi-automatic at the open door.

Footsteps thundered up the stairs, each one pounding like the prelude to bedlam. Nazario gasped, clutching her child close to her chest, wide eyes darting to Huxley. His grip on his Glock tightened as he trained it on the entryway. Four men in black suits stormed in. Three of their faces were concealed by eerie Ronald Reagan masks. Their steps were sharp and synchronized, each armed with suppressed SMGs that glinted under the nursery's light. The fourth man, however, entered last, his face unmasked and his presence more unsettling than the rest. His face was lean, angular, with cold dark eyes that swept the room like a searchlight. A faint scar ran along his right cheek, almost unnoticeable, but it added to the sense that this man had seen violence up close.

Von froze. She couldn't place him, and judging by the perplexed looks on Huxley and Nazario's faces, they likely didn't know the intruders either. Everything about the man screamed authority, the one in charge. Unlike the masked men, who moved with the precision of trained operatives, this one had something else—a quiet confidence that made him stand apart. His black suit wasn't just tailored—it was impeccable. As if creases didn't dare settle on him. He was calm, too calm like he'd walked into this kind of shitstorm a hundred times before.

Then he spoke. "Drop your weapon, Supervising Agent Huxley."

His voice was steady, almost conversational, but the weight behind it made Von's stomach twist. It wasn't a threat. It was a command. The kind that didn't leave room for negotiation. She glanced at Huxley, who hadn't flinched, his gun still trained on the leader. Unable to ignore the directive that shifted the air,

Huxley lowered his gun. Whoever this man was, he wasn't here to take orders. He was the one giving them.

"My name's Lucius Cain—Commander of Operations for Black Nova. There'll be no need for those handcuffs. Our ... Serpent Woman *and* her canine belong to us," Commander Cain said, as though she were property.

"I don't belong to anyone," Von spit out. "Who the fuck are you?"

"The LAPD has not informed me of your ... *group*. You with the CIA?" Detective Nazario asked, turning to the father of her child. "Huxley—you familiar with Black Nova?"

"Negative," he said, "they're not affiliated with the FBI."

"Black Nova is the perfect blend of the FBI and CIA—we're a hybrid, if you will," Cain explained in an even, neutral tone.

"What do you want with our suspect?" Nazario said.

"You're on a need-to-know basis," the commander said. "We'll be in contact."

One masked man shot a tranquilizer dart to the back of Zeus, immobilizing him. Von knew it was the kind of sedatives that put larger animals to sleep and were sometimes used in her clinic on untamed, aggressive dogs.

"You better not have given him an overdose, or I'll kill you," Von warned.

Two of the men threw a black bag over her head and pinned her arms down. She thrashed, kicking wildly, but despite all her efforts and weight training—they were much stronger. Within seconds, a needle pricked her shoulder. The drug, whatever they gave her, began to slow everything down. Von struggled against the encroaching darkness, fighting to remain awake, conscious. She clawed at the fading edges of awareness, desperate to grasp any lingering detail, any fragment of information she could hold onto. Every second mattered—anything she managed to remember now might become her lifeline in the uncertain future.

The last words she heard were "Dr. Wilder Friedrich—Von Schlange—is a federal asset now, protected under classified jurisdiction." *Federal asset?* Von's mind reeled, the terminology jarring. What could it mean for her? For Zeus? The possibilities weighed on her, each one heavier than the next. "Your cooperation, Detective Nazario and Agent Huxley, isn't really required —but it's expected," Cain said before everything went black.

THIRTY-THREE

THE COST OF CONTROL

THEIR HOME WAS NOW a crime scene. The air was a collage of gunpowder and the coppery, metallic scent of blood. Nausea churned in her stomach, visceral and sour. Nazario tried not to squeeze her sleeping baby, not to hold her too tight. They almost took her. Had almost taken everything from Ariabella to leave her motherless. If they'd succeeded, who knew if Nazario would ever have seen her daughter again?

While many stolen babies were found, many were not. The idea that Ariabella was nearly kidnapped was too much to comprehend—it almost didn't feel real. Her breath hitched, and her throat tightened. She and Huxley hadn't addressed the two dead traitors lying in pools of blood—Officers Ronnie Salerno and Marcus Delgado—neither of whom they knew. Nazario, working homicide, didn't always know every single beat cop by name. Different departments and alternating shifts made it hard to know all the blue family members.

But none of that mattered now—Von was gone.

She stood frozen, her mind splintering under the weight of what had just happened. It felt unreal, like she was trapped outside herself, watching it all unfold in slow motion. A battle raged inside of her, a war between duty and gratitude. Feel guilty for trying to arrest Von Schlange, the killer? Or feel even more remorseful for not protecting the woman who had kept her baby alive? They could only watch helplessly as Von's slumped body—and that of her dog—were carted off by the men in black suits and rubber Ronald Reagan masks. The Black Nova men worked with chilling exactitude, their methodical discipline a hallmark of highly trained, specialized operatives, as Von and Zeus were loaded into a black SUV with limo tint that prevented anyone from spying within.

Once the doors to the vehicle slammed shut, that was it. The suspect Nazario and Huxley had been after since the string of murders associated with the Aryan Nation Brotherhood and their illegal sex ring operation was out of their custodial control. Nazario didn't know what this would entail, had no idea what the fuck Black Nova even was, and what this would mean moving forward as they investigated homicides associated with Jaxon Ryker and Merrick Winslow. The chain of command had changed, leaving the investigation in unfamiliar hands. The question of authority hung heavy: who would report to whom now? Did this reshuffling mean Von Schlange—and perhaps even her loyal dog—were poised to become high-level operatives within a shadowy, specialized organization?

"Wait!" Nazario surged forward, handing her baby girl to Huxley. "Why's Von a federal asset? What the fuck does that even mean?"

Commander Lucius Cain squared his shoulders as he stood, observing his men as they slammed the SUV's door. "She's a federal asset because she's valuable in ways you can't imagine, or maybe you've already tasted what that looks like. Her skills, her impressive tenacity, and methodology for accomplishing tasks—or in your language—getting shit done, if you will, are a tad above your pay grade, Detective, and yours,

Agent Huxley," the commander explained, steepling his fingers behind his back as he casually strode toward the waiting SUV. "Of course, please know that the two of you are … appreciated. But there's a time and place for rule-abiders and a time and place for those who know just how to break them."

One of the men garbed in a Reagan mask tilted his head at her, "As we've explained, the Serpent Woman is no longer your concern, Detective. She's ours now. You'll be briefed on next steps, which would entail the LAPD and the FBI's full collaboration with Black Nova."

The masked operative got in the driver's seat and waited for Commander Lucius Cain, who entered the front passenger seat. Huxley stepped to her side, and the two watched the SUV disappear down the street.

Very quickly, the house had been roped off with yellow crime tape. The iron tang of blood thickened the air, the scene around her a blur of bodies and flashing lights. Nazario and Huxley were soon outnumbered as everyone needed on the scene swarmed their home. The crime scene photographer didn't waste time snapping all the necessary pictures. At the same time, Ellen Yang and Chuck Whittier from the Scientific Investigation Division dusted for fingerprints and sprayed luminol across the stairs and nursery, aiming for a clearer picture of how the situation unfolded.

"We'll run the fingerprints, just wanted to make sure there wasn't a third perp on the scene that escaped," Yang said. "SID will examine all the evidence and get back to you if something changes. But it looks like the shots were pretty straightforward."

"They came in to get the baby, and Von shot them," Nazario reasoned. "It's what she told us anyway."

Whittier added, "And from what we gathered, it does look like we've been able to corroborate her statement unless we've managed to pick up fingerprints that don't match anyone on scene."

"Likely not," Huxley said, bouncing the baby just as Detective Wilson showed up.

"Lemme take baby girl off your hands," Wilson offered in a gentle, soothing tone. Huxley thanked him and handed Ariabella over. "Y'all need a moment to breathe. You've had quite the night."

"You can say that again. Don't think we can live here after this," Huxley said.

"We're not getting run out of our home," Nazario returned.

"You really want to stay here after people were murdered?" Huxley's brows rose.

"Where else would we go? I'm not staying at some hotel, racking up debt. It's not like we haven't seen dead bodies before," she said.

"True, but we haven't had people killed in our home until now," Huxley said. "Never had to live where people died."

"It's a good thing you've got wooden floors as opposed to carpet," Wilson said. "A little bleach and some air freshener will fix her up in time for bed."

Huxley groaned a low, reluctant sound that spoke volumes. He wasn't convinced, not by a long shot, but Nazario could see it in his eyes. He'd do as she said. He always did.

After SID was done investigating the scene, gathering evidence, and taking DNA samples from under the nails of the deceased, the coroner and his assistant extracted the two dirty cops in thick blue body bags. After making a call, Chief Johnson arrived in just ten minutes—barely enough time for the tension to settle. Deputy Frost from the FBI wasn't far behind. Huxley hadn't called his boss, but he was there anyway, which didn't surprise Nazario, though it made her suspicious. How much did

Frost know about Black Nova? If there was one person who could clear things up, it was the deputy.

"You're telling me this case," Johnson began, gesturing to the bodies being carted off and hoisted in the coroner's van, "links to something or some group called Black Nova? And you're just now mentioning it?"

Frost hesitated, jaws tightening. "It's not so simple, Chief. Black Nova—they don't exist on any record—top secret stuff. Restricted to the highest clearance," Frost started with a measured tone. He gave Nazario and Huxley a quick glance. "And from what I've heard, they're hunting down Jaxon Ryker. If they're after him, it means his network and influence are greater than we realized—far beyond anything we've dealt with before. This isn't just big—it's a national security nightmare."

Furrowing his brows, Johnson griped, "So why in the hell do you know about it, and we don't?" The chief threw his hands in the air. "Who you think is working those homicides executed by Ryker? Our team—Nazario and Wilson. Now they just up and took Von Schlange before we could arrest her? She was our prime suspect. Chasing her for a couple of years now. Shit, they even snatched up her fucking dog! What're we supposed to do about that? Sit and wait for them to call while Jaxon Ryker runs his own game?"

"I've had ... limited exposure," Frost admitted, choosing his words carefully as the chief fumed, pacing the front lawn. "Only know enough to know conventional boundaries."

"Let's see what needs cleaning inside," Huxley said, heading back toward the house now that everyone had finally cleared out, the coroner's van pulling away last. Nazario, Wilson, the chief, and the deputy trailed after him.

"Best I stay down here with the baby," Wilson said, settling on the couch in the living room where there hadn't been a bloody body to paint the room, a place untouched by the violence upstairs.

A gruesome trail of brain matter and blood streaked the walls along the stairway leading up to the nursery, where one body had been found just outside the door and the other inside.

Hands on his hips, Chief Johnson scanned the aftermath. "Y'all said them two DBs were cops?" Johnson's face soured, the weight of it settling like a bad taste in his mouth.

"Yep, both deceased were blue, sir. Officers Ronnie Salerno and Marcus Delgado—not familiar with either," Nazario said. "Don't know if they were involved in shooting Gus."

"God damn it!" Johnson began to pace. "Salerno and Delgado were beat cops, worked the night shift. That's all I know. Nazario—you're on task to find out who else is dirty. Bring Wilson in when you can, but keep it on the DL. You feel me? No one on the force can know we're sniffing out the rot."

"Stealth is my middle name," Wilson said with a smirk. "No one will know, sir."

"Good. Called the biohazard remediation specialists—our cleaning crew the county contracts with—they'll be here in fifteen. Told me to expect at least three hours for them to really get this all wiped down. Use that downstairs bedroom for tonight since Nazario isn't feeling the hotel idea." Johnson gave the detective a sideways glance, like a father disapproving of their daughter's stubbornness. He turned to Frost, "So we're dealing with another covert government initiative trying to bring Ryker down. A man who already has half of the force on edge. What in the hell is Black Nova anyway? A task force? Some black-ops unit? A rogue agency?"

"Don't know the full scope." Frost rubbed the back of his neck. "But what I do know is this: Black Nova shows up—it's because the stakes are sky-high. Covert operations, classified tech, off-the-books missions. Kinds of things they don't want making the headlines. My guess? Salerno and Delgado got tangled up in something big enough for Black Nova to step in. They operate as an independent third-party. Really hope we don't find more blue folk taking orders from the wrong side."

Anger flashed in Johnson's eyes. "This happened in my city. My jurisdiction. I deserve to know what we're dealing with, dontcha think?"

Frost met the chief's anger with an unflinching glare. The two men locked eyes in a stare-down that lasted for a very long minute of silence before the deputy responded, choosing his words with caution. "I know you don't care for my previous answer, but I'll repeat myself since you seem to think I'm hiding something from you. Trust me, if I could tell you more, I certainly would. Here's what I know: getting combative with Black Nova can be dangerous—for both of us. This isn't a big-dick contest. Once they step in, we're no longer in the driver's seat. And Jaxon Ryker's operation could be anywhere in the U.S., most likely not in L.A. County."

"So, we're taking orders from Black Nova now? This Commander Lucius Cain fellow—never heard of him before, and I got my sources within intelligence, the CIA, and the FBI —and not a one could tell me who this fucker is or what his operatives at Black Nova do." Johnson ran a hand down his face.

"Chief Johnson, I'm in the dark as much as you are," Deputy Frost said.

"With all due respect, sir." Nazario pivoted to Johnson. "I don't think Von Schlange has a choice, nor do we."

"You're right, Nazario," Johnson said, "but I don't like it. Especially when we now have to investigate our own. Don't like it one bit. Ain't nothing worse than the gut feeling—knowing more cops might've flipped to the wrong side."

"Gotta bad feeling we're in for a big power struggle between our departments and this new classified initiative," Huxley sighed.

From her vantage point upstairs, Nazario watched from the nursery window as the white coroner's van disappeared down the street. Resolve hardening, her mind drifted to Von—a killer who'd saved her child and that of her babysitter with nothing but courage and instinct, qualities that were prerequisites Black Nova required. However, the enigma surrounding the clandestine group was obscured, along with its true purpose. Jaxon Ryker's deadly organization was much like a loaded gun, its trigger ready to be pulled at any moment. Everything she knew as a detective, as a member of the LAPD, had been upended since Black Nova entered the picture—along with Von.

But Detective Anaya Nazario wasn't about to walk away.

She'd find Von, and when she did, she'd expose the truth—not just about Black Nova, but about Ryker and the forces that had drawn them all into this deadly game. This was far from over. It was the start of a fight that would force her to forge new alliances—and face new enemies. The lines between good and evil blurred, pressing on her conscience with crushing weight. For the first time in her career, she had to stay guarded against her own. The men and women she once called her blue family were now question marks—trust was no longer a given. Who stood on the right side and who didn't was a truth waiting to be unearthed. The moment of reckoning was coming, and once the light cut through the darkness, there would be nowhere to hide, nowhere to escape.

Sooner or later, everything buried in shadow would be forced into the light.

ACKNOWLEDGMENTS

Twilight of the Serpent was one of the hardest books I've ever written—because it's rooted in real experience.

As someone who has been stalked for seven years, I know the fear, the exhaustion, the invisible weight you carry every day. I also know how rare it is to be believed, let alone protected.

Each year, over 1 in 6 women in the U.S. experience stalking. Yet legal protection remains minimal. Arrests? Rare. Convictions? Even rarer.

Most victims are told to "just block them" or "wait until something worse happens."

This book is for every person who's lived with that fear.

For every survivor who had to become their own shield.

For every voice that was silenced, dismissed, or doubted.

You're not alone.

And you are never invisible here.

ALSO BY S.Z. ESTAVILLO

The Serpent Series

The Serpent's Bridge

The Serpent Woman

Twilight of the Serpent

The Serpent's Order

SZ Estavillo has been passionate about writing since childhood, with a defining moment in second grade when her teacher predicted, "You're going to be a writer someday." Her biracial heritage, being half-Korean and half-Puerto Rican, deeply influences her book themes. As a staunch advocate for diversity and inclusion, SZ works tirelessly to amplify the voices of underrepresented and marginalized communities within the publishing industry.

SZ is not only a feminist whose principles echo throughout her works, but also a true crime aficionado, having devoured every episode of true crime on networks like Discovery ID and Oxygen. Her interest in justice is deeply rooted in her family history. Her uncle, Nicolas Estavillo, retired as the highest-ranking Puerto Rican cop in New York's history, and her father, Jose Estavillo, has served in both the Air Force and U.S. Customs and Border Patrol. These familial connections to law enforcement enrich her storytelling and understanding of justice.

Balancing her roles as a devoted mother and an enthusiastic digital marketer, SZ brings her professional expertise into her personal passion, amassing over 85,000 followers on social media. She uses her platform to inspire and uplift the writing community with motivational and positive content. Along with her two children and two senior dogs, she enjoys the simple pleasures of family sushi outings in their Los Angeles home.

If you enjoyed this book, consider following her on social media or posting a review. Your support helps extend the reach of voices that matter. Thank you for reading and being part of this journey Stay tuned for her upcoming books, "The Serpent Woman" and "Twilight of the Serpent."

Please follow SZ Estavillo:

Goodreads: https://www.goodreads.com/author/show/49349032.S_Z_Estavillo

X: @szestavillo

Instagram: @szestavillo.author

TikTok: @szestavillo.author

Facebook Page: https://www.facebook.com/sonyozofiaestavillo